CORPSE FLOWER

CORPSE FLOWER

A CORNWALL AND REDFERN MYSTERY

GLORIA FERRIS

DUNDURN
TORONTO

Editor: Allison Hirst
Design: Jesse Hooper
Printer: Webcom

Library and Archives Canada Cataloguing in Publication

Ferris, Gloria, 1947-
        Corpse flower : a Cornwall and Redfern mystery / by Gloria Ferris.

Issued also in electronic format.
ISBN 978-1-4597-0712-2

        I. Title.

PS8611.E79C67 2013   C813'.6   C2013-900817-9

1   2   3   4   5   17   16   15   14   13

Conseil des Arts du Canada   Canada Council for the Arts   Canada   ONTARIO ARTS COUNCIL
                                                                    CONSEIL DES ARTS DE L'ONTARIO

We acknowledge the support of the **Canada Council for the Arts** and the **Ontario Arts Council** for our publishing program. We also acknowledge the financial support of the **Government of Canada** through the **Canada Book Fund** and **Livres Canada Books**, and the **Government of Ontario** through the **Ontario Book Publishing Tax Credit** and the **Ontario Media Development Corporation**.

Care has been taken to trace the ownership of copyright material used in this book. The author and the publisher welcome any information enabling them to rectify any references or credits in subsequent editions.

                                                                    J. Kirk Howard, President

VISIT US AT
Dundurn.com | @dundurnpress | Facebook.com/dundurnpress | Pinterest.com/dundurnpress

Dundurn	Gazelle Book Services Limited	Dundurn
3 Church Street, Suite 500	White Cross Mills	2250 Military Road
Toronto, Ontario, Canada	High Town, Lancaster, England	Tonawanda, NY
M5E 1M2	L41 4XS	U.S.A. 14150

For my special loves:
Olyvia, Talia, Dante, Aimee, Rowyn, and Lennon

CHAPTER ONE

FROM NOON SATURDAY UNTIL he was found late that night, Julian Barnfeather lay toes up in the Good Shepherd Cemetery. The ideal place for a corpse, except he was sans casket in the tool shed.

When Chief Redfern learned that I, Bliss Moonbeam Cornwall, spent the day not fifty metres away, he zeroed in on me like a shark eyeing up a sun-baked tourist. How was I supposed to know Julian was dead? I assumed he was in the shed, because he rarely went anywhere else. I thought he was drinking booze-laced coffee and thumbing through his stack of hard-core magazines.

Except for Julian, I liked my Saturday job well enough. There are worse ways to make a buck than raking pinecones and pruning bushes in a quiet cemetery. But, Julian was a four-hundred-pound disgusting pig. A greasy mullet thatched his moon-sized head and his features disappeared into folds of flesh. Between his breath, his sweat-stained shirts, and the odours of whatever else he did in there, my stomach flipped every Saturday morning when I gathered my tools.

That morning was no different. I held my breath and squeezed past his chair. He looked and smelled no worse than usual, certainly no better. He made a few suggestive remarks, as always, his satisfied mirth rumbling out the door behind me. I threw a "fuck you" over my shoulder, and he laughed even harder.

I had to put up with him. If I charged Julian with sexual harassment, the Cemetery Board would find a reason to terminate me. I was a seasonal worker, contracted from April to November, while Julian was a long-time, permanent employee of the Town of Lockport. He was not required to show up on Saturdays, but he always did.

Suing Julian wouldn't help, either. Even if I had the money, there wasn't an ambulance-chaser in town who would represent me. All were colleagues of my ex-husband, Mike Bains — or "the Weasel," as I had come to think of him.

I carried my rake, hoe, and clippers to the newer plots close to the wrought-iron fence surrounding the cemetery. Rows of pines and maples hid the shed from view. I tried to forget about Julian, and relaxed in the tranquillity of the grove, my emotional balance temporarily restored. Julian was really the least of my problems.

The wet southwestern Ontario spring had finally given way to the sunny, mild temperatures perfect for early June. As I worked, I amused myself by reading the words on the epitaphs. "He Loved Too Well" adorned one grave. One had to wonder how he died. Another gravestone read "Another Place, Another Time." Was that a threat, or a promise?

Around four, my BlackBerry chirped, drowning out the birds in the overhead branches. I had been ignoring it all day, but now I pulled it out of the bib pocket of my overalls. I swiped my dripping hairline and checked the display.

Yes, it was Dougal wanting something. What a pain. There was no point putting him off any longer, so I settled myself on Alistair Parks's flat, raised gravestone, 1902 to 1989, and leaned back. The chill from the granite helped to lower my body temperature.

"Bliss? Finally! I've been calling all day. Why didn't you answer?"

I sighed as I squirmed to relieve the knots in my back muscles. "Can I do something for you, Dougal?"

"We can do something for each other, dear cousin. Just wait till you hear my proposition."

Dougal was sounding way too cheerful and calm for someone with his condition. Just last week he had called in a panic, saying a rat was chasing the songbirds in his backyard. I didn't find any rat, but a possum was hanging from the feeder outside his kitchen windows, scooping up the sunflower seeds and smirking at us through the glass. It was more than enough to shake a tightly wrapped thirty-four-year-old ex-high-school teacher who was the centre of his own fast-spinning universe.

"How's the therapy going?" I picked a twig off Alistair's stone and dropped it into the pyramid of pine-cones on the ground.

"Really good. Today, Melanie and I went into the backyard. We only stayed a few minutes, but it's the first time I've been outside in months. The sun felt great."

"Wonderful. You'll be taking a vacation in Costa Rica before you know it." Melanie was a therapist who made house calls, which was fortunate since Dougal insisted he couldn't go to her office. But, hey, that's agoraphobia for you.

"Yes, but that's not why I called. I have a job for you. Thor is going to blossom, within days, and I need you to help pollinate him."

I had never heard of a Thor, and I knew it would be next to impossible for me to pollinate anything. And, as a plant expert, Dougal should know how to do it himself.

After a moment, I responded, "I don't know what medication you're on now, but you better look up the side effects. Have you tried some deep breathing exercises? Do you want me to call Melanie?"

"This is Saturday, isn't it? It's past four o'clock now, so come over when you're done work and I'll explain. I'll pay you a thousand dollars. That should boost your Indict the Weasel Fund."

I bolted upright. "Who do you want me to kill?"

"You're hilarious, Bliss, but that's not the smartest thing to say on a cellphone. I'll tell you exactly what I want you to do when you get here. At the rate Thor is growing, sexual maturity will occur any day."

"I'll be right over." The reference to sexual maturity worried me a bit, but still, a thousand dollars? Despite Dougal's tendency to dramatize every mundane event,

I was intrigued by his offer to pay me mega bucks to pollinate something — how hard could it be, really?

CHAPTER
TWO

AT QUITTING TIME, I dropped my armful of tools outside the shed door to avoid another confrontation with Julian and sprinted to my red Savage. The 1996 650 single-cylinder Suzuki Savage motorcycle was my gift to myself, purchased after I pawned my engagement and wedding rings. It was the best exchange I ever made. From mid-April until late November I was able to ride to my assorted jobs around town, and I could afford to fill up the tank once a week.

Lockport, population 7,021, has the usual mix of well-to-do and poverty-line citizens. Dougal belongs to the former, and so did I until my divorce two years ago. That situation flung me quickly into the latter category. I didn't like it, and I wasn't going to stay there.

Yes, I learned the hard way. Never marry a lawyer while in university, support him through law school, then expect him to be faithful until death. Unless death comes early — during the honeymoon, for instance — it won't happen.

I zipped through the town's one traffic light, keeping an eye out for police cruisers. The red Savage was built for speed, but two recent warnings convinced me to lay off the throttle, since I could barely afford breakfast cereal, let alone a speeding ticket.

Pulling up at Dougal's curb, I enjoyed the sight of the pale yellow bricks of the sprawling ranch-style house gleaming in the late afternoon sun. Immaculate lawns, compliments of my back-breaking labour, spread across a triple-sized lot. The stone drive and path to the front door were bordered by flowering shrubs and beds of early perennials in deep shades of purple and pink. I couldn't help comparing this scene of suburban prosperity to the view from the window of my trailer. Not that I was complaining — okay, I guess I was, but I tried not to be pessimistic about my altered social status. Action yes, whining no, that was the credo I tried to follow.

Dougal was waiting in his arena-sized foyer. "It's about time. Why do you always wear those overalls? You look like a skinny twelve-year-old street waif. I hope you keep your eye out for child molesters in the cemetery."

I resisted the temptation to tell him about Julian's aspirations of molesting his favourite cousin. He wouldn't be interested.

"I'm kind of hungry," I said to him when he started pushing me toward the back of the house. "Is there anything to eat?"

"Later. I want to introduce you to Thor. He's in the solarium." He made it sound like a blind date.

Dougal had the solarium built after his parents died within months of each other three years ago. They left him a great deal of old family money, which afforded him the freedom to quit his position as a high-school science teacher and move back home. Shortly afterward, he announced that he was going to write a mystery novel with a botanical setting, but so far I hadn't seen a single chapter. Then, about eight months ago, he developed agoraphobia and had refused to leave the house since. And guess who became his errand girl, gardener, barber, and junk food delivery slave? Every minute I wasn't working elsewhere, I was doing Dougal's bidding for a pittance. At least he let me do my laundry sometimes and take home the food he didn't want.

"What's the big deal?" I glanced around the ceramic-tiled solarium. An orchid collection bloomed in multi-hued abundance along the perimeter of the room, but nothing else looked ready to flower.

"What's a Thor, and where is it?" I preferred not to hang out in humid places like solariums. They made me sweat like a roofer on a hot summer day, and already my shoulder-length brown hair was frizzing up around my ears.

Orchids aside, Dougal owned a sorry display of horticultural specimens. At the far end of the room, a dozen fern-like plants four to five feet high grew in plastic pots. Groups of buds drooped from the plants, but they didn't look like flower buds. Seed pods?

Dougal's African grey parrot, Simon, perched on top of his multi-level cage, lifting one leg and then the other, as though his feet hurt. The bird eyed me hopefully, but I stayed out of beak range. "Pretty baby," he coaxed, "I love you." He waggled his red tail feathers at me.

"Not a chance," I told him. I knew for a fact that beak was sharp, and as for his love, well, he was probably fickle like most males.

Dougal gazed lovingly at the only other object in the room — a massive concrete pot. It sat in the middle of the tiled floor, shaded by overhead screens that cast filtered shadows on the centre portion of the space while leaving the perimeters of the room in sunlight. A thick stake about six feet high rose from the pot. It was yellowish-grey and looked like a cactus, but smoother.

Dougal gestured dramatically at the container. I stepped closer to the rim. The stake had one continuous pale green petal with frilled edges curling around the base. I backed away.

"That's obscene! What is it?"

"That, darling Bliss, is an *Amorphophallus titanum*, better known as a Titan Arum. The largest flower in the world! My Thor."

"You named your flower? All I see is a huge phallic spike in a skirt. If it gets any bigger, I wouldn't want to be in the same room."

"Well, stand back, because it will probably grow another foot or more in the next few days, then burst into flower. And that's where you come in."

"I've changed my mind. I don't even want to ask what part you expect me to play in this fertilizing business."

"Pollinating, not fertilizing, you ignoramus. Let's go into the kitchen and get some supper, and I'll explain what little you need to do for a thousand dollars."

Dougal hauled a vegetable lasagna and salad out of the refrigerator and deposited them on his antique pine table with a flourish. While waiting for the lasagna to heat, I forked up the wilted salad.

"Where's the garlic bread?" I asked between swallows.

Dougal stopped crunching barbecue potato chips long enough to take a swig of Coke. He stifled a belch and replied, "I ate it for lunch. Want some of my chips?"

He ate nothing but junk food for breakfast, lunch, and dinner, even though the wonderful Mrs. Boudreau, who came in each weekday morning to clean and cook, left him delicious, nutritious meals. I did my best to liberate them, but too many ended up in his garbage bin.

Simon waddled into the kitchen and glared at Dougal.

"Simon wants a chip," he said in what I assumed was Melanie's voice. The voice impersonation was a nice change since the bird's repertoire usually consisted of mimicking the sound of the ringing phone and the chiming doorbell. Occasionally, he bayed like the hound next door or made grunting noises similar to a yeti in heat.

Dougal handed the parrot a potato chip. Simon held his treat in one scaly claw and nibbled at it until it was gone. Then he turned and shuffled out of the room, leaving a gelatinous puddle behind on the oak floor.

I looked pointedly at the mess, but Dougal only shrugged and said, "Mrs. Boudreau will clean that tomorrow."

I got a paper towel and wiped up the slimy deposit. Dougal was finicky about everything except parrot poop. Go figure.

"Can I take the rest of this lasagna home if you're not going to eat it?"

"Go ahead; it's too high in fat and carbohydrates anyway." He opened the wrapper on a Mr. Big chocolate bar and bit it in half.

Chewing noisily, he watched me clear the table and put my plate and cutlery in the dishwasher. "Are you ready to listen now? There isn't much time. Focus on the money."

He settled down on his spine and rested his bare feet on another chair. His long fingers dipped in and out of a second chip bag, the chocolate bar already just a memory, and began to lecture.

"The Titan Arum is indigenous to the rainforests of Sumatra. As far as I know, only a few large botanical gardens and universities have specimens, and maybe there are one or two others in private collections like mine." His almond-shaped blue eyes glittered in his narrow face with the fervour of a fanatic. He scratched at his dark buzz cut, leaving a few potato chip crumbs behind.

I suppressed a yawn, partly from boredom and partly from plain fatigue. Wielding a rake for eight hours was hard work, and, at thirty-two, my muscles took longer to recover than they used to.

"Are you listening, Bliss? Now, I've owned my Titan for about eight years. Every year or so it has produced one huge compound leaf that grows about ten feet tall and then the leaf dies and the tuber lies dormant again."

"Really?" I gave in to the yawn. "I never saw it in your apartment before you moved back to this house. The pot itself would have taken up half your living room. And your ceiling wasn't even eight feet high, so ..."

"Button it, will you? A friend was keeping it for me, okay? Now then, the last month or so, when I was expecting the leaf to start growing again, it didn't."

He pulled a battered cigarette out of his pocket and lit it.

"When did you start smoking? And why? I don't understand you, Dougal. You're going to croak before you hit forty, between your appalling diet and now smoking."

He ignored me and sucked in the smoke. "This time is different. The Titan is producing an inflorescence that consists of the spadix — the tall column you saw in the pot — and a spathe — the green, furrowed structure wrapped around the base. Soon, thousands of tiny flowers, both male and female, will form at the base of the spadix, and the spathe will unfurl around them. The spathe will be dark red on the inside — I saw one years ago when I was in England, at the Kew Royal Botanic Gardens, and it was spectacular. Now, I may have a chance to observe it right in my own house." His eyes sparkled with excitement as he waved the crumpled cigarette in my direction.

"That's fascinating, but I still don't see where I come in. I don't know much about plants, but if this one has male and female flowers, why can't it pollinate itself?"

"That rarely happens, and I don't want to chance it. We need the pollen from another Titan. After a successful pollination, the plant then produces fruit, which, in turn, produces the seeds. The mature seeds are called tubers."

"And that's what you want me to do? Find you another giant, ugly plant? I wouldn't know where to begin to look. I don't think this is a realistic plan, Dougal."

"Will you listen? I know where another Titan is."

"Where? And what makes you think this other one is going to flower at the same time as yours? You said they can go years without …"

"I don't know, not for sure. But the other Titan comes from the same mother plant. Our tubers are the same age, and there's a chance the other one will be at the same stage of sexual development." He took another pull on his unfiltered cigarette.

My ears started to burn. I had the same feeling before when I was about to do something stupid, like the day I got married. I ignored it that time, and look how my life turned out.

"So, Dougal. If I understand the situation correctly, you have a plant that may or may not flower. Someone else, as yet unnamed, has another plant that may or may not flower. You are willing to pay me a thousand dollars to ensure a successful pollination. Sorry, but I think buying a lottery ticket would give me better odds."

"This is a win-win situation for you, Bliss. I will pay you in full if the other Titan is also about to blossom and you talk the owner into pollinating both plants. You'll get the money even if the pollination doesn't work."

"Is there some reason you can't contact the other owner and arrange this for yourself?"

"There's a pretty good reason."

"What is it?"

"I used to be married to her, and she hates my guts."

"Glory? Glory has one of these hideous plants?"

He said reproachfully, "Don't talk like that. They have names."

"Dougal!"

"Okay. Before Glory and I were married, two tubers came into our possession, never mind how. When we split up, I took Thor and she took Sif. I moved into my own place and had a friend with a greenhouse keep Thor for me until I built the solarium here. There, that's the whole story. Once the spathe unfurls completely, the male and female flowers will ripen within a day of each other."

Dougal leaned back and stretched his lanky legs farther out on the chair. He was still smoking and looking unusually relaxed for an agoraphobic whose Titan Arum was about to embark on sexual maturity with no nubile mate in sight. Although he was a foot taller and had at least sixty pounds on me, I sometimes felt like Dougal's mother. Not that I had any experience as a parent.

"What's a Sif? I know Thor was some mythical god, but ..."

"Thor is a Germanic god of war, and Sif is his wife. At the time, Glory and I thought it was romantic. Are there any other questions before I continue?"

"I guess not." Although, considering what happened between Glory and Dougal, naming the plants after a war god and his wife had turned out to be more prophetic than romantic.

"Right. Since you clean Glory's house, you have an excellent opportunity to find out if her Titan is ready to bloom. If it isn't, well, no harm done, and no point even mentioning it to her."

"Dougal, I clean Glory's house on Wednesday mornings. This is only Saturday. I can't go over there uninvited. We aren't exactly social equals anymore."

"You can't wait until Wednesday — Thor might bloom before then! And Sif could be even farther along in development, or behind. I need to know so I can plan. You'll have to find some excuse to go over there."

"But I've never seen anything like your Titan in Glory's house. You can't miss something that resembles a gigantic …"

"Look in the greenhouse at the back of the house. That's where we used to keep the pair."

"Glory never leaves me alone in her house. I've never been in the backyard, not even when you two were married."

"Damnations, Bliss! I'm trying to pay you a thousand dollars. Can't you show a little initiative?"

I was about to tell him where he could stick my initiative. Then I stopped and sniffed. My olfactory sense was second to no one's, at times to a fault. "Something smells funny in here. How old are those cigarettes?"

"Are you going to do it or not? Remember your Indict the Weasel Fund."

As of today, an emergency root canal would wipe out the Fund. "Okay, I'll try. I guess."

"Your enthusiasm is inspirational. No time like the present, so go now, my little minion."

"I can't. Tonight's the only night I have free to do my laundry. And don't call me a minion."

"You can use my washer and dryer later tonight, after you see Glory."

"I'm really tired. I've been working at the cemetery all day."

"Then go tomorrow, but that's leaving it a little late."

"Can't. I have a real estate client tomorrow. I'm showing the Barrister house in the afternoon. And you can't expect me to visit Glory on Sunday morning."

Before he could say anything, I continued, "And I'll be working at the library Monday and Tuesday, and teaching yoga Tuesday night, so I really can't get to Glory's until Wednesday morning."

"Wednesday might be too late. If you want the money, you'll have to get over there right away."

I stopped listening. Something had been niggling at the back of my mind for the past half-hour. The straggly plants in the solarium, the smelly cigarettes without filters ...

I pictured the fern-like plants in their plastic pots, the separate little branches and the clusters of buds ...

"Damn it, Dougal!" I shoved his legs off the chair and kicked him on the ankle, hard. "You're growing marijuana!"

CHAPTER
THREE

AN HOUR LATER, I felt my way through the woods that surrounded three sides of Glory's property. It was silent as a cathedral except for the burbling sound of a small stream. I slapped at the black flies swarming my head and wondered, not for the first time, why the hell I just didn't give up hope of suing the Weasel for my half of our marital property. I could live with my sister in Toronto and work on my master's degree in library science. Blyth even had a job waiting for me as a co-op student at one of the University of Toronto libraries, where she was head librarian. And I wouldn't be crawling around in a bug-infested forest, trying to find a greenhouse. In my opinion, raw nature is greatly overrated.

"Mike will never surrender a dime," Blyth repeatedly told me. "How are you going to beat him on his own turf — the courtroom?" I didn't know how, but I wasn't going to give up everything I helped acquire during the eight years of our marriage.

I finally resorted to inching along on hands and knees. My ex-cousin-in-law, Glory Yates, owned the most expensive real estate on Arlington Mews, a neighbourhood where Donald Trump would feel at home. The pine trees that separated her from her neighbours grew so densely, I soon lost all sense of direction and staggered from tree to tree as the black flies insinuated themselves under my hairline and up my sleeves.

It was ink-black in the woods, and a menacing shadow lurked behind every tree. This was no place for an established coward with a vivid imagination. I chastised myself for not bringing the flashlight from the saddlebag of my bike. It would have been prudent to wait until morning, but Prudence was not my middle name and, once I decided to take the job, I wanted to get it over with. Any conversation with Glory that didn't involve the state of her toilets or the alleged cobweb in the corner of her ten-foot parlour ceiling was bound to be uncomfortable. Before I rang her doorbell on a day other than a Wednesday, I needed solid evidence she was harbouring a fecund Titan Arum.

I found the greenhouse only because it was lit up like a centenarian's birthday cake. I followed a faint glow that grew brighter until I glimpsed steel beams and glass walls blending seamlessly into the forest.

Even before I peeked through the glass, I felt confident I would find a Titan Arum. Although Glory was undeniably rich, she didn't spend a penny more than she had to unless it was on her hair or body. She paid me minimum wage and hadn't given me so much as a box of cheap chocolates for Christmas. Even though, during my former life, we had played tennis together for years at the Lockport Country Club.

So there had to be a good reason why the greenhouse was artificially lighted after the sun went down. I crawled up to the wall and raised myself high enough to peer into the interior.

My mouth fell open. After spitting out either an oversized black fly or an early mosquito, I closed it again and pressed my nose against the glass to get a closer look.

Then I plunked back down on the damp, spongy ground and muttered out loud, "Jee-suz." I batted at the insects and stood up for another look. Still there.

Glory was making no pretence of growing orchids or geraniums or any other normal plant in her greenhouse, which was at least twice as big as Dougal's solarium.

Oh, there was a Titan Arum in there. It sat in the far corner of the greenhouse in a pot identical to Dougal's. The spike reached up, way up. The spathe-thing was barely visible over the rim of the pot and appeared to be at about the same stage of development as Thor.

But, it was the rest of Glory's crop that drew my attention. Weed, pot, Mary Jane, grass. She had twenty or thirty pots of them, far more than Dougal. I almost felt ashamed of myself for yelling at him about his paltry dozen.

While moisture from the soft earth soaked the seat of my overalls, I replayed my heated discussion with Dougal before I left his house.

"Many people, including you obviously, don't know that it's legal to grow marijuana in Canada for personal medical reasons," he told me.

"Dougal, the government has a list of people who are allowed to buy or grow marijuana for specific illnesses, and I don't think agoraphobia is one of them. You can't grow your own unless you're registered, you idiot."

"Well, let me put it this way, you little freak. The cops aren't going to come knocking on my door looking for pot. And, since I find it's the only drug that helps me, I sure the hell am going to keep using it, so mind your own business."

"I wonder how an agoraphobic like you will fare in a nine by nine prison cell. I can just see the police dragging you out of your house, screaming and clinging to the door frame with your fingernails. But you aren't bad looking, so I'm sure you'll find comfort in the arms of a burly Hells Angel. You can be his new bitch."

The conversation went south at that point. Neither of us changed our stance on the subject of home-grown weed, so I had grabbed my lasagna from his fridge and marched out the door. After stowing tomorrow's dinner in my saddlebag, I drove the block and a half to Glory's property and tucked the bike under a towering maple, well away from the streetlights that were blinking on and casting long shadows onto the street.

Now, deep in the bush, the only light came from Glory's grow house. In places, the pines grew tight against the glass, and I was betting the artificial lighting shone during daylight hours as well as the night, so the sun-hungry pot plants could get the energy they needed to mature. I hoped that pilots wouldn't mistake this shining beacon for the small airport west of town.

I hugged the walls, forehead to the glass, until the concrete planter was directly in front of me.

Up close, the Titan Arum appeared to be slightly taller than Dougal's, seven feet perhaps. The spathe was beginning to unfurl and the faintest blush of pink showed on the inside.

A pinecone bounced off my head and rolled across my shoulder as I leaned against the greenhouse wall. I took a minute to reflect. My cell was in the saddlebag of my bike with the flashlight, so I couldn't call Dougal and describe Glory's Titan. Should I go back to his place and tell him what I found, or should I try and broker a deal with Glory right now? She hated Dougal, so there needed to be something in the deal for her. With a last glance into the greenhouse, I followed the flagstone path along the side of Glory's Tudor mansion and ended up at a locked gate. I shinnied over it and climbed the stone steps to the front door.

Glory answered the ring, a glass of white wine in one hand and an exquisitely waxed eyebrow arched in surprise.

"Why, Bliss." Her sea-blue eyes widened and she shook her mane of red waves in sudden understanding. "I forgot to pay you on Wednesday, didn't I? Well, wait right here and I'll get your money. I'm so sorry."

"You paid me, Glory."

"Well, then … I don't understand. It's Saturday evening." She gazed down at me as though she suddenly found the Easter Bunny on her doorstep on Christmas Eve.

"I'm here to discuss business. Botanical business."

"Botanical? Business? You're acting very strangely, Bliss, but come in if you must."

She drifted through the foyer toward her living room of gleaming oak floors and artfully placed furnishings, with me following behind like a stray cat.

She draped herself over a cream leather couch and took a sip of wine. I plopped myself down, uninvited, on a matching loveseat facing her and watched her wince when I planted my soiled runners on her Persian area rug. I remembered my wet, muddy butt and hoped I wouldn't leave a stain on the leather.

"What have you been doing, Bliss? You look more like a hobo than usual."

"Well, let's see. I spent the day tending graves at the cemetery. You do know I work as a groundskeeper in the cemetery on Saturdays, don't you?"

She answered with a slight wrinkling of her nose.

"Then I went to Dougal's, where I ate supper and he offered me a very interesting proposition. Want to hear what it is?"

At the mention of Dougal's name, Glory's face underwent a transformation, like from a human to a werewolf. I suddenly saw, not the socialite who spent her days playing tennis and lunching with her peers, but a primal creature with claws and teeth. And I distinctly saw the whites of her eyes turn red. What had Dougal done to warrant this reaction from his former wife? Nobody seemed to know, but it must have been nasty.

Her fingers squeezed the stem of her glass so tightly I expected it to shatter and splash wine over her turquoise silk trousers, but it remained intact.

"I think you know, Bliss, that I have no interest in anything relating to that worm, Dougal Seabrook. And I wish you would tell me why you are here."

"Yes, well, I don't disagree that Dougal can be a serious pain, but since I was married to a weasel, I think I have the edge on bad marriages. At least Dougal didn't leave you flat broke and living in a trailer in Hemp Hollow."

"I had my own money, don't forget, and that bastard couldn't get his hands on it, not that he was brainless enough to try. Spit it out, Bliss."

"Okay, then. Dougal's Titan Arum is about to blossom, and he thinks yours might be at the same stage. For some reason, he's keen on pollinating his Titan and getting the seeds or whatever happens when two plants mix up their pollen." I still wasn't sure about the mechanics of the whole scheme but, since Glory had the same plant biology degree as Dougal from the University of Waterloo, I figured she would get the idea.

"What makes you think I have a Titan Arum?" Glory got up and poured herself another glass of white wine. She didn't offer me any and I licked my parched lips.

With a sniff, Glory gazed at a twig sticking out from the top of my tee-shirt. Pinky in the air, I pulled it out and placed it carefully on the teak coffee table. Most of my hair had exploded from its ponytail and, given that it had been over a year since I'd seen the inside of a salon, I knew I looked like I had just stepped away from a weed whacker.

"I picked up some brush crawling through your mini-forest. Before disturbing you, I wanted to see if you had a Titan Arum in your greenhouse and, hey, what do you think? You do. So how about it? Would you like to trade pollen with Dougal's Titan?"

Glory shook her glass, but it was empty again. She slammed it down on the coffee table and again it didn't break. Had to be Waterford.

"I hardly know what to say to you, Bliss. You admit you have been sneaking around like a spy? And now you want me to do something that will make Dougal happy?"

"You could say that."

"I can't believe it! I should fire your ass right now. I don't accept disloyalty from my employees." I wondered how many glasses of expensive Chardonnay had passed those glossy lips before I arrived. I really itched to slap her Lancômed face.

"Go right ahead. I have a waiting list of women who would die for me to clean their houses on Wednesday mornings." We both knew I was right. I could clean two houses a day, five days a week, and not make a dent in the list.

"Well, I just think it's rude, that's all." Glory wasn't going to pursue my ass, as in firing of.

"Look, Glory, I don't know anything about these enormous ugly plants, but if they're as rare as Dougal says, wouldn't you like to get some seedlings or saplings from the mother plant you've had for so many years?"

"Tubers," she said absently, tapping her long pink fingernails against the empty glass. "They're called tubers, or corms, once the seeds have matured enough to start growing the plants. And I wouldn't mind having a few new specimens of *Amorphophallus titanum* in my greenhouse, but I don't see why I should do Dougal any favours."

"Okay, so he's a jerk, but if both plants are pollinated,

you'll both benefit. Think about it, lots of little tubers, enough to go around."

She sat silently for so long I thought she had nodded off into a drunken coma with her eyes open. I was ready to get up and pour her another glass of wine to revive her when she glared at me and said, "No, I'm sorry Bliss, you can tell Dougal I'm not interested in his proposition."

"Are you sure?"

"What's the matter with you? Are you deaf or something? I said no deal."

"I know you don't respect me, Glory, because the Weasel dumped me for a politically connected woman five years older, and I ended up with barely more than the clothes on my back. But don't make the mistake of thinking I'm stupid."

"Well, you should have seen it coming and raided the bank account."

We were off topic. And she was pissing me off.

"Here's the thing, Glory. I'm smart enough to know what marijuana looks like. If you co-operate and let me do the cross-pollination, I won't tell anybody about the grass growing in your greenhouse, setting a very bad example for Sif."

Glory's reaction to blackmail was spectacular. I backed away to a safe distance, wishing my old BlackBerry had a camera feature to capture the Kodak moments as they unfolded.

CHAPTER
FOUR

DOUGAL'S FACE WAS BLOODLESS. "I can't go over there! That woman knows I can't go outside. Why does she want to talk in person anyway? I'm paying you to handle it, so go handle it."

He kept shaking his head and backing away like I was threatening to drag him bodily over to Glory's. Although it might come to that.

"I don't know why, but she wouldn't budge on that point. You have to go there tomorrow evening at eight o'clock, or no deal."

Watching Glory throw a tantrum was the most fun I'd had all day. It was the first time I had witnessed someone drumming her heels on the floor while tearing at her hair and shrieking she was going to kill herself. After killing me, Dougal, and, I believe, the Pope for good measure.

Her screams brought Pan on the run, white coattails flapping. Pan was her butler, houseboy, and all-season gofer. Only a few inches over five feet and almost as slight as me, Pan coddled Glory like the goddess she believed she was, pouring and serving and fetching, and God knows what else. He didn't clean though.

Pan gave me a hard look as though he blamed me for the tantrum. I never could figure out how old he was, maybe thirty, or sixty? Splitting the difference, I thought of him as mid-forties. His black hair was brushed back from his face and secured in place with gel. His agate-hard eyes looked like they had seen it all, which was possible working for Glory. But unless he was a martial arts expert, I believed I could take him in a down-and-dirty.

We stood well out of range of Glory's fingernails while she thrashed around and, when she finally slowed down and showed signs of fatigue, we helped her to a sitting position on the floor.

"It's simple, Glory. Dougal wants to propagate his plant, and he's paying me to arrange it, and I need the money. You have the only other Titan Arum in the same stage of development that we know about, so we have to use it. Nobody else needs to know about the marijuana."

There was no point in being discreet around Pan, since he probably tended the crop. A goddess doesn't carry watering cans or snip off dried leaves. And rolling her own joints? Forget it.

With one red eye peering through the curtain of hair and her full lips thinned almost to extinction, Glory finally agreed. But only if Dougal met with her face to face, on her turf. And, yes, she knew but didn't care that he had agoraphobia. That was his problem. He should just get over it. Take it or leave it.

I took it. Now I had to convince Dougal that he could go out into that wide, never-ending world and not die from the experience.

I coaxed, "Look, Dougal, we'll do it like this. Your car is in the garage, right? So we'll get into it there, and you can lie on the back seat with your face covered. When we reach Glory's, you keep your eyes closed while I lead you into the house. That way, you'll never even see you're outside."

His fingers beat a desperate tempo on his chest. "Only one thing wrong with that. I sold my car, and my new Land Cruiser won't be delivered till the end of the month."

"So, we'll walk. It's less than two blocks. You keep your eyes closed, and we'll be there in five minutes. You can stand that, can't you?"

"No, I can't. I've barely been out in the backyard. I can't walk all that way by tomorrow night."

The money was slipping through my fingers. "What if you smoke, you know … before we set out?" I was already a blackmailer, so moonlighting as a drug pusher seemed an attainable career goal.

"I'd have to smoke steady from now right through until tomorrow night to get mellow enough for that. Then I'd be too stoned to talk, let alone think. And you need your wits about you to negotiate with that succubus."

"There's only one thing left. We'll go over on my motorcycle. Wait, let me finish." But he whimpered and wandered away in the direction of his solarium. I followed and found him draped over his concrete pot. I swear he was talking to Thor.

I looked inside and said, "Hey, Glory's spathe is starting to turn pink on the inside, too."

In the few hours I had been gone, Thor appeared to have shot up several inches.

Dougal straightened. "It is? Are you sure?"

I nodded. "Her spadix might be a little taller, but not much." I was tossing off those horticultural terms like nobody's business.

He licked his lips. I knew he tasted the victory of pollinating such a rare plant, a victory that was just out of reach because of a chemical imbalance in his brain.

"How long would it take to get there on your motorcycle?"

"Start to finish? About sixty seconds. And I have a spare helmet."

"Okay, then, I'll try." He reached out toward the unfurling spathe, but stopped short of touching it. "For my Thor, I'll try."

I had to bite the inside of my lip. "I'm sure Thor is grateful. Your country would be grateful if it knew of your courage."

"Shut up and go home."

"Just one more thing. I almost forgot."

He looked at me, his eyes narrowed. "What?"

"Glory wants you to bring Simon with you. For some reason, she seems to miss that bird."

"Simon! Are you sure? What's she up to? African greys only bond with one person, and that's me." He went over to the cage and peered in at the sleeping parrot.

Simon opened one dark eye and said in Dougal's voice, "Gimme some weed."

"Are you letting that bird smoke marijuana? Because I think that's even more illegal than smoking it yourself."

"Of course not. He's a parrot. He used to just repeat what he heard, but now that he's older, he can make up his own sentences, using words he's learned."

"Right. Anyway, Glory wants to see him, so he's coming with us."

"How will we get him there? He can't ride on my shoulder. He'll be traumatized, or else he'll fall off and be killed."

"We'll stuff him in the saddlebag."

Both Dougal and Simon squawked so loudly at that idea, I had to think of another way. "I know. You can put him inside your jacket. How scared can he get in less than a minute?" He might poop himself silly, but that was Dougal's problem.

"If I fall off, he'll be squashed."

"If that happens, a squashed parrot will be the least of your troubles."

"Seeing Glory again will probably finish him off anyway," Dougal grumbled, but I pretended not to hear.

I checked Dougal's fridge one more time for leftovers and acquired a lamb stew meant for his next day's lunch and a carton of milk past expiry date. Stashing these treasures next to the lasagna, I zipped on my black leather jacket and buckled my helmet.

As I came alongside the cemetery on my way home, I noticed three police cars with their lights whirling and several figures milling around in the shadows. I slowed for a better look. Whatever was happening would be all over town by morning, and when I stopped at Tim Hortons before my house showing, I would hear the news. I hoped no gravestones had been desecrated by vandals.

I cruised slowly through Lockport's downtown core, and noticed the dead skunk was still lying in the middle of the road in front of the police station.

It was getting smellier and more bloated each time I passed. I smiled at the probability that complaints had been forwarded to the Town Offices from Public Works. Since the Weasel was also the mayor, any such complaints would wind up on his desk. For a moment, I fantasized about scooping up the skunk myself and depositing it on the Weasel's front step. But no, that was beneath me, if barely.

∎

The Secret Valley Trailer Park occupied a natural dip in the landscape with the Niagara Escarpment looming on the horizon. Mostly retired or single, the residents appreciated not having the upkeep or expense of a big lot in town. The small yards were well-kept and, in summer and fall, flowers bloomed profusely on every window-sill. Front doors competed for the freshest paint and driveways glistened with sealed asphalt. Secret Valley's residents were proud of their humble homes.

I didn't live there.

If you drove through the narrow, winding main street of Secret Valley, the pavement ended abruptly. And, just to emphasize that this was the end of the rainbow, a chain hung between three white wooden posts. Beyond these posts, the ground dropped sharply.

At the bottom, my trailer squatted with two others, like toadstools in a goblin's circle.

Officially, it was part of Secret Valley, but unofficially it was known as Hemp Hollow.

The trailers in Hemp Hollow were real trailers and didn't pretend otherwise. The wheels sunk into the ground and the hitches were propped on stacks of bricks, ready to fall at the slightest shove. All three trailers shared a dirt courtyard where even weeds refused to grow.

My trailer rental was three hundred dollars a month. I hadn't been able to find anything cheaper, not even a room in somebody's basement. From November to April, when the weather made riding a motorcycle impossible, it was a long walk into town and I hoped that, before I had to spend a second winter in the dump, I could find a place in town that was affordable. I was terrified that the rusty gas furnace would malfunction and emit deadly carbon monoxide, so I moved a small electric heater from room to room in cold weather to prevent death by hypothermia. Even so, last winter my bedding froze to the thin aluminum wall more than once.

I rode north past the front gates of Secret Valley and, more by memory than sight, found the dirt trail leading to a dense stand of trees shielding the perimeter of Hemp Hollow.

Food and flashlight in hand, I walked cautiously through the trees to the clearing behind my trailer and listened closely. Except for a few hooting owls and grass-rustling rodents, the night was silent. Then, a faint, earthy odour I had noticed several times lately after nightfall wafted into my nostrils. I whirled around and saw a pair of green, unblinking eyes staring back at me. A bear?

Not wanting that question answered, I turned and ran, aiming the flashlight beam ahead. A garbage can blocked my path, and I'm pretty sure I leapt over it, because the lid flew off, pinging off my trailer and, no doubt, bringing the bear on the run. I knew garbage drew bears like some women are drawn to Chanel No. 5 perfume.

Judging by their darkened windows, both my neighbours had turned in. No help there. I located the keyhole with shaky fingers, my bag of food still intact under one arm. As soon as I rushed inside, I turned on the light and shut and locked the door behind me. While trying to catch my breath, I listened for nails scratching on the outside of the door and peered through a crack in the faded gingham curtains. No eyes, no scratching, no roars in the night. My heart thumped rapidly as I stored my food in a tiny fridge under the sink.

I had running cold water, but no toilet hookup. There was a common bathhouse in the trees behind the middle trailer, and we were expected to take turns cleaning it. After my first look at the place, I never went back. Instead, I used Dougal's bathroom to shower when I could, and if that wasn't possible, I waited for darkness, then made my way up the hill to Secret Valley's recreation building where there were clean showers and toilets.

I was starving again, but before I settled down to eat some of Dougal's leftovers, I communicated with my bladder to determine if it could hold out until morning. It couldn't.

Toiletries in hand, I opened the door. I looked both ways for slavering beasts, then raced up the hill to the rec hall where, after relieving myself, I took a shower and washed my hair. Returning to the safety of my trailer, I was barely able to stay awake long enough to lock my door before falling into bed. My empty stomach gave way to exhaustion, and I found sweet unconsciousness on the lumpy mattress.

It seemed I had only been asleep for seconds when there was a loud thumping on my door. My eyes shot open to find the sun was shining through my bedroom window. It was morning in Hemp Hollow, and my regular Sabbath visitor better be bearing the gift of strong coffee.

CHAPTER FIVE

I THREW AN OLD fleece jacket over my pyjamas and opened the door. My neighbour, Rae Zaborski, usually dropped in on Sunday morning with two cups of coffee. I looked at the old windup clock on the counter and wasn't surprised to see it register seven o'clock. Rae liked to get her visiting done before she left for church at ten-thirty.

"Come in, Rae," I said, "and close the door. It's chilly out there."

"Well, my dear, the temperature dipped a bit last night. Here, this will warm you up." She handed me a large blue mug.

"I hope this is strong."

"Extra strong Columbian for both of us."

She settled herself on my patched bench and pulled her yellow chenille bathrobe more tightly around her toned curves. Sunday was Rae's day of rest, and it was sacrosanct. The bathrobe stayed put until she put on her church-going clothes for an hour, then it returned for the duration of the day.

"I had a really good week," she began. "Fourteen clients."

"Geez, Rae, that's more than two a day. How can you stand it, and where do they all come from?"

"Two a day is usually my limit, but I have my regular customers like Ewan Quigley and some of his friends, and I don't like to turn any of them down. A couple of the guys were willing to pay extra if I fit them in, so I thought, what the heck, it's all money in the bank, right?"

"I guess." Ewan Quigley? Eesh. I guess if you closed your eyes, you could pretend you were doing George Clooney.

Rae was a hooker, and quite a successful one. She charged a hundred dollars a pop, so made at least twelve hundred dollars a week, tax-free. Rae also taught water aerobics to seniors at the high school three afternoons a week for minimum wage. Since her income from this legitimate job was so limited, like mine, she never paid a lick of income tax. But she filed religiously each year to keep Revenue Canada happy — and ignorant of her more lucrative career.

Rae was only twenty-five, but she had been investing her money since she was eighteen. She took endless aesthetics courses and figured that by age thirty she would have enough money to open her own spa. She already had a name picked out: Pamper U.

"Today we're doing your hair, remember?" She indicated the plastic shopping bag hanging off one arm.

"I forgot. I don't think I have time today, Rae. I have a real estate client at one o'clock. Nothing will come of it, as usual, but Elaine Simms made the appointment with people from out of town, so I have to meet them at the Barrister house."

"We'll be done in less than two hours. Come on, quit stalling. I've been dying to get my hands on your hair for ages."

"Rae, I don't think …"

"Come on, Bliss. Don't be such a chicken. I do my own hair and, look, it's fine." She shook her multi-shaded blond mane. It did look good, but I didn't really want to look like the cheerleader Rae once was.

"Look," she coaxed, "I have a base colour that's the same as your own. Then I have two accent colours to highlight with, copper and caramel. It will be subtle, but look gorgeous. And I'll trim your hair just a bit. That way you can still pull it back in a ponytail when you're working."

My hair badly needed a cut, and cheap shampoos and no conditioners had faded my light brown colour to a shade not unlike the lichen on a pile of north-facing rocks.

"Okay, let's do it."

Two hours later, Rae had gone back to her own trailer to dress before church and I was contemplating myself in the chipped mirror in my tiny, non-functioning bathroom. I had to admit my hair looked good. I swung it back and forth and applied lipstick and eyeliner. The mascara and the light green eyeshadow had dried out long ago.

Grabbing a mystery paperback I'd started months ago, I made myself comfortable on the front step and let the sun warm my face and bare arms. Beside me, the shiny purple paint on Rae's trailer shot shards of light into my eyes. I changed position, and this left me facing the Quigley residence.

Ewan and Sarah Quigley's trailer was, like mine, still the original beige it left the showroom in thirty or forty years ago. Two webbed lawn chairs that had seen better years sat out front beside a pile of empty beer cartons. The stringy, sixtyish Sarah was fond of sitting in one of the chairs in her leathery birthday suit, but thankfully she was absent today. Several times, I waved at her and called out a friendly greeting, but she stared silently across the compound until I turned away in embarrassment. Now I pretended not to notice her tanning her wrinkled hide.

I kept an eye on my watch. I wanted my weekly treat at Tim Hortons before the house showing, and for a moment I let myself fantasize about closing the sale. The Barrister house was listed at one hundred and sixty thousand, so if the buyer offered a hundred and forty-five, say, and the commission was six percent, which I would have to split with Elaine, I would get …

Visions of enough money to find an out-of-town lawyer brave enough to take on the Weasel danced in my head. When I heard voices behind me, I turned in alarm, thinking that some of Ewan's disreputable friends might be drunk and ready for love. Not that I could easily be mistaken for Rae.

Instead, I looked up into two sets of mirrored sunglasses, one worn by a female cop and the other by … definitely not a female.

Damn. Somebody ratted on Rae and the cops were here to arrest her for prostitution. I glanced at Rae's purple trailer. Some days you could see the trailer rocking, but since it was Sunday, all was still. I was determined to know nothing and say nothing about Rae's activities.

"Are you Bliss Cornwall?" asked the taller of the two. I noticed that his uniform was a good fit, tailored exactly to his body measurements. His hands rested on his belt, close to his gun.

"Yes?"

He took off his hat, revealing short, spiky blond hair. "Well, you are or you aren't Bliss Cornwall. Which is it?"

"Yes, I am Bliss Moonbeam Cornwall. Can I help you?"

"Moonbeam? Interesting middle name you have." The female cop snickered. She had a slim figure and was close to my age. Dark hair was pinned back under her cap.

"My parents were wannabe flower children. They were too late for the sixties, so they tried to compensate by naming their daughters Bliss Moonbeam and Blyth Starlight. I believe it has strengthened our characters." Celebrate your own uniqueness. That was another of my rules.

She had the nerve to laugh out loud. "So did your parents embrace any other trends from the sixties, like free love or pot smoking?"

Oh. My. God. They knew about Dougal's marijuana! Maybe Glory's too! I tried to swallow the panic caught in my throat.

"Hard to say, I never dared ask. They retired to Vancouver Island where I believe they are camping in a forest in their fifth wheel, or maybe chained to a giant redwood so the socialist developers won't chop it down and build a row of condos." I managed an uneasy smile.

"Please, can we get down to business," admonished the male cop. "Ms. Cornwall, I am Chief Neil Redfern and this is Constable Thea Vanderbloom."

He flashed an identification card. I remembered seeing his picture in our weekly newspaper several times. Since Chief Redfern was relatively young and not ugly, although I wasn't attracted to fair-haired men, he made good media copy. He had left his job as a Toronto detective to take up the post as Lockport's Chief of Police about two years ago.

"Now we all know who we are, why are we here? I lead a blameless life, I assure you. Frankly, I'm too busy to even jaywalk." Shit, it was jail for Dougal and Glory, and I would be forced to appear as chief witness for the Crown.

Constable Vanderbloom pulled a small black notebook and a pen from her breast pocket. She looked down at me and waited expectantly. I was nervous, and desperately tried to think of a way to avoid answering direct questions about two affluent Lockport homes where grass was cultivated and served.

Chief Redfern said, "Do you know Julian Barnfeather?"

That threw me. What the hell. Was the creep accusing me of something?

"Is this a trick question? Because I might want a lawyer, but then again, all the lawyers I know are crooks, so I guess I'll do without."

He tried again. "According to the Cemetery Commission, you work at the Good Shepherd Cemetery on Saturdays from April until October. Is this true?"

"November. Yes?" One word answers were best.

He took off his sunglasses and rubbed his forehead. In an effort to hide the fact that I forgot the question after one glance at his deep blue eyes — they were navy, really — I quickly turned away and scanned the treetops for eagles or buzzards. In the split second those eyes were locked on mine, I was sure all my recent indiscretions had been revealed. Like socializing with pot growers and hookers, and thinking about dropping a dead skunk on my ex-husband's doorstep.

"Yes you work at the cemetery? You don't seem to be too sure about anything this morning, Ms. Cornwall."

"Look, I'm not used to being interrogated before I've had my second cup of coffee." Not so smart, Cornwall, I told myself. When cornered by the law, it's not wise to reveal sarcasm is your first language.

"You call this an interrogation, Ms. Cornwall? These are very simple questions. Now, do you work at the cemetery on Saturdays and were you working yesterday? Yes or no will do."

"Yes. And, yes."

"Good. Did you see Julian Barnfeather during the course of the day?"

"I saw him in the morning, as usual, and that's it."

"So, you didn't see him again before you left the cemetery at the end of the day?"

"No, I did not. I left my tools outside the maintenance shed."

"Was there a reason for doing so?"

"He's a dickhead and I wanted to avoid him. I figured he would put the tools inside before he went home. He's always there when I leave at five o'clock — he locks the gates. My cousin called and wanted me to come right over so I left at five on the dot. I don't know what time Julian left."

"So you didn't see him yesterday before you left. You only saw him first thing in the morning. What time would that be?"

"Eight a.m."

"Did you have a conversation with him?"

"What's this all about? Is it illegal to call that fat doofus a perverted mistake of nature? Because if he's complaining about me, I have grounds to charge him with harassment." I drew myself up to my full sixty-two inches.

A condescending sigh escaped Chief Redfern's lips. The svelte Constable Vanderbloom just kept scribbling in her ratty black notebook.

Then I remembered the flashing lights and activity in the cemetery as I passed it last night.

"Did Julian Barnfeather have a heart attack or something?"

"You don't sound too broken up about the possibility of something happening to Julian Barnfeather, Ms. Cornwall," Constable Vanderbloom observed.

"Look, if Julian is sick or hurt, well, I'm a little sorry, but he won't be receiving a get well card from me."

"A sympathy card to his wife would be more appropriate," said the constable.

"Go on! Are you telling me he had a wife? And he's dead?" Then a sudden thought struck me. "What happened to him?"

Chief Redfern replied, "The autopsy report hasn't come back yet. His wife called us when he didn't show up for dinner last night. We sent an officer to the cemetery."

"Because," I said, like he hadn't spoken, "he could have been lying there dying while I was working. Maybe if I had put my tools away like I should have, I would have found him in time to call an ambulance." I shuddered at the thought of anyone, even Julian, lying in the shed, waiting for help that didn't come. Nobody deserves to die alone.

Suddenly, strong hands gripped my neck and pushed my head so far between my knees that my forehead touched the dirt. The hands held me down and all I could do was flail my arms and yell, "Stop. I haven't done anything. You're hurting me."

"Careful or she'll be screaming police brutality," said Constable Vanderbloom.

I was picked up immediately and held hanging a foot off the ground. I kicked him in the knee.

"Goddamn it!" He dropped me, but I managed to land on my feet. "What did you do that for? I thought you were going to faint."

"I never faint." My heart was beating wildly, and I hoped I wouldn't make a liar out of myself as my vision started fading to black at the edges.

"Then, if you're up to it, I have a few more questions."

"Go ahead." My head still felt like it might fly off into the clouds, but I wasn't going to admit to it.

"Could you see the shed from where you were working?"

I took a deep breath and my vision cleared. "No. The shed is in the middle of the cemetery surrounded by tall shrubs. I was working closest to the fence and Main Street."

"So you didn't see Mr. Barnfeather at all after eight in the morning? What about lunch and calls of nature?"

"I have a key to the bathroom behind the office building at the entrance to the cemetery. You can't see the maintenance shed from there. And I didn't stop for lunch yesterday."

"Did you see anything out of the ordinary?"

Neither cop noticed Ewan Quigley step out of his trailer behind them, take one look, then back quickly inside and close his door. And, between Rae's trailer and the Quigleys', a figure in dusty black leather and multiple chains draped across his chest melted back into the trees.

"No, and I didn't budge from my corner except for one trip to the bathroom. I have excellent bladder control."

Chief Redfern's lips compressed. "Can you describe the people you remember seeing?"

I wasn't going to be much help. I tried to avoid anyone I knew while I was working. It was just too awkward.

"Not really," I said slowly. "The cemetery is a popular place for walking but I didn't recognize anyone. You might ask the Friends of the Settlers, since there are always a few of them in the cemetery, although they probably don't see many folk wandering by their corner."

The glasses came off again. I lowered my eyes and stared at the third button from the top of his shirt. Constable Vanderbloom stopped writing.

"Who are the Friends of the Settlers?"

"It's a volunteer group that looks after the pioneer graves in the northwest corner. That area was the original Lockport Cemetery. The rest has grown out from there. There's an iron fence and pine trees around the site."

"How do we get in touch with these people?"

"There are two or three of them there every Saturday, all quite elderly. You can probably get the names from the Cemetery Board."

I didn't divulge that one of the Friends was Fern Brickle, my Wednesday afternoon cleaning job. I didn't want the police to bother her. She was a nice lady and gave me a fifty-dollar bonus at Christmas.

"So, I'm getting the impression that Julian didn't die from a heart attack or stroke," I ventured, once the notebook was stowed away and both pairs of sunglasses were back in position. The activity in the cemetery the night before made sense, now.

Chief Redfern's lip twitched briefly. "Until the autopsy results are in, we don't know what we're dealing with."

"If the coroner indicates Mr. Barnfeather's death was not due to natural causes, we'll be back for another chat. Don't leave town," said the constable, showing her white teeth in a smile.

"I'll be in touch." Chief Redfern nodded at me.

As they scrambled up the embankment, I sank down on the step. Julian might have been murdered. Lost in thought, I paid little attention to the leather-clad shadow as it emerged from the trees again and slipped into the Quigley trailer.

CHAPTER
SIX

IF THE COPS DID determine that Julian had been murdered, would I be their chief suspect? I tried to put things into perspective. I didn't kill Julian, so I should stop worrying. But memories of Guy Morin, Donald Marshall, David Milgaard, and Stephen Truscott kept intruding on my thoughts. Innocent people did go to prison.

Changing into my real estate agent outfit of white silk shirt, black pantsuit, and motorcycle boots, I rode to Tim Hortons on Main Street and ordered my Sunday favourites. Sitting at a table, I organized my coffee and whole wheat bagel.

I was taking my first bite into thick strawberry cream cheese when a man dropped into the seat opposite me. He placed his coffee mug and cruller on the table and smiled.

I didn't smile back.

"How are you doing, Bliss?" the Weasel asked, his smile still pasted in place. I barely registered the close-cropped dark hair and light brown eyes that, a lifetime ago, could quicken my pulse and send my heart soaring.

"Couldn't be better. And you?"

"Same. You're looking very well." He lifted his mug to his lips, his eyes studying me over the rim.

I swung my tri-coloured hair.

"Sued any widows or orphans lately?"

"Come on, Bliss, when are you going to stop obsessing about the past and move on? You're young and could have a wonderful future." His white teeth bit into the cruller.

"It could be wonderful if I had some money to get on with."

"Let's not go over this again. Our relationship is over, and I have no obligation to continue to carry you financially."

I looked at him through a red haze of rage. "You're an asshole, Mike. I supported you through law school, and yet it's okay for you to tell me to leave our house with three suitcases and two hundred dollars in my purse?"

"You took your jewellery, and I gave you the fifty-acre property."

"Fifty acres of swamp, and we won't even discuss the cheap jewellery."

He deftly changed the subject. "Let the past go, Bliss. I want to tell you something before it becomes public knowledge."

"Don't tell me you and Andrea are having a baby?" The time had never been right for me to get pregnant, and if he told me he was about to become a father, I would stab him with the plastic knife in my hand.

He smirked. "Not yet, but we're hopeful."

"Well, you better get on with it. Andrea is, what, forty? Forty-one?"

"She's only thirty-eight. Now listen. I will be running for federal office in the next election."

I put the plastic knife down and scrutinized the smooth, satisfied face. "You're the Liberal candidate?"

"Yes." He managed to look modest and proud at the same time.

"Bliss." He leaned forward, cupping his hands around his coffee mug. "I was hoping to find you here this morning. I have a cheque for you, for five thousand dollars." His eyes crinkled at the corners but remained watchful as he pushed a cheque across the table.

I inhaled a large piece of bagel and spent a few seconds coughing it back up. It gave me time to think. I didn't believe in the Tooth Fairy, nor did I expect to win a lottery. Therefore, I didn't believe in the Weasel's cheque.

"Five thousand dollars isn't near enough payoff for putting up with you for eight years."

"Bliss, can't you forget your bitterness? You could use the money to relocate, perhaps to Toronto. You might even go back to school."

"With five thousand dollars? You are a very strange man, Mike. I think I can make more money by staying right here in Lockport."

He ran a well-manicured finger around the rim of his cup. "From what I hear, you are working several minimum-wage jobs. I think you can do better."

"I think I can too." I watched his eyes and stuffed a smaller piece of bagel into my mouth.

Mike shifted in his chair and gazed into his coffee. "I hear there was a death in the cemetery yesterday. Weren't you working there?"

"Yes. Apparently Julian Barnfeather was found dead last evening."

"Have the police contacted you?"

"We had a chat."

"I hope they don't think you had anything to do with his death."

"Why would they?"

"No reason, except that you were apparently the last person to see him alive."

"Except for whoever murdered him, assuming he was murdered."

He looked me in the eye. "I wouldn't want to see you involved in a messy murder investigation."

"I'll bet you wouldn't. It wouldn't be good for your public image. Your ex-wife's name in the paper in the same column as that of a murder victim." My mind had been racing and crossed the finish line when I finally figured out why Mike was offering me a cheque to get out of town.

I stabbed my knife into the remains of his cruller, pretending it was his throat. He managed not to flinch.

"Don't you have to be a member of the provincial party first, before you can run federally?"

"Not at all. The party has convinced me that I have an excellent chance of becoming the next MP for this riding. Now, are you going to accept this cheque? If so, I have a waiver for you to sign."

"No thanks. I think I'll hold out for more."

"There won't be any more. This is all I'm going to offer, so take it or leave it."

I tried to look pensive. "I wonder if one of the major newspapers, maybe the *Toronto Star*, will want to interview me."

Mike snorted. "Why would they?"

"Because they like to print controversial articles, especially political ones. They might feel that an interview with the impoverished ex-wife of a Liberal candidate would increase their readership. Their photographer could take my picture leaning on a tombstone with my rake. I'd wear my denim overalls, the ones with the rip in the knee."

I was just yanking the Weasel's balls, but by the look on his face, he wasn't enjoying it. A warm, fuzzy feeling washed over me. Maybe, just maybe, I was on to something. "You're crazy, Bliss. And nobody is going to take a nutcase seriously. You might as well take this cheque and sign the waiver."

I had no doubt he would do well in politics, playing in the big boys' sandbox. Andrea's father was a Liberal backbencher from a neighbouring constituency and would know how to groom Mike for public display. The Weasel might even wind up becoming Canada's youngest prime minister someday and the thought made the fuzzy feeling disappear in a wink. With Mike at the helm, there would be no women and children first into the lifeboats. It was my civic duty to prevent such a catastrophe from happening

"Looks like you have a golden future ahead of you, Mike. But you'll be wide open to public scrutiny if you run. Female voters won't endorse a wife abuser and skinflint."

Aware of curious glances from nearby tables, Mike lowered his voice. "What are you talking about? I never laid a hand on you, and I paid for all your clothes, country club fees, and anything else you needed."

"True, but I didn't even have my own chequing account or a joint account with you. I had to beg every time I wanted money for something other than clothes or country club fees. And I think I can make a case for emotional and verbal abuse."

"I promise you, Bliss, you will not stand in the way of my future." His eyes were as cold as I had ever seen them, and I suppressed a shiver.

Taking my time, I opened my purse and took out a pen and small notepad. I wrote briefly on it, then stood up. "You think about our discussion, Mike. If you want this little piece of your past to go away, then here is what it will cost you." I saw this scene in a movie once.

I handed him the slip of paper and walked off, leaving Mike to stare at the paper in his hand.

A cool breeze had sprung up while I was in the coffee shop. I pulled my leather jacket out of the saddlebag and zipped it up to my chin, trying not to think of the fashion faux pas I was committing. Driving past the town centre, where the skunk still reposed in fragrant death, I turned onto River Road and headed for my real estate appointment.

After my marriage broke up, I had had high hopes of making a decent living by selling real estate. I knew a lot of people and was sure my friends would support me by signing on as my clients. I should have saved the money I spent on the real estate course and the board exam.

Elaine Simms owned the only real estate business in Lockport and she finally confessed, after several client-free months, that the affluent citizens wanted their real estate needs met by Elaine herself, broker extraordinaire. The rest of her customer base was handled by her sister, Rachel. She saw my disappointment and tossed me the listing for the old Barrister house, a property that had been languishing on the market for years.

The property sat on a scraggy seven acres at the junction of River Road and County Road 10, south of Lockport. Once a grand estate, the Georgian-style house now appeared forlorn and neglected, with boarded-up windows and lawns overgrown with weeds. Inside, new plumbing and wiring were needed before the house could be deemed habitable. I had shown the property three times, but each prospective buyer had shied away before even entering the front door. I didn't expect this time to be any different.

Since I didn't have a vehicle to pick up the clients, Elaine had arranged for them to meet me at the house. A silver late-model Volkswagen convertible with red leather seats burrowed into the calf-high weeds. I fluffed up my hair and prepared to dazzle Ivy and Chesley Belcourt from St. Catharines.

Two black-clad figures rounded the corner of the house and moved toward me.

Ivy was tall and fleshy with short grey hair. Her high-necked dress hugged a formidable bosom, skimmed the rest of her body, and ended just above the top of heavy ankles that overflowed sturdy leather flats. A sleeveless vest reached mid-thigh and flapped in the brisk breeze, giving Ivy the air of a huge crow trying to lift off. She relied on a cane to help her manoeuvre the uneven ground and, as they came closer, I noticed the slash of bright red lipstick and the translucent blue eyes. I put her in her mid-sixties.

Chesley was much younger and, assuming he was Ivy's son, he took after his dad. He was a couple of inches shorter than Ivy, and bony. His wide, thick lips opened and closed like a beached bass and, in the absence of words, I surmised he was mouth-breathing. His large round eyes were an unusual shade, and one glance at them turned me off green grapes for life. Medium brown hair, straight and cut to chin level all around, was pushed back behind his ears. A belt and red suspenders secured his pants, and white Nikes peeped out from under the wide hems.

I approached them, trying not to trip on the rough ground, and we stopped a polite four feet apart.

I could see Ivy glance at my silk suit, but couldn't read her expression to tell if she approved of the classic style, or recognized my outfit for what it was — three years out of date on a slightly smaller body than it was meant for. At least it was black, their favourite colour.

"How do you do? Mr. and Mrs. Belcourt? I hope I haven't kept you waiting."

"You must be Ms. Cornwall." Chesley reached out with his thin hand and shook two of my fingers. "We're pleased to meet you, aren't we, Mum?"

"Yes, of course. Now, Ms. Cornwall, Chesley and I arrived somewhat early, so we took a walk around the grounds. We have the specifications supplied by Miss Simms, so we are aware of the property boundaries and don't wish to waste your time, or ours, on exploring any further out here."

"Oh, I understand, Mrs. Belcourt. This property needs a lot of work and not everyone wants to take on a project like this. I'll just give you my card in case you want to look at something else in the area." I stopped when I saw the raised eyebrows on Chesley, and Ivy's pursed lips.

The mother and son looked at each other, and then Chesley said, "We would like to see inside the house now. That is why we came, after all."

"You did bring the key, did you not, Ms. Cornwall?" Ivy's hooded eyes dared me to admit I hadn't.

"Certainly. I have it right here." I threw my shoulders back and led the way through the vegetation sprouting through cracks in the flagstone path.

I inserted the key into the lock box attached to the weathered oak door. This was the second time I had been inside the house. Elaine had shown me around before turning the listing over to me, and I was not hopeful the Belcourts would be any more impressed than I had been.

Entering the hall, I flicked on the lights. The gloom from the boarded-up windows could not be dispelled by electricity. I pulled three small flashlights out of my purse and handed two over to the mother and son.

"Here you go. I don't think there are any holes in the floor, but watch where you step just in case." The place was as sinister as a horror movie set, and I had to shake off a feeling that I would round a corner and find a stack of corpses with an axe murderer standing proudly over his work. Heavy burgundy drapes hung in tatters over the sitting room windows, while the area rugs virtually moved with whatever insect life was living in them. Furniture squatted ominously in the murky shadows, and curls of dark, flocked paper rolled down the walls.

"Good place for a murder mystery dinner," I said, just to break the ice. Neither Belcourt had uttered a sound since we entered the house, unless you counted Ivy's heavy breathing as she stumped along in my wake. I couldn't hear Chesley. He was a quiet mouth-breather.

"I assume this is the kitchen?" Ivy asked, as we opened a door off the main hall.

I flicked another switch and said, "Looks like. I don't suppose you want to see upstairs?"

"We certainly do," came Chesley's precise tones from somewhere behind me.

"Okay, then." I led them back into the hall and headed toward what I hoped was the front door. I was feeling my way, and hoping not to touch anything too gross ... or dead. The air wrapped us in an odour of decay. There were probably dead rats in the walls.

I wasn't keen on taking Ivy upstairs. Considering her bulk, if she didn't put a foot through the treads, she was apt to take a tumble, and I knew whose fault that would turn out to be.

Step by careful step, we ascended what must have once been a beautiful staircase, but was now reduced to a rotting death trap. I turned on all the lights I could find as the three of us stood in a long hallway leading to four empty bedrooms.

Stepping into the bathroom, I said with the total lack of sarcasm I learned in realtor's school, "As you can see, the bathroom needs some updating."

"That's an understatement. The plumbing is archaic and the electrical service is a fire waiting to happen, I'm sure," Ivy noted, her lips thinning as she looked around the dismal room.

No shit, Ivy.

"Well, you can take that into consideration if you want to make an offer," I told her. They would have to be total idiots to even consider buying the dump.

We made our way slowly down the stairs, me in the lead to break the fall of my prospective client, again by the book. Soon we were blinking at one another in the sunlight, like a trio of bears after a long winter's nap. They handed back the flashlights.

"I believe this property is close to Lake Huron, Miss Cornwall?" Ivy thwacked at some nearby weeds with her cane and uncovered part of a small stone fountain, now filled with wild daisies.

"Bird River bisects the northwest corner of the property, as I'm sure you noticed, then crosses the road. It runs into the lake about a quarter-mile away."

"Well, thank you, Ms. Cornwall. We'll be in touch," said Chesley, flicking a strand of stray hair behind his ears.

Yeah, right. I gave them each a card and watched as Chesley helped his mother into the driver's side of the convertible. The tires kicked up a cloud of gravel and leaves as Ivy floored the gas pedal, and the Bug disappeared down the county road toward town.

After locking up, I drove along River Road toward the bridge over Bird River. It was time to check on my swamp.

CHAPTER
SEVEN

IF SOMEONE TOLD ME she was acquiring a fifty-acre waterfront property as a divorce settlement, I would tell her to have the property appraised before signing off rights to any other assets. Not that the Weasel gave me a choice. Apparently, I was the last person in town to know he wanted a divorce, and before my head stopped spinning I was standing on the front porch with my BlackBerry, several suitcases, a couple of cardboard boxes, and the keys to a ten-year-old Nissan. Oh, and the deed to fifty acres on Bird River. Look up *dumb* in the dictionary and you'll find my picture.

My parents were already camped on Vancouver Island, having rented their house out to a retired couple from Hamilton who loved small-town life and weren't leaving anytime soon. So I couldn't stay there, and Dougal was knee-deep in his own marital woes. Not that it would have been a good idea to live with

Dougal anyway. One of us would have ended up buried under the lilacs in the backyard.

While I was standing there on my doorstep, I realized that there wasn't one person in Lockport I could go to for shelter. Each of my friends was half of a couple, and the couples were now Mike's friends. So I slept in my car on the marshy banks of Bird River.

During the next week, I showered at the Y, found myself a job four days a week at the library, a Saturday seasonal job at the cemetery, and persuaded Garnet Maybe, owner of the Golden Goddess Spa, to hire me to teach yoga classes on Tuesday and Thursday nights. The two cleaning jobs on Wednesdays came later.

I drove my clunker to Owen Sound and pawned my engagement and wedding rings, plus a few other pieces, then returned to Lockport's used car dealership, where I sold the Nissan and bought the Savage. I had money left over to pay the first and last month's rent on the trailer in Hemp Hollow. Only then did I call my older sister, Blyth, to tell her what had happened.

Blyth was horrified and insisted I move in with her. I refused for two reasons. First, Blyth's husband, Matt, was working on his psychology doctorate, and they had two small toddlers in day care, so they could ill afford another mouth to feed or another body to bed down in their small semi-detached house in the Rexdale area of Toronto. Secondly, I was out for blood — Mike's blood — and I couldn't get it from Toronto.

So began my campaign of revenge. Both Dougal and Blyth pointed out to me that I was hurting no one but myself. Chances of recovering any assets dimmed with each passing month I stayed in Lockport. I made sure I put a certain amount aside every week and had never once dipped into it. I didn't care that I nearly froze in the winter or would have starved if not for Dougal's leftovers. Revenge was the motivation that spurred me to get up in the mornings.

Elaine and Rachel Simms had both come out to the Bird River property and given me their expert opinions on the value. It was clear why Mike had off-loaded this waterfront property onto me in lieu of money. It was a swamp and no developer would ever attempt to build on it. Sure, this habitat housed cranes, ducks, geese, and other water fowl, but birds don't buy lots or build condos.

I walked back to the road, swung my leg over my Savage, and kicked it to life. As I eased out onto the road, I promised myself that somehow, some way, I was going to pay the bastard back for this little paper trick. He would roast in hell before I was through with him, and he could kiss his political career goodbye.

I decided to go to Dougal's, maybe find a little something in his fridge to eat before we bearded the red-haired dragon in her lair. I passed the Super 8 Motel on the highway into town and noted the silver Volkswagen parked in front of one of the units. So the Belcourts were staying over. Maybe that was a good sign for me, but I refused to get my hopes up. They were probably talking to Elaine on the phone this minute and arranging to see more suitable properties.

The main street was quiet as I drove through town. It was just me and the dead skunk, until I saw Chief Redfern standing on the sidewalk in front of the police station. He waved at me with one of those cop gestures that tolerates no refusal. Still holding my breath against the road-kill stench, I pulled over to the curb.

Before he could open his mouth, I said, nearly gagging over the words, "Can't you get Public Works to pick up that skunk?"

"There appears to be a political issue involved. It should be resolved by tomorrow."

"I think I'm going to barf." If I expected sympathy, there was none forthcoming from this public servant. The indescribable odour clung to the lining of my throat, and it was touch and go for a minute.

"Try and control yourself. I want to talk to you about Julian Barnfeather. Do you want to talk here, or in my office?"

In answer, I ran past him and up the steps, my hand over my mouth and nose. The vestibule of the police station was deserted and nondescript, and I let him take my arm and lead me through into a private office with his name and title stamped on the door.

Collapsing into a straight-backed chair, I took off my helmet, shook out my hair, and unzipped my jacket. As I sucked oxygen into my lungs, I felt my stomach relax, but I could still taste and smell the decay. Just to be safe, I located the waste basket and figured I could hit it if required.

Noting his attention on my pantsuit and silk shirt, I said, "Among my other accomplishments, I am a realtor. I just finished showing a house."

"It's your grave-tending profession I want to discuss." Chief Redfern sat on the front of his desk so his legs were mere inches from my knees. An intimidating stance learned at advanced detecting courses, no doubt.

"Go ahead," I told him, wishing I had a drink of water. Saliva collected in my mouth, and I quickly swallowed.

"We got the autopsy report back. Would you like to hear what it says?" Without waiting for my answer, he picked up a file from behind him, opened it, and glanced over the words, turning a page every few seconds. Another interrogation technique — force the suspect to wait and wonder what evidence has been amassed to throw her in the big house for ten years. Oh wait, that sentence was reserved for serial killers in this country. One murder would get me about eighteen months.

"Are you with me, Ms. Cornwall?" He had left his perch in front of me and was now sitting at his chair, with the desk between us. I relaxed slightly, but was still on guard.

"What I'm going to tell you will be public knowledge by tomorrow. Mr. Barnfeather died from severe trauma to the head."

I looked at Chief Redfern with suspicion. "If somebody hit him over the head, don't look at me. I didn't do it."

A chilly smile flitted across his lips. "Mr. Barnfeather's mortal wound was near the back of the head, close to the top. You're too short to have hit him there unless you were standing on a step stool. And his chair was against the wall, facing the door, so unless you squeezed behind him, you didn't do it that way either."

I shuddered. I actually did have to squeeze past Julian, but I wasn't tightening my own noose. "Not likely.

So you're saying the person that hit him had to be tall and standing behind him?"

"I'm saying nothing of the kind, Ms. Cornwall. You're the one suggesting the victim was hit with something, by somebody."

"What? You said Julian died from a blow to the head."

"The coroner is quite sure that Mr. Barnfeather fell and hit his head."

Was this guy playing games with me? Did he have nothing better to do on a Sunday afternoon than torment innocent citizens? I got up and headed for the door. "So it wasn't murder at all. Thanks for the entertainment. You have quite a way with a story, but if you'll excuse me, I have things to do."

"Sit down, Ms. Cornwall. I'm not finished."

I plodded back to the chair and sat. My stomach was flipping, and I couldn't tell if the smell had permeated the building or was stuck to the mucous membranes of my nose.

"Mr. Barnfeather died from a fall, but not in the maintenance shed. Forensics came back negative on all surfaces in the shed. He died elsewhere and was transported to the shed afterward."

"I don't remember seeing Julian actually doing any work in the cemetery. Maybe he tripped on his way to the washroom and fell against a headstone."

"We've looked at the headstones in the immediate area, but they're clean. But we can't check them all. There must be thousands. In any case, we can't be sure what he fell against. It could have been a rock."

"Okay, without six or seven accomplices, do you really think I could carry Julian's body to the shed, even a few feet? Or drag him? He must weigh four hundred pounds."

"Why do you persist in making this all about you, Ms. Cornwall? I haven't accused you of anything, but I'm beginning to suspect you have a guilty conscience."

"Bull!" Now I was getting angry. "Your constable implied I might be a suspect, and now you're questioning me and tying me all up in knots. If you don't think I did anything to Julian, then why am I here?"

Redfern stood up and came around his desk to stand in front of me again. My stomach burbled.

"Mr. Barnfeather didn't have to work on Saturdays, yet he was there every day you were working. I wonder why that was, Ms. Cornwall?"

"How should I know? It certainly couldn't have been for the few minutes at the beginning and end of the day when he could harass me. He sometimes walked around the cemetery, but he never came near me when I was working. He was probably afraid I'd whack him with my hoe if he tried anything in plain view."

Whoops, I shouldn't have said that, but Chief Redfern ignored my comment. Instead, he dangled a small plastic bag in front of my eyes. His own eyes were hard.

"Do you think it possible Mr. Barnfeather harassed you to keep you away from the shed during the day? By your own admission, you never went near the shed after collecting your tools until it was time to return them at quitting time. Until yesterday, that is, when you left your tools outside for Mr. Barnfeather to put away."

"Yesterday, I had other business to attend to. And I simply couldn't face Julian again. You seem to be suggesting Julian didn't act like a pervert because of my overwhelming cuteness, but for some more sinister reason."

He swung the plastic bag gently, moving it closer to my face. I felt my eyes cross.

"We found this in Julian Barnfeather's hair. Very close to the wound. Do you know what this is, Ms. Cornwall?"

I leaned away from the bag to bring it into focus. It contained a small green-brown object, flattened. I looked up. "I don't know. A piece of fabric? Maybe a leaf?"

"A leaf indeed. Any idea what plant this leaf came from?"

I shook my head, but a horrible glimmer of an idea was beginning to take shape in my brain. Please, no, not again. Surely not.

"This, Ms. Cornwall, is marijuana. Any idea where it may have come from?"

I dove for the waste basket, and just made it. Mostly.

CHAPTER
EIGHT

THE INTERVIEW WAS OVER. Chief Redfern jerked his thumb at the door, and I made a run for it, leaving him to clean off his pants and shoes. You'd think an experienced homicide cop from Toronto would know better than to stand so close to someone struggling to keep her breakfast down.

I retched non-productively while starting my bike and driving away from the skunk as quickly as possible. I detoured off Main Street onto Morningside Drive and stopped in front of my parents' ranch-style house.

Even though the tenants, Joy and Bob MacPherson, emailed my parents routinely with news of their garden and the condition of the toilets, I had promised I would drop in from time to time and check on things. Then I'd text them on my BlackBerry, "All's well here." They would reply, "Thnx, hp yr wl," which was their idea of the hip way to correspond.

They had left town before the Weasel blindsided me, and I had sworn Blyth to absolute silence about my financial predicament. My father had retired early from his manager's position with the Royal Bank of Canada, defiantly bought a gigantic fifth wheel in the face of rising gas prices, and headed for the West Coast. My mother, a homemaker and proud of it, was delighted at the prospect of living unencumbered by eight-foot snow drifts in winter and dried-out lawns in summer.

I hoped they were now strolling along a pebbled beach, listening to dolphins chatter in the distance, maybe drinking a margarita. I wouldn't put it past them to be sharing a joint with real hippies. Apparently the authorities were more relaxed on the West Coast about the weed thing. Still, I couldn't help wishing they would come home so I could move in with them.

Hearing voices around back, I found Joy and Bob enjoying a couple of Bud Lights on the deck. They were a pleasant couple in their sixties, lean and wrinkled from the sun. With matching white hair, they looked like a pair of dandelions gone to seed. Bob was confined to a wheelchair, the result of a three-car pileup on the 401 two years previously. He was forced to retire from his toxicology professorship at the University of Guelph, and the couple had moved to Lockport where they had spent many summers sailing on nearby Lake Huron. Joy rose quickly from her wicker chair and came forward to greet me, with Bob rolling slowly down the ramp to the bricked patio area below the deck.

They insisted on showing me around the garden, and I got a bit of a fright when I spotted some tall ferns enjoying the shade beside the shed wall. I sidled up to them for a better look and satisfied myself the plants were innocent. I had to get hold of myself. I was seeing the demon weed everywhere.

After my brief visit, Joy and Bob accompanied me to the curb and waved me off. Passing the deck again, I glimpsed a couple of burning cigarettes in an ashtray on the small table and managed a good sniff. Bob saw my glance and said, "We only smoke outside. Your parents were quite adamant that they rent to non-smokers."

I kept my face neutral, but the smoke was definitely illegal — I was becoming quite the expert on that.

Dougal was in his solarium spritzing his orchids. Some had dozens of white or pastel flowers on tall stalks; others were only a few inches high and not yet flowering. He had rearranged his marijuana plants, scattering them artfully among the tables of orchids.

"If anyone looks in the windows, they'll see your grass. I'm surprised that hasn't happened already."

He shrugged dismissively. "The gate is locked and no one can get in without coming through the house — and the hydro meter is on the side."

"Someone could climb over the back fence from the cornfield," I persisted.

He snorted. "Who's going to wade through a mile-long cornfield to climb over my fence?"

"Dougal, with this number of plants you could be charged with possession for the purpose of trafficking." It was amazing what I remembered from typing Mike's criminology papers at university.

"Noted."

I walked closer to the Titan Arum. "Hey, this thing has grown a foot since I saw it yesterday."

The spadix was markedly taller, and a pink hue was showing through the cream-speckled green of the frilly spathe encircling its base. Looked at a section at a time, the thing had a bizarre kind of beauty.

"Aren't you worried it will grow up through the glass ceiling and break it?"

"If you look up, dear Bliss, you'll see the container is positioned directly beneath the section of the roof that I can open with this switch here. But it won't grow that tall. You worry about everything. Are you sure you aren't obsessive-compulsive?"

It was my turn to snort at him. "That's pretty funny coming from an agoraphobic."

"Obviously, mental disorders run in the family. Think about it, you're obsessed with getting back at Mike and seem willing to starve yourself to attain some form of justice that isn't going to happen."

"Yes, it will. I'm working on a new plan."

Simon shuffled out of his cage and cocked his head in my direction. "Baby, baby." He opened and closed his curved beak enticingly.

"He wants you to give him one of those jujubes. He likes the black ones."

"Not happening," I replied and reached out to touch the ribbed exterior of the spathe. But before my fingers made contact, Dougal squeezed my hand.

"Don't touch it! Any stress at all could make the whole structure collapse. Do you know how much energy it takes for this Titan to grow tall enough to bloom?"

"Actually, no," I said, wiggling my fingers. "We're due at Glory's soon. Is there anything to eat in the fridge?"

"I think there's a Thai stir-fry. Mrs. Boudreau made it earlier in the week, and I took it out of the freezer this afternoon. As usual, there's enough for an army. Help yourself, but leave some for me."

I took my army-sized appetite to the kitchen, where I ate precisely half the stir-fry and drank a bottle of water. Dougal declared he was too nervous about the upcoming meeting with his ex-wife to eat a bite, but he kept me company at the table and nattered about harvesting his pot crop. I tried not to listen, figuring the less I knew, the less I could testify about, but the odd fact crept in about processing the buds and hanging the plants upside down to dry, and yada yada.

"So, how are Sandy and Randy?" he asked while I was cleaning my plate for the dishwasher. My parents' names are Sandra and Randall, but Dougal seemed to think it was funny to use rhyming nicknames for his aunt and uncle.

"Fine. I've been thinking seriously about taking the money I've saved and buying myself an airline ticket to visit them. Maybe stay for a year or so." Nothing was farther from my mind, but I wanted to see Dougal's reaction to losing his slave.

"Oh. Good idea. I've been telling you to move on and forget about Mike. I'm sure Randy and Sandy will be glad to have you."

I felt mean when I saw Dougal's fingers shaking. He lit up one of his joints, and I felt even worse.

"I was just kidding. You know I'm not going any-where, at least until I force Mike to his knees, and that might take a while."

He smiled faintly and blew smoke in my face. I got up from the table, coughing.

"Let's get ready," I said to him. "Get your jacket and Simon and we'll saddle up."

Naturally, it wasn't that simple. I had to hold Dougal's joint while he struggled into his jacket and tried to force Simon inside. Simon had never been inside a jacket before, and wasn't going there now without a fuss. Dougal told him he would have a nice ride and a won-derful adventure. For a bird that hadn't been outdoors in years, this was not a tempting offer.

"Bad boy, bad boy," he screeched in Melanie's voice, making me wonder anew exactly what kind of relation-ship Dougal shared with his therapist.

"Help! Don't hurt me," the poor bird cried, this time sounding like Dougal. I forced the images of whips and black leather restraints out of my brain.

Finally, the parrot was inserted head first into the jacket. The fabric bulged and strained against the metal zipper. Dougal already wore a pained expression, likely due to the bird poop Simon was depositing inside his cotton cage.

I handed Dougal his joint and smelled my hand. Nasty. God help us if we got pulled over by the police. It was my understanding that police officers were trained to smell pot. Or maybe they just learned to recognize the smell from experience. With my exaggerated olfac-tory aptitude, I should hire myself out as a pot-finder.

The police would save money — I ate less than a sniffer-dog and didn't need an annual rabies shot.

Things got dicey when I put my spare helmet on Dougal. He realized this was it, he was really going out there, and panicked. I pried his fingers away from the knob and pulled him by the arm to the curb, where I had to lift his leg over the seat. He sat stiffly upright, eyes glued shut, clutching my shoulders so hard I knew there would be bruises in the morning.

"Hold onto the bars beside your seat," I instructed him. "You can't hang on to me or you'll pull us both over." We wouldn't be going fast or far, but still, it would hurt plenty if we hit the pavement.

I had to get off and position Dougal's hands in place. Then I started up and we were off, off to negotiate a pollen-swapping contract between a wronged woman and a worm (according to Glory), or a man-eating bar-racuda and a wronged husband (Dougal's view).

My opinion? They were both nuts and somebody better pay me a thousand dollars after this was over or I'd hurt them both.

CHAPTER
NINE

I LEFT MY FACE shield up on the short drive to Glory's mansion, and the soft air cooled my flushed cheeks. It would be a perfect night to drive along the back roads outside of town, enjoying the smell of cedars, hearing the early summer sound of crickets in the grass. That's the way I like to experience nature, whizzing by me on either side of a paved road.

Instead, Dougal ignored my instructions to keep his hands on the bars and relax his body to the rhythm of the bike. He sat rigidly upright and gripped my waist. There might as well be a 165-pound block of cement on the seat behind me. He wouldn't shut up, either.

"I can't do this, Bliss. Take me home. Do you hear me, turn this thing around now. It was a bad idea. I'll have to think of some other way to pollinate my Thor. Maybe I'll call Glory and try and set something up another way." Since we were barely moving, I heard every word in painful clarity.

"Not a chance. We're almost there, and you'll live through it."

"I don't care. I want to go back home. I've changed my mind about the whole thing. Just turn around!"

A lone vehicle passed us and, as it glided by, I saw the familiar squat shape of a silver Volkswagen Beetle convertible. So the Belcourts were taking a night tour of the more upscale part of town. If they were looking at real estate in this district, they wouldn't be interested in the Barrister property. I wasn't disappointed, since the idea of a commission from a sale was a non-starter from the day Elaine handed me the listing.

With Dougal whining in my ear like a neurotic mosquito, I drove through Glory's open wrought-iron gates and parked as close to the limestone steps as possible. Still, getting Dougal off the bike and up those steps to the front door was another challenge, and I ended up giving him a sharp kick on the calf to get him started. Thank God, Pan opened the door immediately. I shoved Dougal in ahead of me and stripped him of the helmet.

Pan and Dougal gazed at one another wordlessly while I divested myself of helmet and leather jacket, astonished to find I was still dressed in my black silk pantsuit. Not much protection if I dropped the bike on the way home.

Five minutes later, Glory and Dougal were squaring off in the middle of the Persian rug, standing six feet apart. Pan and I sat on one of the cream leather couches with a large bowl of popcorn between us, both of us reaching into the bowl without taking our eyes off the combatants. Simon had been fussed and cooed over by

Glory for just under fifteen seconds, then tossed onto the teak coffee table. Simon squawked in protest but uttered no profanities. Yet. I slipped a magazine under his tail feathers just in time.

Hands on slim hips, shoulders back and head high in full battle mode, Glory was the spitting image of Joan of Arc's evil twin. She wore a slinky pink tunic over matching wide-legged trousers. Pink toenails peeped out from three-inch gold sandals. Dougal, on the other hand, was still pasty and sweaty from his terrorizing minute-and-a-half ride. His buzzed hair was getting long on top, and I made a mental note to trim it, barbering being another of the personal services I provided.

Even before the agoraphobia, I doubted Dougal was a match for the hot-tempered Glory, but now I wouldn't have bet a loonie on his chances. The thousand dollars was fading away like mist at sunrise. I jammed another handful of popcorn into my mouth and tried to make peace with that fact. But it didn't work. I wanted that money.

"Okay, start talking and make it fast. You have two minutes to make your case, and then you can get out of my house." Glory looked at her jewel-studded watch, tapped a shapely foot, and glared at Dougal.

Hold on. I was under the impression that I had already blackmailed Glory into co-operating with Dougal's absurd pollinating scheme. But it appeared she thought the blackmail covered talking to Dougal only and not actually agreeing to the pollination swap. Watching Dougal's mouth impotently open and close, struck dumb by his ex-wife's fury, I believed a quick intervention was in order.

I stood up and walked around behind Dougal. Once I knew Glory could see me, I mimed a smoking action and winked at her. She got the message. Her eyeballs turned red as Satan's ass, and I turned away before I burst into flames. I poured two glasses of white wine and gave one to Pan. I decided I better find that list of ladies who wanted their houses cleaned on Wednesday mornings.

Her chest heaving with rage, Glory again addressed Dougal. "Well? Are you deaf? I said start talking."

"I wish I was deaf. Then I couldn't hear you screech like Simon when he wants a cracker." Ah, good, Dougal had found his voice.

"Listen, you worm. Just tell me what you want or Pan will toss you out on your pointy, stupid head. You and your backstabbing nitwit of a cousin."

The diminutive Pan paused with the wineglass half-way to his mouth, looking a bit concerned that he could shortly be called upon to bodily throw us out the door. "As you wish, Miss."

Glory looked at the two of us. "Are you drinking my Riesling?"

"The popcorn made us thirsty," I said, and took another swig in case she took the glass away from me. Pan upended his own wineglass and poured the contents down his throat.

"Okay, Glory, here's the deal." Dougal managed to pull himself together, looking less pasty and sweaty by the minute. "We both have an *Amorphophallus titanum*. Both plants appear to be ready to flower. This is an historic moment, and if we can put aside our differences, we can cross-pollinate these magnificent specimens.

Best case scenario is that both Titans will produce tubers, but there's a good chance that at least one will. We share the tubers equally, no matter which one reproduces. How about it? Just think, Sif and Thor can give us lots of little ones."

Pan and I looked at each other. Good grief, whatever would they name the babies?

As soon as Dougal started talking about tubers, Glory's red eyes turned bottle green with envy. The woman was an emotional chameleon. Dougal knew he had her hooked and moved in to close the deal.

"You won't even have to see me. As soon as the plants are ready, Bliss will transport the pollen between our houses. I'll pollinate Thor, and I'll show Bliss how to pollinate Sif."

Dougal looked every inch the expert botanist.

"Never mind Bliss." Glory spared me one brief, scornful glance. "Just supply the pollen. I'll do it myself. Or Pan will. And if Sif does flower, Pan can collect her pollen and send it over to Thor."

Beside me, Pan stirred uneasily. Probably not a plant biology major.

"Great. Now I just need to see Sif and take a few measurements." From his pocket, Dougal produced a carpenter's measuring tape. His eyes shone and he seemed willing, even eager, to make the trip to Glory's greenhouse. Next stop in his recovery: Shoppers Drug Mart to pick up his own medications.

I glanced at Glory, wondering how she was going to get around Dougal seeing her pot plants. No problem, it seemed.

"Uh uh," she told Dougal. "Tell Pan what you want and he'll do it. Bliss can go with him to help. You stay here and cogitate on your sins, which are many if you recall. If you open your mouth even once, you can wait outside on the front steps."

Take that, you agoraphobic.

Dougal gave us some directions on measurements, then whipped out a small digital camera and gave it to me with instructions to take a few overall shots plus several close-ups of the spathe.

"And don't, whatever you do, touch the Titan. It's so fragile. It could collapse at the slightest stress."

Glory gave Pan a meaningful look and raked me again with her eyes. The irises had more or less returned to their normal sea-blue, so I gave her another wink and followed Pan. Hopefully, Glory wouldn't eviscerate Dougal in my absence with her pink-tipped talons.

On the way to the greenhouse, I asked Pan, "Do you know what Dougal did to Glory? It's strange that no-one seems to have any idea."

He shrugged. "Haven't a clue. Don't forget I've only worked here since Miss Yates tossed your cousin out, and she doesn't confide in me. It must have been something serious, though. If anyone mentions him, her eyes turn red."

"I've noticed. He won't tell me either. He just calls her names and looks scared."

Pan pulled up a tall stepladder close to the concrete planter. With me holding one end of the tape measure to the soil, Pan climbed to the top of the stepladder and called down the number. I found a writing pad and pen on a small table and wrote it down. We did the same for the height of the frilly, red-rimmed spathe, but it was more difficult measuring the circumference without touching it.

Finally, I took the required pictures. Pan insisted on checking the digital images, and I had to delete one shot where a tiny piece of pot frond showed in a corner. I avoided even looking at the crop, figuring if the whole thing went bad and I had to testify in court, I could almost truthfully say I never saw any pot plants in Glory Yates's greenhouse.

"Why is Glory growing marijuana in her greenhouse? I mean, there are a lot of plants here. Surely even the two of you can't smoke all this. And she can't be selling it."

Pan looked at me sideways from his glittery black eyes. "Are you kidding? Can you see Miss Glory smoking anything?"

"I don't understand. What does she do with it all if she doesn't smoke it?"

Pan leaned closer to me. "I shouldn't tell you this, but it's Miss Glory's turn this year to grow the pot. It's for all her friends. And they don't smoke it."

"Then what? And, why?"

He leaned even closer. "They eat it. Because it makes them feel good. And because it makes them feel naughty to get away with it. You sure don't know much about the pot subculture, do you?"

I dared a look at the potted euphoria. The plants were close to six feet, healthy, green and dripping with buds. Running to catch up with Pan, I asked him, "How do they eat it? Do you mean, like, baking it into brownies?" I couldn't imagine Glory and her friends eating high-carb brownies any more than smoking.

But Pan was already opening the front door. We found Glory and Dougal sitting mutely on separate couches. Dougal was chewing his cuticles while Glory tried to bore a hole in his neck with her laser eyeballs. Simon hadn't moved from the table but his head swivelled back and forth between the two. The magazine had collected a six-inch pile of birdie doo.

As I handed Dougal the camera and the paper with the measurements, Simon spoke up. "Anyone for a smoke?" he asked, sounding like a cross between Dougal and Robert DeNiro.

Glory rounded on Dougal. "Are you letting that bird smoke? Surely even you know how dangerous that is for his health. You worm!"

"Tobacco smoke has never entered his lungs," replied Dougal with such an air of innocence that I almost believed him myself.

"Simon obviously heard that phrase on television. He watches *Days of Our Lives* and *General Hospital* regularly. He likes *Law and Order*, too." Dougal managed to look both affronted and pathetic while positioning himself between the bird and Glory.

Simon wasn't through, however. "Oh, baby, that was sooo good. Pass the joint, will you sweetie." I didn't recognize the voice this time, but Glory and Dougal — and Pan — all looked at me with varying degrees of horror.

"What?"

"Are you and Dougal having sex? That's, that's …
it's incest!" Glory sputtered and stepped way back from
our unclean presence.

"*Eeeww,*" I replied in disgust, while Dougal said, "I'd
rather hang myself," at the same time. Pan snickered
until Glory cast him a quelling glance with eyes turning
bloody again. I figured it was time to retreat, and made
for the entrance hall.

While I donned jacket and helmet for the ride down
the block, Dougal was still talking, having never learned
to quit while behind.

"He uses a voice he knows and puts words together.
It's a new thing. He doesn't mimic verbatim." Dougal
tried to stick Simon inside his jacket and was having the
same difficulty as the first time. The parrot's scaly legs
thrashed wildly.

"All I know is someone is smoking a post-coital joint
in front of that parrot." Glory's glossy lips were pursed in
disapproval. "If it isn't you and your undersized cousin,
then who is it?"

"I'd rather sleep with the bird," I called to Glory over
Simon's furious shrieks.

"I told you. It's the TV. Nobody's sleeping with anybody or smoking a joint either," Dougal shouted. I knew
he wasn't lying to save my reputation or even Melanie's.
He'd say anything to pollinate Thor.

"Just get out of my house."

"I'm going. I'll send Bliss over once or twice a day
to check on Sif's progress. She'll have to take pictures
as well. Both spadices are currently between six and six
and a half feet tall, but it looks like Sif might flower a

few hours earlier than Thor, so if you could collect the pollen, Bliss will bring it over to my place …"

"Do what you have to do, just get out now before I snap you in half and toss the pieces in the trash." She could do it, too. Dougal was going to have to bulk up a bit if he wanted to defend himself against his ex-wife.

I stood on the second step of the curving staircase and buckled Dougal into his helmet. The parrot was having a tantrum inside the jacket, and I cautioned Dougal to unzip a little to allow Simon some air.

I figured I would have to boot Dougal out the door and kick him down the steps to my bike, and was rather looking forward to it. But at the open door, he halted so quickly, I hit him in the back with the peak of my helmet.

"Where did you get this?" he asked Glory, indicating an erect plant in a ceramic pot sitting beside the umbrella stand. About a dozen straight stalks rose several feet from the pot in a clump and ended in masses of frond-like leaves. I gave it a hard look to try to burn it into my memory cells. I'd be looking this up on the Internet later, as well as the ferns at my parents' house.

Dougal continued, "It's a magnificent example of *Thamnocalamus tessellatus*, but it needs a lot of direct sun."

"I know what it is, you half-wit. An old friend from school just dropped it off. And I know how to look after a simple Berg Bamboo. Get out."

"Who was it? Is it anyone I…?"

The door slammed me on the butt and caught the edge of Dougal's helmet, propelling us both down the steps to the Savage. This time, I had no trouble getting

Dougal on the jump seat. He was obviously bemused by his reunion with Glory. The growl of the motor and Simon's muffled squawking sounded like music to my ears after Glory's angry screeching. God, whatever Dougal did to get kicked out of her house and bed, it had been his luckiest day ever.

As we rode down the street past the woods, I saw the dark shadow of a vehicle pull away from the curb and fall in behind us. Headlights reflected yellow light into my mirror, effectively blinding my left eye. I attempted to move as far right as possible to allow the vehicle to overtake and pass. But the headlights behind me did neither, and, as I coasted under a streetlight, I dared a quick look in my mirror.

There was no mistaking the Beetle shape behind the glaring lights. The top was down, and I could see one narrow head. Chesley Belcourt was on a breakaway from Mum.

Enough was enough. Did the Belcourts want to buy the Barrister house so badly they were prepared to follow me after dark to close the deal? Not likely, but only one way to find out.

I turned the Savage around, planning to confront Chesley. I have short legs and, with Dougal squirming and twisting my jacket in a clenched fist, it took a few seconds to make the one-eighty. By the time I re-balanced and pointed in his direction, Chesley had shot past me and was speeding off into the night, probably making for the highway and the Super 8 Motel. This time, I didn't try to turn the bike on the road, but drove over a lawn and double driveway. I was just a few hundred yards behind

Chesley when he turned right onto the highway that bisected the town.

Ignoring Dougal's bleating and the death grip he had on my stomach, I flipped my face shield down, leaned over the handlebars, and turned the accelerator toward me.

A surge of wanton recklessness suddenly washed over me and I forgot Dougal and Simon were on the seat behind, forgot even my own safety.

For a few enchanted moments, I wasn't anything-for-a-buck Bliss Moonbeam Cornwall, rejected wife and trailer park dweller. I became Indiana Bliss, saviour of the world, hurtling through the night with 350 pounds of steel between my thighs.

CHAPTER
TEN

THE METAL FOOT REST scraped the pavement as we took the corner onto Highway 21, but I managed to pull the bike upright coming out of the curve. I had never driven the Savage at this speed, and wasn't sure I could maintain control. The cemetery whizzed by on my left. The streets of Lockport were as silent as the tombs within.

Dougal's grip had loosened and his helmet was bopping the top of mine, as though he had given up all hope of survival. I hoped this ride wouldn't set back his recovery. Something was pushing frantically on my back, probably Simon trying to free himself, but at least he and Dougal had ceased their screams of indignation. Or maybe both of them were still shrieking their guts out, but the wind rushing by overpowered the sound.

The blood lust was abating and I geared down to seventy, still too fast entering the town centre. The Beetle also slowed, and I was about fifty yards behind as we neared the police station. Rotting skunk odour filled my nostrils.

The Beetle tried to veer, but its left tires hit the skunk dead on. Black and white and red chunks of gore shot from under the tires, flying into the interior of the convertible, smashing onto my windshield, and skidding across the roadway. Luckily, I was barely moving when my front tire hit a lump of slimy black and white fur.

The wheel slid sideways, but just before the bike went down, Dougal swung his long leg over my head and jumped free. The crash bar saved my own leg, and I clambered out and crawled to the curb.

The Beetle kept on going.

Dougal fell on his hands and knees and barfed in the gutter. I felt like doing the same, even more so, when I recognized the uniformed man standing over us. He must have seen the whole thing.

Taking the offensive, I said to Redfern with as much indignation as I could muster, while trying not to regurgitate the popcorn, "Did you see that! If you want to put out an APB, I can tell you exactly who he is and where he's staying."

"Cornwall. Why am I not surprised? I think you've been watching too many American cop shows. We just call them plain old Alerts in these parts, and that driver who hit the skunk will be punished enough when he realizes he has a car full of decomposed animal parts."

Was Redfern kidding me?

"You mean you aren't going to arrest him? He was stalking me."

We were standing under a streetlight, and I saw his blond eyebrows rise. "Looks to me like you were stalking him."

"Get real! He followed us from my ex-cousin-in-law's house, so I turned around and followed him. And why was the skunk still in the middle of the street?"

"As I told you earlier today, it's an internal municipal dispute. The carcass was going to be removed in the morning."

"Well, now I guess Public Works doesn't have to bother."

"There's skunk parts everywhere," Dougal mumbled from the gutter, before going off into another paroxysm of vomiting. I gagged involuntarily at the sight of a long strip of red gristle swathing the top of Dougal's helmet. I unbuckled my own helmet and tossed it onto the grassy boulevard.

"Are you going to puke on me again?" Chief Redfern asked, stepping back.

"I'm not sure yet."

He took another step away. I remembered the glass of wine I had consumed at Glory's and tried to suck in a lungful of air to stave off the urge to heave it up.

"And who would this gentleman be?"

"He's so not a gentleman. That's my cousin, Dougal Seabrook." Just then, Simon stuck his black beak out the top of Dougal's jacket and cried, "Help me! Help me!" The voice was cracked and barely comprehensible, probably his own birdy voice.

If Redfern was surprised at the sight of a parrot bobbing out of a jacket and asking the police for assistance, he showed no sign. He said, "Looks like we better get your bike off the street, Cornwall."

"I can do it myself," I replied, which was a bald-faced lie. After buying the Savage, I had dropped it a few times before learning not to put the kick stand down on soft gravel or sloping ground. And I was never able to pick it up by myself. A couple of men were always around to help out a little lady in distress.

Maybe adrenaline would see me through. I braced my legs close to the undercarriage and heaved. Something ripped in my shoulder, but the bike didn't move one iota.

"Dougal, get over here. Take this other end and help me lift."

Dougal edged closer to Redfern. "She's crazy," he told the silent cop, whose eyes were undoubtedly rolling wildly in his head. "She almost killed me and poor Simon. Can you take me home, please, or call me a taxi? I have agoraphobia and need to take some medication."

The pathetic excuse for a moron was actually plucking at Redfern's trousers. His "medication" was probably in his pocket, and he better hope one didn't roll out at Redfern's feet.

Shaking his leg, Redfern detached himself from Dougal's fingers and said, "The Lockport Police Department is not a taxi service."

He sauntered over to me and, with one swift tug, set the Savage upright. I grabbed the handlebars and pushed the bike to the curb and kicked the stand down. Picking up a twig from the curb, I flicked the piece of skunk pelt off Dougal's helmet and checked mine before donning it. I spent a few minutes prying out putrid bits from the front end of the bike, trying to keep my stomach contents down by thinking up ways to kill Dougal and not get caught. The bike would have to be hosed down and cleaned thoroughly, but at least the visible pieces were out. Finally, I clasped Dougal by the arm and pulled him to his feet.

"Come on, Braveheart, it's past your bedtime. One more little ride and you'll never have to get on a motorcycle again. At least not on mine."

I was halted by Redfern's voice.

"One more thing, Cornwall. Where will I find you in the morning? I have a few more questions about Julian Barnfeather's death." A narrow smile budded on his lips but died on the vine.

"I can be found every weekday morning, except Wednesday, right across the road at the Public Library."

Simon chose that moment to stick his head out from Dougal's jacket again and cry, "Par-tay! Reefer time!"

This time, I recognized my own voice. If the subject matter hadn't been such a threat to my freedom, I would have enjoyed the sight of Redfern's face. It was probably one of the few times in his life he was struck speechless.

I followed Dougal into his house, where I retrieved my extra helmet and cautioned him that Simon's imprudent words regarding marijuana were apt to land us in a whole heap of trouble with Redfern who, unless he was lower on the food chain than a puffball, was going to start regarding us with suspicion. A former big-city cop likely had radar where drugs were concerned.

Since Simon's ill-advised words were not uttered in his voice, Dougal remained unconcerned now that he was back in his own house with the door closed on the scary universe. Actually, I thought he had done well on his first excursion in almost a year and told him so. He gave me a dirty look and told me to please let the door hit me on the butt on the way out. He pulled a joint out of, yep, his jacket pocket, and went to lie down on the couch and watch the Discovery channel on his sixty-inch TV. I started to tell him to change his clothes and take a shower first, but decided I didn't give a rat's ass about his furniture. Simon was still entombed in his jacket, and I cared even less about that.

I took a pasta salad and two pears from his fridge before heading out.

Dougal lived south of the cemetery, while my humble home was due north. Therefore, I had to ride through the town centre again after I left Dougal, keeping my speed to the posted fifty. No cops lurked and the warm air still held a strong whiff of eau de skunk, but that might have been me.

My right shoulder had grazed the pavement and was further strained trying to lift the bike back up. It throbbed with every vibration of the motor, and I was glad to dismount behind the trailer. I was pretty sure I had some road rash on my thigh, as well, since my bottom half was protected only by thin silk, a serious no-no when riding a motorcycle. The fabric had split and seemed to be sticking to my skin in spots, signalling the ruin of my only realtor outfit. I was trying to remember if I had any antibiotic ointment among my meagre medical supplies when I heard loud noises coming from Rae's trailer.

Rae kept pretty regular hours, but once in a while she would entertain a client later in the evening, though always before midnight in deference to her neighbours. I couldn't see my watch but figured it had to be at least nine-thirty.

I started to hurry past her trailer, not wanting to hear the sounds of whatever the hell was going on in there, but my steps slowed as a woman's voice cried out in agony. Then, she screamed, "Stop! Please stop. You're hurting me." I heard fists on flesh and something heavy hit the wall. More screams followed the sound of furniture overturning.

Dropping the bag of food, I ran around the front of Rae's trailer and tried the door. It was locked. I hammered on it, shouting, "Stop that. I've called the police and they'll be here any minute. Leave her alone." The cries of pain and distress continued.

I was reaching for my BlackBerry when I was seized roughly from behind and tossed aside. As I lay on the ground, stunned, I saw two men forcing Rae's door open. One had long, stringy grey hair and, in profile, I saw a hawk-like nose jutting from the lined face. I recognized Ewan Quigley from Hemp Hollow's third trailer, but the other man was a stranger — tall, dressed head to toe in black leather and a silver-studded belt with a snake's head buckle as big as a saucer. The snake's ruby eyes glittered in the light streaming from Rae's windows.

With the door torn away, Ewan rushed in immediately, but the second man turned and looked at me. He growled, with a voice sandpapered down from years of smoke or drink, "Get out of here."

I finally found a smidgeon of courage. "But Rae is hurt. I'm calling the police and an ambulance."

He pointed a grease-grimed finger at me. "We'll look after Rae. And don't call the police or you'll be one very sorry little girl." The upper part of his face was shaded by a leather biker's cap, the lower covered in black stubble.

I believed him. I lingered at the doorway until I heard Rae say she was all right. When I heard a man pleading for mercy and dragging sounds coming back toward the door, I scuttled over to my own trailer. With trembling fingers, I managed to unlock the door and barricade myself in by shoving a chair under the handle. Leaving the lights off, I parted the curtains an inch and saw a naked man with a bundle of clothes in his arms being hauled away by the biker. I hoped his body wouldn't be found in the river with rocks tied to his feet. Being a witness to a crime was not a long-term vocation.

A few seconds later, Ewan led Rae out and across to his trailer. She had a blanket wrapped around her shoulders and seemed to be walking steadily enough. When the two reached the Quigley's trailer, the door opened and a woman was silhouetted against the lighted interior before the door closed again.

For another hour, I peered through the curtain into the dark night, but didn't see the leather-clad man or Rae's attacker again. Finally, shaky with exhaustion, I replaced the torn silk trousers with old sweat pants and fell into bed. Throughout the night, I jumped at every owl hoot and rustle in the grass.

If I had to sleep in a tent on my swamp land, I was not going to spend another month living amongst that nest of criminals. Quigley and his pals were up to no good, and Rae, for all her lofty dreams, attracted the worst scum walking upright. It was only a matter of time before her lifestyle either earned her a prostitution charge or landed her in the cemetery. Maybe my life sucked, but I didn't want to die, at least not until I completed my mission of retribution.

With arms wrapped around a scarred wooden baseball bat, and my eyes wide open, I waited for the night to end.

CHAPTER
ELEVEN

I WAS LATE FOR work Monday morning and deeply pissed when I got there. The rose-tinged tendrils of friggin' dawn had already touched the treetops before I gave up any hope of sleep and crept out to use Rae's hose at the back of her trailer to rinse off the Savage. The early light was bright enough to confirm I had missed plenty of gory skunk bits with the twig. That done, with some gagging involved, I went back into my trailer and dropped the ruined silk trousers into a garbage bag along with the matching top. The leather jacket I draped over a bush behind my trailer until I could figure out how to remove the smell.

Since Secret Valley's shower facilities weren't open until ten o'clock, I shoved my bedding into another garbage bag, gathered an old denim jacket and some clothes for work, and headed over to Dougal's. Letting myself in with the key he had given me when I first became his drudge, I discovered Dougal snoring on his living room couch, still wearing the jacket from the night before. Simon appeared to have escaped, and I saw small puddles leading away in the direction of the solarium. I left the puddles; not my problem. The house reeked of skunk.

I threw my bedding and yesterday's underwear in the washer with plenty of bleach. In the guest bathroom, I ran into a problem with the road rash. The night before, I had been too scared over Rae's drama to think about my leg, but now I found that the fabric of the sweat pants was stuck to my skin. I had to get in the shower with the pants on and soak them off. I almost screamed when the hot water hit the injured skin. Once the pants were off, I remained under the pulsating water for at least twenty minutes, shampooing and rubbing a floral-scented body wash over every inch of non-injured skin.

I found a hand mirror and had a look at my right leg. The abrasion stretched from hip to just above the knee and oozed a clear liquid. The dress pants I had brought to change into would simply stick to the fluid, and I would wind up having to soak them off again later. If I kept that up, I would never heal.

Taking a day off was not possible. If I didn't work, I didn't get paid. Wrapped in a large towel, I passed Dougal, still dead to the world, and crept into the walk-in closet in his bedroom. Somewhere in that mess of shirts, pants, and piles of jockey shorts, I hoped to find — aha!

The elusive Melanie had left behind a few garments on her visits to counsel the afflicted Dougal (and that relationship had to be wrong on all sorts of levels). Sorting through a blouse, a pair of jeans, and various tee-shirts, I found a flowered skirt with an elastic waist.

It was probably calf-length on Melanie, but skimmed my ankles and flowed loosely around my thighs. With any luck, I wouldn't have to peel the skirt off later.

So, I rode to work wearing a skirt and ankle-length leather boots, with a ripped denim jacket to complete the ensemble. Granny Clampett was coming to town on a motorcycle.

I wasn't a pretty sight, judging by the heads that turned as I drove into town. I had to drive with one hand and use the other to hold my skirt down. By the time I reached the back of the library, where I parked the Savage, I had decided to stop at the Liquor Store after work, buy a bottle of cheap red wine, then go home and drink the whole thing at one go. Maybe then I would be able to sleep.

Clomping into the employees' bathroom, I removed the jacket and changed the boots for sandals. I applied lipstick and brushed my helmet hairdo into a ponytail. There, much better. Throw a bonnet on me and I could pass for an Amish ho.

Allison Seymour, the librarian, was off on two weeks' vacation, leaving me in charge of our summer student, Bailey Russi. Thankfully, Allison had given Bailey her key, so my late arrival inconvenienced neither Bailey nor readers eager to nab the latest Mary Jane Maffini or Louise Penny novel. If Bailey squealed on me to Allison, well, frankly, I didn't give a shit.

Dropping onto the chair behind my desk, I gestured at Bailey to continue applying bar codes to new books. She overflowed with teenage angst most days, and I just wasn't in the mood for it. I hiked the right side of the skirt up to my waist so the fabric wouldn't stick to the road rash and turned on the computer. First, I logged on to my bank account and checked my balance. Since my only expenses were rent, gas for the Savage, and a modicum of food if I couldn't get enough from Dougal's fridge, there were no surprises. I just needed regular reassurance that the balance was growing, if at the pace of an icicle melting in January.

Then I Googled "marijuana." After looking at a multitude of sites and dozens of pictures, I was pretty sure the ferns growing against the tool shed in my parents' backyard were really ferns. And the plant in Glory's foyer was bamboo. I looked up every few minutes to make sure Bailey didn't sneak up on me and catch a full screen view of the pot. That's how I spotted Chief Redfern before he reached me.

I logged out of the Internet and feigned interest in a catalogue of new publications, letting him stand for a few seconds before looking up and smiling at him.

"Ms. Cornwall."

"Hey, Redfern," I replied. "Nice morning."

"Is there someplace we can talk?" He looked at Bailey, who was openly gawking at the Chief of Police in his carefully pressed uniform, blond spikes gleaming. As I said, he was no ugly duckling. "In private?"

"Sure." I carefully pulled down the skirt before pushing my chair back and leading the way to the staff room. I sat down in a chrome chair and pushed out another one with my foot. "Have a seat. Can I get you some coffee?"

"No thanks." He looked me up and down, either admiring my outfit or sizing me up for a prison jumpsuit.

"You look, uh …" He was again at a loss for words.

"Like a hillbilly?" I suggested.

"I was going to say nice."

"Sure."

His eyes lingered on my fingers as I pulled the skirt away from my leg. "Road rash?"

I looked at him, surprised. "A little."

"I've seen more than my share of motorcycle accidents, and I have a Honda Goldwing. It's the 2005 Anniversary Edition. Red."

"Nice. I haven't seen you riding around on it. I'd have noticed that bike."

"Well, I haven't had much leisure time since I moved to Lockport."

"Yeah, I imagine that the crime rate here in Lockport must keep you up nights."

He looked at me, hard. "I think, Ms. Cornwall, you might be surprised at what goes on in a small town, one that is three hours from Toronto, two and a half from Hamilton, four from the border."

"Well, now you have a murder to solve. But that doesn't happen very often," I replied, feeling I should defend my home town.

"Nobody says Julian Barnfeather was murdered."

"You did. You said that Julian Barnfeather didn't die in the maintenance shed. That he was put there afterward. What else could it be? If it's not murder, why are you trying to pin it on me?"

He watched me as though trying to make up his mind about something. Maybe whether to arrest me, or just threaten me some more.

"Cornwall, do you recall the marijuana leaf found in Barnfeather's hair? It didn't jump in there by itself. You may be the best possible lead we have to his death."

I said indignantly, "Why don't you question the staff that digs the graves, or the people in the office? They're all regular employees, like Julian. I'm just a seasonal worker."

"The fact remains, Cornwall, you were the only one there on Saturday when Julian Barnfeather met his untimely end."

To my everlasting shame, I burst into tears. I'm not generally a crier, but the violence of Rae's attack, followed by a night without sleep, had shaken my emotions loose. During the past two years, I had ignored the hunger, the cold in winter, and the veiled contempt from former friends. Yes, it was my chosen path, but it wasn't fun.

Now, not only was I terrified for Rae's safety, I was furious with Dougal for risking his health and freedom by growing marijuana.

And now I was suspected of murder. The tears flowed faster than I could wipe them away with my forearm, and I was making a disgusting hiccupping noise. Redfern reached over and snatched a box of tissues off the counter, practically throwing it into my lap.

"Come on now, Cornwall, there's no need to carry on like that. I'm simply saying that, since you were at the cemetery the day Barnfeather died, you may have noticed something that could help us. That's all I'm trying to get from you."

I blew my nose and threw the tissue in the wastebasket.

Through clogged nostrils, I said to Redfern, "I already told you I left Julian in the shed about eight in the morning and never saw him again. I never went near the shed all day. What more do you want from me?"

"I want you to explain to me how a marijuana leaf wound up in Julian Barnfeather's hair."

I was sick of marijuana. I didn't grow it, I didn't use it, I didn't endorse its use for any reason and, seriously, I didn't give a shit what other people did unless it impacted my life.

I stood up. I pointed my finger at Redfern. "Do I look like a pot head? Look at me?" I even pulled up my skirt to show him the road rash. "Do I look like somebody who deals in drugs? Do you think I'd be living in a crappy trailer with no toilet or shower, or cleaning other people's houses, or teaching bitchy women how to do the Downward Dog if I had a steady income from drug sales? Do I?" The last words were pretty close to a screech.

Redfern stood up as well, leaning down so his nose was inches from mine. "I don't know what your problem is this morning, Cornwall, but I haven't accused you of drug dealing. Obviously, you have some issues to resolve. I haven't the time now, but you and I *will* talk again."

He turned and strode to the door. I was right behind him and, when he stopped abruptly, saying, "One more thing, Cornwall," my lips met the middle of his back, leaving a perfect pink lipstick imprint on his shirt.

"You might want to put some antibacterial salve on that abrasion before infection sets in. Oh, and cute will only get you so far." Then he was gone, and I kicked the metal waste basket against the wall. Bastard!

I was beyond the point of exhaustion and in no state to meet and greet the public. I took the trolley of returned books and spent a couple of hours restocking the shelves, assigning Bailey to deal with library patrons. At noon, I left her in charge and went down the street to DeLong's PharmaSave where I bought antibacterial spray.

The Second Hand Rose Shop was next door to the drugstore and, on impulse, I went in, hoping to find a replacement for my silk suit.

The store manager, Holly Duffett, smiled as the bell over the door jingled. She was a volunteer, one of Lockport's wealthy, and more civic-minded than most. A striking woman in her mid-thirties, Holly was a little taller than I, only a smidge heavier, and had straight blond hair expensively cut. She smelled pleasantly of a natural, clean scent that seemed familiar.

"Bliss! I haven't seen you in ages. You look great." Her smile faltered there at the end, but I didn't hold it against her. She glanced up and down my body, looked confused, then turned her hazel eyes back to my face.

"Hi, Holly. Do you have any double sheet sets?" I was pretty sure my worn sheets would not survive the bleach bath in Dougal's washing machine. I was running short on undies too, but second-hand underwear was a destination I hadn't quite reached.

"Sure, lots. Over here." After selecting a pair of faded pink sheets and a yellow pillowcase, all for three dollars, I browsed through the racks of women's clothing, trying to find an outfit that would take me through any future showings of the Barrister house. I managed to find a cobalt blue pantsuit in my size and set it beside the sheets on the counter. The outfit was a synthetic blend that resembled silk and, bonus, I could rinse it out at home and it would dry overnight.

"Bliss, I know you have one already, but this jacket came in a few days ago. It's your size, I think. It's twelve dollars." Holly was holding up a black leather jacket. I tried it on and, while the sleeves almost reached my fingertips, length was a plus in a motorcycle jacket. The lapels and cuffs were loaded with silver studs. I was fond of bling.

The jacket joined the sheets and polyester-wear on the counter. While I was adding up the total, Holly called from the back of the store, "Bliss, we got a big donation of canned goods this morning. Everything is fifty cents, if you need to stock up on anything."

I almost drooled looking at the shelves of baked beans, pasta in tomato sauce, soups, stews, and vegetables. I collected an armful and deposited them with the other items at the cash register.

"Let's see. I can give you everything for twenty dollars, Bliss." Holly packed my bargains into two plastic bags and rang up the sale. As I turned to leave, I found myself toe to toe with a tall woman carrying a pile of towels in one arm and several pastel garments in the other. She sucked in some air and closed her eyes. She had to be hoping she would open them to find herself somewhere else. She was face to face with her worst nightmare.

CHAPTER
TWELVE

YOU CAN'T PRACTISE THE lawyer trade and remain thin-skinned. Andrea, the new Mrs. Bains, showed her mettle by hardening her eyes and softening her thin lips into a professional smile.

I waited for her to speak, wondering why she hadn't had those lips enhanced with collagen. Fine lines webbed the skin around her light blue eyes and grey streaked her red-brown hair. The fifties bob hairdo could use a little updating, too. I noticed she was wearing pumps of conspicuous quality, Chanel in fact. I think the Weasel had been telling a fib about his trophy wife's age — she would never see forty again. If she expected to grace the arm of a federal Member of Parliament, she better get herself a makeover.

I had never felt bitchier.

That reminded me of my mission: getting my fair share of the marital estate and, if possible, keeping Mike Bains out of politics. It wouldn't be easy to discredit him, and I knew from years of living with a lawyer not to say anything even covertly litigious. After my dark night of the soul, I knew that justice would not come my way in a court of law. Let's face it, I didn't have a chance of saving enough money to take Mike to court before he won an election and became virtually untouchable. My blackmail plan needed to grow some fangs, and soon.

I looked around the small store. Good, an audience.

"Hi, Andrea. Say, those look like my towels."

"Oh, these? Yes, well, we've redecorated and these don't fit in with the new colour scheme." Andrea started to put them on the counter. Then she stopped and looked at me. "Would you like them back? They're a little thin now, but you could still get some use out of them."

The bitch had balls.

"Sure, thanks." I took the pile of pale blue towels from her. "I can always use some extra towels around the old trailer."

She shifted and placed the clothing on the counter. "Well, nice to see you again, Bliss."

"What have you got there?" I asked her. "Can I see them? Maybe there's something I could use." I sorted through the pile of neutral outfits. "Oh, this is nice." I held up a pale pink pullover with beige trim. I held the matching pants up to my waist and let them pool onto the floor. "Darn, way too big." I pawed through the pile, saying, "too big" or "too long" at each item. "It's a shame we aren't the same size; I could use some new outfits and your clothes are really good quality."

By now you could hear a hair fall to the bare wood floor in that place.

"What are you doing, Bliss?" Andrea whispered.

"What do you mean?" I asked, not lowering my voice. "I just thought that, since you were my lawyer when Mike and I divorced, you might still be interested in my welfare. For instance, if you need to buy a new tea kettle, I wouldn't mind having the old one. Or an iron. Actually, the ones you're using now probably used to be mine so, I'm just saying, if you get new ones, I'd be happy to drop by and pick up the discards. It would save you bringing them here. I can't carry anything too big on my motorcycle, but small appliances and blankets would be great. You wouldn't believe how cold that trailer gets in the winter." I smiled bravely up at her.

She was too smart to take the bait. She was thinking fast, but before she could move or speak, I upped the ante.

"Listen, Andrea. When you were my legal aid lawyer, I thought we were becoming friends. Sure, I was a little surprised when I found out later you and Mike were, well, better friends — even before he told me he wanted a divorce — but I know you gave me the best legal counsel possible. I don't believe for a minute there was any conflict of interest on your part." I let my voice break a little. "It wasn't your fault I wound up with nothing but fifty acres of swamp south of town. And, I'm serious, if you have anything you don't need any more, give me a call and I might be able to take if off your hands. Here, I'll give you my cell number."

Andrea turned and walked out the door, her head held high.

I gazed after her, forlornly waving a piece of paper in the air, the receipt Holly had just given me. When the door closed, I pulled some change out of my purse and handed two loonies to Holly. "Here, this is for the towels. Is it enough?"

Holly pushed my hand away. She said, "Are you kidding, Bliss? I should give you your twenty dollars back, just for the entertainment."

"Thanks, Holly. I hope, if anybody asks, you can truthfully say I never made any threats or accused Andrea of being unprofessional."

"I remember every word, Bliss, and you have nothing to worry about. Have you heard that Mike is going to run in the next election? He's really reaching for the stars, isn't he? If he wins, he'll be one of the youngest Members of Parliament in history."

"Oh, he'll win." I rammed the towels into the bag on top of the canned goods. "With Andrea's father grooming him, he's a shoo-in. Next stop, 24 Sussex Drive."

"He'd sell our oil rights to the States … or our water. I hope somebody stops him."

"Maybe somebody will." I wrestled the bags toward the door and waved at Holly with one free finger.

As I reached the alley between the library and the video store next door, Andrea stepped out of the shadows and blocked my way.

Surprised, I let go of the bags and they slipped to the ground. Darn, I hated dented cans, but perhaps it was just as well my hands were free. Andrea had six inches and at least fifty pounds on me, and by the flush high up on her cheeks, she was pissed. I looked around. No witnesses.

Arms crossed over her chest, Andrea leaned toward me. "Mike told me how you threatened him, trying to extort money. That could be construed as blackmail, and you could wind up with legal problems. Take my advice, as your former lawyer. Stay out of our way, or you'll think a juggernaut ran over you."

Adrenaline flowed, making my heart race and my body ready to do battle. I tried to damp it down to keep the oxygen in my brain. This fight required wits, not muscle.

"I don't know what you mean, Andrea. As Mike probably told you, I gave him a figure I thought was a fair share of the estate we accumulated during our marriage. I'd be more than happy to give back the fifty acres in exchange."

"You signed off all rights to any other properties at the time of the divorce. We owe you nothing."

"Well, at the time I thought my lawyer was looking after my interests. I didn't realize she was sleeping with my husband. Did you know I registered a complaint with the Law Society of Upper Canada?"

Andrea snorted. "Of course I know. They contacted me. How did that go for you?"

"Not so well. They sent me a nice letter saying they would look into the matter, then a couple of months later another letter arrived dismissing the complaint, but telling me I had the option of suing you. Anyhow, there will always be a record of the complaint, with your name on it. It would be such a shame if that came out during Mike's campaign."

"Do you really think we'd let that happen? We could make you look like a total nutcase."

"Don't be ridiculous, Andrea. The ex-wife of the Liberal candidate is living in a trailer, working several minimum-wage jobs, buying food and clothes from the second-hand store." I nudged the bags with my toe. "Why, I could supply pictures of me in my overalls, raking up the cemetery, or cleaning houses. Goodness me, whatever would the voters think? Let alone the party officials. They might consider Mike a risk they don't want to take. I told Mike all this, but he's a stubborn guy."

"Mike offered you money, but you refused to take it. How does that look?"

"You mean yesterday's offer at Tim Hortons? I don't believe there were any witnesses to that offer. The amount on the cheque was an insult, and expecting me to sign a waiver means you underestimate me. You can tell Mike to shove both the cheque and the waiver so far up his ass he'll need surgery to retrieve them. I believe I forgot to suggest that to him."

"Mike and I are deeply committed to one another. We have a brilliant future, and we won't let you spoil things for us. This is your last warning."

I held up my hands. "Hey, I'm not planning to interfere with your future. I just want what's fair, and you know what that is. Think about it, and I'm sure you and your true love will do the right thing."

I bent down and picked up my shopping, relieved when Andrea didn't swing her brown Louis Vuitton bag down on my head.

"Andrea, don't get your hopes up about becoming the wife of the prime minister of this nation. Once Mike gets to the first rung and feels he can do without your father's connections, he'll dump you without a backward glance. He'll marry some pretty little blonde who will give him a couple of cute little blond children to grace his Christmas card photo. Don't kid yourself; Mike is only thirty-two and you're, what, forty? You may be in love, but to him you're only a means to an end."

I took five minutes to unpack the bags and resettle the items in the saddlebags of the Savage after watching Andrea march away. After that, I felt calm enough to finish off the afternoon scanning out books for patrons. Dougal called twice to make sure I was going to measure Glory's Titan and report my findings before I went home.

The Liquor Store was my first stop after work. Bypassing the Vintages section where I shopped during my marriage, I checked out the Ontario reds and chose a Niagara merlot that cost twelve-ninety-five. A slight splurge, but well-deserved. Next, I bought a copy of the *Lockport Sentinel*.

Now, I had wine to drink and something to read while eating the canned beans. Or maybe I'd have the stew, or even the Chef Boyardee. With a can opener and a microwave, any option was possible.

The wind had picked up during the day so the short drive to Glory's was even less pleasurable than the morning's run. The skirt ballooned and flapped, but at least my road rash got a good airing.

Pan answered my ring, but instead of inviting me in, he stepped out and closed the door quietly. He looked at my outfit, started to say something, then shook his head slightly.

"We'll go to the greenhouse this way. You don't want to risk running into Miss Glory today. She's in a very bad mood."

"How can you tell? Any special problem or just the usual princess syndrome?"

We had left the ladder in place beside the Titan Arum the night before and Pan climbed to the top with the tape measure. I held the end of the tape to the dirt.

He called down a number to me and I wrote it down. The spadix had shot up several more inches overnight.

Pan said, "Glory's still in a rage about Dougal. She must seriously want this pollination to work. It's hard to understand why. This is the ugliest thing I've ever seen. Who'd want more of them?"

"It's not pretty," I agreed, "but apparently it's rare, and pollination is difficult, so maybe the seeds are valuable. Or, since neither Glory nor Dougal need money, maybe they hope to publish in the Botanical Geographic."

Pan snickered. "More like Botanical Playgirl. It looks like a big—"

"Yeah, yeah, I know."

We decided not to try and measure the circumference of the spathe, lest we cause the structural collapse Dougal was so concerned about. Neither of us wanted to be responsible for that.

I took pictures, with Pan again censoring them. I stole a glance at the pot plants while he arrowed through the shots. Glory's marijuana was thriving, seeming to match the Titan Arum in growth ratio. Maybe they were companion plants like onions and marigolds.

Before I left, I glanced into the spathe, feeling as wicked as a maiden peeking up a piper's kilt. "Hey," I called to Pan. "Look at this. I think there are flowers forming down there."

He took a polite glance. "Yeah, great, we're moving right along. Here's your camera."

I aimed the camera into the spathe and took a few more shots, hoping Dougal would be able to figure out if anything was happening that might speed up the pollination process. The sooner I was done with this pot palace, the better.

When I arrived at Dougal's, he jerked the camera from my fingers and demanded to know the height of the spadix. He thumbed through the pictures and, in my opinion, got unreasonably excited about the last shots I had taken of the spathe's interior.

"This proves it," he said, heading off down the hall toward his solarium. He put his hands on either side of the concrete planter and stuck his head into the spathe.

"Yes, Glory's Titan will blossom before mine, possibly only a few hours, certainly not more than a day. Perfect."

"Perfect," I repeated, with my back to his marijuana plants.

Reminded I was there, Dougal rounded on me. "You didn't touch Glory's Titan, did you?"

"Of course not. We didn't even measure the spathe."

"Now listen, Bliss. Tomorrow, don't measure the spadix either. I don't need any more measurements, I just need confirmation there are no signs of collapse, so take lots of close-ups."

"I got it, but ..."

He looked directly at me for the first time. "What the hell kind of outfit are you wearing? You look like you should be ploughing the fields hitched to a horse. You're really letting yourself go, Bliss. I hope you don't tell anyone we're related."

"Everyone knows we're related, moron. And I'm the one they feel sorry for."

I led the way to his kitchen and began telling him about my day, including the face-off with Andrea. All he heard was I borrowed a skirt from his closet.

"That was you in my bathroom? I should have known. There were wet bath towels and sweat pants on the floor. And what gives you the right to waltz into my closet and help yourself?"

"Who did you think was in your bathroom, you idiot? I needed something to wear and figured Melanie might have left something I could borrow."

"What makes you think it's Melanie's skirt? You're jumping to conclusions, Bliss, and I'd thank you to stop making accusations about my therapist."

"Have it your way. If it isn't Melanie's skirt, you must be a secret cross-dresser. I found a bra in there, too, right beside your pile of Speedo bathing trunks."

By this time, I had removed a foil-covered casserole dish from his fridge as well as a large chunk of chocolate cake. I got a plastic grocery bag from under the sink and piled the food inside, adding half a flaxseed loaf from the bread box.

"I forgot to mention, Bliss," Dougal said, in a tone that suggested he wasn't going to talk further about Melanie or bras. "You'll need to go to Glory's twice tomorrow and from now on until we pollinate. I'll need pictures and first-hand reports."

"Come on, Dougal, when am I supposed to find time to do that? I'll go right after work, like today. Isn't that good enough?"

"We're getting close now. You'll have to stand by and be ready to pick up the pollen at Glory's as soon as her Titan blossoms. There's only a small window where the pollen is viable, so you'll have to drop whatever you're doing as soon as I call you. Meanwhile, get me pictures before and after work."

"Swell. Pollinating two freaks of nature is taking up more time than I expected. I better get that money."

"Stay on track and it will happen, darling Bliss. Insulting such beautiful specimens is beneath you. Now, are you ready to leave? Can you fit any more food in there or should I get you another bag?"

He tried to propel me out of the kitchen, but I stood firm and said, "Listen, I need to tell you something else that happened last night after I dropped you off." I related the incident with Rae and the tall goon who had pushed me roughly to the ground.

"So, can I stay here tonight? Just until things get back to normal at the trailer park?" Prostitution and whatever Quigley was up to, maybe running a meth lab, were normal at Hemp Hollow, but the guy with the snake's head belt buckle, and Rae's attacker, were not.

"No, you can't. Sorry. I'm having company any minute, none of your business who. And you need to get out of that trailer, Bliss. It's dangerous. Too bad you don't have any friends you can stay with."

"Wait," I struggled to free my arm. "My laundry. I put it in the washer this morning."

"And I put it in the dryer for you myself. That's the kind of cousin I am. You can pick it up tomorrow, but I'm afraid those sheets have had it. They're full of holes and your underwear is a disgrace. You better get some new ones, Bliss, or the next time you bend over you're going to moon somebody."

He looked at me accusingly. "Mrs. Boudreau had to put my laundry through twice, it smelled so skunky. And she helped me haul the couch out to the garage. She says there's nothing that will take the odour out, so now I have to buy a new one. Do you know how much that will cost?"

In the hall, I nearly stumbled over Simon who was lurching from side to side like a drunken sailor, probably stoned again. He hummed something that sounded like "Dancing Queen."

"He likes Abba," Dougal said fondly, as the parrot looked up Melanie's skirt and whistled.

"You're both certifiable," I said to Dougal, and slammed the door.

I was tempted to hang around outside and catch Melanie in the act, but I was anxious to get home and barricade myself in before dark. Before leaving Dougal's doorstep, I tucked the skirt as tightly around my legs as I could. I likely wasn't doing the road rash any good, but at highway speeds, it wouldn't do for the skirt to blow up over my face.

Passing the Super 8 Motel, I saw the silver Beetle still parked in front. The top was down and Chesley was barely visible bobbing between the seats, still cleaning the red leather. I wanted to stop and ask what he and his mother were up to, but I wasn't dressed for the occasion and sunset was imminent. I felt like a freaking reverse-vampire.

On the ground behind my trailer, I found the bag of food I had brought from Dougal's last night. The pears were squishy and the pasta salad would be toxic after lying out in the sun all day. I smelled the leather jacket still draped on a bush, and immediately removed my nose. No way was that scent dissipating anytime soon. If I left it any longer, it might attract another skunk. I dropped the jacket and the bag of food into the metal trash container between my trailer and Rae's. At least I had a replacement for the jacket.

Before moving to the front of the trailer, I stopped and sniffed. A faint odour seemed to be coming from the woodland, and it was disturbingly familiar. Like wet dog and dead groundhog combined. The skin on the back of my neck tightened. Clutching the fresh food from Dougal's and the two bags from The Second Hand Rose, I hurried around to the front.

I wondered if I should knock on Rae's door. From the little I saw of her condition last night, she would be in no shape to service customers. After a moment's hesitation, I walked over and rapped lightly. There was no response and I heard nothing when I placed my ear against the door. She could still be at the Quigleys' — and I sure wasn't going over there.

Inside my trailer, I wedged the chair under the door-knob again, though a fat lot of good that would do if someone wanted in, as proven by how easily Quigley and the other guy had broken Rae's door down. I hung up my new outfit and leather jacket, arranged my canned goods in the cupboard, and stacked the blue towels on the miniscule bathroom counter. Then I made the bed up with the pink sheets. My chores done, I heated a portion of the chicken and noodle casserole and sat down at my tiny table with the *Sentinel*. Better to eat the fresh food now and save the canned stuff for the times when Dougal closed his kitchen to me. Reluctantly, I decided against the wine. It looked as though the sunrise and I were going to be BFFs for the next few days at least, and a hangover would make an unwelcome third wheel.

I opened the paper, hoping that reading the classifieds for places to rent might help keep me awake long enough to get undressed. Sitting with the skirt tucked into my underpants on my bad side and forking up the food, I unfolded the newspaper.

Before I could turn to the classifieds, an article on the front page caught my eye. It was about the mayor of Lockport's political future. So the word was officially out that the Weasel was on his way to Parliament Hill.

I continued to read until I came to a paragraph halfway down that made me forget my exhaustion and the plate of cooling food on the table.

"What the hell!"

CHAPTER
THIRTEEN

PUSHING THE PLATE ASIDE, I read the article again. It seemed Mr. and Mrs. Weasel were donating fifty acres of wetland, a haven for the endangered spotted turtle, to the province. The exact location was to remain private until legal arrangements with the Ministry of Natural Resources were complete, but it was believed to be somewhere along Bird River.

I thought about that for a minute, then read the article a third time. Apparently, this environmental philanthropy was to be the platform from which Mike Bains would be launched into political celebrity.

Questions flooded into my tired brain. Did Mike have another fifty acres of land somewhere near mine? He didn't have while we were married. Was a wetland the same as a swamp?

I didn't have a dictionary in the trailer, or a computer, so I called Dougal, forgetting he was getting some after-hours therapy from Melanie.

"What?" he snapped into the phone. "This better be good, Bliss."

"Listen, I just need to know the difference between a swamp and a wetland."

A moment's silence followed. I peered out through a tiny gap in the curtain, but nothing stirred in the darkness. Across the dusty compound, a shadow moved inside the Quigley trailer, but the window covering hid any details of size or gender. I couldn't tell if it was Rae or one of the Quigleys. Or someone else.

"You better not be drinking, Bliss. Remember, you need to get up bright and early. But if it will get you off the phone, the terms swamp and wetland are used interchangeably these days. Theoretically, a wetland has more mature trees growing on it, trees that can withstand a lot of moisture. An authentic swamp is usually under water, so the roots of most trees will drown. If you see an area with lots of dead tree stumps, that would be a swamp. Both swamps and wetlands are home to many varieties of plant and wildlife. Now if there's nothing else, can I get back to what I was doing before you called?"

"Say hello to Melanie for me," I said, and we both disconnected together.

I recalled the thick canopy of deciduous trees that covered the property, all thriving and seemingly happy in their marshy soil. So, I was the owner of fifty acres of wetland. Funny that Mike was too.

Once in bed cuddling my baseball bat, I found that, tired as I was, I could not relax enough to sleep. I kept listening for footsteps outside my tiny bedroom window. I wished I had a dog, a big dog. Maybe I would stop by the animal shelter and see if they had anything available in a German shepherd or Rottweiler model. But, then I'd have to buy it food and walk it, and a dog that big would poop a lot.

Behind all these conscious thoughts, my subconscious must have been working on the wetland puzzle. Flipping on lights, I trotted to the kitchen and pawed through a junk drawer full of twist ties, pencil stubs, takeout menus, and my divorce documents. Ignoring the latter, I threw everything else on the countertop and sorted through the various pieces of paper.

I sank onto the stained bench and spread a small pile of official-looking pages and one unopened envelope out on the table. All were from the town offices demanding payment of property taxes on the swamp. I hadn't paid a dime of it, and each subsequent notice of taxes due simply added that quarterly installment, plus interest, onto the total.

The fact that the taxes hadn't been paid for a year before the Weasel and I divorced infuriated me. How he and his wily bitch managed to transfer ownership with back taxes still owing was a mystery, but I had ignored those demanding letters arriving four times a year like clockwork and hadn't even opened the last. Now I did.

The property tax on fifty acres of soggy land near a river that flowed into a lake was surprisingly low. It appeared the universe was giving me the finger, since the total for three years plus interest was within a few dollars of what I had in the bank. I glanced at the date on the letter. This was Monday and, according to the small print on the bottom of the page, the property would be confiscated by the County of Bruce to be sold to any interested party on — this coming Friday! Three days from tomorrow.

A loud banging on the front door sent me flying back to the bedroom for the baseball bat. Armed and dangerously shit-scared, I crept to the front of the trailer where more fist-hammering was followed by a female voice calling out.

"Yo, Bliss, are you in there? I saw your lights on and figured you were still up. I've brought you some Earl Grey tea."

Rae. But a Rae I wouldn't have recognized if she had tripped me on the street. Her face was swollen to twice its normal size and a Band-Aid covered one eyebrow. Both eyes were purple and her lower lip was puffed into a shocking pout. I stood aside as she slowly climbed the two steps into the trailer.

"My God, Bliss! What happened to your leg? That looks awful!"

I had forgotten I was wearing only underpants and a tee-shirt. The abrasion had started to scab over and I was hopeful that I would be able to wear pants the next day. I gave my leg another spritz of antiseptic.

"My bike went down. It was Dougal's fault. But what about you? Have you been to the hospital? You look like you can hardly move."

"I'm doing okay. I'll have a few weeks' vacation, I guess. Not too many men want to have sex with a woman who looks like this. And I'm not my usual nimble self right now, I have to say."

"If you don't mind me mentioning it, Rae, you seem a bit cavalier about what happened. Don't you think it's time you looked for another career? You could open that spa; maybe start small with nail care and facials."

"This is an occupational hazard, Bliss. Something similar happened a few years ago, so now I've got a special fund set aside to keep me going until I heal. I'm careful to take a new customer only when he's been recommended by a regular, but sometimes a wing nut slips through no matter how careful I am. Jerry is a friend of Ewan Quigley, and I thought he was okay. Like I said, it's an occupational hazard."

"But the spa ..."

"I'm not quite ready for that yet. I need a few more pesos in the old bank account. But soon."

Neither of us spoke for a few minutes. We drank our tea and I tried to think of something supportive and upbeat to say, but came up empty. Each of us had our eye on a personal prize. Only time would tell if either of our improbable dreams would materialize.

"So, are you staying with the Quigleys again tonight? I didn't know you were friends with Sarah Quigley, too." That was a back-handed way of asking if Sarah knew Ewan was boffing Rae.

"Well, they're kind of rough, but they've been good neighbours. And, in case you're wondering, Sarah knows Ewan is a customer. She's cool with that. Saves her from having to do the dirty deed herself, I guess."

I saw Sarah's point, but *eeewww*.

"We just sat around and ate some cookies last night after Sarah fixed my cuts. That and a shot of Southern

Comfort, and I slept like a baby in their spare bed. The only down side is that Sarah doesn't wear clothes in the trailer."

"She doesn't wear clothes outside the trailer, either. What's with that, anyway?"

"I'm not sure. Sarah has some mental problems, I think. Ewan doesn't pay much attention to her, so maybe it's her way of getting him to notice her."

As a psychologist, Rae sucked, but I had no better explanation for Sarah's penchant for nudity.

But, cookies and a shot of booze? Maybe I should try that to help me relax enough to sleep. There were no cookies here, but I did have that bottle of wine.

I asked Rae, "Who was that big guy who ripped off your door, the one with the snake belt buckle? He was plenty scary, even though he came to your rescue."

"Oh, that's Snake. He's new around here. I think he helps Ewan with some business."

"And what business is that?"

Rae looked at me through her swollen eyes. "I think Sarah and Ewan have a little … uh … produce company. Nothing big, but apparently they have a loyal client base in the area."

"What about Snake?" Seriously, how ridiculous was that name. "What does he do for the Quigleys? Is he an enforcer or a distributor?"

"Don't know and don't want to know. I'm just glad he was around last night."

"What happened to the guy who assaulted you?"

"Jerry? Hopefully he's folded up in a shallow grave somewhere."

At my expression, she added quickly, "Not really. I imagine Snake just laid a beating on him and let him go."

I yawned, feeling more relaxed now that I had company.

"Well, listen, Bliss. I won't keep you up. I just wanted to ask you something. You'll probably say no, but I know how hard up you are right now so maybe you'll consider it."

I yawned again, almost dislocating my jaw. "What's that, Rae? Anything I can do, you just name it. I could take your laundry and do it with mine at Dougal's. Or I can fit some groceries in the bike."

"No. Listen, would you take a few of my customers for me while I'm laid up? Just a couple of my better ones? No more than one or two a day. I'd make sure they weren't kinky, and give you some pointers on what they like. You could fit them in between your other jobs. I wouldn't ask you, but I don't want to risk losing good clients."

After opening and closing my mouth a few times, composing and rejecting several answers, such as, "I'll do your laundry but absolutely will not do your customers" and "Yuck, yuck, a thousand yucks," I finally replied, "Sorry Rae. I can't do it. It's not my thing, so, sorry."

My future might include dying of starvation in a ditch, but it was better than turning tricks in Hemp Hollow. The horny pervs would have to go elsewhere for service.

She sighed and stood up. "That's okay, Bliss. I understand."

I stood on my stoop and watched as Rae painfully climbed the steps to her own trailer. Either Ewan or Snake had repaired Rae's door. I shivered at the thought of either of those two creeps working so close to my place.

After locking myself in, I took a last peek through a slit in the curtains. Across the compound, a figure stood silhouetted against the Quigleys' open door. The man, or woman, handed a large paper grocery bag over to Ewan, who unfolded the top and peered in. He nodded and stepped back, but before he closed the door on his visitor the light widened momentarily and I caught a quick glimpse. Slight build, short, slicked-back hair. I didn't need to see the agate-black eyes.

Pan. What was Glory's manservant doing here, on the wrong side of the tracks?

He had dropped something off. Rae had more or less confirmed that Ewan was dealing marijuana, but Pan wasn't picking up a stash, he was delivering something. Could it be Glory's pot in that bag?

I remembered the cannabis leaf stuck in Julian Barnfeather's greasy hair. Was everybody in town involved with the stuff? Neil Redfern seemed to think so.

I scooped up all the overdue tax papers and shoved them back into the drawer, except for the final notice, which I folded and tucked into my purse along with the newspaper article. I didn't know what I was going to do about the swamp, but I had only a few days to decide.

It seemed unlikely that Mike owned another section of wetland he was donating to the province. Was he waiting until Friday to buy my land back? He could probably get it for little more than taxes owing. But, in that case, wasn't the article in today's paper premature?

If someone else bought the property first, Mike would be in big trouble. And with the Liberal nominations coming up fast …

During our conversation in the alley this afternoon, I had offered Andrea the swamp back and she hadn't reacted. Was that legal training or ignorance?

In bed with my face resting against the bat, I felt a faint stirring of hope. Nothing concrete, but the beginnings of a plan. The Weasels were not going to make the giant leap to Parliament Hill by stepping on my neck. Not without a fight.

Maybe the universe wasn't giving me the finger after all. Maybe I had been given a sign.

CHAPTER
FOURTEEN

TUESDAY I GOT FIRED.

Allison Seymour, the town librarian, interrupted her vacation to come in and hand me a letter. The board regretted that, due to financial constraints, they were forced to cut back part-time staff.

"I'm really sorry about this, Bliss. Walt Sheffield dropped this off at my place last night and directed me to give it to you this morning. I didn't know anything about it, honestly."

Walt was the Library Board head and a major butt-kisser. I saw the Weasel's hand all over this. As the mayor, Mike would only need to put a word in Walt's ear and, poof, one troublesome ex-wife gone. Andrea was on the board, too. It was a wonder it hadn't happened sooner.

"Listen, Bliss, you have two weeks' notice, so that will give you time to find another job. I'll give you an excellent reference, and you can take time off for inter-views if you want."

I could have fought it. I had seniority, but who would I complain to? Certainly not the municipal leaders. The Ministry of Labour? If the paperwork didn't kill me, the phone bills would.

I thought about options. There were none. Finally, I said, "I think, Allison, instead of putting in the two weeks, I'll just leave now. I'll start job-hunting immediately."

"Wait, but Bliss! You have to stay for two weeks. I'm on vacation and so is Cheryl. Bailey can't cover the library alone."

I opened my desk drawer and looked in. Funny, there was nothing personal in it, not a photograph, not a lipstick, or a Band-Aid. I closed it again. Picking up my purse, I walked toward the coat room where I gathered up my boots and jacket. Allison followed me, wringing her hands.

"Bliss, you know that if you leave now, the board won't give you any severance pay."

I said to Allison. "I won't get any severance at the end of two weeks either. I believe the library owes me for last week, yesterday, and three hours for today. You can mail it to me."

In the parking lot, I was snapping on my helmet when a tall shadow blocked out the sun. I looked up to see Thea Vanderbloom, cap tucked under her arm and mirrored sunglasses folded into her breast pocket. Without the glasses, I could see she had pretty eyes, dark grey, with thick, curled lashes.

"Hey, Moonbeam, where are you off to?"

"No place in particular. I've just been fired." For some reason, I handed her the letter and removed my helmet again. My head felt like it was going to explode. Maybe from anger, maybe from fear, I couldn't tell.

"That's cold. I suppose the mayor is behind it." She handed back the letter while I looked at her in surprise.

"No doubt in my mind, but how did you know?"

"Hah! Everyone knows about what happened to you. Mike Bains is pretty slick. So where are you going, really?"

"I guess I'm as free as a bird, so if you've come to arrest me, I've nowhere else to be at the moment. Break out the handcuffs."

Officer Vanderbloom slapped me on my bad shoulder so hard I almost flew over the seat of my bike. "I've met my arrest quota for the month. Since you aren't doing anything, how about I buy you a cup of coffee?"

Why not?

"I'm here on a goodwill mission," she said, once we were seated in a corner booth at the back of the Mason Jar Cafe, next door to the police station.

After the waitress laid our coffee cups on the table, I set to work opening two packets of sugar and three 18 percent creamers. I needed the calories. Officer Vanderbloom watched and, when I had finished stirring and took my first sip, she tried again.

"Are you with me, Moonbeam?"

"Oh, sure, sorry. What did you want to say, Officer Vanderbloom?"

"Call me Thea. Okay, Neil sent me on a, well, kind of diplomatic mission to smooth the waters with you."

"Pardon?"

"Oh, brother, he's such a guy sometimes. He thinks I'll automatically know the right thing to say to another woman."

I took another cautious sip of my coffee but found that, thanks to the three creamers, it was lukewarm. I took a bigger swig. "I don't think I follow you, Thea."

"Okay, the heck with it. I'll just say it in my own way, which is probably not subtle but will save time. Neil says that every time he tries to talk to you, you either puke on him or cry. Or yell. You have him on the run, so he sent me to say you aren't a suspect in Julian Barnfeather's death, and we don't think you're dealing drugs."

"I don't get it. How can you just arbitrarily decide I'm innocent?"

What?

"You're losing it, Moonbeam. You don't have to get it. Let's just say that the police in this town know more than we let on. So, all you have to do is let us question you and answer to the best of your knowledge. Because of where you work, the cemetery I mean, and where you live, you probably know more than you think."

The waitress refilled my cup. Thea waited patiently while I doctored my coffee again. This time, I only used two creamers.

"You want me to be your stooge?" I asked finally.

Thea pressed her full lips tightly together. "The word would be *stoolie*, if we even had such a thing, which we don't. And we're not asking you to be one. But I'm beginning to see what the chief means."

"What's he so sensitive about, anyway? Hasn't he been thrown up on, or cried on, or yelled at before?

He was a homicide cop in Toronto, wasn't he? You'd think he'd be used to the earthier parts of the job."

"He was on the drug squad, actually. So he knows his drugs, and knows there's stuff going down in Lockport that needs to be stopped before this town becomes the Gateway to the North for drug trafficking."

"The True North Strong and Stoned?"

"Nice one, Moonbeam, but yes, Lockport is perfectly situated. We're just down-peninsula from Tobermory. Beyond that, the North is wide open."

"Wait," I said, "are we talking about things like meth or heroin?" I was thinking of Ewan Quigley. If ever there was a disreputable character, it would be Ewan, and he was up to something besides supplying Rae with reefers. What if he was into worse stuff than pot? I didn't think he had enough room in his trailer for a meth lab, but he might have another location for the actual manufacturing. I hoped so, or else my innocent ass could be blown sky-high while I slept some night.

"Not specifically. Why, do you know something you need to tell me?"

"Of course not. But if you don't tell me what you're looking for, how will I know if I have relevant information?"

"Just answer our questions. And right now, I have only one for you. Have you ever seen anything unusual in the cemetery?"

"No, never. Redfern asked me that already. What kind of connection could there be between the cemetery and drugs?"

"Marijuana, Moonbeam. Marijuana. We are specifically concentrating on pot."

I was confused, but at least she wasn't asking about Hemp Hollow. I didn't know how I could possibly steer the police to Ewan Quigley without mentioning seeing Pan dropping something off. A bag of money? Snitching on Pan would lead to Glory, then probably to Dougal, then directly to me.

"There's no pot growing between the tombstones, that much I can tell you. I've groomed the whole place at one time or another, and there's no pot."

"Sheesh, Moonbeam, we know the stuff isn't growing merrily among the epitaphs, at least not out in the open. But, as Neil told you, Julian Barnfeather had a marijuana leaf on his person, and it was fresh, so he came into contact with it shortly before he died."

"Maybe he was smoking it and he dropped some."

Thea shook her head. "Are you for real? You don't smoke it right off the plant, you have to dry it first."

"So what was a fresh leaf doing in Julian's hair?"

Her hands balled into fists and she leaned into me. "That's my question. Do you know the answer?"

I leaned away. Boy, she was getting as cranky as Redfern. "No, I don't."

"Okay, just for the record, Ms. Cornwall, did you see anyone approach the maintenance shed at the Good Shepherd Cemetery last Saturday at any time during the day?"

"No, I did not."

She wrote in her notebook, then sat back.

"It must have been you that left a pink lip print on

the back of the chief's shirt yesterday."

"It wasn't my fault. He stopped without warning. How did you know it was me?"

"Elementary, my dear Moonbeam. I know he went across to the library to see you, and he came back with lipstick on him. And, you're the right height."

"Well, congratulations, Officer Vanderbloom, I believe you're ready to sit for the sergeant's exam."

"Don't be flip. The chief was not amused when one of the guys pointed out the lipstick and ventured a guess as to how it got there."

"Well, too bad. I was hoping his wife would be the first to notice."

"His wife died three years ago, before he left the Toronto force."

"Oh, I'm sorry, I hadn't heard about that. Was it an accident?"

"She had a congenital heart defect that she didn't know about. She got pregnant and for some reason just died in her sleep one night when she was three months along. I didn't hear this from him, by the way. He never mentions her."

"That's horrible. No wonder he's so ... uh ..." I searched for a more charitable word than I usually used when thinking of Chief Redfern.

"Rigid?" Thea drained her cup and gestured to the waitress for a refill. "I didn't know him before, so I don't know how, or if, he's changed."

"Well, you'd think he'd have a girlfriend by now. Somebody to mellow him out."

She looked directly at me. "What about you? Have

you found yourself another man to take your mind off your ex?"

"Hardly. Look at me. I'm one step from living on the street now that I've been fired from the library. Even if I wanted a man, which I sure as hell don't, what man would want me?"

"Ah, Moonbeam, there are plenty of men around who would be interested if you'd just pull your head out of your butt and stop trying to get even with Mike Bains. Get on with your life, why don't you?"

I was sick of being told what to do, and practically sputtered at her, "You haven't heard the latest. Look at this."

Opening my purse, I unfolded both the final notice of taxes and the article from that week's *Sentinel* and shoved them across the table.

Thea might have been quick, but she wasn't that quick. "What am I looking at here? An article about the mayor running for MP, which is no shock, and a tax notice from the Town of Lockport."

"Read the part about Mike donating fifty acres of wetland to the province. And this notice is for a fifty-acre property I own down by the river."

Now she got it. "Are you saying he's donating your land? Maybe there's another property. Although, if you don't pay this by Friday, Bains could buy this piece of wetland before it goes to public auction."

Thea folded up the papers and passed them back. Standing up and placing her cap perfectly straight on her head, she looked out the window at the street and said, "Moonbeam, it looks like you're finally getting screwed again, but not in a good way."

CHAPTER
FIFTEEN

FOR THE FIRST TIME in two years, I didn't know
what to do with myself. There was no place I had to be.
It was too early to make my second trip of the day to
take pictures of Glory's gestating jungle monstrosity.
And it was way too early for the yoga class I taught on
Tuesday evenings at the Golden Goddess Spa.

Then I thought of something constructive to do. I
should be calling prospective cleaning customers. Initially,
I had been desperate to fill my empty Wednesdays with a
paying job, so, playing a long shot, I responded to an ad
placed in the *Sentinel* by Fern Brickle who required cleaning help four hours a week. Fern, well-to-do but not part
of the country club set, had agreed to give me a week's
trial. To my surprise, and probably hers, I turned out to
be superb at cleaning. Toilets I wasn't so crazy about, but
they came with the territory.

Glory heard about my success at Fern's and, when
her own cleaning lady quit on her, she begged me to

step in. Despite her complaining, I knew Glory never had her house cleaned so thoroughly, but now I wasn't sure if she wanted me back at all.

Allison must have been watching for me to return for my bike. As I zipped my jacket and tucked my hair into my helmet, she came sprinting down the steps to the parking lot.

"Wait, Bliss. Please, can I talk to you?"

Determined to stand firm, I waited for her to reach me.

"Bliss, I called the board, and they agreed to keep you on till the end of the month. That should give you more time to line up something else."

I seriously considered it. I would be crazy not to. Continuing to work a few more weeks at the library would give me a chance to resolve some key issues without worrying so much about money, issues like pollinating two giant plants, finding another place to live, extricating myself from marijuana purgatory, screwing the Weasel right back ... Actually, these issues were so pressing, I didn't have time to work at the library.

I hopped on my bike and called to Allison over my shoulder, "Gotta go. Oh, and thanks for the offer, Allison, but I've made other plans."

It was peaceful and quiet at the back of my trailer, but I couldn't shake a feeling of unease. There was no smell of four-legged carnivore and no sinister rustlings in the underbrush. I was fishing at the bottom of my purse for my key when I emerged from the shade of the trees into the bright sunlight of the courtyard. A sense of being watched forced my eyes upward from the key in my hand.

Snake was staring at me. He wore his dusty leathers and chains, with a skull-patterned do-rag wrapped around shoulder-length, greasy black curls. I froze for a second, then darted up the two steps to my door and tried to open the lock. My fingers wouldn't grip the key and I dropped it twice onto the platform porch. I looked behind, but Snake hadn't made a move in my direction. Neither had he taken a step back. Finally, on my third try, I jammed the key home.

Locked inside, I watched through the narrow slit in the curtain as Snake opened the Quigleys' door without knocking. He looked up once toward my trailer before closing the door. God, where was Rae? Should I check on her? No, I didn't think Rae was in immediate physical danger from Snake. But I could be. Who knew what was going on in that shack built onto the back of the Quigleys' trailer?

With the baseball bat securely between my knees, I sat on my worn bench and contemplated the bottle of wine tempting me from the counter. I looked at my watch and sighed. Pretty soon I had to do the ugly plant run, then I was due at the spa. I wasn't looking forward to returning to the trailer after dark tonight.

With fingers still shaking, I pawed through the junk drawer again until I located the list of potential cleaning customers. Within the hour, I had booked two clients for Fridays, starting next week. The rest of the list had found alternate cleaning help but would keep me in mind if circumstances changed. Two phone calls went unanswered and I left messages.

A stomach rumble sent me to the fridge. Empty. Not even a cracker. Simon probably had more crumbs in his cage than I did in my whole trailer. I perked up when I remembered the stacked cans in my cupboard.

Somehow I had to find work for Mondays, Tuesdays, and Thursdays. Suddenly, my hasty decision to walk away from the library before the end of the month didn't seem like such a smart move.

I turned over one of the old tax notices and, with my pencil stub, wrote the total of my bank account on the top of the page. Then I wrote down what I could reasonably expect to earn in the next three weeks before rent was due again. I could probably make the rent payment without dipping into the bank account, but it would be close. I still had to buy gas for the Savage. And, if I wasn't mistaken, Dougal was starting to take note of the amount of food I was removing from his fridge. Well, I would cut back on food for a while if I had to. And there was the slight possibility I could coordinate the pollination of the two Titan Arums, but I shouldn't count on that money. The whole thing seemed too quixotic to actually work.

So, without touching my bank account, I could survive for a month. Put another way, if I paid the back taxes on the swamp, I had a month to sell it back to the Weasel. Or I'd threaten to blow the whistle on his crooked scheme to donate land he didn't own to the province.

On the other hand, I could let the swamp go, allow the Weasel to take it away from me, and use my savings to keep myself going for six months while I tried other means of squeezing my share out of him. I could even find a safer place to live.

Turning my hands on the table, palms up, I looked at them, envisioning one choice in each. I had to make a decision now, and it had to be a choice I could live with, no matter what happened. I looked at the numbers written on the paper.

What the hell.

Tomorrow afternoon, when I was finished cleaning Fern Brickle's house, I would stop by the registry office and pay off the taxes. Then I'd wait for the Weasel to find me and offer me a deal. Let next month take care of itself. And the month after that. Who cared? No pain, no gain, Cornwall.

At Arlington Woods, Pan looked alarmed when I asked to speak to Glory. I still had half an hour before my class at the spa.

"You might want to think twice about that, Bliss. The Mistress of Darkness is still chewing nails, and I don't mean her own."

Pan was walking me around the side of the house to my bike after visiting the greenhouse. We had taken our look at the plant, and I had snapped the required pictures. The pot crop was coming along well, too.

"I need to know about tomorrow, Pan. It's my morning to clean, and I want to know if Glory still wants me to come."

He whirled to look at me. "What do you mean? Of course she wants you to clean the house. You know I don't clean."

"I've noticed that. But after the other night, I got the impression she was really angry. She yelled at me to get out."

"Mostly she meant your cousin. Just the sight of him sends her into a frenzy. She's been eating her special food like crazy, but it hasn't helped."

"What special food? Oh, you mean … *special?*"

Pan nodded his sleek head. "Cookies, casseroles, dips, you name it."

"You can make all those kinds of food from … you know?"

"Certainly. But it's very rich, and Miss Yates is going to hate herself when she comes out of this, then she'll hate your cousin even more when she has to go to a fat farm to lose the ten pounds she put on." Pan pressed his fingertips to his temples and looked every inch the overworked servant.

"So, are you the creator of all these special dishes?"

"I don't cook."

"You don't clean, you don't cook." I was afraid to pose the obvious question, and instead asked, "Who does the cooking, then?"

"Herself doesn't eat breakfast, eats lunch only on occasion with her closest female friends, and eats dinner at the Club. Unless a gentleman takes her out."

"Well, I know that, Pan. I mean, who cooks these special meals? I'm pretty sure the Glorious One doesn't slap on an apron and start chopping up the pot and other herbs."

He smirked. "I'd love a picture of that."

I thought about telling him I had seen him the previous night, dropping something off at the Quigley trailer. Trouble was, I didn't know if his errand had to do with Glory's diet or something more personal. If Pan was there on private business, it was probably in my best interest to keep quiet.

Pan seemed to make his mind up about something. Moving closer until our noses were almost touching, he whispered, "The less people who know about this the better, but since you keep asking questions and you know about the stuff, I'm going to explain a few things. But if you blab, we could both get hurt."

I could tell he was serious, so I didn't laugh. Honestly. This was Lockport. Then I thought of Snake and Ewan Quigley and lost even the desire to smile.

He whispered, "Okay, there's a person in town called the Baker. The Baker takes private stashes and turns them into gourmet meals to die for. A lot of the influential people in town use the Baker's services."

"It must be expensive."

"The Baker takes a cut of the stash. No money changes hands."

"Then what does he do with his cut?"

Pan shrugged. "I don't know, but I'm guessing the Baker sells it."

I sucked in a breath. "Okay, we've crossed over into serious criminal activity here."

"That's what I'm saying. Now you know how dangerous this whole thing is."

"I never doubted that. I don't even like being in the same room with those plants. I keep thinking the feds are going to come smashing through the glass windows with guns blazing."

"Well, how about me. I have to water and feed the stuff." Pan managed to look highly affronted at his servitude to the Cannabis Queen.

"Glory must pay you well."

"I do all right. So, you see what I'm saying here?"

"Not really."

"We're both in this, right along with Miss Glory and all her society friends. Maybe more so. Who do you think is going to do more time if they catch us?"

"You. They won't charge me just for being in the same room, especially if I plead family connections. You, on the other hand, will be kissing your ass goodbye for a few years." I didn't add that I could be forced to testify against him. No point branding the words *Witness for the Crown* on my forehead.

He nodded and stepped back. "I guess. Anyway, remember what they said during the Second World War, 'Loose lips sink ships.'"

I agreed. I didn't want to be the torpedo aimed at anybody's ship.

CHAPTER
SIXTEEN

THE CLASS WAS PERFORMING the Tree Pose, and two of the fifteen participants had already fallen over onto their yoga mats. This pose promotes balance but is not one of the more simple yoga moves. Staring at a spot directly in front helps and, to maintain my own equilibrium, I was concentrating on the sweating nose of the thirty-something woman who had positioned herself in the middle of the front row. She was doing pretty well, although yoga consists of slow movements and if you sweat you're probably trying too hard.

The perspiring woman crashed to the floor, followed by several others. My line of sight was now cleared to the back row where I noticed that one of the few still standing was a male. As the woman on either side of him fell over in unison, I saw he was wearing black bicycle shorts and matching muscle shirt. This was not a good look for …

Chesley Belcourt. Now he was standing like a lone sapling in a fire-ravaged forest. We both stood firmly, one foot high on the inside of the opposite thigh, arms reaching ceilingward with palms pressed together. Our eyes locked.

Chesley held onto that pose like he could do it forever, but I drew a bead on his eyes. I always won the blinking contest against Blyth and Dougal, and I knew how to stare without blinking. Chesley's eyes moved away slightly and I followed them. When he moved them back, I was there too. Within seconds, it was over. His concentration broken, Chesley's left foot fell off his right thigh and impacted the floor. That was good enough for me.

"Okay, everybody. Good session. Now lie flat on your mats for the Corpse Pose. Eyes closed and let your hands and feet open naturally."

After five minutes, I dismissed the class with a bow over pressed palms. "*Namaste,*" I said, and they repeated the salutation.

Usually I hit the shower facilities before leaving the centre, but I didn't want to take a chance on losing Chesley. I retrieved my clothes from the women's locker room and dressed in the hall, replacing my yoga pants with a pair of jeans and shoving sockless feet into my boots. I was relieved no one saw my tattered French cuts.

Holding my small gym bag, I took up a position in front of the men's locker room door. I figured it would take Chesley a few minutes to wiggle out of the tight bicycle shorts, an image I didn't dwell on.

Garnet Maybe came by and handed me a twenty she took out of her pocket. Then she drifted back to her office, not even curious as to why I was loitering outside the men's locker room.

The country club set attended exercise classes at their exclusive club house, leaving everyone else to drop in at Garnet's Golden Goddess Spa, so I wasn't concerned the Weasel's influence would get me fired here. Still, I had no qualifications as a yoga instructor and I knew that when Garnet found an instructor who did, I was out on my keister. Until that day arrived, however, I just tried not to cause anyone permanent physical harm.

Just when I was ready to storm the locker room and drag Chesley out by his lips, the door opened. His head eased out and, when it swivelled far enough to catch sight of me, he jumped back and tried to close the door again. I put my weight against it, which, admittedly, didn't do much, but just the gesture seemed enough to show Chesley how silly he was acting.

Holding his canvas carryall to his chest, he stammered, "Oh, hello, Miss Cornwall. Very nice class." He didn't move from the threshold.

"Call me Bliss. And may I call you Chesley?" I put on the fake realtor's smile and captured his elbow, propelling him into the hall and away from the safety of the smelly locker room. "Are you and your mother planning to stay long in Lockport? If so, I'm sure Elaine Simms can show you more suitable properties than the Barrister house."

Chesley trembled in my grasp. "Well, Mum and I are just trying to get a feel for the area first. And we haven't totally discounted the property you showed us, Miss Cornwall, ah, Bliss."

I'll bet. "You have my card if you want to reach me, Chesley. I'd like to stay and chat a bit longer, but I have an errand to run."

I released his arm, but, just as he tasted freedom, I asked, "Oh, I do hope you were able to get the pieces of skunk and the smell off your lovely leather seats."

He made an involuntary gagging sound, then caught himself and swallowed.

"Well, not quite. I'm still working on it. The clerk at Canadian Tire sold me a bottle of solution he guarantees will make the leather smell and look as good as new."

"Hope that works for you. Personally, Chesley, I had to throw out my leather jacket and my cousin needs to buy a new couch."

Chesley's eyes popped a bit more. "Your cousin?"

"Yes, my cousin Dougal. He was on the back of my bike when you ran over the skunk. We got the stuff all over us, too."

"I'm truly sorry you were involved, Miss, er, Bliss."

"Well, no lasting harm done, Chesley. But why were you following me from that address in Arlington Woods?"

"Following you? I wasn't following you, Bliss. Why would I be following you?"

"I don't know, Chesley, but you pulled out behind me from the wooded area and nearly blinded me with your headlights."

"Ah, I was just re-setting my GPS. As I said, we're trying to familiarize ourselves with Lockport and I was cruising that section of town to see if any properties are for sale."

I know a liar when I hear one. But, I still had to drop off pictures at Dougal's, so I let Chesley off the hook for the moment.

"Give your mother my best regards, and tell her I hope we'll meet again before you leave town," I told him.

Chesley made a dash for the stairs. The rubber soles of his white Nikes squeaked on the wooden steps, and my leather boots clattered close on his heels. At the bottom, he didn't wait for further pleasantries, just ran for the Beetle parked in front of the building. I noticed every window was opened wide on the convertible.

Performing an expert U-turn in front of the police station, Chesley headed north in the direction of the Super 8 Motel.

"Well, good night, Bliss. See you on Thursday," Garnet called to me as she locked the street-level door to her studio. She sped down the sidewalk, her short blond curls glowing under the streetlights like the head of a marigold on a slender stalk.

It was another mild night and I left my face shield up to allow the silky air to enfold my face as I made the short drive through peaceful streets.

The peace only lasted until I walked through Dougal's front door.

"Where the hell have you been? I've been calling you for hours and you didn't pick up. This is a critical stage and we need to be in constant communication. Well?"

"I left my phone in the bike, I guess. Here you go." I pushed the camera into his hands and ran to the kitchen. "I'm starving. I don't know when I last ate, so get out of my way. Oh, and I got fired today."

"If you'd get a phone with a camera feature, you could email me the pictures." Dougal fiddled with the camera as he followed me.

"If I had a pig with wings, I'd be rich. Then I could buy myself a brand new Smartphone. And I got fired today."

Dougal was panning through the latest pictures. "Didn't you take any of the interior of the spathe? Oh, here they are. Did you smell anything when you had your head in there?"

"I didn't stick my head in. You said not to touch the plant, so I just aimed the camera inside and hoped for the best. I got fired today."

I had been pulling out various covered bowls and plastic containers. One looked like mashed potatoes with gravy, so I nuked that first after spooning it into a glass bowl from the cupboard. No sense ingesting all those toxins from the plastic. Figuring I had to be dehydrated too, I poured myself a glass of water from the reverse osmosis tap.

"Everything looks like it's coming along on schedule. Did you see any signs of collapse, either at the top of the spadix or at the spathe level?"

"What you see in the pictures is the status at about six o'clock this evening." My stomach must have shrunk. After swirling the gravy into the potatoes and eating it with a tablespoon, and downing a second glass of water, I wasn't sure I could manage the chicken breast revolving inside the microwave.

Dougal jumped up as the timer went off. Sticking a fork into the chicken, he handed it to me, and said, "Come with me. I need to see through your eyes."

He hauled me to the sun room while I nibbled on the chicken.

"Now, look at Thor. Look hard. How does he compare with Sif? Take your time, but, for instance, is he as tall? Does Thor's spathe grow up the spadix as tightly, or does Sif's spathe look a little looser and can you see the red colour inside?"

"Okay. As near as I can tell, they look about the same height, although Sif's spathe looks a little frillier at the top and is starting to curl outward. And, yes, as you can see by the pictures, the inside is a rich burgundy colour. By the way, I got fired from the library today."

Simon was sitting on the top perch outside his cage and had been mercifully silent. Now he decided to join in the conversation, if you call clucking like a broody hen conversation.

Dougal looked over at Simon and said, fondly, "That's enough, buddy. Maybe if you ask nicely, Bliss will share her chicken with you."

"Bliss bloody well won't," I replied and moved a few feet farther away from the perch.

"Aw, come on, darlin', take one for the team," begged the bird in Dougal's wheedling tones.

Dougal reached over and broke off a piece of chicken and handed the morsel to Simon.

"Does Simon know he's eating poultry, effectively committing cannibalism?" I asked.

"Simon isn't poultry. Now, can you pay attention here?"

"I never knew it could be like this," Simon said in a female voice. It sounded familiar, probably Melanie again.

I glared at Dougal, but since he was such a self-absorbed snot, he didn't notice. At least the parrot wasn't yelling about pot.

I took a closer look at Dougal. "Hey, what happened to you? You look, uh, not bad today."

Actually, he looked better than I had seen him in over a year. His hair was expertly buzzed, without the dips and rises I left when I used the manual clippers on him. And he had doffed his usual baggy shorts and stretched tee-shirt for pressed trousers and a short-sleeved red shirt. He still wore sandals, but his feet were …

"Did you get a pedicure? Dougal, you've been out!"

"Calm down, will you. I finally found a hairdresser in town who would send someone in to cut my hair. She also gave me a pedicure and manicure." He stretched out his hands and I could see that someone had filed and buffed the nails.

"That's wonderful. You're really coming along."

"Yeah, I'm doing great," he said modestly. "Pretty soon, you won't need to run my errands or pick up my food for me. Although, I'll still need someone to weed my gardens and cut the grass. And take the trash to the curb."

"You honour me." It looked like the pittance I earned from Dougal would soon be a half-pittance. Well, things were changing fast and I had better be ready to make the most of the emerging opportunities. I made a mental note to find a nice park and stake out my bench for the winter.

Dougal assumed his lecturing stance, or, as I liked to put it, went into snore mode. "From these latest pictures,

I now believe that Thor and Sif will flower within an hour or two of each other, with Sif perhaps slightly ahead. This couldn't be better. The female flowers mature first and about twenty-four hours later the male flowers produce pollen. I'll gather Thor's pollen and Glory will do the same for Sif's." Dougal put out his hand as though to touch his palm to Thor, but stopped short of making actual contact. "I'm going to be videotaping it all on a time sequence. Are you getting this, Bliss?"

I nodded, although it was beginning to sound more like a porn movie than a botanical experiment.

"Let me recap. The female parts of both plants will flower within a few hours of each other. We wait approximately twenty-four hours for the male flowers to produce pollen. You will stand ready to take Thor's pollen to Sif, where Glory will immediately pollinate Sif's female flowers. You will return here with Sif's pollen, and I will manually pollinate Thor's female flowers. Hopefully, the female flowers of both plants will still be receptive, keeping in mind that they have been ripe for twenty-four hours. Got that, Bliss? Do you understand how crucial it is for you to be on standby and deliver Thor's pollen to Glory, then Sif's here to me?"

"Yeah, crucial. Standby. Got it." In truth, Dougal lost me way early in his lecture, but my role seemed to be limited to making a few trips between the plants to deliver pollen. And someone would no doubt tell me which way to go first, so there was no need for me to get overly involved in the science.

"Okay, you can leave now. I'm having company, so take your shabby underwear out of my dryer and whatever food you haven't eaten, and go." Dougal shooed me out of the room.

"Your other plants look ready to pollinate too, Dougal. Don't you have to do something with them, like get them the hell out of the house? I'm telling you, the police are very interested in marijuana these days."

"It's ready to cut and dry. I'm doing much better now, with the therapy, and a Valium now and then to take the edge off. I think this will be my last harvest."

"Glad to hear that," I said, relieved he was coming to his senses. "Why don't you just get rid of it now?"

"What am I supposed to do with it? If I burn it in the backyard, the whole neighbourhood will be high. And I can't exactly put an ad in the paper: Mature Cannabis Plants for Sale. This crop will last me a few years, and by then, who knows, it might be legal to grow your own."

"I thought you said you weren't going to smoke the stuff anymore."

"When did I say that? I'll still smoke once in a while on social occasions. What do you think people do when they have a party?"

"Uh, eat, drink, talk?"

"You are quite the little innocent, aren't you? What did you do at university when everyone else was stoned?" Dougal was shoving items from the fridge and cupboard into a plastic bag and glancing at his watch every few seconds.

"Worked in my spare time to help the Weasel through law school," I replied, thinking I could remember every party we attended at university, there were so few of them.

"Well, that worked out well, didn't it? You would have been better off having a little more fun." He shoved the bag and a bottle of water into my hands. "Here, drink this. You're looking a little dry around the edges. Got your underwear? Good. See you bright and early in the morning. Don't be late again."

I sniffed my armpit.

"What are you doing that for?" Dougal backed away quickly.

"I can't remember when I had a shower last. I have to use your bathroom before I go."

"Oh, no you don't. You'll just have to smell yourself until tomorrow. Company's coming, and I have a few preparations to make."

"Like lighting some candles and uncorking the wine? Or maybe rolling a few?"

"None of your business." He shut the door on me, an affront I was growing used to.

I did consider, once again, hanging around to catch Melanie in the act, at least see what she looked like. But something Dougal had said about the parties at university triggered the ghost of a memory. It was a long shot after so many years, but suddenly I was in a hurry to get back to the trailer, my fear of Hemp Hollow's threatening shadows forgotten for the moment.

Maybe, just maybe, I had a spare ace up my black-mailing sleeve.

CHAPTER SEVENTEEN

I NOTICED THE STENCH first. My preoccupation nearly caused me to miss the low growling, but even had I been in a coma my nose would have detected the fetid reek emanating from the forest behind me.

Hugging my bag of food close to my chest, I turned my neck and saw the unblinking green eyes cutting through the black night. A snarl preceded another wave of wild animal scent. Bear!

My feet flew between the trailers and around to my stoop. I was certain I heard the bear crashing through the underbrush, snapping at my heels. This time the key found its mark at first try. Lucky, since I wouldn't have had a second chance. As soon as I slammed the door shut and shot the bolt, a heavy thud sounded against the trailer wall, followed by a menacing growl. Starving bears were known to move down the Bruce Peninsula this far south in search of food, and I had heard stories of bears actually tearing doors right off their hinges.

The skin on my neck tightened as I waited for another assault on my aluminum door. I should have my bat, I thought, but the logical part of my mind knew a bat was no protection against a bear. I ran to my bedroom to get it anyway, stealing a peek out the tiny window. Nothing.

The bat under my arm, I pulled out my cell to call 911. I punched the 9 and the first 1, and stopped. The police would come around in response to my call. They would look for a bear, which they may or may not find. But the police might notice something suspicious around the Quigley trailer. When Ewan and Snake were released on bail, they would be really angry.

Bear or Ewan and Snake? The choice could kill me. I closed my BlackBerry and sat on the floor in the dark, my ear pressed against the door. It may have been hours, it may have been ten minutes, but I heard no further rumbling, and nothing clawed at the door from the other side.

I was still holding my plastic bag. Knowing bears could smell food from miles away, I got up and stowed the bag in the fridge. I called Rae's number, but there was no answer. I left a message warning her about the bear.

I really, really hated nature. I could hardly wait to move back to town where sidewalks and pruned bushes discouraged wild animals, and the worst thing you could meet in the dark was a Doberman on a leash or your neighbour mooning you in the backyard. I'd take a bare ass over a wild bear any day.

Even though I had to pee, I didn't dare go outside and climb the hill to the recreation building. A full bladder and terror are not conducive to restful sleep, but exhaustion finally claimed me and Morpheus held me in a steely grip until a pain in my abdomen woke me at first light.

The pain was my bladder about to let go. Frantically, I tried to think of something to use as a receptacle. Pulling open the only cupboard in the trailer, I surveyed the possibilities. One small pot and one plastic bowl. Not enough, even combined.

Unlocking the door, I stuck my head out and sniffed. Cooking odours drifted from the Quigley trailer. Vanilla and some other unfamiliar seasoning. No musty bear odour.

Bat in hand, I scurried around back and sought out a suitable spot. Not that I had time to be fussy, but I needed privacy. Finding a clump of low-growing wild junipers, I climbed into the middle and hunkered down to business.

Junipers have short, scratchy needles, and the dried leaves I was forced to use in lieu of two-ply were going to leave serious scars. Just as I pulled up my undies, which were beginning to resemble a shredded thong, I heard crackling nearby. Something was shuffling through the deep blanket of pine needles that carpeted the forest floor. And it was coming my way.

I squatted down again and my fingers found the bat. Dragging it behind, I crawled deeper into the junipers. I couldn't smell the bear, but if it was out there it would be able to smell me. It was too late to run.

The shuffling became louder and closer and, just as I imagined the pain of thick, sharp claws closing on the skin of my neck, someone spoke.

The voice was no farther than five or six feet from my juniper cave. I scrunched up in a ball and tried not to whimper.

"You shouldn't be here, man. It's too close to ground zero. We could meet somewhere tonight." The voice was low and gravelly.

Oh boy. Snake. I could only pray that my red tee-shirt didn't show through the branches of the junipers. I pulled the back of the shirt down over my rump.

"I parked on the concession road and walked in. I know it's dangerous, but you need to know what's happening in town."

I clapped my hand over my mouth to thwart the cry of surprise that almost leapt from my throat. It couldn't be …

"I'll walk back to the road with you. It's almost sunrise and Miss Bliss, for one, is up pretty early." Snake sniggered.

Chief Redfern laughed right along with his friend. "We'll be lucky if she doesn't screw up the whole deal. She hasn't mentioned you, which makes me suspicious. Any other woman would run screaming to the cops about the big, bad biker in the woods, but not her. I think …"

The words faded out and I lay shaking on the damp ground under my green canopy. Redfern was crooked. Who would better know the intricacies of the drug trade than a former drug cop from Toronto? Maybe the years of watching endless amounts of illegal money flow around him, combined with the unexpected death of his wife, made him cynical, and he had turned into one of the bad guys. Thank God I hadn't confided in him about my fear of Ewan and Snake.

I remembered the bear and shot up out of the junipers. Ignoring my bare feet, I ran back to my trailer where I pulled on my overalls and started stuffing a change of clothes and some toiletries into a plastic bag. I locked the trailer behind me and fled to the clearing where my Savage waited. Barely taking the time to buckle on my helmet, I pushed the bag and my leather jacket into the saddlebag and sped away from Hemp Hollow.

CHAPTER
EIGHTEEN

PAN TOOK A STEP back when he opened the door. He didn't exactly hold his nose, but he didn't take any deep breaths either. It wasn't my fault I smelled bad. After the Night of the Bear and the Dawn of the Crooked Cop, I was lucky I wasn't followed to Glory's by a pack of dogs.

"It's pretty early, Bliss."

"I know what time it is, Pan. There's a bear living behind my place, and I wanted to get away while it was still sleeping."

"A bear?" Pan didn't look convinced. "I don't think so. I haven't heard any reports of bears being spotted anywhere near town."

"I know what I saw. And smelled. Anyway, here I am, ready to clean. So, out of my way."

I wasn't going to mention the conversation I heard between Snake and Redfern. In this case, a burden shared was not necessarily a burden lightened. I was beginning to think there was an organized drug ring operating in Lockport and, for all I knew, Pan was part of it. He had visited the Quigley trailer on at least one occasion.

Edging Pan aside, I surveyed Glory's palatial foyer. There was a faint shadow in one corner. The shadow was slowly fluttering, set in motion by the current of air from the closing door. A cobweb.

Glory was known to foam at the mouth when confronted by a cobweb, invariably followed up by her trademark high-pitched shrieking. But, before dealing with cobwebs, I had to clean myself up.

"Is she sleeping?"

Still standing upwind, Pan nodded. "Lady Gloryness won't be up for another hour or two."

"Good. Is there coffee on?"

In the kitchen, I drank a mug of water, then poured coffee into the same mug from the European carafe on the counter. Carrying the coffee, I nabbed my canvas bag from the foyer floor and headed up the curved staircase.

"Wait," Pan called anxiously behind me. "She's still sleeping, and believe me, you don't want to wake her up."

"I won't. I'm going to start on the guest bathrooms, well away from the Queen's hive."

I chose the bathroom farthest from Glory's master suite and stripped down. Stepping into a shower spacious enough to hold the entire Lockport High football team, I used the shampoo, conditioner, and body wash from the supply on the built-in shelving. My road rash was pretty well scabbed over, but the hot water stung some fresh scratches from the junipers, including a few where the sun never shines.

After dressing, I finished my coffee and tied my wet hair back in a ponytail. Then I got out the cleaning supplies. Pulling rubber gloves over my moisturized hands, I set to work on the bathroom, moving on to the other three in record time.

Until Glory was awake, I couldn't clean her bathroom or use the vacuum cleaner upstairs. I dropped my carry-all near the door and surveyed the cobweb. The aroma of eggs and bacon hit me like an invisible force, and my stomach contracted painfully.

Pan stood behind me, chewing rapidly and cradling a napkin-wrapped breakfast burrito in one fist. He sniffed.

"Did you take a shower up there?"

"Better you don't know. Then Glory can't extract the information under torture."

The smell of the burrito was torment. But, eating on the job was pushing it, so I didn't ask for a bite. Pan offered me the object he was holding in his other hand.

"Here. I thought you might want to get that cobweb right away."

I accepted the duster, duct-taped to an old mop handle. Glory didn't waste money on tools for the help. "Thanks." I took one last sniff of Pan's burrito and turned to the waiting cobweb.

"Wait a minute." I stepped closer to the corner and looked up. "There's a spider in there. It's huge." I backed quickly away and handed Pan the duster. "Get it."

He handed it back. "You get it."

"One of you twits better get it." Glory came up behind us, having silently descended the staircase on bare feet.

She was wearing an emerald satin robe over matching pyjamas and looked better with tangled hair and half-awake eyes than I did after my forbidden sojourn in her guest shower.

"That would be you, Bliss," she said, in case I had forgotten my place. She looked me up and down but didn't comment on my wet hair or squeaky-clean complexion. I probably even smelled expensive, thanks to her complimentary skin care products. "By the time you leave, there better not be any spiderwebs in this house."

She turned sleepy eyes on Pan, whose cheeks were bulging with the last of his breakfast. "Is my coffee ready, Pan?"

"Right away, Miss."

Pan sprinted to the kitchen. He better have his mistress's coffee poured and delivered to the breakfast room by the time she got there. Until her eyes were fully open, Glory wasn't able to drill holes in your brain with them, so I turned into a cleaning machine to get as much done as possible before she swallowed the last of her second cup of caffeine.

Even with the pole attached, the duster didn't reach the ceiling. I leaped at the corner, lunging and thrusting, until the web was dispatched. I lost the spider, but didn't pursue him. Four hours later, I was done.

Glory's castle was web-free and gleaming. Even the magazines in the sitting room were stacked with meticulous care. I managed not to run into Glory again, but found my pay on the antique buffet in the foyer.

Pan accompanied me to the greenhouse to snap pictures of Sif. The pot plants drooped under the weight of their buds and, in an opposite corner, the Berg bamboo stood stiff and lonely. Something about that bamboo almost triggered a thought, but it slipped away and I didn't have time to think about it.

On the curb beside my Savage, I took out my phone and checked it. And sighed. Dougal had left four messages. He started yelling the second he picked up.

"Bliss! Where are you now? You didn't report in this morning, and it's critical you stay in touch. I haven't heard from you since yesterday."

"I just took some pictures but can't get them over to you until I'm through at Fern Brickle's. Sorry, but I can't spare the time. I'm due there now."

"Bliss, get your ass—"

I hung up on him and swung my leg over the seat. It took me less than a minute to reach Fern Brickle's bungalow. She greeted me at the door dressed in Capri-length leggings and a long v-necked tee-shirt in turquoise. Silver hair flowed to her shoulders, the layers cut with precision and style. As always, she wore lipstick and eyeshadow in glossy pastels. If you didn't know she was seventy-eight, you would take her for sixty, tops.

"Bliss, my dear. Come in. You're looking very nice today. How are you?"

"I'm fine, Mrs. Brickle. You look great, as usual."

The joints in Fern's hands were swollen and misshapen. Rheumatoid arthritis had taken its toll, and I often wondered how Fern was able to comb her hair or put her makeup on, let alone dress or make a meal. But she managed, and never complained. Her only concession to the disease was someone to clean her house for her.

"Where do you want me to start, Mrs. Brickle?"

"About that, Bliss. We'll have to do things a little differently today, if you don't mind. You may not know, but I usually have my friends over for a dessert party every Thursday afternoon. Well, for reasons that won't matter to you, I am hosting it this afternoon instead. Everyone will be here at one o'clock, so if you would just clean the guest bathroom and run the vacuum cleaner over the living room rug, I'll pay you as usual, and you can do a more thorough job next week."

I whizzed through the bathroom, wanting to ask Fern if she needed help dressing, but knowing the offer would not be accepted. The bathroom done, I went to the kitchen pantry where the vacuum cleaner was stored. With my hand on the doorknob, I paused, my head turning to stare at the counter.

A glass plate was heaped high with chocolate squares, so rich and gooey that the pile almost looked like a pyramid-shaped cake. The icing ran off the tops of the squares and drizzled down the sides. My stomach gave an angry growl. It would no longer be denied.

I looked around and listened. The only sound came from the ticking grandfather clock in the dining room.

I considered the plate of chocolate squares. I didn't see how it could be done. If I took the top one, its absence would be immediately apparent. And if I took one out of the middle section, or the bottom layer, the whole structure might collapse.

I licked my bottom lip and reached out. Before I could stop myself, a delicious morsel was in my mouth, plucked from the bottom. My eyes closed in wanton ecstasy.

I hadn't had sex in so long, I didn't even miss it anymore. Not until that moment, the moment when the piece of chocolate heaven entered my mouth and melted on my tongue. Then, I remembered what it had been like when Mike and I were still in love and could hardly wait for class to be over and we were alone, our hands ripping away clothes and our …

But, given a choice between that moment and this one, I'd have to say, give me another hunk of chocolate square.

Another piece followed the first, just as wonderful. But the pyramid was listing a little to one side, so I turned the plate around and carefully extracted a square from the opposite side. I popped that one into my mouth and chewed more slowly. What was that, three?

The pile was still a little lopsided. I was unsure how to straighten it out. Fern would notice if I kept eating her dessert. But, maybe just one more piece from this side and everything would be even again.

Just as that square was about to follow the first three, I heard Fern's voice.

"Bliss? How are you coming along, dear?"

There was a box of plastic wrap sitting beside the pile of treats. Not wanting to be caught with my mouth full, I quickly tore off a strip of the wrap and wound it around the square. My overalls had a handy chest pocket, and, in no time at all, the little parcel was out of sight. By the time Fern reached the living room, I was plugging in the vacuum cleaner. I was a little worried about the leaning tower of chocolate squares in the kitchen, but I didn't think Fern would begrudge me a wee snack if she knew.

And the chocolate was just what I needed. As I finished up the vacuuming, I was feeling great, stronger than I had in days. Sure, it was just a sugar high, but it would keep me going until I could get some lunch at Dougal's when I dropped off the pictures. He would be really glad to see me, so much earlier than he expected. And I was looking forward to seeing Thor. I really missed that plant.

Fern was wearing to-die-for jeans and a beaded tunic top. When she paid me, I gave her a hug. She looked a little surprised, but, what the hey, there's not enough love in the world, that's what I always say.

At the curb, it took me a while to get my leather jacket on. I couldn't get the little thingie in the zipper to stay inside the little hole while I pulled on it. And people kept stopping in Fern's driveway or on the street in front of, and in back of, my motorcycle. I had to wave at them all. There were the MacPhersons, their dandelion hair drifting gently around their heads. Once Bob was settled in his wheelchair, they gave a friendly wave back.

Then a man I didn't know got out of his cute little Yaris. He didn't wave back, which I thought was rude until I realized he couldn't take his hands off the two canes that were holding him up. I gave him an extra wave.

Four or five other people went into Fern's house. I waved at all of them and most of them waved back. I finally got the zipper up and picked up my helmet. I couldn't figure out which side was the front. I decided the peaky thing should be at the back to catch the wind and was trying to force it over my ears when a pair of hands pulled the helmet off my head.

I turned around to give the person what for.
Bummer.

CHAPTER
NINETEEN

HOLDING MY HELMET UNDER one arm, Redfern said, "Have you been drinking alcohol, Cornwall?"

"No! 'Course, if I had the time, I would." I observed the crack in the sidewalk under my feet, wondering how they got all the cracks the same width like that.

"Explain why you were trying to jam your helmet on backwards."

"Seriously? So, that's why it didn't fit."

He leaned closer and peered down into my face. I stepped back, trying to remember why I needed to avoid this man. Oh, yeah. He was a dishonest cop. He was bent. That's what the British called it. A bent cop. I liked that word. The British were so descriptive. I smiled.

"Let's go at this another way, Cornwall. Have you been smoking something? Anything?"

"No! I have never smoked something. Or anything, either." I lifted my face to the sun, feeling its nurturing warmth in every cell of my body.

He leaned over me again. "What's that on your face?"

He reached out a hand and, before I could pull away, he wiped his finger across my upper lip. He looked at the finger for a second before holding it out to me. I jumped back.

"What's this, Cornwall? Chocolate?"

"No! Well, maybe. But I only ate one. Did Mrs. Brickle call you?"

"What did you eat? Tell me the truth. Was it a brownie?"

"Hah. If what I ate is a brownie, then may my lips fall off." Funny thing, my lips did feel kind of heavy, and bigger than usual. I stuck my tongue out and swept it back and forth across my bottom lip. Then I did it to my upper lip. Yeah, my lips were big.

Redfern didn't say anything for, like, hours, although his mouth opened and closed a few times. I just waited patiently. Had to, since his car was parked in the middle of the street, inconsiderately blocking my Savage.

Finally, his lips parted. He had really nice lips for a bent cop. Too bad he was bent.

"Can you focus here, Cornwall?"

Somebody else was always telling me to focus. Who was it? Oh, yeah.

"Listen, Redfern, I gotta go. Dougal is waiting for me and I'm late." Late for what? Something, though.

"Dougal can just wait a minute or two longer. Tell me what you ate."

"Okay. It was the best, most delicious chocolate square I ever had. Oh, man, it was better than sex. I'd take another one of those over sex any day, even though I've been a virgin for more than two years." I patted my chest.

"Good to know. Just how many did you eat, Cornwall?"

I held up one finger. Then, before my startled eyes, a second finger rose. And a third traitorous digit joined the team. "I had one." I smiled.

Redfern's blue eyes raked me from hair to boots. He took off his hat and tossed it through the open window of his car. Good thing I didn't like bent blond cops. I giggled — that was a good description I just made up. I was almost British.

"What have you got in there, Cornwall?"

As Redfern's hand reached down toward my chest, I tried to lean away, but my back was against his cruiser.

"Whoa, back it up there, Skippy." I slapped at his hand.

"I need what you have in your pocket, Cornwall."

"You men are all alike. Only after one thing, and when you get it, poof, you move on to greener pastures, someone older and better connected." I yanked my helmet from under his arm and tried to put it on.

Redfern took it back. "Cornwall, pay attention. I'm not after your virtue. I just need that brownie in your pocket, and for you to verify you got it from Fern Brickle."

"Listen up. I told you it's not a brownie, and you can't have it. It's mine and I'm going to eat it as soon as I get to Dougal's. And he isn't getting any, either."

Redfern stepped over to the Savage and turned the key that I had already placed in the ignition, back when I thought I was going to get out of there sometime today. While I stood in amazement, he rolled the Savage over to the alley that ran between Mrs. Brickle's house and her next door neighbour's. He parked the bike under a tree and hung the helmet on a handlebar. Rummaging in the saddlebag, he pulled out my jacket and purse and walked back to the curb.

"Get in, Cornwall. I'm driving you home." He opened the passenger side of the cruiser and placed his hand on my head.

"No way." I wrapped both arms around the window frame and hung on, kicking backward at his knees. "I'm making a citizen's arrest. You're going down for this, Redfern, and in case you didn't notice, people are looking out Mrs. Brickle's front window."

"I noticed. I want them to see this. And if you kick me again, I'll arrest you for assaulting an officer. Or maybe for being under the influence of a controlled substance."

Somehow, I found myself in the passenger seat, and Redfern was speeding away. He stopped on Evening Star Road and barked, "Put your seatbelt on."

"No." I folded my arms. How embarrassing was this? A woman walking her two-pound froufrou dog stared at us. I gave her the finger before recognizing her as a friend of my mother's.

While he was reaching across me for the belt, I noticed the back of his neck. It was smooth and tanned, not all wrinkly like some men. But bent! Bent cop.

"I don't want to go home. There's a bear in the woods behind my trailer. I want to go to Dougal's house." And I didn't want to be in Hemp Hollow with this guy.

"Whatever. Where does he live?"

When I told him, Redfern made a dangerously tight U-turn in the street and roared back up Evening Star, then careened onto Pinetree before jamming on the brakes in front of Dougal's. Good thing I was wearing a seatbelt.

"Whee. That was fun." Another giggle escaped.

"Glad you're enjoying yourself. That's what we cops are here for, to provide citizens with entertainment."

He lunged at me again, but I was able to get out of the car with my jacket and purse before he made actual contact with my chest.

Sticking my head back inside the car window, I said, "Trying to force yourself on a citizen is not entertaining for the citizen. Why, I'm practically a virgin again, and trying to compromise a virgin cannot be within the code of honour for a police officer."

Then I remembered that this particular police officer possessed no code of honour, and added, "You're still young. You have a chance to turn your life around, to turn back from the road to perdition. Do it now, before it's too late." I gave him a compassionate smile and ran up the steps to the front door.

The look on his face was forever branded on the memory lobe of my brain. Right next to the lobe that controls the urge to shoot myself.

CHAPTER TWENTY

DOUGAL WAS IN HIS study, bent over his keyboard.

"Hey, sweetie," I called from the doorway, "ready for more pictures?"

He looked up at me briefly, then held out his hand for the camera. While he downloaded, I floated to the kitchen and opened the fridge. By the time Dougal joined me, I had pretty much polished off a roasted chicken. Only the wings and tail were left and, as Dougal stared wordlessly, I started gnawing on a wing.

"Oh, I'm sorry," I said. "Did you want some of this chicken?" I held up the spare wing.

"That was my dinner. You ate the whole damn thing."

"Don't you have any potato chips or chocolate bars, or any other junk food you can eat? I'll toast us a few cinnamon bagels, if you want."

Dougal pulled out a chair beside me. His ears were turning flamingo pink.

I burped. "Oh, excuse me." I burped again. "Well, if you don't want this wing, I'll just finish it off."

"Are you drunk, Bliss? Is that what this is all about? You better let me have the key to your death machine."

I tried to chortle at him, but I fear it came out as a giggle. Which, for some reason, reminded me of my recent conversation with Redfern.

"I don't have my motorcycle any more. Redfern took it away and drove me here. But, listen, there's some stuff ..."

"What!" Dougal stood up so fast his chair crashed to the floor. "You led the cops to my door? And not just any cop, the Chief of Police! Are you trying to get me thrown in jail? What if he wanted to come in? Would you have taken his hand and led him into the solarium?"

"Someone hasn't had his smokie-wokie today. Anyhow, I didn't have any choice, and he didn't ask to come in. It wasn't a date, sweetie. Although, he did get a little fresh. I think he's hot for me." I contemplated the chicken's tail, then picked up the rib cage and stripped it with my teeth.

"Hot for you? You are a whack job, Bliss. You said yourself he's on a crusade to end all cannabis use in this town. Why the hell would you think he's got the hots for you?"

"Well, sweetie, he kept trying to grab my boobs." I put my hand over my chest and felt the bulge in the front pocket. "Oh, well, maybe not."

I pulled out the packet and set it on the table. The contents were flattened and oozing through the wrap, but I threw the rib cage over my shoulder and picked up a fork from the table. Chicken and chocolate. *Mmm-mmm-mmm.* I unfolded the wrapping carefully.

Before I could stick my fork into the chocolate goo, Dougal's hand shot out and his fingers encased my wrist.

"Not so fast, Bliss. Tell me what it is, and where you got it."

I explained as quickly as I could, eager to taste the chocolate. It seemed so long since the last yummy square in Fern Brickle's kitchen.

"So, you ate some of these desserts from Mrs. Brickle's kitchen, wrapped one up to take home, and Chief Redfern nabbed you outside her house and tried to take it from you. Does that about cover it?"

I nodded and plunged my fork into the melted dessert. Dougal ripped the fork from my hand and transferred its contents to his own mouth.

"No more for you," he said, chocolate oozing out the corner of his mouth. "Let the expert determine if this is what I think it is."

My eyes followed every crumb as Dougal lifted the fork to his mouth again and again. He let the chocolate melt on his tongue. God, I knew what that was like. At one point he got up, went to a cupboard, lifted down a box of cookies, and dropped it in front of me. Simon joined us, shuffling into the kitchen and looking terribly lonely on the floor. I lifted him onto the table and shared a cookie with him.

"Here you go, baby," I said, stroking the red tail feathers. He wasn't such a bad bird.

Every time I fed him a tiny piece, Simon would flap his wings and shout, "Do it again, do it again!" Good old Melanie.

The plastic wrap was finally scraped clean by Dougal's fork. He sat back and sighed with contentment.

"Okay. Now we wait."

"Wait for what?" I asked him, ramming home another cookie.

We listened to the ticking of the kitchen clock. At least I did. Dougal was in some sort of meditative trance and wouldn't answer any of my questions, not responding even when Simon fluttered onto his shoulder and pecked at his ear. Time passed.

Finally. "Oh yeah. This is good stuff. I guess the rumours are true."

"Rumours of what? Of your death? And are they greatly exaggerated?" I laughed uproariously at myself.

"You're stoned, Bliss. If you ate three of these, you have to be higher than a kite. I'd say this is the Baker's handiwork."

"I know not what you mean, you miscreant."

"I've heard about a group of elderly Lockport residents, all with medical challenges, who grow their own weed and give another local citizen, known as the Baker, the raw product to cook up into brownies."

"That was not a brownie," I told him. "That was sheer heaven, admit it."

"Okay, whatever it was, it was good, and it was loaded. And Chief Redfern knows, or he wouldn't have tried to take this one away from you."

"Are you saying Redfern wasn't making a pass at me?"

"Sorry."

"He's bent, you know."

"Bent?" Dougal looked confused. I wished he'd try

and keep up with me and the British."

"And there's a bear living behind my trailer. So I have to stay here tonight. Maybe forever."

"No. I'm having company later tonight. You can walk over to Glory's and get this evening's shots, then take a taxi or something home after you deliver them here. I'll even pay for it."

"That's very generous, sweetie, but Hemp Hollow, for reasons I can't remember at the moment, is a very dangerous place."

"And, please, go back to calling me moron so I know the planets are spinning in their appointed co-ordinates."

"As you wish, moron. I think your parrot just pooped on your shoulder. Maybe he shouldn't have eaten so many cookies."

I skipped to Glory's house and took pictures of Sif, who was really strutting her stuff now. Her spathe was half-opened, the interior blood-red and inviting. While Pan looked through the shots, I touched my fingertips to the spathe. It was velvety and spongy, and I understood, on a primal level, why Thor's pollen would be welcomed by this jungle beauty.

Back in Dougal's solarium, I took a few minutes to visit with Thor. While Dougal's back was turned, I stroked Thor's spadix, whispering, "Not much longer now, Dark Prince, before you and your lady will be as one." Finally, I understood how Dougal felt about Thor, the spiritual union of human and plant.

It was twilight when I left Dougal, telling him I was going to walk home. As if. I had another key to the Savage in my purse and it took only a few minutes to reach Fern Brickle's house. Her visitors had all departed, and a lone light blinked on as I passed the front of the house. My bike was still in the alley.

Soon, I was rolling along the trail to Hemp Hollow, through the dark woods, singing "Over the Rainbow" loudly to frighten away the bear. The clearing behind my trailer was devoid of wild smell or green eyes, so I picked up a stick and swung it in the air, yelling, "Fuck you, bear," before scurrying around front.

An envelope was taped to my door. It was from Rae, telling me she was going to stay with her sister and brother-in-law in Owen Sound for a week or two. "Things are kind of crazy around here," was how she put it. She didn't know the half of it.

I hadn't realized how much I depended on Rae for company until she was gone. Just knowing she was a few feet away had been a comfort. I didn't blame her for making herself scarce, but now I was truly alone.

My eye fell on the bottle of wine on the counter. Red wine was supposed to be cooled for twenty minutes before serving, I seemed to remember from dinner parties a thousand years ago. But then, I wasn't going to serve it. Good thing the bottle had a screw top, so easy to open.

There were no glasses in the trailer, only a couple of ceramic mugs, and red wine was never to be drunk from a mug, another wine rule. So I upended the bottle and took a swig. Not as good as chocolate, but not bad.

I extracted the two-day-old newspaper article from my purse and reread the piece on the Weasel and his political aspirations. That's right. Tomorrow, I had to pay the property taxes on my swamp before it magically turned into a wetland. And there was something I needed to look for that might help with my Weasel problem.

Taking the bottle with me, I went to the bathroom and inspected the two small boxes stacked in the shower stall. When I left my former home, I had thrown a few keepsakes like year books and albums into those boxes and hadn't touched them since. I was afraid to open them now in case I was wrong.

Taking another sip before setting the wine in the sink, I pulled the first box out. Unfolding the top, I found report cards from high school, transcripts from university, and a few programs of concerts Mike and I had attended during our engagement.

The second box was packed to the top, mostly with photographs. A couple of albums held casual snaps of my growing up years, of birthday parties and Christmases with friends or Blyth and my parents. Digging deeper, I found a dozen loose wedding pictures. They were taken by a professional photographer and had initially been secured in a large white album with a hundred others.

On that last day, I had whipped through the wedding album, pulling out pictures taken before the church ceremony. These didn't include Mike.

I looked at one photo where I sat in shadow looking out a window. It was posed, of course, but the expression of happiness and hope on my face was genuine.

Only ten years ago, but I was so different now. A better person, or just stronger?

Was I wrong to spend so much time and effort on recovering material assets? Dougal and Glory seemed to think so, but then they both had financial security. And, quite frankly, neither of them worked a day of their lives for what they enjoyed. So, why the hell should I listen to them?

Only a few older photos remained in the box and there was no reason I would have kept the picture I was thinking of. The Weasel was in it.

Reaching up, I hauled the wine bottle out of the sink and tipped it up, letting the lukewarm liquid run down my throat. Okay, one moment of truth coming up.

I lifted up the half-dozen or so photos from the bottom of the box. Shuffling through them, I discarded all but one.

Here it was. And there I was, in all my nubile glory, laughing at the camera, holding up a glass of spectacularly cheap red wine, showing at least twenty-eight perfect white teeth. No wonder I took it with me. I would never look so good again.

Behind me, impossible to confuse with anyone else, even though it was at least eleven years ago, was the Weasel. And now I had him right where I wanted him. If paying the property taxes didn't convince him, this would.

Oh, yeah.

CHAPTER
TWENTY-ONE

THAT NIGHT I SLEPT the dreamless sleep of the optimistic. A pack of grizzly bears could have joined a biker gang in a hoedown outside my trailer, all smoking reefers, for all I cared. If I had known two-thirds of a bottle of wine would send me off to sleep like that, I would have done it a long time ago. My head was banging a bit when I woke up, but it was well worth it for a full night's rest.

When memories of yesterday's encounter with Redfern threatened to surface, I washed them away with pleasant thoughts of the Weasel's face when he handed me the cheque. I should get a picture of that. Mrs. Brickle's chocolate desserts were not going to enter my consciousness again, ever. I can't say it was a bad experience, just not one I cared to repeat. Except for wine, I swear no mind-altering substance would ever pass my lips again, so help me God.

Fresh from a shower in the recreation building, I zipped on my leather jacket and started to head around back to the Savage.

"Yo, Bliss. Wait."

Rae slammed her trailer door and joined me by our communal garbage can.

"Rae. I thought you were staying with your sister in Owen Sound?"

"I was, but Suze and Jason, her husband, got into a huge fight, so I got the heck out of there. I figured it was safer here, know what I mean? I got back late last night." Rae pulled a pink knapsack slowly over one shoulder. Under the heavy coating of foundation, the bruises were still puffy, but she looked much better than two nights ago.

"Do they have any children?"

"Who, my sister? Not yet, but they're trying."

"Are you going to the pool to teach a class, now?"

"That's it, girlfriend. As long as I'm back, and still out of commission, I might as well pick up some extra money at the community centre. The water helps ease the muscle soreness, too."

"Listen, Rae, I don't want to scare you, but have you heard the bear outside your trailer at night?"

"Bear? I've heard something, snapping noises, like that. And twice I heard a high-pitched howl. I was thinking there's a coyote out back. But coyotes won't hurt you. They usually run away when faced by a human."

"A coyote." I considered that. Possible. "I hope you're right, Rae. I haven't heard the howling, but I've seen green eyes watching me at night when I come home, and there's the smell too."

"Smell?" She turned her nose to the wind and sniffed. "Oh, you mean, like that?"

"What?"

But now I detected it, too; the earthy stench of a primitive creature. I stepped closer to Rae and we scanned the trees. Then we heard a low growling.

Rae dropped her knapsack and picked up a hefty stick. She started toward the woods and I tugged on her arm.

"Rae, wait. What are you doing? You don't know it's a coyote. It could be a wolf, or a bear even. We better call someone."

"Who are we going to call, Bliss? The police? Do you really want them poking around Ewan and Sarah? Or Snake? With us right in the middle?"

That had been my argument for not calling the police before, and now that I knew Redfern was crooked, I was even less eager to call 911.

"We can contact the Ministry of Natural Resources," I told her, fumbling for my phone.

"As soon as we see what it is, we'll call them. They won't come unless there's a confirmed sighting. I'll try to get a picture of it with my cell. I don't mind going alone. You wait here."

"Just let me get a stick, Rae. I'll come with you." I couldn't let Rae become a dead hero on her own. But goddamn.

Picking up a stick, I followed her onto the trail. Halfway through the woods, she stopped and held up her hand. We listened but heard no further growling. The animal reek, however, was stronger.

"This way," Rae whispered and headed off-trail into the trees. The woods were thick and dark as dusk.

Rae stopped, and I slammed into her back.

"There he is," she whispered, and by her movements I figured she was reaching for her cellphone. Since she was four or five inches taller than me and standing between two sturdy tree trunks, I couldn't see over or around her.

I ducked under her arm. "Where? And why are we whispering? Don't we want to scare him away?"

"Not until I get a couple of pictures. Here, hold my stick."

Peachy, now I had two sticks. Some protection. I was content enough to take a subordinate role in this safari, since the world of nature was not my area of expertise, and Rae seemed to know what she was doing.

"I still can't see it," I whispered. Was it a bear, or was it a wolf, that's all we needed to know, and, yes, a picture would be nice, but getting the hell out of the woods would be nicer. I hoped it was a wolf, since they couldn't climb trees like bears. But, looking up to the lowest branch, I realized it didn't matter. No way could either of us shinny up one of those pines to reach a branch growing well above our heads.

"It's right there. Just a couple of shots and we can chase it away with our sticks. To sort of discourage him from trespassing on our turf."

In the sudden flash that followed, the creature was outlined in white light, not fifteen yards away. The eyes glowed yellow, then green, and still glowed when the flash faded.

Rae's cell flashed again, and this time the animal uttered a menacing sound from low in its throat. By the third flash, I knew this wasn't a bear. I didn't know how big wolves were in relation to coyotes. If it was a coyote, it was a big one and a mean one. The bottom half of its face was black, and it turned to face us.

"Okay, give me back my stick. Now we chase it away."

Rae uttered a high-pitched shriek. I almost dropped my stick, stunned by the unearthly sound. She stepped forward into battle, stick held in both hands over her head. I was beginning to think she was crazy, but I followed her anyway, proving I was the crazy one.

We moved ahead, her in front, me trying to edge around her body in the tight space. We waved our sticks in front of us, advancing on the wolf like a skimpy army.

We were less than ten feet from the creature when I tugged on Rae's tee-shirt to stop her.

"Wait, Rae. It's not backing away, and that's blood on its mouth. It's eating something. Move back!"

"Probably a deer." But she stopped and lowered her stick slightly.

I stepped up beside Rae and for several seconds we faced down the beast. We were close enough that, even in the gloom, we could see its dripping maw move menacingly and hear its deep-throated snarls.

I dared a quick glance at the creature's feed. The motionless heap was half-hidden behind several trees.

"That's no deer," I screamed at Rae. "It's wearing a plaid shirt."

CHAPTER
TWENTY-TWO

RAE TRIED TO TAKE a deep breath, but it turned into a gurgle in her throat. She dropped like a rock, pulling me to the ground. I fell on my skinny stick and heard it snap into two equally useless pieces.

Fuck. I sprang to my feet and tore Rae's stick from her limp fingers. When I looked up, the beast had advanced several feet. Rage poured from its primitive eyes. Its blood-stained jaws snapped once, and again. The stench emanating from its matted fur did as much to strike me numb with fear as its menacing stance. The lips curled back on fangs drenched with gore.

Prodding Rae with my foot, I said, "Get up. Get up, now."

She lay as still as the plaid mound only a few feet away. You're fucked, Cornwall.

I weighed my options. There wasn't even one good one.

I opened my mouth and screamed. Lowering my head, I charged the animal. I'd go down swinging.

Nobody would ever say that Bliss Moonbeam Cornwall gave up without a fight.

My flash of courage didn't last long. I closed my eyes as I swung the stick, expecting yellow fangs to sink into my calf or throat. Again and again I swung, once connecting with something solid, maybe the animal, maybe a tree. When I opened my eyes, I was swinging at the air. The beast was gone. I quickly turned in a circle, watching for those glowing eyes, listening for snarls. But even the rank odour was dissipating.

Rae was stirring, whimpering softly. I helped her up, saying, "We have to get out of here. Hang on to me." I avoided looking at the body on the ground and Rae was too confused to notice anything. She let me lead her back to the trail and from there we stumbled to my trailer and locked ourselves in.

I took out my phone. "Okay, who do we call? We can't let that animal run loose in the woods. Now it's killed someone."

Rae moaned and leaned back on the bench, her head rolling back and forth.

"I'm so scared. How did everything get so bad?"

"Don't ask me," I said. "Maybe we're both dead and in hell. But I have to call the police. No choice." I punched 911, all three digits this time, quickly before I changed my mind.

Police cruisers, ambulances, and even a fire rescue truck cluttered the rocky, weed-filled area behind Hemp

Hollow. Thankfully, we hadn't been asked to lead the first responders into the woods to show them the body. The forest wasn't very big and with my general instructions they found it within minutes.

Now, uniforms of different colours ran in and out of the trees. This may be just my jaded opinion, but it looked like they were enjoying themselves. Except for Redfern. He was casting frequent scowls at the large rock where Rae and I had planted our butts.

We were told to stay there and not move by Thea Vanderbloom, one of the first to arrive at the scene. She hadn't asked for many facts, leaving the interrogation to her boss. Redfern had just left us, after wringing out every last detail of our ordeal. He didn't seem impressed by our actions, and just barely stopped his eyes from rolling when we described heading into the woods armed with sticks. He confiscated Rae's phone and reiterated Thea's instructions to stay put. Then he swaggered off to take charge of the show.

A white Ministry of Natural Resources truck pulled in and a large man in a windbreaker and ball cap got out. He exchanged a few words with Redfern and was handed Rae's phone. I really hoped Rae didn't have any photos of her clients on that phone.

Redfern and the MNR guy disappeared into the trees. Now that I wasn't under Redfern's scrutiny, I turned my back and pulled out my own phone.

I called and explained to Dougal why Sif's morning report hadn't been delivered yet.

"But I'll be there as soon as I can," I assured him.

Did he hear any part of the account of my dangerous

adventure or commiserate with me for enduring such trauma? Not Dougal.

"Honestly, Bliss. If it's not one thing, it's another with you. All I asked is for you to focus for no more than a week. And I'm paying you a lot of money for your time. I thought you were more reliable. Well, get your ass over to Glory's as soon—"

"Go fuck yourself, Dougal." I clapped the phone closed and jammed it back into the inner pocket of my jacket. It was warm in the sun and I started to take it off. Then I remembered what I had hidden in another pocket. I poked my finger in, to ensure the photograph was still there.

That reminded me that I was supposed to pay my property taxes today. And, didn't I promise Fern Brickle I would come back this morning and finish cleaning her house? Did she know I helped myself to her desserts? And that Redfern was onto her? Although, if he was involved in Lockport's pot trade, it probably didn't matter who knew what.

My head swam. Without a program, I could no longer tell the good guys from the criminals. For instance, Fern Brickle was the sweetest, most giving woman in town. She was on every benefit committee from Toys for Tots to the Food Bank. But she served pot to her friends.

Was it a co-op thing? Like Glory's circle, did Mrs. Brickle and her friends take turns growing the weed they used at their afternoon teas? Everyone I saw getting out of their car at her house yesterday was either elderly or infirm. Some were both.

Rae elbowed me, and I looked up to see Redfern bearing down on us again. He hooked his thumbs on his belt and waited. I stood up, not enjoying such a height disadvantage. But he was still a foot taller. I sat down again.

"Well, ladies, you might be interested in what Chad Ames from the Ministry told me." He put one foot on the rock beside me.

"Chad is almost certain that you saw a coywolf, a product of crossbreeding between coyotes and wolves. These hybrids are showing up in urban areas since they have the wolf's aggression but the coyote's lack of fear of humans. The size is larger than a regular coyote as well. They prefer hunting in packs, but this one seems to be a loner. At least, we hope it's not part of a pack."

"I sure hope so, too. It stinks so much, I don't think I could stand more than one," I said.

"Yeah? Perhaps it's diseased or has an infected wound. The Ministry is going to try to capture it."

"I hope they shoot it. It killed a person. Do you know who it is?" I asked.

"Yes. He had identification on him. Fitzgerald Corwin. Ever hear of him?"

Beside me, Rae gasped. Both Redfern and I looked at her, but she shook her head and tried on a smile through shaking lips. The smile failed and Redfern gave her a speculative look.

Trying to distract him, I said, "Fitzgerald Corwin? Never heard of him. Is he local?"

"No." He turned to Rae. "Miss Zaborski? I believe the paramedics would like to check you out, to make sure you aren't in shock. If you wouldn't mind stepping over to that ambulance?"

Rae left so quickly she nearly came to grief on the stony ground. But, once leaning forlornly against the back door of the ambulance, she was soon surrounded by several medical personnel who, it must be assumed, cared deeply about her condition. Her cheerleader looks might have had something to do with their solicitous attention. No one seemed concerned about my shock.

"I want a private word with you, Cornwall."

"We've had nothing but words in the past few days. What is there left to say?"

"Do you remember yesterday's conversation?"

"Certainly, I do." I thought for a minute. "A lot of it didn't make sense, though."

"Exactly. So, I'd like to start again. But, before we begin a discussion that will probably end in yet another argument, I'm suggesting very strongly you find someplace else to live. Hemp Hollow is not safe for an innocent like you."

"Hey, watch your language, Chief. It's been some years since I was an innocent."

"Yesterday, you told me you were a born-again virgin. Remember that?"

"Well, aren't my cheeks red as tail lights?"

"They should be. Now, let's move on to the brownie you ate at Fern Brickle's house."

"It wasn't a brownie. And let's stop beating around the bush, Redfern. I don't know what your game is, but what I ate in Mrs. Brickle's kitchen did not have a label on it. Therefore, I can tell you nothing. So, now, ask about something else."

"You're tough, Cornwall. I can't decide whether you're a lamb in a fox run, or you're in this mess up to your pretty little neck."

Choosing my words carefully, something I should do more often, I said, "You'll have to be more specific. I'm involved in several personal messes at the moment, but I don't believe any of them are of an illegal nature."

That sidetracked him. He didn't want to hear about my personal life, but if I had to, I was prepared to go on at length about my living conditions, marital woes, cousin commitments, and so much more. Anything to stay off the subject of drugs and drug dealers.

Removing his hat, Redfern looked toward the trees and said, "That wasn't so smart, Cornwall. Confronting a wild animal like that."

"What was I supposed to do? Rae was unconscious at my feet, and the wolf was only a few yards away. I couldn't leave her and back away from it. And if I'd run, it would have chased me down, or killed Rae."

"I guess you did what you needed to. You've got guts, Cornwall, but you'd drive a saint to drink. And your mouth is world class."

"Good to know I'm skilled at something. Now, if we're done here, I have to go into town and pay my property taxes."

"I have a feeling we'll never be done, Cornwall."

Redfern's eyes were fixed on a spot over my shoulder, and I turned to see the Weasel standing a few feet away, probably here as mayor to see what all the fuss was about.

Had he heard my comment about paying my property taxes? Didn't matter. I stroked my jacket with its secret treasure and gave him a polite smile. Then I turned away and left him in Redfern's official hands.

Right now, I needed to address a more pressing dilemma.

CHAPTER
TWENTY-THREE

MANOEUVRING THE SAVAGE THROUGH the field littered with vehicles was difficult enough without the possible humiliation of tipping the bike in front a dozen men to consider. Not for the first time, I wished I was six inches taller and fifty pounds heavier.

Redfern ambled through the field looking at the ground with his hands in his pockets. I stopped the bike beside the ambulance where Rae was hooked up to a blood pressure cuff. Two firemen and three emergency responders were standing so close to her, they were undoubtedly hogging her oxygen supply, and one comely youngster was actually holding her hand, pretending to take her pulse. It was a safe bet I wouldn't have earned as much attention if I'd been torn limb from limb by the coywolf. I winced, reminded that Fitzgerald Corwin had met that very fate.

I had to clear my throat a few times before Rae noticed me.

"Hi, Bliss. Are you going somewhere?"

"Things to do, places to be. Do you want to stay with me tonight? I thought we could be company for each other, especially if they haven't found the, well, you know."

"Yes, I'd love that, Bliss. It's pretty scary in that trailer right now."

Murmurs of empathy and support followed this statement. Oh, to be twenty-five again. And curvaceous.

"Right, then. I'll be back about nine o'clock and knock on your door."

Out of the corner of my eye, I spotted Redfern coming my way. I remembered my bike was supposed to be parked in Mrs. Brickle's alley. My tires kicked up some stones when I took off, but I didn't look back to see if any hit him in the eye. Boy, wasn't I the wild child?

As I approached the exit to the concession road, I was forced to stop. A Harley Fat Boy blocked my way. Snake.

The abundant chrome on the low-slung bike shone like mirrors. I noticed the bike had showroom exhaust pipes, not the customized straight drag pipes that infuriated lovers of peace and quiet and earned the biker regular fines for noise infractions.

His bike might be immaculate. Snake was not. Tendrils of greasy black hair had escaped from his helmet and hid a large portion of his face, the rest covered by wrap-around shades. The helmet sported a death's-head embellishment and too many nicks and dents to count. Either Snake collected a lot of pebbles as he rode, or he got knocked off his bike a lot. Remembering the rough treatment I suffered at his hands the night Rae was attacked, I hoped the latter.

"Yo, little sister. What's going on over there?"

The gravelly voice was affable enough, but he wasn't charming me.

"A wolf killed a man in the bush behind Hemp Hollow. And ate him."

If Snake was unnerved, he concealed it well.

"Who's the guy? Anyone we know?"

"Nobody I know. Fitzgerald Corwin. Do you know him?"

"Nope. Nice bike you have there, for a girl. Ever ride a Harley?"

I snorted. "A Harley? That's so yesterday."

Snake appeared not to have heard the insult. He rolled his bike forward a few feet and I squeezed by him, missing his shiny chrome fender by inches.

I stopped at the mail kiosk near the main entrance to Secret Valley. A couple of flyers for pizza specials and upholstery cleaning sat atop one white legal-size envelope from the Town of Lockport. Throwing the flyers into the trash barrel, I ripped open the envelope.

The Cemetery Board no longer required my services. Would I please drop my key to the office washroom at the municipal offices at my earliest convenience?

Crumbling the letter, I threw it into the barrel. So be it. The Weasel wouldn't know what hit him.

The silver Beetle was still parked outside the Super 8 Motel. Again, Chesley was bobbing up and down between the seats. On impulse, I pulled the Savage into the parking lot and stopped beside the vehicle.

"How are you coming with the seats?" I asked Chesley, removing my helmet. He was bent over in the back seat and his bony butt seemed to be rocking in time with the heavy metal music blasting from the CD player.

Chesley's head shot up and he whirled around. In one hand he held a cleaning cloth, in the other a large bottle labelled "Odour Gone." He reached over and turned down the music.

"Miss Cornwall. Bliss …" Chesley swallowed audibly and his prominent eyes blinked at me. A crimson flush dotted his cheekbones.

"Is that stuff working?" I asked. I could smell skunk from where I sat.

"It's coming. One more treatment should do it."

"Great. Chesley, have you and your mother found a suitable property yet?"

"We've looked at a couple more with Miss Simms, but none of them are exactly what we're looking for. The property you showed us is the most promising so far, though."

"Well, let me know. I'd be happy to show you around again, if you want a second look."

"Wait, Bliss. Mum and I were wondering about another piece of land across the road. You can see it from the Barrister property. The one with a river flowing through to the lake. Miss Simms said you owned it."

Now I noticed Chesley was wearing a red sweatshirt and green flannel pyjama bottoms. Who dressed this boy? I preferred him in black. Before I could ask why he wanted to know about my swamp, a sound not unlike a sonic boom echoed from a nearby unit of the motel.

"Chesleeeeee!"

A sharp pain pierced my left eye and my feet left the ground. The bike wobbled. It was touch and go, but I managed to get my toes on the asphalt again before the bike went over.

"There you are, young man." Ivy stumped over to us, in flowing black shift and signature red lipstick. "Oh, Ms. Cornwall. You're here, too."

"I just stopped by to see how Chesley was doing with the leather cleaner."

Ivy didn't look thrilled to see me, but in real estate school they told us to get used to rejection. I was already there, and just smiled.

"What do you think about my son running over that skunk in the middle of town, Miss Cornwall? We saw it earlier in the day when we stopped to speak to Miss Simms. Disgraceful that such a horrible thing was allowed to rot there."

"I'm sure Chesley did his best to avoid it, Mrs. Belcourt. Apparently, there was some sort of internal dispute about jurisdiction."

"Disgraceful," she said again. "We may sue."

"Mum." Chesley's eyes pleaded with me not to rat him out. Obviously, Ivy didn't know the whole tale.

"If you're serious about suing, Mrs. Belcourt, I would suggest you go out of town to retain counsel. Our lawyers in Lockport aren't so hot."

"Hmmph."

"Mum."

"Well, Ms. Cornwall, Chesley has work to do here. I'm not setting foot in that vehicle until the smell is gone. We'll be touch in due time about the property we looked at."

Dismissed, I turned the bike to leave, but not before catching Chesley's mouthed, "See you later."

Something was up with Chesley, but I forgot him and tried to concentrate on Sif and Thor. Watching those two ugly plants for symptoms of impending ovulation or, conversely, signs of collapse, was getting old. Whatever they were going to do, I wish they would just do it, so I could collect the money and never have to see them or pot plants again, ever.

The whole damn town was growing pot, or eating it, or both. And the one person who was supposed to be putting a lid on it was up to his badge in the whole business.

CHAPTER
TWENTY-FOUR

SIF HAD SHOT UP another foot during the night. The interior of the spathe glowed blood-red and displayed a ring of tiny cream-coloured flowers at the base. These were the male flowers, according to Dougal, and underneath would be another circle of pink female blossoms. I walked around the planter, snapping a dozen pictures of the inside of the spathe.

While waiting for Pan to edit them, I sniffed. Something. I glanced at the other plants, ripe buds hanging, but it wasn't the pot. I couldn't place it.

"Pan, do you smell something in here? Is there a dead mouse somewhere?"

He took a perfunctory sniff and handed back the camera. "No. Smells okay to me."

I shrugged. Maybe it was just a memory of the coywolf in my brain. As we left the greenhouse, I said to him, "I need to talk to Glory for a minute."

"I don't know, Bliss. She'll just be finishing up breakfast."

"What, you mean two cups of black coffee? Never mind, I know the way."

Glory was sitting in her breakfast room at the back of the house, flipping through a magazine. The floor to ceiling windows overlooked terraced flower beds, with the pine forest as a backdrop.

I pulled out a white wrought-iron chair opposite her and waited. She glanced up, froze, then a curl of her lip dared me to sit down. So I did.

"Glory, we need to discuss your pot."

"What? My pot? That's got nothing to do with you, so butt out."

"Yes, I probably should. But, for some reason, I don't want to see you spend your remaining youthful years behind bars."

"Are you threatening me? How dare you."

She crossed her legs at the knee and one foot began to waggle back and forth.

"The police are hot on the trail of anything resembling cannabis in this town. They're cracking down big time, and I don't know why you think you're so special you can't be charged. Just get rid of the pot, and buy it off the street like everyone else."

"You have no idea what you're suggesting, Bliss. The commercial plants are full of pesticides and other horrible things. At least I know mine don't have toxic residue."

"Well, here's an idea. Don't use it at all."

The foot swung faster. I stood up.

"Have you told that worm about my pot?"

"I haven't told anybody. But, like I said, the police are all over this town searching the stuff out. What if the Baker snitches on you?" Perhaps I exaggerated, given the Chief of Police was involved and I wasn't sure of the identity of the Baker, but sometimes you need to hit those born to privilege with a mallet to get their attention.

The foot stopped. "What do you know about the Baker? Who told you?"

"Glory, I am everywhere. I hear things, and I know the police are ready to move in and make arrests. Get rid of the pot in your greenhouse."

"I'll think about it."

"I guess that's it, then. Now, I have to show Dougal the latest pictures of Sif. It looks to me like—"

"Dougal!"

Just the sound of his name threw Glory over the edge. Her eyes completed their transformation and were blood red. I looked away from her face, not 100 percent sure she couldn't turn me into a pillar of salt if I gazed directly into those eyes.

The high-heeled mule flew off her wildly swinging foot and came straight at me. I ducked and the slipper hit the sideboard, where it landed in a nest of sherry glasses.

The sound of expensive crystal shattering sounded more like an explosion than a tinkle, and Pan came on the run. We passed at the door of the breakfast room, where he gave me a quick accusing glance and rushed over to the Princess of Petulance who was winding up like an air raid siren. The second slipper whizzed through the doorway as I ran out of the room. It hit a mirror in the hallway, but I kept going.

If this was Glory on a steady diet of grass, I feared

for my life, and Pan's, if she had to give the stuff up. This afternoon, when I came back for the day's second photo shoot, I would suggest Pan serve her an extra helping of marijuana alfredo. Just to use up the supply in her freezer. Once Thor and Sif were pollinated, and I had my money, Pan could cut her off.

Before driving away, I called Fern Brickle. I couldn't fit her in today and wanted to suggest Friday instead. There was no answer and I continued on to Dougal's.

"What part of twice a day don't you understand?" was his greeting.

I looked at my watch. "It's only a little past one o'clock. Here's the camera."

"How's she looking?"

I assumed he wasn't referring to his ex-wife. "She's getting really tall, maybe eight feet."

Dougal looked concerned. "Oh God, I hope they both have the energy to sustain that rate of growth without collapsing. It would be a tragedy if the blossoming failed now."

"Well, look inside the spathe. Those male flowers are visible. What more has to happen?"

"The male flowers have to release their pollen. And that happens when the spathe is completely unfurled. By these pictures, that should happen within the next thirty-six hours. Now I'm beginning to think Thor is possibly ahead of Sif."

"But thirty-six hours would bring us to late Friday night or early Saturday morning."

"Titan Arums traditionally blossom around midnight, so, yes, what's your point?"

My point? "You mean I have to run pollen back and forth in the middle of the night? You didn't tell me that."

"What, do you turn into a witch and fly away on your broomstick at sundown? I always suspected as much." He laughed. "I know you don't have a love life, so why do you care what time the Titans blossom?"

Another glance at my watch reassured me that I had time for a quick bite before visiting the municipal offices. But, as I turned to leave, a scent like the one in Glory's greenhouse wafted through the air. I lifted my nose and sniffed. Gone. There was nothing.

"What's wrong with you?"

I walked closer to the orchids. Putting my nose inside a lavender blossom, I breathed in. That wasn't it.

The pot crop, like Glory's, was fecund with ripened buds. But they weren't the source of the elusive scent.

"I smell something," I finally admitted. "It happened at Glory's, too."

"What? What kind of smell?" He clutched me by the collar and dragged me back to Thor. "Smell."

"I don't know. It comes and goes."

Dougal pushed my face to within an inch of Thor's mottled spadix.

"Now?"

"Oh, yeah, there it is. Barely. I think Thor needs deodorant, Dougal. Or else you have a sewer leak."

Dougal jumped up and down and, since I was attached to his left hand by the scruff of my neck, I found myself bouncing right along with him.

Kissing me on both cheeks, he took my hands and swung me in a maniacal square dance, around and around Thor. My feet left the floor, and for a minute I was in danger of flying through the solarium windows and taking a few orchids and pot plants with me.

"Enough, Dougal. Put me down."

He did, so abruptly that I skidded along the tiles toward the door. But I managed to stay on my feet and just kept going, heading toward the kitchen. Dancing always gives me an appetite.

"There's nothing in here." Standing in front of the open fridge, I stared in amazement. "It's empty."

"The Titans are going to blossom, Bliss, and very soon. There's no doubt now. I think this is a first in the botanical world. Two Titan Arums belonging to private collectors will blossom. And if they are successfully pollinated and bear fruit, who knows how many more Titans I can grow?"

"Great, Dougal. But why isn't there any food in the fridge?"

"Mrs. Boudreau hasn't been in for a couple of days. What's today, Thursday? She was here Tuesday. If she doesn't show up tomorrow, you'll have to buy me some groceries."

"Where is she? She's supposed to come in every day." I went into the pantry and surveyed the tidy shelves full of canned goods. I wanted fresh.

"Well, you've been taking food out of here lately like you were stocking a bunker. Get a frozen dinner out of the freezer and nuke it."

Packaged macaroni and cheese from the freezer would have to do. While I ate, Dougal babbled on about how he was going to surgically cut into Thor to dab male

pollen from Sif onto the female flowers. It sounded painfully clinical, and my mind wandered back to the scene
outside Fern Brickle's house yesterday as I watched her
visitors arrive. Mrs. Boudreau was definitely there. She
even waved at me.

I interrupted Dougal's discourse on how and when
to re-pot Titan corms, a subject even more boring than
how to harvest the fruit. "Do you remember telling me
about the group of people with disabilities who grow
their own cannabis, then take it to the Baker to be baked
into desserts?"

"Sure."

"Then, you must know that Mrs. Boudreau is one
of them."

"I never said that."

"She's in your house five days a week. She has to know
about your plants in the solarium, so I'm assuming you
two talk about harvesting your crop. I bet you've been
giving these people botanical advice."

"Bliss, you're ignorant about the subculture. Okay,
Mrs. Boudreau knows about my pot, and once in a while
I give her a few doobies. She suffers from severe anxiety
and smoking helps her. But I didn't know she belonged
to a dessert ring. And it's her business. So mind yours."

"Dougal, listen up. The police …"

"No, you listen. I told you I'm not growing any
more after this crop is harvested. It's almost ready now,
but I don't have time to deal with it until I complete the
cross-pollination. So, put a lid on it and get out. But come
back before dinner time with another report. I'm having
company tonight and don't want you underfoot."

"And, that's another thing. Melanie—"

"Don't say her name again."

"But you have to know how unprofessional a relationship is between a therapist and client."

"Bliss, stop trying to control other people's lives. I'm not your child, so stop mothering me. Why don't you find a man, any man, and get pregnant. Then you can smother the poor kid with unwanted advice and leave me alone."

"Fuck you, then."

"No, fuck you. And get out."

I was fuming. From here on, Dougal and Glory could smoke and eat cannabis until their ears fell off, or they were arrested, whichever came first.

CHAPTER
TWENTY-FIVE

I PUSHED MY DEBIT card and the notice of taxes across to the teenaged clerk behind the counter. She glanced at them, then said, "I'm so sorry. Would you wait one moment, please?" She turned back to her desk and picked up her phone. I tried to relax. I had time to kill before I could check on Sif again and report back to Dougal, then instruct the Thursday evening yoga class at the Golden Goddess. After that, both Rae and my part bottle of wine would be waiting for me in Hemp Hollow to keep the haunts away.

The size-zero teenager finally put the phone down and returned to the counter.

"I'm sorry, Mrs. Bains, but the debit card reader is malfunctioning." She had trouble with the last word, and I wondered if she knew what it meant.

"You can call me Ms. Cornwall. And you are…?"

"Oh, hi. I'm Alyce. With a Y."

"Hi, Alyce. If your debit card machine isn't working, then I'll give you a cheque." I reached into my purse and pulled my chequebook out. "Do you have a pen?"

"Yes, but you'll have to come back tomorrow."

"Okay, why? Don't you accept cheques?"

"Well, yes, but only if it's post-dated."

"How about if I write tomorrow's date on the cheque?"

"That would only work if your taxes were due today."

"Excuse me? You mean I can't give you a post-dated cheque today that's dated tomorrow? Alyce, that's a post-dated cheque."

Alyce's eyes welled up.

"I'm sorry, Mrs. Bains, I mean, Mrs. Cornwall. You'll have to come back tomorrow."

"How about if I go across to the bank and get the cash? Then you can stamp this notice as paid and I won't have to come back tomorrow."

"We don't accept cash, Mrs. Cornwall." The blue, mascara-rimmed eyes overflowed.

"Since when did cash become non-legal currency?"

"Pardon?"

"Can you get your supervisor, Alyce?"

"No. There's nobody here but me."

"Never mind, Alyce. I'll come back tomorrow. If you can guarantee that my taxes will not be overdue."

"Oh, certainly, Mrs. Cornwall. I'm sure tomorrow will be fine."

"It's *Ms.* Cornwall, Alyce. I'll see you tomorrow."

Not at all sure that tomorrow would be fine, I left Alyce in her Wonderland and sped down the hall to the mayor's office.

The Office of Mayor of Lockport was just a part-time job. Running Crooked Lawyers R Us with his wife from a sleek office in a professional building at the south end of town monopolized the rest of the Weasel's week.

On the off chance that he was putting in one of his mayoral hours, I knocked and turned the knob.

Mike looked up as I dropped into the visitor's chair and breathed out a dramatic sigh.

"Boy, wasn't that something in the woods this morning?"

"What do you want, Bliss?"

"Just my half of our assets."

"We don't have anything left to discuss. I made you an offer and you turned it down. End of story."

"*Au contraire, mon ennemi.* Let's discuss the wetland you are reportedly donating to the province. That wouldn't be my swamp, would it, Mike?"

"That has nothing to do with your settlement."

"I'm so glad to hear it. I was afraid you thought you still owned that habitat for endangered spotted turtles."

"Don't be ridiculous." Beads of sweat popped out on Mike's tanned forehead.

"What happened? Did the paper leak the story a week or two early?"

He lifted himself halfway out of his chair, then subsided and pasted a look of practised detachment on his face. I hid my satisfaction.

"Did you think I would forfeit the land and you could swoop in and pick it up for taxes owing?"

He didn't respond. His air of indifference might be an effective strategy in a courtroom, but I was immune to the ploy.

"Andrea and I will publically refute any claims you make regarding mistreatment or illegalities. Your mental instability is public knowledge."

"Andrea can kiss my ass. And so can you, Mike."

"Point proven."

"That I'm unstable? Maybe. But even if I end up in the psych ward, I promise that you will not be elected to any office other than this one." My eyes swept the shabby room.

He sneered. "You're out of your league, Bliss. Andrea and I are on our way to Ottawa, and there's nothing you can do to stop us."

I pulled the picture out of the inner pocket of my jacket.

"You might want to look at this before you make such a rash statement, Mike. Remember this? It was taken in our last year at university."

He reached for it, but I pulled it back. Twenty-one-year-old Bliss, sexy as hell, sat on Mike Bains's lap. Mike was wearing a top hat and holding a cigarette to his lips. But, wait. The cigarette was misshapen, discoloured, impossible to mistake for anything than what it was.

"Remember that party at your frat house, Mike? You had a lot to drink and smoked a doobie. And here it is, captured for all time."

"You smoked one too!"

"Actually, I didn't. Not that it matters, since I'm not running for public office."

"Everybody was smoking. I shouldn't be penalized for doing what everyone else was doing."

"I agree. And you can have this photo, with one wee string attached."

Before I closed the door on his stricken face, I said, "For the price I wrote on that piece of paper at Timmy's, you can have the swamp and this picture. A bargain. Run it by Andrea."

CHAPTER
TWENTY-SIX

WHEN I REACHED THE street, I sat down on the curb beside my bike. My hands shook so hard I was afraid the key would fall from my fingers.

What if Mike offered me a settlement? I would have no idea if it was fair, and, knowing him, it wouldn't be. What figure did I write on the piece of paper at Timmy's? Some forethought would have been wise, Cornwall.

"There you are, Moonbeam."

"Thea. Hi."

The municipal offices and the police station shared a building. It was necessary to walk by the police nerve centre to reach the staircase to the second floor where the mayor and councillors met once a month to draft by-laws the townspeople ignored.

Thea had changed to her summer uniform of a short-sleeved light-blue shirt. Her gizmo-laden duty belt had to weigh twenty pounds, and from my vantage point I could see dangling handcuffs, baton, flashlight, a radio, and, of course, the holstered gun.

"What, no shorts, Thea? You must be really warm in those long pants."

"No warmer than your jeans, Moonbeam. By the way, you're looking even more fractured than this morning in the field. Has something else happened?"

"I refuse to think about this morning. Anyway, things are coming together for me, Thea. A few more days and I should be solvent and able to decide what to do with the rest of my life."

"Sincerely glad to hear it. But why are you sitting on the curb in full view of Chief Redfern's office window?"

I looked up at the first-floor windows, but with the sun reflecting off the glass the entire Lockport force could be watching and I wouldn't see them.

"Ah. So he sent you out here to move me along. Okay, I'll go. It won't do to have a vagrant littering the streets of Lockport."

"Not at all, Moonbeam. I think the chief prefers you under his watchful eye rather than running around ingesting illegal substances or pitching epic fits. That's a direct quote, by the way, not necessarily my opinion."

"I appreciate it."

"He suggested we attach a tracking device to your ankle, and I'm not sure he was kidding."

"Thanks for the heads up."

"Okay, Moonbeam, now that my attempt at humour has so clearly relaxed you, I have something more serious to discuss."

"Shit, you're not going to arrest me for Julian Barn-feather's murder, are you? I thought we were past that."

"What? No."

I stood up. "Okay, what is it?"

"That man you found in the woods today, name of Fitzgerald Corwin?"

"I remember."

"Well, the coywolf didn't kill him."

"It was eating him, Thea."

"There's no denying that. But Mr. Corwin died from multiple blows from a sharp device like a hatchet or axe. You're not going to faint, are you?"

"Hardly. Why didn't Redfern tell me himself this morning in Hemp Hollow?"

"We didn't know until the coroner examined the body. You need to be aware that the killer has not been apprehended, and to take care. The chief suggests you stay with a friend or relative for the time being."

"Can't do it, Thea. I hate to admit this, but there isn't a soul in Lockport who would give me a bed. Even my cousin, Dougal, is conducting a secret love affair and regularly throws me out of his house. It's my own fault — I've been so intent on making the Weasel pay up that I've neglected relationships, career, everything. But it's almost over now."

She shook her head. "I don't like this, Moonbeam. There's something going on in Hemp Hollow, stuff I can't share with you, and you need to get out of there. You and that hooker friend of yours, what's her name, Rae Zabinski?"

"Zaborski." I didn't ask how she knew about Rae.

"One more thing. Keep what I've just told you about Corwin to yourself until it's made public. The chief only wants you to know so you'll be careful."

As Thea backed away, the Weasel walked past us to cross the street. He was pulling a black suit jacket over his white shirt. As our eyes met, it was all I could do not to shiver, but I held his gaze. A palpable wave of ruthlessness touched me.

Thea watched him for a minute, then shifted her belt, hand automatically resting on her holster.

"If I were you, Moonbeam, I wouldn't turn my back on your ex."

"He can rot in hell. But not before writing me a nice big cheque."

Thea shook her head again and bounded up the steps, the belt hugging her trim waist. I liked Thea and hoped she wasn't involved with Redfern and Snake.

The Quigleys were running some sort of drug depot. I preferred to think their business involved marijuana and not crystal meth. As far as I knew, pot wouldn't blow you sky high. And Snake was their … their what? Assistant? Enforcer? Delivery boy? Perhaps the Quigleys' business had expanded to the point where they needed a partner.

And I had no idea how Redfern fit into the picture. Maybe he simply looked the other way, for a price, and all his talk about cleaning up the gateway to the North was just a smokescreen. He was right about one thing, though. Hemp Hollow was no place for me and Rae.

Unfortunately, both of us were fresh out of options.

I crossed the road and headed for the Second Hand Rose Shop. Holly Duffett was just finishing up with a customer. As I approached her, I realized that the large-boned woman was not a customer, but was donating a stack of cardigans and wool skirts.

Holly greeted me with a "Hi, Bliss" and turned back to the middle-aged donor. "Thanks, Melanie, I'll keep these in back until September."

The woman headed for the door, but gave me a swift, appraising look on her way past.

"Did you call her Melanie?" I asked Holly.

"Sure. Melanie Davies."

"And, is she by any chance a therapist?"

"Well, yes she is. She's on the Board of Community Assistance, which oversees the management of this store."

I was shocked that Dougal was having an affair with a woman at least fifteen years his senior. And, not to be rude, but she didn't look like the type a younger man would find attractive. Ergo, Dougal was stringing me along, and his paramour was somebody other than his therapist. I realized that Dougal had simply let me hang myself with the rope of conjecture. I had to hand it to him, he was almost as devious as his favourite cousin.

"Did you know today is Julian Barnfeather's funeral, Bliss? The service was at St. Luke's, but the burial should be taking place about now."

On the street outside again, I looked down at myself. My jeans, pink tee-shirt, and motorcycle boots were fairly clean.

I'd go. I wanted to see who would be there for Julian's send-off.

CHAPTER
TWENTY-SEVEN

THE WORDS OF THE 23th Psalm wafted toward me, and a dozen mourners stood around the open grave. Julian was being buried only yards away from Alistair Parks's flat stone where I had rested my back just five days ago.

I stood beside a cedar hedge and, for a moment, felt sad that I would never trim it again. A man wearing a black suit and a woman in a beige shift stood with their backs to me. She had her arm threaded through his and, once, she put her head on his shoulder, just for a second. He moved slightly, and as she straightened up I recognized The Weasels. Mike couldn't take the chance of being criticized for ignoring the funeral of a town employee.

Thea had been teasing me about Redfern watching from his window. He stood directly opposite me now, sunglasses in place. His chin lifted in my direction, and I knew he had spotted me.

From my vantage point, I had a good view of the other mourners. The large blond woman in a black pantsuit seated with her back to me was surely Julian's wife. Her shoulders heaved, and two younger women comforted her. I hoped she never found out what a pig her husband had been.

Fern Brickle and Joy MacPherson stood beside Bob in his wheelchair. I recognized Mrs. Boudreau and a couple of other people I had seen arriving at Fern's yesterday.

Then the truth hit me like a sledgehammer. Fuck.

Seeing them together in the cemetery, I realized Fern's dessert group were all Friends of the Settlers. The very Friends who spent every Saturday tending the graves of Lockport's homesteaders.

It hadn't occurred to me before, but the settlers' graves in the far corner of the cemetery should not have required weekly attention.

The area was enclosed by a tall wrought iron fence with a locked gate. And a thick line of pines hid the interior from view. A curious sightseer could only place an eye to the gate and catch a glimpse of ancient tombstones, words etched neatly with black paint to preserve history. The Cornwalls were one of Lockport's founding families, and their graves lay inside.

My mother once mentioned that, although the lock had been put on to keep out vandals, the area was open to the public every day. But those gates had never been opened during my employment at the cemetery.

It would be interesting to know how the Cemetery Board justified closing the Settlers' Plot to the public.

Unless — and this was pure speculation — one or more of the dessert club were members of the Cemetery Board.

Which meant what?

Perhaps … Dessert Club *are* Friends of the Settlers *are* Cemetery Board. No problem keeping the public out of the Settlers' Plot.

Why go to all that trouble? Because they had to grow their freaking pot somewhere, didn't they? I would have thought the Settlers' Plot would be too shady to grow marijuana. But, as had been pointed out to me several times, I knew squat about marijuana.

I considered climbing over the fence and checking out my theory. Right here, right now. The Friends were gathered around Julian's casket, staring into the hole in the ground.

Too late. The mourners, including the Friends, were lining up to drop yellow roses onto the lid of the casket. Soon they might wander off to check on their crop.

Whoops.

Redfern strode purposefully in my direction, and one conversation per day with that bent cop was all I could handle.

I fled the scene.

CHAPTER
TWENTY-EIGHT

"MISS GLORY WANTS A word with you, Bliss."

"I'll pass, thanks, Pan."

It was my second Titan run of the day, a bit early, but it's amazing how many hours there are in a day when you don't have a real job.

Sif seemed to be more or less the same height as this morning, but her spathe had further opened and her inner lining of deep red velvet cupped thousands of miniature cream flowers at the base. The odour in the greenhouse was stronger than even a few hours earlier, and brought to mind a fresh load of manure spread on a newly ploughed field. Pan noticed the smell this time and threw me sidelong glances until I told him that it wasn't me, for God's sake.

The pot crop was high and verdant, obviously ready for harvesting. I was thankful that, soon, I would never have to set foot in Glory's greenhouse again. I needed the money now more than ever, but I hoped she would tell me she no longer required my services to clean her house. The woman either ingested too much pot, or not enough.

"She was really insistent," Pan wheedled.

After a moment's thought, I decided to comply. Until I transported Sif's pollen to Thor, and Thor's back to Sif — or the other way around — it would be in my best interest to stay on Glory's good side. Well, that was a stretch. Glory had only a bad side, and a worse side.

"Lead me to Her Weedness then, but shouldn't I get a last meal?"

"You're quite amusing at times, Bliss."

It looked like my amusement factor wasn't getting me any food. It was just as well. I'd had my quota of special ingredient for the week, and it apparently featured in every dish prepared in Glory's kitchen.

Glory sat on her terrace, in a wicker armchair pulled up to a round table. She was dressed in white shorts and a sleeveless tee-shirt, and I was happy to see she wore tennis shoes. At least she wouldn't be hurling high-heeled slippers at my head, but I kept my eye on the tennis racquet propped nearby.

A bottle of white wine in an ice bucket sat on the table. Two long-stemmed glasses waited nearby. I looked around for a bowl of chips or beer nuts. Nada.

"Sit down, Bliss."

"Here?"

"Of course."

I pulled out the chair opposite her and sat on its edge. I shot Pan a glance, but he looked as perplexed as I felt.

"I hope you like Riesling?" She waved Pan away with one hand and he left the terrace with unflattering speed. There would be no help from that houseboy if I needed rescue.

Glory expertly poured wine into the glasses and handed one to me. I took it but didn't sip.

"You've been on my mind all day, Bliss." She tossed her tangle of fiery hair back and aimed her sea-blue eyes at my own regulation brown ones.

"Oh?"

"Yes. I realize you were only showing concern for me, and I reacted badly. You may be poor, and not too smart in the marital department, but you're sincere. I promise you that the crop of marijuana in my greenhouse is my last. The next time it's my turn, I'm going to tell my friends I won't do it. I'm quite high-strung, and I need my special food to relax, but I'm sure I can find another source."

"I'm glad to hear it, Glory." I wouldn't bet the family silver on that promise.

"To make up for being so cross with you, I'm going to tell you something. Something I haven't told another living soul. Except my therapist."

I took a healthy gulp of wine and stayed on the edge of the chair. I had a premonition Glory was going to tell me she slaughtered her previous house cleaner and buried the body in the forest behind her house. Or she had a crazy old grandmother stored in the attic. Or, more probable, she was sleeping with Pan and was pregnant with his triplets.

"I'm going to tell you why I threw Dougal out of my house, and why I would cheerfully castrate him given a clear shot and a sharp knife."

All right! I drained the glass, then poured myself a wee drop more.

"My therapist wants me to tell someone I trust, to share the pain. It's been eating at me for three years and he says that if I share it with a friend, the burden will be lightened. But I can't trust my friends not to laugh or spread gossip, so I'm going to tell you."

"Does Dougal know why you threw him out?"

"Of course he does! It happened on my birthday, my thirtieth. You probably remember how you felt when you hit thirty. Unattractive, over the hill, incipient wrinkles, the whole bit?"

I nodded, although the memory I had of that landmark birthday was spending it in my parked car at the Bird River swamp. And, until now, I hadn't given significant thought to wrinkles. I fingered the skin at the corner of my eyes.

"Well, Dougal and I had dinner at the Club that night. He had been excited all evening, and I suspected he had something special for me."

Glory's fingers were wrapped around her wine glass, but she was too engrossed in her story to drink. I poured another smidge into my glass.

"I thought maybe it was a diamond heart pendant I had been hinting about, or a pair of emerald drop earrings. Instead, he pulled an envelope out of his pocket and gave it to me, with his typical stupid grin. Well, then I figured the envelope held tickets for a trip. We hadn't been to Florence since our graduation year and … Guess what it was?"

Hell, I had no idea. I just shrugged and poured another nip.

"It was a gift certificate. My loving husband gave me…. Guess."

"Don't know, Glory."

"Breast implants. The worm had bought me breast implants. All I had to do was phone the surgeon's office and book the appointment. He was so pleased with himself."

Now Glory drained her glass and reached for the bottle. It was empty. It couldn't have been a standard-sized bottle, probably one of those small bottles from France, or Bulgaria.

Glory snapped her fingers and Pan magically appeared with another chilled offering wrapped in a cloth napkin, resting along his arm like he was some goddamn maître d' at the Château Laurier. He refilled her glass halfway and was going to place it in the ice bucket, but I held my empty glass out. He glanced at his mistress and, at her regal nod, poured me a couple of inches.

She waited until Pan disappeared again. He probably was hiding around the corner of the terrace, ears flapping like sails in the sunset. If he had any decency, he'd have brought out some chips with the second bottle of wine. I could feel the alcohol hitting my empty stomach and my near-empty brain. But this stuff was so much smoother than the red I drank the night before. I reached into the ice bucket again.

"Do these look like they need to be augmented? Tell me the truth, Bliss, do they?" Glory had her hands over her girls and was shaking them up and down. "Don't these look perfect to you?"

"Of course, they're perfect, Glory. If they were any bigger or firmer, they'd be just trashy. I can't believe Dougal would try and buy you bigger ones. Isn't that just like a man, only thinking of himself? He needs a brain transplant."

"I know!" Glory reached over the table and filled both glasses to the brim. Oh, my kingdom for a sandwich.

"You know, Glory? That is the most insulting thing a husband can do. It's like he doesn't think you're good enough the way you are. I don't blame you for throwing his selfish ass out. No kidding, that was purely evil, what he did."

"I know!" She snapped her fingers, twice, and Pan ran up with a third bottle, this time some kind of Chardonnay. I much preferred Riesling.

"I'm really sorry, Glory. But I'm glad you didn't give in and have the surgery. A lesser woman would have gone through with it, just to please her selfish husband. Bastards."

"I know. But you don't mess with perfection, Bliss. Now, if the worm suggested you get implants, that would be different. No offence, Bliss, but you could use a little help in that department. Although, maybe if you put on a few pounds, your va-voom factor would increase exponentially. I don't remember you looking so flat before."

What? I cupped my hands over my va-vooms and gave them a jiggle. Those puppies were as firm as apples but, I couldn't deny it, about the same size. It would probably be rude to ask Glory what she did with the gift certificate.

"There's something I must chastise you for, though." Glory waggled a finger in front of my face. "You didn't tell me you are no longer working at the library. I had to hear it from the grapevine."

I looked at the grapevine that had come out of hiding and was hovering nearby. He just shrugged and tucked a string of gelled hair behind his ear.

"Anyway, Bliss, I have a proposition for you."

"Yeth?" My tongue was numb and my lips were thick, or the other way around.

"Since you have so much free time now, I want you to come over three mornings a week to clean — Monday, Wednesday, and Friday."

It was hard to contain my joy. "I already lined up two custer … customers for Friday."

"I'll pay you more."

"No way!"

"Yes way."

She named an hourly rate that was twice what she paid me now.

"Pan isn't much good at cleaning, and I need somebody reliable. That's you. I've entrusted you with my deepest secret, so you can't say no."

"I can't come tomorrow. Dougal says the Titans will blom … blom-som soon, and I have to be ready to run po … mmen back and forth." Okay, you try pronouncing those consonants on a snootful of wine.

"Monday then. Be here."

It was rude to leave unfinished wine behind, but now my toes were numb. Pan helped me through the front gate to the curb.

"You shouldn't drive, Bliss."

"Aren't going to, my little buddy. I will roll my bike along the sidewalk to Dougal's house."

"I hope you realize you just agreed to work for the Fiery One three mornings a week?" He hung the strap of Dougal's camera around my neck.

"I am too dizzy to argue that point at the ... *mo* ... *mom* ... *min*-ute. I will recon*shider* in the morning. And she knows you heard about the fake boobs. So we should never speak again. Of it. Ever."

"Don't worry about me." He mimed sharpening a knife and stabbing his own heart.

I nodded, solemnly as befit the occasion. "Exactly. Now we know the secret, and our souls belong to the Duchess of Devilweed."

CHAPTER
TWENTY-NINE

"WOULD YOU SCAN THIS *pic*-ture for me and file it someplace safe?" I asked Dougal once he detached the camera from my neck and sat down at his computer to download the latest shots of Sif. I planted my legs wide apart to keep from swaying.

He glanced at the photograph in my hand, then leaned across the desk for a closer look.

"This is Mike with a reefer in his mouth. Where did you get it? I thought you burned all his pictures. And who's the hot babe on his lap?"

"Very hilarious. This *pic*-ture is going to get me my fair share of our mooch-ual worldly goods."

"Has he seen it?"

"Yes, and I am happy to retort ... I mean *report*, that the blood drained instantly from his face. Even his ears were tight ... white."

He gave me an up and down gaze, but said merely, "Interesting. Anyway, sure, I'll do it right now while you go look at Thor and see how he compares with Sif."

Thor looked, and smelled, pretty much the same as Sif. I wasn't tempted to linger in the solarium, but got sidetracked by Simon who was sitting on top of his condo glaring at the Titan.

"Help me!" he shrieked when he realized I was leaving him alone with the stinky plant again.

"Well, plop down and come along, then," I said.

Simon fluttered to the tiles and beat me to the door. "I don't know what your problem is," I said to the bird. "Thor is a jungle plant and so are you. A jungle bird, I mean. You should be thick as thieves."

Simon turned his head and stabbed my ankle with his curved beak. He lurched rapidly down the hall, clipped wings flapping impotently and red tail feathers lifted high off the floor.

By the time I reached the study, Simon was perched on the back of Dougal's chair, opening and closing his beak in silent laughter.

"Simon bit me."

"Don't be ridiculous. He was probably rubbing his beak against your skin as a sign of affection. Like this." Dougal and Simon demonstrated a cross-species kiss, beak to lips.

"It's nice outside. Why don't we put Simon out on the patio and see if an owl comes by to visit? Or a coywolf?"

"Here's your photo of Mike and his doobie back. I've filed a copy on several different drives as well as a memory stick."

"Doobie doobie doo," sang Simon, not sounding like Dean Martin. He jumped off the chair back and skittered across the desk toward me.

I backed away. "Thanks, Dougal. Did Mrs. Boudreau bring any food yet?" The thumping headache I woke up with this morning had returned tenfold, and I knew I had to eat something. My Thursday night yoga class was in less than two hours, and I wouldn't get through it unless I sobered up.

"So, is Thor about at the same stage as Sif?"

"Looks the same, smells the same. About that food …"

"We're on our way, then." Dougal's eyes were shining like a kid's on Christmas morning. "Nothing can stop the blossoming now."

"Actually, they both look pretty blom-somy already. How come you can't do the pollination now?"

"They aren't quite ready. I'll know the perfect moment, and that may very well occur tomorrow around midnight, but you better make yourself available all day tomorrow, just in case."

"Sure, I'm there. But Dougal. Food?"

"Mrs. Boudreau didn't come again today. I tried to call her, but had to leave a message. I hope nothing's happened to her, but if it has, you'll have to bring in groceries. You're not a great cook, but you may have to pinch hit for awhile. I've eaten all my convenience food and I'm starving."

"I am not cooking for you. I draw the line in the sandbox." I leaned on the desk to stop the floor from shifting under my feet.

Dougal threw me another onceover, but said nothing more. Soon we were in his kitchen surveying the still-empty fridge. After closing the door on that depressing sight, we moved to the cupboards.

"There's some spaghetti. You can cook that."

"I can't remember how to turn on a stove, so move on." I tried to walk in a steady line, which had me bumping into chairs and appliances.

The walk-in pantry still held the motherlode of cans.

"I have a pooper-scooper idea," I said to Dougal, trying to pronounce my words carefully. He was watching me closely, but I gathered a selection of cans into my arms and called over my shoulder, "Fetch a bowl and some can openers."

Soon, we had a production line going. I sat at the table and drank a bottle of water while Dougal opened cans, poured the contents into bowls, and heated them in the microwave. From all the hissing and popping sounds, that microwave would be a bitch to clean once it dried out.

We dispensed with plates and just used one fork each to spear whatever we fancied out of the dozen bowls arranged in the middle of the table.

"What's this?" I asked, looking at a bright red ball on the end of my fork.

"Beet." Dougal was shovelling up ravioli, and changed to a spoon to capture the sauce.

I ate a beet. It wasn't so bad, so I ate a couple more before deciding to switch to a different colour group.

"What's this?" It was long and green.

"Asparagus. But it's from China, so I wouldn't eat too many."

I spat it out beside my plate.

"Bliss, what the hell are you doing?" Dougal handed me a napkin and I wiped delicately at the corners of my mouth.

"Bliss, are you high again? Or drunk?"

"Drunk. What's this?"

Dougal leaned over to view the white chunks floating in gray liquid.

"How should I know? Try it and tell me what it tastes like."

I snickered. "Yeah, right. Here, taste it yourself." I shoved the purported food across the table and had a go at what was left of the ravioli.

"What's going on, Bliss? Yesterday you show up stoned, today drunk."

"It wasn't my fault. Glory gave me some lovely Riesling, then we switched to Chardonnay. And since I haven't had a bite of food since forever, it went right to my head. Now I'm enjoying this yummy buffet. Pass the stew and your spoon, please."

"Glory? Glory voluntarily served you wine. That's not a very credible story, Bliss."

"It's true. She said she was grateful for my concern about the mari ..." Oops, almost spilled the beans, there. "Let's just say I did her a favour and she was grateful. So we sat on the terrace and enjoyed a couple bottles of wine."

"You're not making any sense, Bliss."

"And she told me why she threw your ass out. How about that?"

"You're both crazy."

"I've been called that a lot lately. Anyway, you showed an uncanny lack of sensitivity, even for you, buying your wife a set of fake boobs for her birthday. Shame, Dougal. Shame!"

His face now resembled the lone beet left in its bowl. I jammed my fork into it and shook it at Dougal. The juice spattered the front of his spanking white tee-shirt, leaving a track of red stains that looked a lot like blood. I shook my fork again and a disappointingly smaller spatter overlaid the first.

Dougal looking speechlessly down at his chest, and I was recovered enough to realize it was time to leave.

Chewing the beet, I said, "I'm throwing myself out this time, to save you the bother. See you in the morning."

I was a little wobbly, but made it to the front door without major incident, although the umbrella stand tipped over as I was trying to step into my boots.

"Your skin is so soft," insisted Simon who had followed me from the kitchen. He jabbed his beak at me again, but I fended him off with the curved handle of an umbrella.

"Fuck off, bird." I slammed the door on him.

I should have brought the umbrella with me. While I was inside enjoying Dougal's hospitality, the fine weather had ended, and the angels had opened the taps.

I was in no shape to operate a motorized vehicle, so, scurrying to my bike, I tore off my leather jacket and replaced it with the top of a bright yellow rain suit I kept stored in the saddlebag. Slinging the canvas bag holding my yoga clothes over my shoulder, I set off for the Golden Goddess Spa.

The ten-minute walk did me good, but I was still unsteady as the class began. I learned that the balancing poses such as the Tree, the Standing Lotus, or any of the Warrior Poses required the blood to run alcohol-free as it was really embarrassing for the instructor to fall over before the students. We spent the hour on our mats performing poses that kept the whole body on the floor.

Throughout the session, I kept my eye on Chesley in the back row. I wanted to make sure he didn't slip away after class. Ivy and Chesley Belcourt were up to something, and I was going to know what that was before the night was over.

CHAPTER
THIRTY

CHESLEY DIDN'T TRY TO escape. He was waiting in the hall as I turned off the studio lights and locked the door. Up close, Chesley in spandex bicycle shorts was not a maiden's dream, and an image of those bad boys, Snake and Redfern, popped into my head. Horrified, I figured I was experiencing alcohol poisoning.

"Do you by any chance cycle, Chesley?"

His grin spread outward from the middle until it reached his ears.

"How did you know that? I belong to a small racing club in St. Catharines."

"Oh, I guess it was the muscle development in your legs." A glance down to his lower limbs confirmed that Chesley had, indeed, well-developed thigh and calf muscles.

If his smile got any wider, he was in danger of swallowing his nose.

I said, "I'm glad you waited. I thought our discussion was just getting interesting this afternoon when your mother showed up."

"I'm afraid Mum and I haven't been totally forthright with you, Bliss."

"You really aren't interested in the Barrister house, are you?"

"We are. But Mum doesn't want me to say anything yet about our plans. We still have funding considerations that need to be weighed. We should have an answer for you tomorrow or Saturday. Anyway, that's not what I meant when I said we hadn't been forthright."

"What? Is there another property you want to see? I'm the agent for the Barrister property only, so if you're interested in looking at something else, you'll have to talk to Elaine Simms."

"I know, but it's not that."

Getting Chesley to the point was proving a time-consuming activity. The coywolf, not to mention a murderer, was at large in the vicinity of Hemp Hollow, and the sooner I was locked inside my trailer with Rae, the better.

"Tell me what's on your mind, Chesley." And snap to it.

"Okay, but don't be angry with me."

"Chesley."

"Here goes, then. You know how you thought I was waiting for you outside Glory's house on Arlington Woods? Well, I was." Chesley uttered the last sentence like it was a hanging offence. His shoulders hunched, making him look like a green-eyed buzzard.

My head throbbed with every beat of my pickled heart. I wanted to feel sorry for him, but if he was stalking me, I'd take him down and smack him silly.

"Would you care to explain your actions?" Then, something occurred to me. "And how do you know Glory? Wait, you were the one who dropped off the Bern bamboo."

"Berg. And yes, I did visit Glory and give her the plant. I wanted to see if her Titan Arum was still alive and healthy. She said that Sif was doing well and was even going to blossom. You can imagine how excited I was."

Chesley's eyes were gleaming with a fanatic's fervour, much as Dougal's did every time he mentioned Thor. I made a let's get this story on the road motion with my hand.

"When I was driving away from Glory's house, I saw you on your motorcycle. I thought your passenger looked like Dougal, although it was hard to tell because of the helmet. Anyway, I waited under those trees for you to come out again. I wanted to see if it really was Dougal, and if so, where he lived. He isn't listed in the phone book, and I didn't want to ask too many questions of the local people. Not until Mum and I have completed our business dealings. Anyway, when you turned around and followed me, I panicked."

I didn't speak.

Chesley said, "I think that's all."

"No, it's not. What have Glory and Dougal got to do with ... anything?"

"Oh, didn't I say? Sorry. I knew Glory and Dougal

at university. We were all enrolled in the same B.Sc. program."

"So, why are you here now?"

"I can't tell you everything, not right now. And we — that's Glory, Dougal, and I — agreed we would never talk about this since what we did was illegal. But I'm pretty sure the statute of limitations has run out, so I can tell you, generally, what happened."

"Chesley, I've had a rough day, so if you don't tell me what you're talking about, I'm going to do some damage to your person."

"Okay, Bliss, but you're sworn to secrecy. Now, only four people will know the whole story. Well, after graduation, the three of us went to Europe for two months. We saw the usual sights, visited some European countries. One night in — I can't tell you the country — we got blasted and stole ... took three Titan Arum tubers from a botanical garden. We brought them back to our hostel and bagged them up. Then we stored them in our backpacks under our dirty laundry and flew home."

"You three crazy kids just strolled through Customs, each with a stolen botanical specimen in your backpack? Did you ever think what might have happened if you had been caught?" Shit, there I went again, acting like a mother.

"Not really. You know, at that age you think you can do anything, get away with murder. Now, of course, you can buy Titan Arum tubers on the Internet. Although the quality is suspect if you buy them that way."

"You're sidetracking me, Chesley. There's no reason you shouldn't visit Glory or Dougal, but why the cloak and dagger stuff?"

"When Mum found out what we did back then, she blamed Dougal, and rightly so. She always thought he was a bad influence on me. After that, we lost touch. But, almost three years ago, Dougal contacted me and said he and Glory were splitting up and asked me to store Thor in one of my greenhouses temporarily. A year later, he said he was moving into his parents' house again and was building a solarium. He wanted Thor back, and I reacted, well, rather badly, I have to say. I was reluctant to part with Thor, and Dougal threatened to kick my ass."

Seems I wasn't the only one who felt that urge in Chesley's company.

"So, you two did not part on good terms," I finished for him, anxious to move this slightly interesting, but ultimately insignificant, story to its climax.

"Exactly. But Mum and I remembered Thor, and Sif of course, when we discussed opening a new mail-order business."

"Chesley, I am running out of patience. And I admit to a world-class hangover. Tell me, what the hell does a new business have to do with two jungle plants?"

"Sorry, Bliss, I'm not telling this coherently. Mum and I have been planning to expand into a specialized market for a few years now. We could have used Jarnsaxa as our flagship plant for the new business, but she didn't make it. She passed about four years ago. Just withered away. We—"

"Wait. Wait just a minute, Chesley. I'm taking a quantum leap here, but is Jackassa your Titan Arum? Raised from the baby tuber you smuggled out of some nameless foreign country twelve years ago?"

"Jarnsaxa. Thor's mistress. Yes, so that's why I wanted to keep Thor. Anyway, now Mum and I are ready to proceed with our venture. But what a coup it would be if our new greenhouse showcased a mature Titan Arum. That's as far as we thought, at first. But, now that we know both Sif and Thor are blossoming, the possibility of a multitude of new tubers is mind-boggling."

You would think that two jungle plant enthusiasts would be enough for one small town, but now we had three. Or four, if you counted Mum.

"This is all mildly interesting, Chesley. I suggest you walk up to Dougal's front door and tell him about your new business. Who knows, he might not kick your ass."

"But this is where you come in, Bliss. Mum and I want you to negotiate a deal with either Dougal or Glory, or both. When I visited Glory, she became furious when I mentioned Dougal's name. The whites of her eyes turned blood red. She scares me, and I would rather you did the negotiating."

"She scares everyone, Chesley, but I can't help you." Glory was possessive about her Titan Arum, and Dougal really loved Thor. No way would either of them part with their plant. I was not going to use Glory's pot growing to blackmail her again, and as for Dougal, he seemed incapable of giving a shit about consequences of any type.

"But, Bliss, you haven't heard our offer yet. If we can get one of the Titan Arums for our new greenhouse—"

"I don't care."

I dashed down the hall to the women's change room. The others had left long ago, so I had the place to myself. I should have showered before getting back into my street clothes, and God knows I needed it, but I was anxious to get indoors with Rae and lock the door. My jeans and tee-shirt were still damp, even though I had spread them out over a bench. Stuffing my yoga duds into the bag, I left the change room to find Chesley waiting for me, still in his spandex.

"Forget it," I said before he could open his mouth. "I don't want any part of your scheme. Grow a pair and ask Glory or Dougal yourself. You're a businessman. If there's something in it for them, they might come around." And good luck with that.

Garnet was working at her computer, half glasses on her face. She gave me a quick smile and handed me a twenty dollar bill. That's the way I liked to do business. Service provided, money exchanges hands, no talk necessary.

Chesley was blocking the exit door. I could easily knock him down the stairs to street level and be on my way. He must have seen the possibility on my face, for he stepped aside, but followed as I took the stairs two at a time.

It was raining harder than ever, and I had to stop in the entrance to don the raincoat. Chesley began yammering in my ear again.

"Bliss, you didn't let me tell you what the offer is. I believe you will find it worthwhile to expend just a little time in convincing your cousin or Glory to either loan their Titan Arum or sell me some of the new tubers."

"We don't know if the pollination will even work yet. Listen, Chesley, if you and your mother are interested in buying the Barrister property, let me know. Otherwise, good luck with your future plans, and bye-bye."

I started toward Dougal's, head down against the driving rain. In the dark, I probably resembled a yellow ghost floating several inches off the ground. And, man, did that almost come true.

CHAPTER
THIRTY-ONE

THE COACH LIGHTS MOUNTED under the eaves of Dougal's garage threw a diffused glow onto the driveway, outlining a dark-coloured vehicle that could have been a Volvo. If it wasn't raining, and if the Rockettes weren't performing high kicks in my brain, I might have walked up and taken a closer look. The vehicle must belong to Dougal's girlfriend who wasn't Melanie, and I was curious about her.

However, satisfaction would have to wait. By the time I took the cover off the bike and pulled the raincoat off in order to put on my leather jacket, I was soaked through again. Even my boots had taken on water. I quickly replaced the raincoat and pulled the helmet over the hood. The helmet fit a little tight, but at least water wouldn't run down the back of my neck.

The rain looked like an all-nighter, so the smartest thing I could do was get home as quickly as possible.

Lockport's stoplight was situated on the highway just past the Petro Canada station. A man in a green poncho who was walking two sodden pit bulls had pressed the walk button, forcing me to stop. He flicked a condescending glance at my bike as he passed, so I revved my motor in response. The unmuzzled dogs turned and growled at me, and I took my toes off the pavement and inched forward in case I had to take off quickly. An SUV pulled out of the Petro Canada and stopped behind me. When the light changed to green, I took off carefully.

I saw in my mirror that the SUV had narrowed the gap between us. Thinking I was driving too slowly, I increased my speed slightly. The vehicle moved up, but I had to slow again to make the turn onto the concession road. I signalled right and turned, careful to avoid the patch of gravel at the intersection.

The SUV turned with me. Alarms began ringing in my brain. The SUV was too close, and, other than the back entrance to Hemp Hollow, there were only a couple of farms farther on that were more easily accessed from the next concession road.

I sped up again as I came up on the rough trail leading to Hemp Hollow. With the rain an impenetrable curtain, my headlight scarcely made a dent in the darkness. The SUV moved up beside me and swerved. I veered sharply, hoping to avoid a collision, and the front wheel of the Savage caught in the sucking mud of the trail. The handlebars quivered under my hands.

As the Savage fell, the SUV roared away. I bounced and rolled, my helmet striking the mud grooves. The final bounce hurled me into the deep runoff ditch.

As I lay on my back, my head vibrated inside the helmet. Water swirled over my body and lapped against my face. But despite my addled state, I realized that I shared the ditch with something … something that smelled very dead. My overactive olfactory sense shuddered in distress and my pounding heart threatened to explode as I recognized the stench: the coywolf.

CHAPTER
THIRTY-TWO

THE REEK OF DECAY surrounded me. I moved my arms and legs. Check. I was almost afraid to turn my neck, but my vertebrae seemed intact.

I sat up and noticed the ditch was filling up fast. If I had landed on my face and been knocked out, I would have drowned. I unbuckled my helmet and pulled it off. With water running over my face, it was impossible to tell if my head had sustained any bloody wounds. Nothing hurt and everything hurt.

Another stinking wave hit me and I froze, knowing the coywolf had to be very close.

I looked at the walls of the embankment and realized how far down I had fallen. The creature was trapped there with me.

I stood up slowly and was grateful to feel my legs plant themselves firmly in the muck and hold. It was silent except for the sound of the rain hitting the rushing water. I let myself hope that the smell was coming from a roadkill casualty, perhaps a long-dead deer.

The walls of the ditch were higher than my head and too slippery to climb. I needed to find the drainage pipe running under the concession road. But which way? Crap, my internal GPS was screwed.

I picked up my helmet, poured out the water, and plunked it on my head. Pulling my feet out of the mud one by one, I turned left and, after three squelching steps, collided with something solid.

Feeling with my hands, I determined that I had found the drain pipe. But it was flush to the opening under the path. Nothing for me to climb. No way out.

A sudden flash of lightning was followed almost immediately by a crash of thunder so loud my ears were ringing inside my helmet. I quickly released the metal pipe.

I stood ankle-deep in water in a ditch too deep to climb out of. The epicentre of a thunderstorm was directly overhead, and a malodorous animal, hopefully dead, was close by. If I believed in the modern translation of the Old Testament, this experience would be payback for wishing vengeance be heaped upon the Weasel — and maybe for using the F-word so often lately.

The lightning flashed again and, in the nanosecond before the illumination faded, I saw a motionless mound parting the stream of water as it rushed toward the drain. It was about ten feet away. I had to have been almost nose to nose with it when I landed in the ditch. One good thing — it looked dead.

Another lightning and thunder duo passed before I remembered my BlackBerry. I reached through the raincoat to the inner pocket of my leather jacket.

Careful not to drop the phone into the swirling rain-water, I hit 911.

The dispatcher tagged me as a prank caller at first. It took a minute before I could convince him that I was stranded in a ditch and was in imminent danger of: a) drowning, b) electrocution, or c) both. He promised to send help.

I thought I heard thunder again. Then I recognized the sound of a motorcycle engine. Help was coming, but until it arrived I was at the mercy of anyone with wicked motives. The chance that a passerby would stop to rob or rape a woman in a ditch was pretty remote, but I felt around in the water for a rock anyway.

The sound of the motor stopped above me. Footsteps slid along the path that had to be a sea of mud. I didn't call out, hoping he would leave.

"Hey! Anyone down there?"

Snake's deep, rasping voice. It was one of those "life sucks but wait and it will get worse" moments.

"Kiddo? You okay?"

I remained silent. The fire department was coming.

I heard the sound of another engine. Thank God.

A car door slammed.

Snake spoke. "Do you have a flashlight, Neil? I think she might be down there, but I can't see anything."

I was shit out of luck tonight.

Redfern called out, "Cornwall, can you hear me?" The beam from a flashlight hit the running stream of water, lingered on the dark shape, and moved on.

Then the light struck my eyes.

"Why didn't you answer me, Cornwall? Are you hurt?"

"Aren't you ever off duty, Redfern?"

"Don't you ever sleep, Cornwall? What happened?"

"Is my bike okay?"

It was Snake who answered. "It's fine, little lady. It's muddy, but listen, the engine turns over."

The sound was music to my ears. I had been so afraid the Savage was totalled. Now I just had to get myself out of this ditch.

"Smell that?" Redfern appeared to be talking to Snake. "I think there's something dead down there."

"No fucking kidding, Sherlock," I said, immediately thinking I should shut it. One, maybe both of them, had a gun. I might as well find an alligator and poke it with a stick.

I could hear Redfern's condescending sigh.

"Stretch your arms out as far as you can, Cornwall. We'll grab your hands and pull you out."

"Not happening. I'm waiting for the paramedics."

"Paramedics? Are you hurt?" He said to Snake, "I'm going down. If she isn't hurt too badly, I'll boost her up and you grab her. Otherwise, I'll call in a rescue team."

I said, loudly, "Call the paramedics, fire department, even the army. I don't care. I'm not coming up until somebody else gets here. So just stay where you are."

In the brief lightning flash that followed, I could make out two heads high above me, one bare, the other helmeted. The thunder blunted Redfern's next words.

"Is this because of what happened yesterday, Cornwall? You still think I was hitting on you? That was the last thing on my mind."

"Thanks so much. How come you responded to my 911 call anyhow? That was quite cavalier of the dispatcher to send you when I might have needed medical attention."

"You told him you weren't injured."

"I need a ladder. Do you have one?"

"Cornwall, I'm soaked and I feel like a lightning rod up here. If you don't let us pull you out, I'm coming down."

My BlackBerry rang. "Just a minute, I have to take this call."

"Hi, Bliss, how's it going? Are you getting the storm they predicted? It's not too bad here, but I hear your area is getting the brunt of it. I hope you're someplace safe and dry."

Blyth always had the worst timing. "Yeah, it's coming down pretty good here at the moment."

"I haven't talked to you for a while, Bliss. I just wanted to make sure you're thinking about my offer."

What offer?

"Oh, right, about coming to stay with you while I work on my masters."

"Geez, that was a loud one, Bliss. You must have the window open. Well, what have you decided?"

"I think that might be something to consider. But I have to let you know later in the summer. Mike might finally cough up some money for me, and I should know one way or the other in a week or so. I really appreciate your offer, Blyth, but I have so many things going on right now, I can't give it much thought. Can I get back to you soon?" Another clap of thunder eradicated her answer.

"What?" I crouched in the ditch, my butt dipped in the rising stream that rushed toward the drain pipe.

"You must be having some storm there, Bliss. But, everything's okay, right?"

"Things are going great."

"I'll let you go then, but call me soon."

"Love you. Bye."

As soon as I closed the cell, it rang again.

"Cornwall, if you answer that, I'm going to rip your phone apart with my fingers. Now, which will it be? You help me pull you up, or I come down there."

I heard scrabbling noises, and gave in.

"Okay, stay there. You can pull me up."

Raising my arms up felt like surrender. Snake held the flashlight and Redfern knelt on the edge of the ditch and reached down. He grasped my hands and with one swift tug I was standing beside my Savage.

"What happened?" asked Snake. "Did your wheels grab mud at the corner?"

"I was run off the road. By an SUV. On purpose." As soon as the words were out, I regretted them. I feared that my ditch experience was linked to the drug situation in Hemp Hollow. Which Snake and Redfern were involved in.

Redfern took my elbow.

"Come on, Cornwall. I'm taking you to the ER to be checked out."

I pulled away. "Uh uh. I'm not hurt. Thanks for the help, but I'm going home."

Sheets of water blew at us, and the lightning and thunder continued. Redfern wore a slicker, but the water ran in rivulets down his face. Snake's helmet kept his head dry but water poured down the back of his neck. Both looked as miserable as I felt.

I hopped on the Savage and turned on the motor. Neither man stopped me.

The path was deep, rutted mud. I found it easier to drive on the field to reach the small clearing behind my trailer, where I covered the Savage. It was saturated already, but if the storm lasted any longer, it might be hard to start in the morning.

If the coywolf was still alive, it would have sense enough to find shelter from the storm, but it was impossible to forget that a killer was still on the loose. Casting a look behind me at the Quigley trailer, I banged on Rae's door. Worried she wasn't home, I kept up the barrage until the door opened.

In the two years I had known Rae, I had never been inside her trailer. After I closed the door behind me, I stood speechless, filled with a sense of awe.

Either I was in a whore's bedroom or Barbie's Dreamhouse.

CHAPTER
THIRTY-THREE

OF COURSE IT *WAS* a whore's bedroom. Rae may look like Malibu Barbie with a domestic problem, but she was still a hooker.

She had ripped out every fixture in the trailer except the miniature sink, fridge, microwave, and furnace. The walls were painted a lighter shade of purple than the outside, and pink, custom-made blinds closed out harsh sunlight and curious eyes. Two purple tufted chairs were pulled up to an equally purple round table. The only other piece of furniture was a king-sized bed pushed against the far wall. The bed was covered in a puffy pink bedspread and strewn liberally with pink and purple cushions. A tiny white table beside the bed was loaded with coloured tubes and small jars. Gels? Best not to think about it. But everything was scrupulously clean.

A polished chrome post, reaching from floor to ceiling, was the focal point of the trailer. I dragged my eyes away and tried not to imagine Rae hanging upside down from the pole wearing nothing but a garter belt and fishnet stockings.

Rae stared at me in horror.

"Bliss. Look at you." She fluttered around me like a fairy trying to comprehend the sudden appearance of a hobbit. "What happened?"

"I got run off the road at the corner. Are you ready to come over and spend the night?"

"You have to get cleaned up, Bliss. You are absolutely filthy."

"Easier said than done, Rae. Maybe I could take off my clothes and stand in the rain."

"Don't be silly. We'll just go to the centre and wash you up."

"The centre will be locked."

She reached into a hanging purple cupboard and pulled out a pink ribbon. Attached was a key.

I didn't even want to ask if she had some sort of arrangement with the manager of Secret Valley. But I changed my mind about minding my own business. If it killed one of us, I was going to get Rae into another line of work.

Rae slipped on a pair of rain boots and grabbed an umbrella from under the bed. We stepped into the storm and, as the lightning flashed, I saw a figure standing under the roof overhang of the Quigley trailer. A cigarette tip glowed. I grabbed Rae's elbow, but she merely gave the figure a friendly wave and kept going.

"Lead on, MacDuck," I hollered as we clambered up the slippery bank. By the time we turned on the lights in the centre, Rae's shorts and halter top were almost as mud-smeared as my clothes.

Rae had her own locker containing toiletries galore. Both of us shampooed and showered. Rae dressed in clean clothes from her locker and offered me a spare thong, but I passed. I donned the oversized yellow raincoat.

While I opened my trailer and turned on the lights, Rae ran next door. By the time I was dressed in an ancient set of gray sweats, Rae was back with a covered dish and a bottle of wine. The sight of the wine made my stomach lurch, but to my surprise I was hungry again.

While Rae bustled around, heating the shepherd's pie and opening the wine, I tried to come up with a diplomatic way of broaching the subject of the dead guy in the woods.

But, hell, it had been a really long day.

"So, Rae, I believe you know the man we found in the bush this morning."

She paused with a large serving spoon in her hand. Avoiding my gaze, she said, "What makes you say that? We couldn't see his face."

"I don't think he had a face anymore. And you heard the cops identify him as Fitzgerald Corwin."

"Oh?"

"Fitzgerald. Your abusive client. The one who beat the hell out of you. Wasn't his name Jerry?"

"Well, it could have been him, I guess."

"Snake dragged him away. Now he's dead. Death by hatchet, according to the police."

"Bliss, you don't think that I ..."

"Of course not. I'm thinking Snake."

I was trying to watch Rae's face while digging into the casserole. She looked troubled, but not frightened. Me? I was just the opposite, scared as hell but not giving a shit who did it as long as he was caught, and soon. And I didn't tell her about Redfern's involvement with Snake. Sometimes the less you know, the safer you are, and I hoped this was one of those times, for Rae's sake. She seemed too friendly with the Quigleys as it was.

"Bliss, you may find this hard to believe, but Snake is really a kind person. He looks rough and talks like a tough biker, but he's been looking out for me."

"Is he one of your clients?"

"No. Only because he's never asked."

"Maybe he's gay."

"Bliss, stop it. You're suspicious of everyone."

"It's been that kind of day. Anyway, now that we know that Jerry is the dead man, what should we do about it?"

Rae sat opposite me and poured herself more white wine.

"Honestly? I don't know what we should do. If I tell the police I knew him, they'll find out pretty fast he was a client. Then, there goes my business."

"You were going to quit anyway."

"I know, but my plan calls for me to work another couple of years."

"You might not have any choice, Rae." An idea was germinating in my brain, but now wasn't the time to pursue it.

"I just don't know what to do," Rae repeated. "The Quigleys have been good to me, but there's something funny going on over there."

"You've spent a lot of time in their trailer. Have you seen anything suspicious?"

"Like what?"

I helped myself to another portion of the shepherd's pie, but left the wine alone. One hangover per day was plenty.

"Well, why is there so much traffic at the Quigley trailer? Boy, this food is really good, Rae. I don't know how you cooked this with only a microwave."

"I don't cook. I nuke a lot of frozen foods, but Sarah made this dish. Isn't it great?"

My first impulse was to spit out my mouthful of food, and my second was to punch Rae in the face. I controlled both impulses, swallowing and keeping my hands in my lap.

"Uh, Rae, did Sarah use her special ingredient in this dish?" I already knew the answer. Now I was a pro, and recognized the boneless, floaty sensation that was moving up my body from my legs. I still wanted to strangle her, though, so it hadn't quite hit my brain yet.

Rae looked guilty.

"Oh, I guess I should have told you, Bliss. I'm sorry."

"I just ate two bowls of this."

"Sorry."

"Let's get this on the table, Rae. Sarah Quigley is the Baker, right?"

She nodded unhappily, but didn't speak.

"So, did it ever occur to you that Sarah's cooking is the reason so many people come by their place for a short visit?"

"No. No. Wait, Bliss, calm down. You're right. People

bring their own weed for Sarah to mix in with the food. But that's not all of it. You don't think all those bikers eat shepherd's pie or coconut cookies, do you?"

"No, they probably eat pretty little hookers and innocent short women." I was bellowing at her. I didn't feel the same as yesterday after Fern Brickle's chocolate squares, not nearly as relaxed. And my skin crawled. "Why do you think Snake hangs around here? He's the Quigleys' enforcer."

"Enforcer for what?" Rae asked.

"Well, I don't know! For whatever it is they do over there. Maybe a meth lab, a nice companion business for the pot baking."

"There's no meth lab, Bliss. There was one in my old neighbourhood until the cops shut it down. It smelled horrible, and the equipment takes up more space than one of these trailers has."

"You've just fed me marijuana, you empty-headed dolt."

"I said I was sorry."

I needed some fresh air. I didn't care if a pack of coy-wolves or ten murderers were waiting outside the door. I could run through the rain and the wind and laugh at the lightning bolts as they tried to strike me.

I jumped up from the table and threw myself head-long at the door. Rae dragged me back.

"Bliss, you can't go outside. The storm's worse. It sounds like a hurricane."

I shoved her away from the door just as a powerful hammering sounded from the other side.

CHAPTER THIRTY-FOUR

I SLAMMED MY BODY to one side of the door and flipped off the light.

"It's the murderer. Get a knife." I wasn't getting enough air in my lungs.

Rae peered between a slit in the threadbare curtains.

"It's Chief Redfern."

"Get away from that door, you fucking idiot. He's one of them."

"Ms. Cornwall. Open the door. Now." Redfern rattled the knob.

Rae pushed me away from the door and turned the light back on. I tackled her, but too late.

The door flew open and I landed against Redfern. My weight forced him back a half-step, but he braced himself against the frame and caught me under the arms.

I wrenched away and dove for the junk drawer. There was a paring knife somewhere in the mess.

I never made it. Redfern wrapped his arms around

me from behind, pinning me helplessly against him. I kicked and squirmed, but he held me tighter.

He asked Rae, "What's happened to her?"

"It's the food." Rae sounded frightened, but I was still going to punch out the bitch's teeth. She had no right to let the enemy in.

"Does she know what she ate?"

It was time to get involved. "She does now! It's everywhere I look and in everything I eat. Instead of solving the problem, you're part of it. You should rot in jail with the rest of the crooks, Redfern."

"This must have something to do with the road to perdition I'm on, Cornwall. But right now you need to listen to me."

In answer, I gave a mighty heave and managed to break free from his grip. But an instant later his arms wrapped like steel cables around my body again.

"Is there anything else in that food besides marijuana?"

"No." Rae's voice was shaky, the stupid bitch.

"Okay, listen, Bliss." Redfern sat down on the bench seat and pulled me onto his lap. He held my wrists in his hands and crossed our arms over my chest. "You're having a bad reaction to the weed you ate. I know it's hard, but try and relax and it will pass sooner."

"I ate it yesterday, but I liked it then. This is awful." My entire body was shaking and I could feel a pulse beat under my chin, ready to burst through the skin.

"The effects can vary. You were just in an accident and your body still contains stress hormones. If I were you, I'd stay away from weed from now on."

"Oh, like I run around buying it on the street. I had a bit of wine this afternoon."

"That wouldn't help."

"That wasn't my fault, either. God! If Glory had just given me food instead of three bottles of white wine, I might have been able to ride my bike home sooner and missed that crazy driver who ran me off the road."

"Let's talk about that. Tell me about the vehicle. When did you first notice it?"

"After I pulled away from the traffic light. It must have come out of the Petro station."

"Colour, make?"

"SUV. Light, maybe white or cream. Or even light blue or green. It was raining so hard I couldn't see and, before you ask, I didn't get the licence plate number."

"Not any part of it? Close your eyes and think about that. You looked in your rear-view mirror and …"

I closed my eyes. I was shaking all over and still wanted to run away into the night and never stop.

"It was maybe a Tribute or even a Tucson. There was an A and an H on the licence plate. And a 7, I think. But that's all I remember."

"That's good, Bliss." To Rae, he said, "Please get her some water."

Rae found my one bottle of water in the fridge and opened it.

Redfern said to me, "You won't try and get away if I let go of one of your wrists, will you?"

"I would not consider it," I said carefully. When he released me, I grabbed the bottle, upended it, and drained it in three or four gulps. "Shit. Now I'll have to pee and it's still raining outside. Rae, can I borrow your key to the rec hall for later?"

Redfern said, "Rae, can you get the key and some more water?" She scurried out the door without a word.

Redfern said, "Tell me what you know about Fitzgerald Corwin."

"Bet you didn't know that Rae sleeps with men, though. For money." Well, fuck, I probably shouldn't have mentioned that.

"I know. And, you might tell her that I won't be able to look the other way much longer. She needs to get out of the game before she's charged."

"The whores have always been amongst us," I intoned. "Seriously, can you imagine having sex with, like, two strange men a day? Isn't that gross?"

"Hard to believe, isn't it?"

"I've tried to talk her into another occupation, but she says she needs more money to open her spa. Sometimes, I think that's just a pipe dream to justify what she's doing, as if the end justifies the means."

"Are you still talking about Rae? Or yourself?"

"I'm not breaking the law to achieve my goal. And I know when to change tactics."

"How so?"

"I was trying to save enough money to hire a lawyer so the Weasel would have to fork over a fair portion of our assets. You know he totally screwed me over?"

"I heard the rumours."

"I realized that it would take me years to save enough money, so when a fortuitous turn of events occurred, I seized the moment."

"Really?"

I found myself telling Redfern about the article in the paper prematurely announcing the Weasel's impending run for office and his donation of fifty acres of wetland to the province to save the spotted turtle habitat.

"The thing is," I said, "I own that land. It was my divorce settlement ... and worthless. It's a swamp, and nobody will ever buy it for development. I realized the other day that if I don't pay the back taxes by tomorrow, the property will go to public auction. I think that's what the Weasel is counting on. He'll swoop in and buy it, then give it to the province."

"You must be feeling better," he said. "You're starting to make sense."

I realized I was still sitting on his knee. I slid over to the bench, but he pulled me back.

"Did you say you have to pay the outstanding taxes by tomorrow?"

"I tried this afternoon, but their debit machine was down, and the clerk said they didn't take cheques, or cash. I'm pretty sure she's the missing evolutionary link."

"So you plan to try again tomorrow?"

"I have no choice. If I don't pay by the end of business tomorrow, I lose the property and the Weasel wins. I stopped at his mayor chambers today and told him I was onto his game. I told him he could have the swamp in exchange for a fair settlement. I only wish I could remember what it was. I sort of pulled the figure out of my ass."

"Quite the picture."

I didn't mention my piece of insurance. Loose lips sink ships, as some famous person once said. Or maybe it was Pan. The photo of Mike and his reefer would remain a secret, unless I had to send it to all the major newspapers, or learn how to upload it to the Net. That would depend on Mike's decision.

"Where's Rae?" I asked.

"I'll go look for her if you'll be okay by yourself for a bit."

I was uncomfortably aware that my thighs were growing warmer against Redfern's. It wasn't like he was glad to see me, as the saying goes, but it was time to get off the man's damn lap.

Redfern lifted me onto the bench beside him as Rae came back in, her arms juggling bottles of water. She was soaked through again, her streaked blond hair lying in wet wisps against her cheeks. It occurred to me I hadn't told Redfern about Jerry, a.k.a. Fitzgerald.

"Sorry," she said breathlessly, "I thought maybe you wanted to talk to Bliss alone."

Redfern stood up. His short hair had begun to dry and was standing up in spikes again. I wondered if they would be soft or hard to the touch. Probably soft.

"Actually, I came over to tell you both that you can stop worrying about the coywolf. The carcass in the ditch is the coywolf. In the morning, I'll call the Ministry of Natural Resources again. They'll want to take it for testing. There is still a killer at large, so I want you two to stick together as much as possible. Understand?"

He pulled a baggie out of an inner pocket and spooned some of the shepherd's pie into it. "Miss Zaborski, can you confirm who prepared this food?"

Rae's eyes surveyed the room, as if seeking help from an unseen source. Redfern waited, and at last she said in a small voice, "Sarah Quigley made it."

"Thank you, Miss Zaborski."

"I wish you weren't bent," I said as Redfern put his hand on the doorknob. He turned back to look at me, then his eyes swung to Rae. She shrugged.

"You know, like the British."

Redfern ignored me and said to Rae, "I thought she was lucid. If she gets panicky again, call me at this number." He handed Rae a card and stepped into the driving storm.

Even a murderer wouldn't be out on such a night, so Rae and I took turns holding the flashlight while the other made use of the small clearing inside the juniper bushes.

Rae was clearly worried over her admission to Redfern, and fretted about what the morning would bring.

"You didn't have any choice," I told her. "He already knows what Sarah is up to. He just needed confirmation. If you hadn't told him the truth, he'd have arrested you instead."

"Do you think he'll arrest her tomorrow?"

"I have no idea." Redfern probably found himself in quite a dilemma. Or not. I wasn't sure anymore what was going on. Even the Sopranos showed a human side occasionally.

"But," I cautioned Rae, "if I were you, I'd avoid the Quigleys' trailer for a while and let this play out. You warned Snake, didn't you?"

"I tried to, but he wasn't there, so I asked Ewan to give Snake a message."

"You told Ewan the cops know Sarah is the Baker?"

"Yes. He said he would give Snake the message."

I was way too tired to smack her around, or even yell. Let Redfern figure it out.

I merely said, "Well, I'm staying away from Hemp Hollow tomorrow. And I suggest you do the same."

With that, I pulled the thin blanket over my shoulder and Rae turned her face to the wall. We went to sleep with my baseball bat between us.

CHAPTER
THIRTY-FIVE

EVERY MUSCLE, BONE, TENDON, and eyelash
screamed in agony when I tried to get out of bed.

Rae crawled over my pain-wracked body and stood
over me, looking concerned.

"I have some important errands to run today," I said.
"Take my hand and pull."

"I'm two-thirds through my registered massage
therapist course. I can try and work out some of the
knots in your muscles."

"Do what you have to. Right now, I can't function,
and I need to get mobile."

Rae kneaded my head, neck, arms, legs, and even
feet. She pointed out my back was bruised from shoulders to tailbone. I refused to let her look lower than my
tailbone, so who knows what my posterior looked like.
It felt like freshly minced hamburger.

"Bliss, can you sit up now?"

I could, barely.

My cell rang as I was carefully tying my runners. My boots were history.

"There you are, Bliss."

"No place I'd rather be, Dougal."

"What? Never mind. Don't bother going over to Glory's or coming here this morning or evening. The female flowers reached maturity last night and now we have to wait for the male flowers to produce pollen. And that should occur around midnight. I don't know the exact time, so you have to be on standby."

"Sure."

"I'm serious, Bliss. I talked to Glory last night and, this is really strange, both Sif and Thor are, near as we can tell, blossoming simultaneously. We're both filming with a time-lapse recorder and are thinking about collaborating on a documentary. This will astound the botanical world."

"Do you think it will astound the botanical garden where you stole the pods from?"

"Tubers. That botanical garden closed its doors years ago. Anyway, we aren't going to divulge the origin of the plants. You can actually buy seeds on the Internet these days, so who's to know?"

"I've heard that."

"So keep your phone on. We expect to move quickly, sometime around midnight, but it could be sooner. Or later. So stay close."

"I got it, already. I'm practically on your doorstep."

"Stay away from my doorstep until I call you."

As I closed the BlackBerry, I caught sight of Rae rooting through my cupboards, probably looking for food.

"Rae, Redfern knows about you. He says you need to quit the business unless you want to be charged. You could spend all your savings on legal fees, have you considered that?"

She gave up on finding a crumb or a teabag and sank onto the bench.

"I guess I can start up in another town. I want to avoid big cities — they have pimps and organized crime."

"Or you can go legit. You might not make as much money, and it will take slightly longer to open your spa, but at least you won't get charged with prostitution."

"Bliss, you know better than anyone how hard it is to even get by with minimum wage jobs. How much money have you saved the last few years?"

"About enough to pay my property taxes. I know of one perfectly respectable line of work where you can make more than minimum wage without training. Maybe not as much as sleeping with creepy, strange men, but at least you wouldn't be sleeping with creepy, strange men."

"Really? I want to complete my massage therapist course, so I can't work a nine-to-five job."

"Then what I have in mind will be perfect for you. But for now we both have to get out of Hemp Hollow for a day or two. Do you have enough money to stay at the Super 8 Motel for a few nights?"

She nodded. "But, Bliss, you haven't told me what the job is. And if it pays so well, why aren't you doing it?"

"I am, but not charging near enough. Let me work it through in my mind before I tell you more. Get your clothes packed and follow me to the motel."

It took Rae an hour to gather enough supplies for a couple of nights away. I helped her carry two suitcases, a duffle bag, three cosmetic cases, and a large canvas book bag through the woods to her car. I almost crossed my fingers in an anti-hex sign when Rae offered a prescription painkiller. In the past few days, my body had been subjected to enough chemicals, both legal and illegal, to begin a search for a liver donor.

The dirt compound had turned into a brownish pond, and the water lapped at the bottom step of all three trailers. Rae put on her cute rain boots and I rolled up my jeans and slipped my feet into flip-flops. Every time I lifted a foot, the flip-flop remained in the mud, so, in the end, I waded barefoot to the edge of the clearing where we only had to deal with fallen branches and a couple of large limbs that had barely missed the roof of my trailer. Nature really sucks sometimes, or have I mentioned that before?

Entire sections of the path were washed away and the rest rendered impassable by pools of mud. With me leading the way on the bike, and Rae following in her Echo, we bumped over the field to the concession road. Two Ministry of Natural Resources trucks were parked nearby, and four men with coils of rope hanging over their shoulders stood looking down into the ditch. They didn't look at us as we passed, no doubt busy trying to decide who wasn't going down to retrieve the dead coywolf.

The only available room at the Super 8 was next to the Belcourts' units. After unloading Rae's luggage, we had coffee and a muffin in the motel's small restaurant.

I sat with my back to the door in case Chesley or Ivy came in.

Rae offered to pay for our breakfast, and I let her. After I settled up my taxes, I would be back to where I was two years ago. I had to shake the Weasel loose from my money in the next few days, or me and my Savage would be sleeping on that park bench. On second thought, gas for the motorcycle would be out of reach and I would have to sell it.

"What's wrong, Bliss? You look almost as bad as last night. Are you sure you don't want a painkiller?"

"I have to get going. I need to stop in at the municipal offices and pay my taxes. You stay here and have another coffee, but remember, don't leave."

"I won't. Bliss, do you want to stay here with me until we can move back home? I really don't want to be alone."

Yes! I figured I would have to either wander the streets all night or slip back into my trailer, hoping the Quigleys and Snake wouldn't notice me.

"I'm doing some work for Dougal later, and it might be late when I'm through, but I'll call you if I can make it. In the meantime, park your car around back where it can't be seen from the highway. No point advertising your whereabouts."

CHAPTER
THIRTY-SIX

I RAN INTO CHESLEY at the door. He held a plastic tray heaped with two Styrofoam containers and two paper cups of coffee. A bag hanging from a fingertip dropped at my feet.

"Let me get the door for you, Chesley." I picked up the bag, opened the door, and gave him a shove in the back to propel him outside before he noticed Rae. Until the Barrister house deal was officially dead, I didn't want either of the Belcourts getting friendly with Rae and learning about my personal circumstances — or her business.

"I didn't expect to see you here, Bliss. But, I was going to call you anyway. Mum and I want to talk to you."

"Maybe I can stop by later, Chesley. I have some business in town right now."

"This is important. Here, we'll go into Mum's room."

He stopped in front of door number six and gave it a soft kick with his foot. I glanced at my watch and saw it was barely ten o'clock, still plenty of time to get to the municipal offices before noon. Once there, I planned to throw the mother of all scenes if Alyce still didn't accept cash or cheque.

"Okay, Chesley, let's do it."

Ivy opened the door, every grey curl in place and lips carefully filled in with cardinal red colour. A long satin garment, black, covered her ample figure.

"You found her. Good. Come in, Miss Cornwall."

Two beds covered in plaid spreads, a round table, and two orange armchairs almost filled the room. Usual motel decor.

Ivy seemed to be reading my mind. She said, "Miss Cornwall, this is not the sort of place I'm used to. I want to complete my business here in Lockport and go home where my hot tub and a bottle of Shiraz are waiting. Sit down, Miss Cornwall, and let's get to it."

I sat in one of the orange chairs and waited while Chesley deposited the tray on the table and took the covers off their breakfast containers. There were scrambled eggs, crisp bacon, and whole wheat toast with little packets of jam on the side. My stomach threatened to rumble.

"I'm sure you've already had your breakfast, Miss Cornwall, so you won't mind if we eat and talk?"

"Not at all. I couldn't eat another bite."

Chesley kept his huge eyes on my face as he ate his breakfast. I wasn't sure if he was trying to warn me not to mention anything we had discussed yesterday, or he just thought I was pretty. I figured the former.

"Chesley and I are considering opening a new greenhouse here, Miss Cornwall."

"Why?"

"What? Why?" Ivy asked.

"I mean, what's here in Lockport? It's just a small town like hundreds of other towns in southwestern Ontario. It's several hours from any major population base like Toronto or Hamilton. Why would you want to open a business that depends on a large customer base?" Guess I shouldn't apply for a job with the Lockport Chamber of Commerce.

"Valid point, Miss Cornwall. I can see we've chosen well. Let me put my cards on the table."

Both Ivy and Chesley had finished their food and were now sipping coffee. I glanced under the table at my watch and, by a hair's breadth, restrained myself from sighing.

"I'm not sure if you are aware of this, Miss Cornwall, but Chesley and your cousin, Dougal Seabrook, were roommates at university. They, along with a young lady who subsequently became Mrs. Seabrook, acquired some Titan Arum tubers overseas and brought them home. Chesley's tuber languished for a few years, then perished. I understand the other two plants are now blossoming and will be pollinated by your cousin and his ex-wife. Are these facts correct as you know them, Miss Cornwall?"

"I admire your grasp of the situation, Mrs. Belcourt."

"And I admire your work ethic and your loyalty to your cousin. We can certainly use you in our organization. But, to answer your question as to why we have fixed on Lockport for our new venture, the facts are based on fiscal acumen and geographical requirements."

"What do the Titan Arums have to do with anything?"

I avoided looking at Chesley, who had spilled his guts on that subject yesterday. I wanted to hear from Ivy, who obviously ran the show.

"I'll come to that. Chesley and I own two large greenhouse operations, one in St. Catharines and one in Niagara Falls. We have been dabbling in exotics for a few years now and are at the point where we need to expand one of our facilities to accommodate them, or build a new one dedicated to exotics only. Chesley, in particular, has an interest in domestic endangered flora."

"You mean, like swamp plants?" I was beginning to get the picture.

"The Barrister property is extensive enough to accommodate several large greenhouses. And the house itself can be renovated into office and living spaces. It might be possible to rent out space to another business or two to generate extra revenue. Land is cheaper here and the property taxes are substantially lower."

"What about the domestic endangered flora?"

"The Barrister property is adjacent to a piece of wetland with a river running through to Lake Huron and plenty of tree cover. Perfect to propagate plants that would be made available to universities and individuals interested in preservation of endangered species."

"My swamp."

"Exactly, Miss Cornwall."

"You want to buy it?"

"I want to buy your land and the Barrister property. Before we looked at the Barrister house, Elaine Simms told us you owned the land across the road."

"And the Titan Arums? Where do they come in?"

"It's very simple, Miss Cornwall. I'm only interested in the house and wetland if you can guarantee at least one of the Titan Arums is part of the deal."

"Glory and Dougal don't need money, so I doubt they'll sell their plants. Are you willing to settle for an alternative arrangement, Mrs. Belcourt?"

"Like what, Miss Cornwall? Chesley and I have our hearts set on having at least one mature Titan Arum as a draw for the new greenhouse."

"You mean, if you can't acquire one of the Titans, you will pass up Lockport as your new location?" I wanted the bottom line.

"Come now, Miss Cornwall. I believe you are a clever woman. I am coming up to retirement age and eventually want to leave Chesley in charge of the entire Belcourt Corporation. My personal plan is to build a summer home in Lockport near the lake and spend winters in Florida or Costa Rica.

"Sounds like a nice plan."

"Although I won't be spending my winters here, Chesley will. We plan to run a year-round operation. We have excellent managers for our businesses in St. Catharines and Niagara Falls and will concentrate our efforts on Lockport for the next year or two. We plan to lead the world in mail-order exotics. And we expect the endangered flora side of the enterprise will create international interest."

"Well, Mrs. Belcourt, you've taken me by surprise. It would be an exercise in futility to try and buy Sif and Thor outright, but perhaps you would consider something a little different?"

"You mentioned that earlier, Miss Cornwall. What do you have in mind?"

"I haven't had time to think this through, so I'd prefer not to speculate just yet. I'm assuming Chesley has already approached Glory and Dougal?"

Chesley found his voice. "I asked Glory the other night when I dropped off the Berg bamboo. She refused to sell, and wouldn't even let me see Sif. I was reluctant to approach Dougal since we parted on bad terms a few years ago, but I did go over to his house last night after yoga class. I never got farther than the front steps. He didn't invite me in, and I never got a chance to ask if he would consider selling Thor."

"We're going back. This afternoon."

Chesley opened his mouth, but Ivy quelled him with one look, and he sank back into his chair. I could learn a lot from this woman.

I told him, "I'll meet you in front of Dougal's house at six o'clock. Don't go in without me. Together, we will come up with a solution to benefit everyone." I had no idea how to accomplish that, but something was bound to occur to me.

Somehow, I had to avoid passing title of the swamp to the Weasel until the Belcourts made up their minds to buy property for their new venture. I just wasn't sure they wouldn't run for the county line if they got their hands on a Titan Arum, and build their new greenhouse elsewhere. Things were getting so complicated that one false step now and I could end up with nothing. Not so different from present circumstances, but I was so close to solvency that I couldn't bear to start all over again.

Sitting in Ivy's motel room, I had stiffened up considerably, and the sweat beaded on my forehead as I swung my leg over the bike. Neither Belcourt came out to see me off, and I was glad they didn't witness my discomfort.

Getting off the bike in front of the municipal building hurt even more, and as I shuffled across the sidewalk towards the steps, a voice called out, "You're hobbling like a bride the morning after her wedding night."

"Nice, Thea," I answered and put one foot on the first step. When the pain died down, I dragged the other foot up beside the first.

"Sorry, Moonbeam. I heard you were in an accident last night."

"Yes," was all I could manage as I reached for the doorknob. Thea followed me into the building. I expected her to disappear into the police offices, but she remained near as I tried to manoeuvre the first step to the second floor.

"Oh, for God's sake." She wrapped her arms around me, pinning my arms to my side, and carried me up the flight of stairs.

"There." She set me down and reached up to straighten her bun. She wasn't even puffing.

"Well, thanks, Thea. That was helpful."

At the battered wooden counter, I waved to Alyce, who was again holding the fort down single-handedly. She approached at a snail's pace and even more slowly blinked her black-rimmed eyes.

"Oh. Mrs. Bains, isn't it? You're back."

"Ms. Cornwall. Good to see you, Alyce. I'm here to pay my taxes. Here's the notice and here's my debit card. Let's get keying and swiping and whatever else needs doing."

"Um, could you excuse me for a minute, Mrs. Cornwall? I have to make a quick call."

"No you don't, Alyce. That's your debit machine, isn't it? And that's your computer. Type in this tax number you see here. All my information will come up on the screen and we'll go from there. What are you waiting for?"

The blue eyes filled with tears. "I really have to make a call. Then I'll be right back."

"Alyce. Type. I'll even read the numbers for you, but you are not using the phone until we complete this transaction. Got it?"

"Take it easy there, Moonbeam. Maybe this young lady's supervisor can help."

I turned my neck slowly to find Thea had been standing at the doorway throughout my exchange with Alyce. I turned back to the girl.

"What about it, Alyce? Where's your supervisor?"

She burst into tears just as a small octogenarian with a bulbous nose came through the door behind us, clutching a sheet of paper.

"I've come to pay my house tax," he announced. "Get out of the way, there, Missy. Oh, hello, Officer Thea. What a pleasure to see you, my dear."

"Good morning, Mr. Thiesson," replied Thea. "If you'll just wait a minute, I'm sure this young lady will pull herself together."

"She's a nitwit," the old gent whispered loudly. "But, she's related to the mayor's wife, so they gave her a job here. Flunked out of college. You have to speak slowly to her."

Both Thea and I turned toward Alyce, who looked like a racoon in the headlights of a transport truck.

"I think you should get your supervisor. Now." Thea's tone was quiet, but Alyce ran sobbing from the room.

"Can't I pay my tax?" asked Mr. Thiesson. "This is the last day. I always wait until the last day just so they think I forgot."

"You'll pay your taxes, Mr. Thiesson, don't you worry. And so will you, Moonbeam."

Alyce, still crying, came back in the wake of a large woman in red jeans and a black, rhinestone-studded tank top.

"I'm the office manager, Delia Melancourt. Why is this child so upset?"

I said, "Alyce doesn't seem to know how to use the debit machine or access the property tax program on the computer, Ms. Melancourt. Perhaps she needs more training, but in the meantime, both this gentleman and I are anxious to take care of our business and be on our way, so I assume you can help us?" I double-dog-dared Ms. Melancourt to put more obstacles in our way. Thea was formidable, but my money was on Mr. Thiesson.

With a quizzical look at Alyce, the office manager took Mr. Thiesson's debit card and processed him out the door in under three minutes. Then she did the same for me. I had the PAID stamp on my form and the debit card receipt to prove I was still the legal owner of fifty acres of the finest swampland in Bruce County. I tucked these treasures into the inner pocket of my jacket, next to the precious photo.

"Thanks for your help, Thea. I didn't realize Alyce was related to Andrea Bains, but now I understand why she gave me the runaround yesterday."

"The Chief suspected as much after you told him what happened. Are you going to sit back and wait for your ex to make an offer?"

"Wait a minute. Did Redfern send you here to make sure I didn't run into a repeat of yesterday?"

"Can we keep that to ourselves? I wasn't supposed to let on. He told me to wait around for you and follow you up to the tax office. Apparently, you spilled your guts last night, not his words by the way, and he seems to feel some responsibility for you." Thea looked me over with new interest. "Do you two have something going?"

I almost choked on my own tongue. "Hardly. I thought maybe you and he ... you know?"

She looked horrified. "I already told you Dwayne and I are an item."

"Who's Dwayne? You never mentioned Dwayne."

"Dwayne Rundell. Don't you know him? He's on the job too. We're keeping it quiet, for now, or the other guys will make our lives a living hell."

"Mum's the word. And you're not carrying me down the stairs like a sack of carrots. So, thanks again. I'll make it down on my own."

"Okay then, if you're sure. Call me if you need anything."

I went back into the municipal office and stood at the counter until Alyce looked up at me, the inevitable tears pooling in her eyes. Ms. Melancourt had disappeared again.

"I want to look at the lists of board members, Alyce. Can you pull that up for me on your computer?"

Without protest, Alyce made a few efficient tapping motions, then turned the monitor to face me. She walked over to a desk in a far corner of the room and picked up the phone. I shrugged and reached for the mouse.

I advanced through the various screens until I came to the Cemetery Board. Three members of the Friends of the Settlers were also on the Cemetery Board: Joy MacPherson, Elise Boudreau, and Fern Brickle. They would ensure the Friends had a free hand in the management of the Settlers' Plot, including access and distribution of keys. I understood then how short-sighted it was to underestimate a gang of senior citizens.

Nodding to Alyce, I shambled out to the hall. I put my hand on the newel post and prepared to take the first step.

"Bliss!"

The Weasel was steaming down the hall from his office, brows hooding his eyes like his Neanderthal pre-human ancestors, lips drawn back over unnaturally white teeth.

I stepped away from the top of the stairs.

CHAPTER
THIRTY-SEVEN

"WHAT THE FUCK ARE you doing here again today?"
The Weasel's hands were curled into fists, clenching and unclenching.

His dark eyes held a burning fury instead of the usual calculating coldness. Had he known my jacket still held his future secreted in the inner pocket, I believe he would have ripped it from me and shoved me down the stairs to my death. He may or may not be sorry afterward.

I inched away until my back was against the wall.

"I take it you've paid the taxes on the fifty-acre property."

"Guess you got the call from wee Alyce in there. Nice work, Mike, planting a mole in the tax office."

"Don't be ridiculous. Alyce has worked here for two years."

"Really? Convenient. Well, I hope you have another wetland lined up to donate to the Province of Ontario.

If it's any consolation, the spotted turtles will be safe with me." Whether they'd be safe with the Belcourts was a separate issue.

"We can't discuss these matters in the hall. Come back to my office."

"The 'S' stamped on my forehead stands for short, not stupid, Mike. We can talk right here."

"Maybe I no longer want the fucking property. I can come up with some reason not to donate the land, and nobody is going to listen to your lame fucking story."

"Sure. Whatever you say. I have another offer on the property anyway. Let's discuss the photo then. I hope you realize, Mike, that I'm not threatening or black-mailing you. I'm offering to return to you a precious memento of our past. I look incredibly hot in that photo, don't you think? I suppose I could have it scanned first so we'll both have a copy."

"What do you mean you have another fucking offer on the property? From whom?"

"Can't make that public just yet. We're still in nego-tiations. You know how it is. Now, the other matter ..." I can't say I was exactly enjoying myself, and I wasn't dumb enough to think Mike couldn't lose it completely and attack me. But, for the first time in two years — even longer, since I had held no power in our marriage — I felt strong. Looking up into my ex-husband's enraged face, I felt no fear. Even the F-word seemed to have fled my vocabulary for his.

A vein throbbed in the middle of his forehead, and I hoped he wouldn't stroke out before we completed our negotiations.

"What do you want, Bliss?" His mouth formed into a tight bud, rather like the asshole of a weasel.

Capitulation? Not yet. I envisioned Mike's razor-sharp mind running through options. I had to tread carefully. All I had to bargain with was an old photo of my ex-husband with a reefer in his mouth. If the photo went public — Facebook sprang to mind — my face would be out there too. Did I mind? Uh-uh. Would Mike? We'd see.

From Mike's excessive use of the F-word, I was fairly certain he wasn't taping our conversation. Still, I quickly reached out and patted his chest, pulling down the neck of his polo shirt to check inside.

"What the hell!" He shoved my hands aside like a Victorian maiden while I scanned the walls and ceiling for surveillance cameras. Paranoid? Maybe. But now was no time to get careless.

"Remember that figure I wrote on the piece of paper for you last Sunday? Well, add twenty thousand and we'll call it a deal." Geez, I hoped that was enough.

"And just what do I get for this fucking deal?"

"The satisfaction of knowing you've done the right thing, Mike."

"So I'm supposed to just hand over five hundred and twenty thousand dollars to you?"

Whoa. Did I actually write a half a million dollars on that piece of paper? Serious money.

"You're right, Mike, that's just silly. Make it an even five hundred thousand and we'll forget the twenty. That was a joke, but you aren't laughing, so forget I even mentioned it."

"You won't get away with this, Bliss."

"Blah blah blah, Mike. I've heard it all before, from you and from your wife. Here's a card with my cell number in case you change your mind. Bye now."

To my relief, he stalked back into his office without hurling me down the stairs. He took my card, though.

I remembered the twenty dollar bill that Garnet Maybe had given me the previous night after my yoga class. Lunch was on me. Until I checked my bank balance on Dougal's computer, I didn't want to make any withdrawals. Paying my taxes must have all but wiped me out, and in three weeks the rent was due on my trailer.

I had cast my bread and the tide better wash something up, fast.

CHAPTER
THIRTY-EIGHT

TIMMY'S WAS BUSY WITH the lunch crowd, but I snagged one of the last tables. I had just taken the first bite out of my egg salad sandwich when I spotted Redfern at the order counter. I kept my head down and hoped he wouldn't see me.

I shoved a large portion of my sandwich into my mouth just as Redfern plunked down a plastic tray on my table and dropped into the opposite seat.

"I'm glad to see you looking so perky after your ordeal yesterday, Cornwall."

I swallowed my mouthful before it was thoroughly chewed and had to force it down with my scalding coffee. Redfern was poking at his bowl of chili with a plastic spoon and appeared not to notice my near expiration.

"'Tis a manly lunch," I gasped, indicating the chili, "but you should have some vegetables with that."

"Beans are vegetables. And don't be taken in by my apparent disinterest. I was ready to jump in with the

Heimlich if required, but you'll understand my reluctance to appear to hit on you again."

"It's rude to keep your sunglasses on when speaking to someone. I can't tell if you're looking at me or scanning the room for Canada's ten most wanted."

"Oh, I'm looking at you. But you're right, it is rude."

He took off the shades and hooked them onto his breast pocket. Now that those eyes were fixed on me, I wished he would cover them up again.

"What are you staring at?" I asked. "Staring is rude, too."

"I can't win with you, can I, Cornwall? You have a piece of egg at the corner of your mouth. I'd wipe it off, but you'd probably bite my fingers and yell rape."

I scrubbed furiously at my entire face with a paper napkin. Embarrassing memories of sitting on his lap surfaced. I had told him practically every detail of my life including how I played the Butterfly Queen in my kindergarten pageant. But I hadn't told him about Jerry a.k.a. Fitzgerald Corwin. Why? Because he was a crooked cop? Something felt wrong, but I didn't know what it was.

"Now you're staring, Cornwall. Do I have chili on my face?"

Not a chance. I had never seen anyone eat a bowl of chili so neatly. "I was just wondering whether to thank you for sending Thea to cover my back today, or tell you to butt out."

"I know which I'd prefer."

"Well, forget it. Anyway, why are you here? You told me last night to get out of Dodge, I mean Hemp Hollow, and I have — for the moment, at least. So, what now?"

He wiped his completely clean lips with his napkin. "I see foreplay is over."

Shocked, I looked around to see if anyone was within earshot.

"Don't be such a prude, Cornwall. You can't deny there's something going on between us. Once I have a few matters settled, we'll have to explore those possibilities."

"What? What!" I sputtered.

"I finally figured out that bent thing. And the road to perdition you said I was on when you were high on Fern Brickle's brownies. I'm not quite sure where all that's coming from, but I guess I'll have to convince you otherwise. Right now, though, we have to discuss Julian Barnfeather."

Was this a good time to tell him I wasn't attracted to fair-haired men who called me by my last name and talked openly about foreplay? I could feel the heat move up my ribcage and engulf my face. For two years I had been too busy to notice any man, and now, when I had more pots on the stove than burners to cook with, I had one hitting on me. Because I might be out of practice, but I recognized the vibes. Coming from him, that is, not me.

"Speechless, Cornwall? As I told you a few days ago, we've determined that Julian Barnfeather's death was not murder, but death by misadventure. That means there was no deliberate intent to do harm."

"You mean the Friends of the Settlers accidentally killed Julian? Did you find marijuana growing in the pioneers' plot?"

He lowered his voice further, to the point where I had to lean closer to hear him. Our heads were almost touching.

"So you do know more than you said, Cornwall? How long have you known about the Friends?"

"Don't go all conspiracy theory on me, Redfern. I just guessed. You didn't answer me about the marijuana."

"Keep your voice down. We shouldn't be discussing this here, and I shouldn't be telling you anything at all. But since it will be all over this gossipy town by tonight, yes, we found a healthy crop of marijuana growing in the old section of the cemetery. I have to give those people credit, either for guts or stupidity, I haven't decided yet. The surrounding coniferous trees are so thick, the only way they could grow the plants to maturity was to scatter them in the centre among the graves where the sun could get at them. This was only their second crop, and it still had a couple of months to go before it was ready for harvesting. Apparently, last year's harvest didn't yield very much and the brownies you consumed were part of the last of it."

"I'm assuming you've uprooted the plants and burned them?"

He made an "are you nuts" noise in his throat. "The plants have been taken away to a disposal facility. Burning them would require a self-contained air supply to prevent the officers from being affected." I remembered Dougal used that same excuse for not burning his crop in his backyard.

"The whole area is probably a real mess. Someone will have to clean it up, but I suppose the Cemetery

Board won't allow the Friends of the Settlers in there now," I said. Even though half of the board were Friends.

"You bet your big brown eyes they won't. I suppose that can be your job on Saturdays now that you have the rest of the cemetery in such good shape."

"Hah! I've been fired from there, too, thanks to the Weasel. What's going to happen to the Friends? I know they were growing marijuana for medical reasons, but since they weren't licensed, you'll have to charge them."

"How do you know they were growing it for medical reasons?"

"Don't be so suspicious, Redfern. I noticed that everyone visiting Fern the other day was either elderly or infirm in some way. Fern has severe arthritis, and Bob MacPherson is in chronic pain from his back injury. The others I didn't know, but I'm guessing they have some medical problems, too."

"One has multiple sclerosis, one has cancer. Most of them could have registered with the government and bought marijuana legally, but it's a tedious process, and I think they decided that growing their own would be easier. But in a public cemetery?"

"What will happen to them?"

"I've passed the evidence to the Crown Attorney. He can decide whether to charge them or not. I'm guessing he'll mull it over long enough to let public interest move on to some other topic, then bury it. Nobody wants to take sick old people to court. They weren't trafficking."

"But they did kill someone. What about Julian?"

"Well, now, Cornwall, that's the most interesting part of this amateur crime spree."

My cell rang. It was Dougal, naturally, and I mouthed "Gotta take this" at Redfern who impatiently surveyed the parking lot for litterbugs.

"Yeah, yeah, I know. I'm at your beck and call as usual, and ready to do your bidding. I did not tell Chesley to go and see you, but we're coming over at six. He has a proposition for you. I know you hate him, but he's not a bad guy, and no, you can't kick his ass. Just listen to him. Sure, if Thor's pollen is ready we'll postpone it, but you said midnight, so ..."

Redfern was listening openly by this time. Dougal squawked for a few more minutes until I got tired of hearing his lunatic threats to throw both of us off his property if Chesley dared show his face again.

"Take a couple of pills and relax, why don't you? We'll be there at six." I disconnected Dougal in mid-diatribe.

"This is the cousin you almost killed on your motorcycle Sunday night, I take it?"

"It was his fault the bike went over. Well, him and the skunk. If Dougal hadn't moved around so much behind me, I could have kept my tires on the road."

"You're a regular Evel Knievel, Cornwall. Tell me, who is Thor and what is he pollinating?"

Ah well, the international statute of limitations on jungle plant theft probably expired years ago. "Thor is a flower and Dougal thinks it's going to blossom tonight. Which means its pollen will be ready to pollinate another plant. Something like that. Dougal is a botanist."

I smiled as innocently as possible at Redfern, knowing he would tell me if something was stuck in my teeth. At least that might distract him.

"I see. Can we get back to Julian Barnfeather now?"

"Right. Are you at liberty to tell me how he died?"

"Again, yes, since our investigation into his death is complete. You're good at guessing. Care to give it a try?"

"Sure. Julian found out what was really growing in the Settlers' Plot. He was pretty lazy, but he did walk around the cemetery once in a while. He wanted a share of the crop, either to sell or for his own use. One of the gang whacked Julian in the back of the knees with his cane, Julian went down, and they all jumped on him and he hit his head on a tombstone and died."

Redfern looked at me, whether in appreciation or disbelief, I couldn't tell.

"You were doing pretty well until the end there, Cornwall. Julian did find out and he did want a cut. There are some details I can't share with you, but he shoved one of the group and was pushed back. A man of his size is top-heavy and his foot turned over on the uneven ground. He fell and, you were right about this part, he did strike his head on a tombstone."

I looked him over for a few seconds. Sitting at a cozy corner table in Timmy's, I had almost forgotten his involvement with Snake. Could I trust that what he said about anything was the truth? My instincts said yes, but my common sense told me to shut up and get the hell out of there. Curiosity won out.

"You told me Julian was hit on the top of his head. How could he have sustained an injury there if he fell backward onto a tombstone?"

"I said the wound was near the top of his head. We

found hair and blood belonging to Mr. Barnfeather on a tombstone. We made a mould of the stone and compared it to the indentation on the skull. They match."

I thought for a minute. "Those old stones are small compared to modern ones. Someone could have picked it up and bashed Julian over the head."

Redfern had the audacity to laugh outright. "You should write for *CSI*, Cornwall. The stones in that area are cemented to a base. And not recently," he added, as I opened my mouth to ask if the cement was fresh. "I don't know why you're so anxious to make a bunch of harmless seniors into ruthless murderers."

"I'm not," I protested. "I just want to make sure you covered every angle."

"Your attention to detail would make you an asset to the force, Cornwall, but I'm afraid insubordination would get you fired the first time you spoke."

"Ten-four, sir. But, however accidental, Julian's death occurred during the execution of a crime. Doesn't that mean it's automatically manslaughter, at least?"

"Sometimes I forget I'm dealing with the ex-wife of a lawyer. Since I'm quite sure these people will never be charged with growing marijuana, no crime has been committed. Therefore, accidental death is what we have here. Now, just for fun, can you guess how Julian's body travelled from the farthest side of the cemetery to the maintenance shed during the day when any number of people were in the area?"

I thought hard for a moment. Those frail seniors would not have been able to carry Julian's enormous body all the way to the shed. Even if they could drag him, someone would have seen. Then I had it. It was really so simple.

I said to Redfern, "They have a gardening cart. It has a flat bed and is only about a foot from ground level. They were able to pull Julian's body onto the cart. Then they covered him with a tarp and hauled the cart to the door of the shed. Someone acted as a lookout while the others rolled him inside. Why didn't I think of that before?"

"I wish you had. It would have saved me days of speculation about how the body was moved."

"How did you know about the Friends?"

"Let's see. Got a list of names from the Cemetery Board of people who have access to the locked, fenced plot. Found marijuana growing in plot. Questioned names on list. All felt extremely guilty and confessed. Stories all match."

"You're a modern Sherlock Holmes, Redfern."

"You've mentioned that before, and you're quite the little Watson yourself. But, I haven't told you all this because I admire your sexy smile and killer cheekbones. The Over the Hill Gang caper is just a sidebar to the real drug crimes in this town."

"You mean Hemp Hollow?" Again, where was my brain? As soon as I said those words, I wondered if I had some secret death wish. Redfern might be up to his elbows in whatever was going on in Hemp Hollow.

"Exactly. This is confidential, and I'm only telling you because somehow you seem to show up all over town at all the wrong times. I suspect Julian Barnfeather was involved in more than just minor extortion of senior citizens. That's all I can say at this time, but stay away from the cemetery as well as Hemp Hollow for the next few days. Will you promise to do that?"

"Sure." Tomorrow was Saturday, but I had been fired and wouldn't be working at the cemetery anyway, so that promise was easy. As for Hemp Hollow, I might need some clothes later today, but I could be in and out in minutes. No need to even mention it.

"I hope you mean that." He gave me another hard look, but I tossed him one of my killer smiles. Or, was that a sexy smile? Right, it was killer cheekbones and sexy smile.

Without another word, Redfern departed Timmy's, and I watched as he pointed his cruiser toward town. I looked at my watch. Still a few hours to go before I refereed the reunion between Chesley and Dougal.

CHAPTER
THIRTY-NINE

DEEP PUDDLES DOTTED THE overgrown lawns of the Barrister property. Last night's storm had done little to flatten the wild grasses that flourished over the seven acres.

I imagined the property through the eyes of a developer. Front-end loaders and graders could clear the land in days. Bird River crossed the road under a crumbling cement bridge and bisected the north edge of the property, leaving plenty of room for greenhouses. I wasn't sure about the house, though. It was in bad shape.

I crossed River Road to where century-old deciduous trees guarded the entrance to my swamp. As I slipped between the trunks, the place didn't seem as gloomy as I remembered.

A few shafts of light beamed down between the branches and scattered tiny sun drops on the forest floor. When I looked closer, I saw they were yellow lady's slippers and I knelt on the soggy earth for a closer look.

Reaching out to gently touch one specimen, I realized some things in nature weren't so bad.

Bird River flowed quietly through the trees to a small inlet off Georgian Bay a quarter-mile away. I stepped cautiously to the river bank and looked down at the water. The river was a few hundred feet across, and one tall tree had, many years past, fallen over the bank to lay partly submerged. Now it was just a dead log for birds to stand on while they hunted small fish or insects in the water below.

Suddenly, part of the log seemed to move. A head on a scaly neck swivelled in my direction, like some alien life form scenting an intruder. When I realized it was a turtle as big as my head, I prepared to run. I'd heard stories of large turtles taking the legs right off geese and ducks.

As I looked, four more turtles, smaller than the first, turned and blinked up at me.

The big one began to pull its cumbersome body along the log in my direction. I wasn't up for an attack by a herd of turtles, but, on the other hand, I needed to verify that my swamp was indeed home to the infamous spotted turtle, endangered and ugly as hell. I needed to see if these had spots.

I picked up a small branch and banged on the log. That stopped the turtle's advance. It looked at me and I sensed the gears in the primitive brain turning.

"Bad turtle. Jump."

One of the little ones obliged and, just before it plopped into the water, I saw its shell was black and orange, but not spotted. The monster lumbered closer.

I banged the log and plop, plop, two more dropped into the river. Those two had yellow spots.

Plop. I heard the fourth small one hit the water, but I didn't take my eyes off the leader coming at me.

"Back. Back, turtle." It was close enough for me to see its shell was black and it had yellowish spots, not just on the shell, but everywhere. As it crawled closer, I saw a large orange spot on either side of its head. Turtles have ears?

Not only were its ears orange, but its eyes were as well, and, holy shit, it had an orange beak, like a bird of prey!

That was enough detail. I ran until I reached River Road, where I had to stop or be flattened by a pickup driven by a good old boy with a black lab hanging out the passenger window. I berated myself for fearing all things that slithered, scampered, or jumped.

Now I had another dilemma to add to my list. The spotted turtles were endangered, and, although I wasn't personally fond of the prehistoric creatures, they apparently needed to be protected. If the Province of Ontario acquired their habitat via the Weasel, there would be spotted turtles for everyone's grandchildren to enjoy.

The Belcourts' motives were unclear. They said they planned to grow rare, native wildflowers as a business venture. But if they planted things willy-nilly throughout the swamp, would that destroy the turtles' habitat? An environmental assessment would take forever, and I didn't have that long. I would be forced to take up residence under a bridge unless I made some serious bucks soon.

And the swamp was my primary ace. Sell it to the Belcourts or sell it to the Weasel. I had, at this moment, no firm offer from either, so should I accept the first one and devil take the turtles? On the other hand, I didn't want to be known the length and breadth of Bruce County as the mercenary who dispatched an endangered species into full-blown extinction.

Hell. Before I saw those ugly animals on the log, their existence was just academic. Now I had their very survival on my conscience. Stupid damn turtles.

CHAPTER
FORTY

THE SILVER BUG GLEAMED beside the curb in front of Dougal's house, the odour of skunk drifting from its interior. No Canadian Tire product would win that battle. Chesley leaned on the hood playing with a cellphone.

"Hi, Chesley. Rehearsed your marketing strategy?"

"Bliss, I was afraid you wouldn't make it." Chesley's eyes were bright with anticipation. I almost felt sorry for the shit-kicking, figuratively-speaking, he was about to experience at the end of Dougal's tongue.

"Let's go see if we can bag you a Titan Arum for your new nursery."

I took his arm and we walked along the stone path to the front door. I saw Chesley's expert eyes flick from side to side and wondered how he rated my gardening skills.

Dougal waited until I rang the bell three times. He opened the door, eyed us briefly, then turned without a word and walked away. I took this as a good sign. At least he didn't slam the door in our faces.

We found him in his living room. There were two armchairs and a hassock in the space. Simon fluttered up to the hassock and glared at us.

"I see you haven't bought a new couch yet," I said to break the silence. I sank into one of the armchairs and left the other two to stand or sit. Who cared.

"Good eye," Dougal observed. "I told you I had nothing to say to this jerk."

When Chesley continued to stand like a mute swan, I was forced to speak for him.

"He wants to buy Thor," I said bluntly. Why did everyone expect me to be their go-between? Negotiating was not my speciality.

"He can kiss my ass," Dougal replied.

No rebuttal from Chesley.

I stood up and stepped between them. I've noticed that my subconscious is smarter than my conscious mind, and it was time to let the smart one speak. I opened my mouth and let 'er rip without trying to filter the words.

"Chesley and his mother are going to open a new business here in Lockport. The new nursery will specialize in foreign exotics and native wildflowers." I hoped that was in the ballpark.

Dougal looked incredibly underwhelmed, so I blundered on. "They need a signature plant, something spectacular. The plant will appear on the letterhead and as a banner on the web page. A Titan Arum, as impressive in leaf as in flower, would be a perfect flagship plant for Belcourt Exotics." I thought Dougal began to show some interest, and Chesley blinked once.

"Thor is going to be a father, or mother, or both, and his little corms will fetch a pretty penny on the market. I know you can buy the seeds on eBay, but how often do they actually grow into mature plants? Imagine a business where discriminating buyers can browse among lovely orchids and other rare flowers. Imagine Thor standing proud in the luxurious greenhouse, his little corms sprouting in clay pots beside him."

What I knew about horticulture could dance on the head of a pin, but both men were staring at me with open mouths. A little drool collected on Dougal's lips.

"Imagine a wetland directly across from the greenhouse where local wildflowers, like the yellow lady's slipper I saw this afternoon, flourish amidst other rare specimens. The area is fenced to preserve the sacred spotted turtle in its natural habitat …"

"Wait. What? A yellow lady's slipper?" Dougal had me by the shoulders and was shaking me. I ground my heel into his toe and he stopped.

"You saw a yellow lady's slipper?" Chesley actually spoke out loud and stopped blinking like an owl in daylight.

"Well, yellow with reddish twisty things growing out the back of pouches," I replied. "But there was this enormous turtle with an orange beak. Did you know turtles had ears?"

"*Cypripedium parviflorum,*" both idiots said in unison.

"How many did you see?" Dougal advanced on me, and I backed up.

"Dozens."

"Did you get any shots?" asked Chesley.

"She has the oldest cell on the planet," said Dougal. "I'm surprised her charger still works."

"I have a charger?" I said. Then "Just kidding. What's the biggie on the lady's slipper?"

"The *Cypripedium parviflorum* is quite rare in this area," Dougal responded. "Where did you say you saw them?"

I watched Chesley. His thick lips were sucking in air, and he seemed to be gearing up to say something momentous. I think I closed the deal when I said, "Well, I was strolling in my wetland out by River Road. I was so surprised when I saw all these tiny yellow lady's slippers. So pretty."

Dougal said with disbelief, "You own property? You don't own yesterday's dinner."

That was rude, and I would make him pay.

I ignored him and spoke to Chesley. "I don't know how long the flowers will last. They seem to be in full bloom now. I can take you out there if you want to snap a few photos. Maybe Mum would be interested in coming along?"

Chesley wiggled all over. "Oh, would you, Bliss? I would love to see the lady's slippers. And I'm sure Mum would too. Can we go now?"

I glanced at Dougal. He seemed about to cry. Served him right. "Well, I don't think we can go today, Chesley. Thor is going to bloom any minute, and I have to stand ready to transport pollen back and forth between here and Glory's house."

This news was too much for Chesley. Tears leaked from his eyes and ran down his thin cheeks as he turned back to Dougal. "Thor is going to blossom? Oh, please, can I stay and watch? This is a once in a lifetime opportunity, Dougal, and you know how I grieved for Jarnsaxa."

"Sure, sure, buddy." Dougal punched Chesley lightly on the arm and turned away. His eyes were wet, too.

Nobody cared about the spotted turtles, but the lady's slippers were a big hit. Somehow, I could turn that to my advantage.

"Just remember," I said to Chesley. "I'm getting paid to deliver the pollen from Thor to Sif and the other way around. So, when magic time rolls around, get out of my way."

"You can stay and help me with Thor tonight, if you want, Ches," Dougal offered. "I have to surgically cut through the spathe to brush on Sif's pollen. Bliss can do the grunt work by transporting the pollen between plants, but you and I will suit up and perform the pollination. Glory will do the same at her end."

"Uh, Dougal?" I flicked my head and rolled my eyes toward the solarium where Thor shared his digs with other, worldlier members of the flora species.

"You all right, Bliss? ... Oh. Never mind, Ches is cool."

A voice behind me called, "Reefer time, man. Who's got the lighter?"

"Get lost," I told Simon, as he skated through the solarium door.

Chesley went directly to the Titan and looked up. His face had that beatific look you see in old paintings, where the saints are illuminated with the knowledge of the cosmos. He was taking in air in great gulps and, fearing he would hyperventilate, I slapped him on the back.

Dougal stood by, as proud as if he had personally fathered this giant freak of nature instead of stealing it.

Then Chesley caught sight of the marijuana. He walked over to the tall plants, ignoring the orchids now bunched together near a window.

Fingering a cluster of buds, Chesley turned and looked at Dougal.

"Dude."

"Yeah," Dougal responded modestly, "prime."

"It stinks even worse in here than it did last night," I observed, sniffing the humid air. "Are you sure you don't have a sewer backup? There appears to be essence of cannabis mixed in with a dead rat in the wall smell again."

"This crop is ready for harvesting," said Chesley.

Dougal nodded. "I might get a chance tomorrow. Thor's taken up all my time lately. I've documented his progress, and plan to write an article for one of the Geographic magazines."

"I've been thinking, too," I interjected. "Dougal, I'm sure you don't want to sell Thor. And, you've done a wonderful job coaxing him to blossom and, hopefully, the pollination will be successful. But have you thought about afterward?"

"What do you mean, afterward? Thor will go dormant for a time, then his leaf will grow intermittently for a few years, then, if I'm lucky, he'll blossom again."

"But, in the meantime, think of this scenario. Thor resides at the entrance of a vast greenhouse built of soaring steel and glass. A large brass plaque is affixed to his burnished pot. The plaque reads: On Loan from Dougal Seabrook. Visitors will line up to see Thor, even in his leaf stage. A legend on a stand describes the life cycle of the Titan Arum, with pictures of each stage of development. And when Thor blossoms again, the excitement will rival that created by a blossoming Titan in any botanical garden in the world. Everybody wins. You still own Thor, and the Belcourts have their flagship exotic."

"Or," said Dougal, "how about if the plaque reads: On Loan from Published Author and Renowned Botanist Dougal Seabrook?"

Chesley and I both stared at Dougal.

"Well, you'll have to wait and see if *National Geographic* accepts your article," I said. "And, as for the renowned part, you aren't exactly in that league yet …"

"I'm not talking about a magazine article. I heard this morning that a Canadian publisher has accepted my manuscript, *Death in the Conservatory*. I told you I was writing a mystery with a botanical theme." He looked at me reproachfully.

"But I didn't know you even started it."

"You've been preoccupied lately, Bliss. I would have appreciated your opinion on my draft, but you were always in such a hurry."

"Because you kept me on the hop every minute of the day, you numbskull. Weeding, mowing, fetching, delivering, trimming your damn hair! I would have read it."

"Uh, I hate to interrupt, and congratulations, Doog, that's great news about your novel. I always knew you'd be a writer some day," Chesley said. "I'll have to discuss this with Mum, but I'm sure she will agree with me that leasing Thor is acceptable if you aren't willing to sell outright. Of course, we would expect to purchase a percentage of any viable seeds that may result from this current pollination."

"Pull the stick out, Ches," Dougal replied. "Thor is a lot of work, and I feel confident you can care for him. As a loan. So, once tonight is over, we'll discuss business with Mum."

"I have another idea," I said.

Both goofballs looked at me condescendingly.

"Just listen. Dougal, you need something to do with your life other than sit in this house and grow pot. Okay, and write mysteries. How about you invest in this latest Belcourt operation, the greenhouse and wetland, for exotics and natives? This is a new type of venture for them, and you can help with the new Titan Arum tubers."

Becoming involved in affairs outside his own head might also help Dougal overcome his agoraphobia without the use of illegal herbs.

"I'd have to think about that," said the tightwad who still had every nickel his parents had left him.

He turned his back on me and spoke to Chesley. "I've been feeding Thor with a high potash liquid fertilizer. I wouldn't doubt it had an impact on his energy levels."

"Did you give some of this yummy fertilizer to Glory?" I asked. "Sif looks exactly the same as Thor, so their diet ..."

"Shut it," Dougal told me.

He said to Chesley, "I have some other ideas for potting the corms in larger containers so they don't have to be disturbed later on. If we can increase the energy stores in the corms, they might bloom sooner and more often. Several universities have done some interesting work on Titan Arums and they might be willing—"

"I have to call Mum," Chesley interrupted. "I'll tell her I'm staying here tonight to help you with Thor and Sif. Tomorrow, we can talk about the business after Mum and I finalize our financial arrangements. Oh, and Bliss, can we visit the *Cypripedium parviflorum* tomorrow? Maybe in the morning? I don't want to risk missing the blossoming of the Titan."

I looked at my watch. "Not a problem." I was relieved that Chesley was content to wait until morning to see the tiny lady's slippers in their boggy beds.

It was almost dusk. I knew turtles sometimes crawled up on land, and if I saw one trudging through the lady's slippers, there better be daylight between me and the exit. I didn't figure I could count on Chesley in a crisis.

As events played out, it wasn't a homicidal turtle that Chesley was forced to confront.

CHAPTER
FORTY-ONE

BEFORE LEAVING "DOOG" AND "Ches" to renew their friendship and no doubt smoke a calming joint, I decided I better check my bank balance in case my bike needed fuel.

I called over my shoulder to Dougal, "I'm going to use your computer for a minute, okay?" I tried to close the solarium door on Simon, but his scaly legs were faster than they looked and he managed to get his tail feathers out before the door slammed.

In Dougal's office, I studied his laptop. I was used to the desktop at the library and wasn't sure I could figure out how to access my bank account. Sitting down on his swivel chair and shoving Simon away from the mouse, I tentatively pressed a key. The display showed a plethora of shortcuts. My hand was wrapped around the mouse, index finger poised to make a selection, when the finger was seized.

"Ow! Ow!" I stood up. Dougal applied more pressure and I stomped on his manicured toes. Simon squawked and fluttered, dislodging a stack of CDs, which flew across the room like miniature Frisbees.

"Ouch." Dougal let go of my finger and collapsed onto his chair. Cradling his foot, he looked up and screamed, "You could have broken my toes, you freaky midget."

"Well, consider yourself lucky I'm not wearing my boots. What's the matter with you, anyway? I only wanted to check my bank balance."

"My manuscripts are on there …"

The altercation brought Chesley to the door of the office. He took one look and disappeared again.

"Did you ever think of asking?" Dougal was breaking the municipal noise bylaw, and I hoped one of his neighbours would call the cops. I was through giving a shit if Dougal was hauled off to jail.

"Never mind. I didn't know it was such a big deal. I'll wait and go into the bank tomorrow."

He tapped the keys, then said, "Here, you can put in your password now."

"Well, thanks. You don't have to look over my shoulder. This is my personal business."

"Get real. I'd be surprised if you had the price of a doughnut." But he moved away and surveyed his damaged toes.

My balance confirmed I did have the price of a doughnut, barely. Something better happen before my rent was due, or humiliation at the gas pump would be the least of my problems.

"Thanks, and sorry about your toe." I wasn't sorry at all, but had kept to my promise not to drop the F-bomb today, and apologizing seemed to be in keeping with the new me. I was beginning to think that my involuntary ingestion of pot — twice — had mellowed me out. It better be temporary.

"Whatever. Just make sure you keep your antique BlackBerry on," Dougal responded. "Tonight's the night, and I don't want to have to wait for you. Actually, it might be better if you stay right here. I think there's a piece of take-out pizza left in the fridge if you're hungry."

"Tempting, but no. I have things to do. But I won't be far away, so just call and I'm here."

"You better be." He logged off and limped away to the solarium. Simon was still sitting on the edge of the desk, regarding me with his black-pebble eyes, head cocked to one side.

"I couldn't go on without you," he said solemnly, then jumped off the desk and skittered down the hall in Dougal's wake. The female voice he used was familiar, and once I placed it I suspected I would have the name of Dougal's paramour. Hopefully, some skank wasn't planning to take advantage of him. Dougal was no dummy, but he hadn't been what you might call emotionally stable since Glory threw him out.

I inched my way along Dougal's front walkway. The sky was dull, without stars or moon, and the street lamps lining Pinewood Avenue flickered to life as I started the Savage. Thick fog lay close to the ground, disappearing and recurring so sporadically that, by the time I reached the end of Dougal's street, my eyes were burning from the strain of seeking substance within the mist.

When I saw Fern Brickle getting out of her car in her driveway, I steered the bike to the curb.

"Mrs. Brickle. Hello." I walked closer so she would be able to see me through the haze.

"Bliss? What are you doing out on such a nasty night? You should be snug at home with the fire on and some hot food inside you. That air off the lake feels just like October instead of June."

"I could say the same thing to you, Mrs. Brickle. This is not the weather for you to be driving around."

"Oh, I wasn't driving very far, dear. I was just over at the MacPhersons'. I guess you heard what happened at the cemetery?"

"I did. But I understand no charges will be laid, so you and the others shouldn't worry."

"I know that, dear. That nice young police chief explained that the Crown Attorney was unlikely to prosecute. But our group wanted to meet to discuss our path forward."

"What did you decide?"

"There is no point in pursuing the cultivation of our own medication. The police took down our names and, no doubt, they will be keeping an eye on us."

You think?

"I don't believe Chief Redfern would tolerate a second transgression by our little group. But he's a very good-looking young man, don't you think?" She peered into my face.

"He's not ugly, I guess. Anyway, what happened with Julian Barnfeather? Did he find where you were growing it?" I had the official version from Redfern. But I wanted the truth.

Fern leaned more heavily on her cane. "We started growing cannabis in the Settlers' Plot last year. We barely harvested enough to meet our needs, and it wasn't terribly effective since we just chopped up the whole plant and used it in baking. Then we tried to smoke it, but some of us had never smoked before and we made quite a mess of it. It didn't feel right either. Somehow, if we put it in our food, it didn't seem so unlawful."

"What happened when Julian found it?"

"That man was evil. I'm sorry he's dead, and even sorrier that his death was at our hands, however inadvertently, but once he found our cannabis, he just took over. He told us he would keep our secret for a share of the harvest. In a way, he helped by taking the plants to someone who actually baked the resin from the buds into desserts for us — a stronger product. Julian delivered the baked goods to me, and the group met every Thursday to play a little bridge and sample the dessert of the week. Then each member of the group took home a supply. But with Julian's share, our medicine just didn't go as far as we needed it to. In any case, a scuffle ensued last Saturday. I don't want to go into details, but I hope you believe we never meant for Julian to die."

"I believe you, Mrs. Brickle. What are you going to do now?"

"Those of us with chronic conditions, like my arthritis, will register for the government program. First, we have to find a doctor to prescribe cannabis as a medication, which we couldn't do before. The legally grown cannabis is said to be inferior to the kind you can buy from dealers or grow personally, but now we have no choice. Those with more acute conditions, like cancer, well, they will have to rely on drugs that will affect their cognitive functions and make their remaining months or years less tolerable."

We were both silent for a moment as the mist gathered around us like a third entity silently eavesdropping on our discussion.

Then Mrs. Brickle said, "I know what people will think of us. Cannabis is an illegal substance and we misused it, or that's what they will believe. But I would do it again, and, as a matter of fact, our group decided we'll join an organization to actively promote the legal use of marijuana as a medical drug."

A picture of Mrs. Brickle and her cohorts marching on Parliament Hill was a vivid one. Maybe I could drive the bus.

"Mrs. Brickle, I'm sure nobody is going to judge you. If anyone gives you a hard time, just call me and I'll take him down for you."

That was the best I had to offer, and to my surprise she laughed.

"Bless you, Bliss, you are a true warrior. Now help me with my key and then get yourself home. I'll expect you next Wednesday afternoon, as usual."

After I saw Fern safely indoors, I called Rae to tell her I wouldn't be at the motel until quite late and possibly not at all that night. She sounded bored with motel living, but said she would leave a lamp lit in the window in case I made it.

I rummaged in my saddlebag for my leather gloves and pulled them on. I had lied to Dougal when I said I had things to do. I just didn't want to hang around old home week in the solarium, listening to frat house stories or learning how to grow bigger, faster-growing Titan Arums.

I planted my warrior butt on the damp seat and aimed the Savage into the fog.

CHAPTER
FORTY-TWO

MY STOMACH FOCUSED ON the hot coffee and buttery croissant I planned to order at Timmy's. It was the perfect place to hole up until Dougal's call summoned me back to transport the sacred pollen. Already I had forgotten which pollen was to be gathered first.

As I turned onto Main Street, I noticed a dim light radiating from within the heart of the Good Shepherd Cemetery.

I pulled the bike to the curb and tried to see through the fog. At that time of the evening, there should be no one working in the cemetery. But the light seemed to come from the area between the squat office building and the maintenance shed where Julian had been found.

My footfalls sounded like thunderclaps in my ears. I ran across the road and pushed my face against the locked gates. The iron bars felt clammy against my skin.

I pulled my head away and looked around at the empty street. No footsteps, no voices penetrated the white fog. In the parallel world of my imagination, this could be a London streetscape at the end of the nineteenth century, smog-bound and silent, with only dim illumination cast from hissing gas lamps. Jack the Ripper might glide up to me any minute and introduce himself.

In the real world, I easily fit through the junction between fence and gate post. If teenagers were knocking over headstones, they would soon face the wrath of Bliss Moonbeam Cornwall.

White puffs of mist floated among the graves, as ethereal as the spirits of those who rested there. I kept my eye on the light ahead, still unable to gauge its origin.

The patches of fog interfered with my sense of direction, and the cemetery that was as familiar to me as the back of my hand became a minefield. Tombstones slammed me in the stomach. Claw-like branches raked my face and neck.

With a grunt, quickly muted, I slid over the top of a rectangular stone — is it you, Alistair Parks? — and landed heavily against a smaller marker. Rolling away, my fingers sank into soft earth, newly turned.

Fucking hell! A new grave. It had to be Julian Barnfeather's. Ordinarily, the cemetery held no fears for me, but rolling around on Julian's grave conjured up every horror movie I had ever seen, as well as the entire *Buffy the Vampire Slayer* series. With visions of a grisly hand reaching up to pull me in, I took off on all fours.

At that point, I knew what a stupid decision it had been to enter the cemetery. Damn my impulsive nature. I was fucked.

I turned until I located the yellow orb, enticing as a fairy light. Voices murmured through the mist. They seemed to come from behind me, in front of me, even from the treetops.

Reason told me to find the fence, follow it to the gate, and get the hell out of there. But curiosity compelled me to find out why people were talking in the cemetery on a foggy evening. I hoped to find a couple of kids sitting in a circle with an Ouija board, trying to raise a spirit.

Placing one foot carefully in front of the other and feeling ahead with my hands, I moved between the markers of the dead.

I stood behind a massive monument to the affluent Bowles family who were related to Glory on her mother's side. The fifteen-foot-high obelisk was wide enough for me and two of my best friends to hide behind, if I had that many friends stupid enough to accompany me to the cemetery in the dead of night.

Two mausoleums stood straight ahead. I recalled that the iron doors of both structures were fitted with modern padlocks, the keys probably resting with the Cemetery Board or the families. And perhaps available to the cemetery's maintenance supervisor, Julian?

My mind apparently had already made the leap between Julian's activities in the cemetery with the Friends of the Settlers and what Redfern had told me at Tim Hortons. Like, there were things about Julian he couldn't yet divulge. And he told me to stay out of the cemetery.

For some reason, I had been leaning away from the notion that Redfern was a crooked cop. Unless he was here in the cemetery.

I glanced around the monument. Two figures bobbed in and out of the haze, their forms too indistinct for me to recognize.

Then one of the figures spoke again and my blood stopped circulating.

"Is that the last of it?" Snake's gravelly voice travelled through the mist.

Crap.

For a moment, the fog parted and I saw the mausoleums clearly in the illumination of a Coleman lantern. The door to the one on the right hung agape. Two men stooped over the ground, their backs to my hiding place.

The mist enfolded the scene again. Only the lantern continued to throw its feeble glow toward me.

"We're done here. Let's pack up and get the hell out. The whole police force could be watching us." The second man spoke, but I didn't recognize the voice. Not Redfern, I realized with relief.

At that moment, my cell rang.

CHAPTER
FORTY-THREE

"THE COPS. MOVE!"

"Not cops. Wait here."

If I had the brains God gave a flounder, I would have dropped the BlackBerry on the ground and high-tailed it out of that cemetery.

I managed to silence the phone before the third ring, noting that Blyth, not Dougal, was trying to reach me. I flattened myself against the Bowles memorial and tried to become part of the stone.

I hoped the fog had thrown the shrill sound of the cellphone far across the cemetery, so the two men would head away from me. I tried to still my breathing, but instead took a huge gulp of air. I was afraid the sound would lead the men directly to me.

The remnants of my courage took flight as I heard a twig snap within a yard of my hiding place. I stepped back to get my bearings, and the hesitation was nearly my undoing.

A menacing shape loomed out of the fog. A hand brushed my jacket as I yelped in primal terror and sprinted into the dark. I wasn't sure if Snake or the faceless accomplice was after me. It didn't matter.

I hoped I wouldn't knock myself senseless trying to blindly run through the randomly placed tombstones. My pursuer followed close behind me and I nearly impaled myself on the stony sword brandished by a seven-foot angel who, I knew from experience, was glaring down at me, eyes aflame with righteousness. The sword scraped my temple, but I now knew I was close to the entrance gates.

Heavy footfalls pounded toward me — too close. I dropped behind a headstone and lowered my chin to my knees. Panting, the man paused, inches away, his boots twisting and turning, searching for me. I pulled my jacket over my face, hoping to muffle my own breathing.

Finally, he moved away, his footsteps scuffing through the grass, until the sounds of wheezing and shuffling were swallowed by the curtain of vapour. I heard a muffled yelp, followed by a string of obscenities. He must have fallen over a headstone. I crawled from stone to stone, pausing behind each to listen, expecting at any instant to collide with my pursuer.

At no time during this terrifying hunt did I consider confronting the man. Every instinct demanded flight and evasion.

I smothered a cry of relief when I felt the brick path beneath my scrabbling fingers. I was in a dangerous state of panic, no longer caring if my ragged breathing gave away my position. As the last vestiges of reason collapsed, I leaped to my feet and ran.

I was approximately three feet from the iron gates. The impact dropped me to my knees, while the night blazed with a thousand sparkling lights.

I lost the will to resist the F-word, and used it several times as I clutched the bars to pull myself up. Heavy hands gripped my shoulders, and I twisted around in horror.

"Got you!"

I recognized Snake's raspy voice.

As the hands tightened, I did what every threatened, red-blooded woman would do in my place.

I kneed him in the nuts and, with all my remaining strength, gave his chest a shove. He hit the ground with a satisfying thud.

He writhed at my feet, groaning, while I frantically searched for the gap in the fence. Hesitation was a mistake. A hand encircled my ankle and tightened. I kicked him in the head with my free foot, struggling to maintain my balance. He howled in agony and released me. I squeezed through the opening.

Freedom was fleeting. I barely had time to absorb the sight of lights and movement when another figure materialized out of the shadows and grasped my shoulder.

Reason deserted me. Did Snake de-materialize in the cemetery and reappear on the sidewalk? A hand covered my mouth and I was lifted off the ground.

I bit down, and my captor pulled his hand away but didn't release his grip. I dangled several feet off the ground, and the situation seemed painfully familiar.

"Goddamn it all to hell. I might have known it was you." Rage and frustration radiated from the voice near my ear.

"Oh, fuck."

CHAPTER
FORTY-FOUR

NO WORDS WERE EXCHANGED while an officer opened the rear door of the squad car and Redfern tossed me in. At least he didn't handcuff me. I tried to tell him I was expecting a call and might have to leave soon, but he slammed the door so hard I was surprised the window held up.

Someone arrived with a key to the cemetery gates and, after it was opened wide, men and women rushed in and out like crazed shoppers on Boxing Day.

It started to rain and, between the water running down the windows and the fog, I wasn't able to see what the cops were doing. I assumed they were hunting for my attacker, although nobody had asked about that. As a matter of fact, Redfern hadn't asked me anything. I gnawed my nails and hoped I would be released before Dougal called, or I could kiss my thousand dollars *arrivederci*.

After what seemed like many hours, but may have been less, I had to pee really badly and was starting to worry about the air quality in the vehicle. Redfern could have cracked a window at least. I was about to hammer on the window to attract attention when the big chief himself opened the driver's door and jumped in.

I scratched on the grill separating me from the front seat.

"Listen, Redfern, I have to go to the bathroom, so could you let me off …"

"Shut. The. Fuck. Up. Cornwall."

The volume at which my name was roared rattled my eardrums, and I sat back in shock. The blood rushed to my head, but before I had time to throw a fit, we arrived at the police station.

Redfern slammed the brakes on and leaped out of the vehicle, almost in the same motion.

"Out," he ordered.

"Give me a minute while I peel my face off the grill." There had to be a law requiring the drivers of police cars to belt in their jailbirds.

He pointed at the steps. "Up."

In the vestibule, I tried again. "I have to go to the bathroom. Seriously."

"In. My. Office. Now."

"Okay, then, but remember what happened last time I was here? Try getting pee off your boots."

He marched me down the hall to a small, unmarked door.

"In."

It was a unisex bathroom that didn't smell great, but any port in a storm. I sat down and sighed in contentment. There was a small mirror fastened to the wall over the sink, and I caught sight of my reflection while washing my hands. My hair stood out around my face in a wild tangle of witch locks and dried blood streaked my forehead — a souvenir from the angel's sword in the cemetery. It was impossible to distinguish darkening bruises from the graveyard grime that tinted even my lips. Roadkill looked better after three days by the side of the road. I sniffed my armpits. At least I didn't smell quite as bad as roadkill. I thought about trying to wash my face, but figured it wouldn't help much. Fuck it.

I was surprised to find Redfern waiting for me outside the door. I thought he'd lose interest and wander away to supervise the takedown in the cemetery.

His arms were crossed, his fair skin the colour of rosy bricks in the sunshine. I acknowledged to myself that he might have a small point to his anger but had no intention of telling him that.

"My. Office. Now."

"Right."

Thea and another officer were already in Redfern's office, leaning against the wall. Redfern pointed at the chair in front of his desk. He saw me looking at his waste basket and said, "Don't. Even. Think. About. It."

He sat in his chair, with the space of the desk between us.

"Are you going to keep talking like that?" I asked.

"Like. What?"

"Like, with a big space between each word. It's creepy."

He swung his chair around until he faced the window. The blinds were closed, so he had a great view of muck-brown vertical slats. He rocked rapidly back and forth.

I watched Thea and the other officer. They were shooting apprehensive glances at each other, and I noticed their shoulders were close, but not quite touching.

"Hey," I said. "You must be Dwayne. Thea's told me about you."

They looked apprehensive, but since Redfern continued to stare at the blinds, I tried to keep the conversation going. I remembered in time that their relationship might be a secret from their boss.

"Yes, Thea has told me about all her co-workers. You guys must have had quite a time in the cemetery tonight, eh?"

I barely had time to intercept a mouthed "Shut up" from Thea before Redfern swivelled to face me.

"Just exactly what *was* going on in the cemetery?" he asked.

His skin was less rosy and he was speaking in whole sentences, so I deduced the danger of Redfern going postal on me was diminishing. Thea and Dwayne seemed more relaxed, so I followed suit and zipped open my jacket. I felt for my cell and pulled it out to make sure I hadn't missed any calls from Dougal. No way was I going to lose out on that money now, not after all I had been through to get it.

"Put that away, Cornwall, and answer the question."

I took a second to formulate a lucid answer, one that would save us all time and get me the hell out of there before Dougal called.

"When you're ready, Ms. Cornwall."

"Well, it's very simple, Chief. I was riding by, saw a light in the cemetery, and decided to investigate. I feel quite protective toward the cemetery residents, and thought vandals might be tipping over gravestones. That's about it, I guess. Somebody chased me, I kicked him in the balls, you threw me in the back of your car, and here we are. I'm always happy to cooperate with the authorities, as you know, but I have a pressing engagement and need to leave now."

He ignored everything I said.

"I should arrest you right now. You have single-handedly jeopardized a six-month investigation and put the life of an officer in danger."

"What the hell are you talking about, Redfern? Arrest me for what? Okay, maybe you can get me for trespassing, but good luck with that one. Don't forget, I was married to a smart, slimy lawyer, so don't try to intimidate me. I know what you can and can't do. You can throw down a summary offence for trespassing if you want, but I'll raise you an assault charge, which would be an indictable offence."

I could feel Thea and Dwayne stiffen beside me. Redfern's face started to redden again and he shouted, "Assault? For what? If you could read my mind, maybe!"

"You didn't fasten my seatbelt. And I smashed my face against the grill. Look." I pointed at the small cut on my forehead from the stone angel. I was lying like the pro I was, but Redfern was being an asshole.

"There are no seatbelts in the back of cruisers, you little menace."

Dwayne's and Thea's eyes were pivoting back and forth between me and Redfern. They had moved away from the wall and were standing by the side of his desk. The door opened and a head peered in but quickly disappeared after one glance at Redfern's face.

"That's cold," I said. "What happens during a high-speed chase? The poor suspect can take quite a beating."

"We don't take our suspects on high-speed chases," Thea said.

"Yeah, once we bag one, we usually bring him right in," Dwayne contributed.

Redfern snapped a pencil in two and threw the pieces. I felt them wing by my ear.

"Can we all get back to the cemetery, if you don't mind?" he asked, with murderous calm.

"I'm not quite sure what was happening in the cemetery," I said with total honesty. "But if there was some kind of sting operation happening, why didn't you have officers inside? Really, letting innocent citizens wander into a crime scene can't be regulation. Geez, I could have been killed, Redfern."

His mouth tightened, and he looked like he was trying to swallow a baseball.

"Cornwall, I wish I had time to deal with you, but at the moment I—"

My BlackBerry rang.

"For the love of God, don't answer that, Moonbeam," Thea entreated.

But it was too late.

"Hey there, cousin," I said brightly.

"It's time. Get over to Glory's and pick up Sif's pollen. Bring it here."

Dougal's voice was excited and too loud, and I put

my hand over the cell. "I'm on my way," I whispered between my fingers.

"What's going on?"

"Nothing." I cupped my hand around my mouth. "I'll be at Glory's in a few minutes."

Redfern was staring at me like my hair had turned to Medusa's snakes, which gave me an idea. After closing the cell and slipping it back into my pocket, I tried a cute smile on Redfern. When his face didn't change for the better, I stood up quickly and brushed at my shoulders, then pulled at my hair, squeaking, "Is there something on me?"

I bent over and shook my head as though trying to dislodge an entire battalion of spiders.

"Get it off me." I skipped closer to Redfern. "Can you see it?" I continued to shake and pull.

Thea and Dwayne backed away. Redfern's new expression told me he wasn't fooled but didn't have time for any more nonsense.

He pointed at the door. "Go. We'll continue this discussion tomorrow afternoon."

"What's his problem?" I asked Thea on my way past, but she closed her eyes and didn't reply.

"And stay out of Hemp Hollow." Redfern's bellow followed me outside. A quick glance at my watch showed Dougal had been right in his prediction that the Titan Arums would blossom around midnight.

The rain had ended, but the fog still filled the street, creating an unnatural stillness, and I picked my way along the sidewalk. I wanted to avoid the cemetery, but my bike was parked across from the entrance gates. I took a deep breath and darted across the street, chancing that an eighteen-wheeler wouldn't suddenly burst out of the haze and flatten me.

I made it across but wondered if it wouldn't be safer to leave my bike where it was and make the pollen run on foot. Well, safer for me maybe, but not my bike. I wasn't going to leave it parked where it could get smashed to smithereens by a police car backing out of the cemetery. I knew from personal experience that cops drove like maniacs.

I hadn't been totally putting on an act in Redfern's office about the spiders. Before clamping on my helmet, I performed another check through my hair.

The Savage was facing the wrong direction, and I needed to make a U-turn. I fumbled with the key as a shape materialized out of the fog. A leather vest over a skull-covered tee-shirt. Ruby eyes gleamed dully from the belt, and my own eyes travelled up to the unshaven face and do-rag–wrapped head.

I didn't need to hear the hoarse voice with the sardonic undertones.

CHAPTER
FORTY-FIVE

I LIFTED MY TOES off the pavement and turned the accelerator. Shooting past Snake, I made a wide U-turn in front of the cemetery and drove south a few hundred yards, trying to see Evening Star Road. Visibility was less than a foot and I overshot the turn and had to make another U-turn. By now, my life was in the hands of the angels, who had done a pretty good job so far tonight. But it was midnight and a celestial shift-change might be occurring, which meant I was off the heavenly radar for the next few minutes. Cold sweat dampened my armpits.

By the time I cut the engine outside Glory's mansion, I was shaking all over. Should I call Redfern and tell him I spotted Snake on the street opposite the cemetery? If I did that, Redfern might insist I come in and make a statement. Not happening tonight.

After my pollen duties were over, I'd make an anonymous call to the police station.

Glory opened the door holding a white pail in her hand. A lid was snapped on and further secured with grey duct tape. I looked down at the white cotton booties on Glory's feet, then up along white coveralls that covered her to the neck. A purple shower cap topped her abundant tresses, but the cap was not up to the task and thick red strands had escaped and were cascading over her shoulders. A green surgical mask hung around her neck. Once again, I wished my elderly BlackBerry could take pictures.

"Is that a scalpel, Glory? You aren't dismembering Sif in there, are you?" Then another thought occurred to me. "Where's Pan? What have you done with him, you monster?"

"Shut up, Bliss. I'm in no mood for your pitiful humour. Now, take this pollen to Dougal at once. Do you understand?"

I nodded, not wanting Glory to go red-eyed with a scalpel in her hand. Guess our all-girls-together relationship was over.

"Good. Dougal is gathering Thor's pollen right now, and when it's ready, bring it directly here. Do not stop to take a bath or wash your hair, even though you look more disgusting than usual. Got it?" She handed over the pail.

I snapped my heels together and saluted with my free hand, then turned to run when Glory's eyeballs took on a pinkish hue.

When I hit the sidewalk, I kept going on foot. Dougal's house was only a short walk away, and the fog showed no sign of abating. I had been hearing sirens in the distance for some time and figured the cops at the cemetery were ratcheting up the hunt for Snake and his accomplice.

But now the sirens sounded much closer. I was a half block from Dougal's house when a squad car drove up alongside me, siren screaming and roof lights flashing. It was still impossible to see an arm's length ahead, so while the cruiser was creating a lot of fuss, it crawled along like a hornet after a frost. Was I on the most wanted list again? Well, they wouldn't take me in, not before I got my thousand bucks.

Sprinting ahead with my pail of pollen, I searched through the fog for the low columns marking Dougal's driveway. When the cruiser pulled to the curb, the headlights and flashing roof lights illuminated them.

I dashed up the driveway and slammed into the garage. By the time I reached the front door, the beam of a powerful flashlight moved slowly along the brick path from the sidewalk.

"Cornwall!"

The flashlight backed me against the door. I cradled the pail of pollen in my arms.

Fuck it all to hell. Was the man never off duty?

"What have I done now? You said I could go. Is it necessary to chase me around in this pea-souper with sirens and guns and everything?"

"Don't give yourself airs, Cornwall. I'm not after you — this time."

I clutched the doorknob behind me with one hand to prevent myself from buckling at the knees. Someone had ratted on Dougal, and he was about to be hauled away. I had joked about that when I first found out about his marijuana, but it was all coming true. Dougal would never survive the trip to the police station, or the subsequent night in jail before I could bail him out. Then I remembered something. Redfern needed a warrant to enter the premises unless he was granted permission ...

"What's wrong with you, Cornwall? This is your cousin's house, isn't it?" Redfern asked, mounting the last step to stand over me.

"Yes."

"When did you see your cousin, Dougal Seabrook, last?"

"I don't know. A couple of hours ago, maybe around six o'clock, or maybe eight o'clock. I can't really remember."

"Was anybody with him when you left?"

Hell. Now Chesley would be involved. If he was charged for possession or trafficking, there went any possibility of a commission for the Barrister house. And I could forget entirely the long shot of selling the Belcourts my swamp.

"Well?" Redfern's hand was inches from mine on the doorknob.

"Yes, Dougal's friend from university, Chesley Belcourt, is visiting." The two morons were probably in the solarium, happily gathering pollen with joints hanging out of the sides of their mouths.

"Belcourt must be the owner of the Volkswagen parked out front. Did you notice an unusual smell earlier?" Redfern's fingers hovered over mine, but I clutched the doorknob tightly. He'd have to go through me. I took Snake down in the cemetery tonight, so I was no pushover. And there was the warrant requirement.

"Smell?" Did he mean the distinctive odour of the cannabis plants standing tall and healthy against the windows? Or … I would go with the other, stinkier one. "Now that you mention it, there was a bit of a sewer odour, or maybe a rat died in the wall. I have a super sense of smell, so nobody else would notice it."

"Somebody else noticed. We received a complaint from a neighbour of an odour of putrefaction, like that of a decomposing body."

"No way. Nobody was dead in there a few hours ago. It's probably a sewer backup."

"We have to investigate all complaints. Now, either step aside and let me enter, or go get your cousin."

I clutched the pail tighter to my chest with one hand. "How come you're here? Why didn't you just send one of your officers?"

He smiled without humour and I saw the dark smudges beneath his eyes. "Everyone else is either off-shift or involved with other duties. Busy night. The fog has caused a few fender-benders on the highway, and Thea and Dwayne are on their way to the scene. So, that just leaves me to respond to a simple odour complaint. But finding you here, Cornwall, makes me think something else is going on." His lips twitched, briefly, like a nervous tic.

"No," I said, quickly. "It's the sewer, like I said."

"Are you going to let me in?"

"Have you got a warrant?" There, I said it.

"No. Have you got something to hide in there? Or, maybe your cousin does."

"Why don't I go in ahead and check it out? That way you don't have to be bothered."

"Please get your cousin and bring him to the door." This time the words and tone were official.

My left hand was still wrapped around the doorknob. Redfern stepped closer to me and his fingers, warm and firm, touched the skin of my hand. A weird current ran through my body, and the brass knob appeared to take on a life of its own. It turned under our entwined fingers and the door swung quietly open.

Our combined weights propelled us into the foyer.

"Omigod." I clamped a hand to my nose and Redfern's head slammed back as though he had run into a wall. A solid wall of stink.

I sprinted down the hall toward the solarium. What I hoped to accomplish with a two-second warning was not apparent, even to me: Run, Redfern is right behind me?

The solarium door had a stained glass window insert. It was impossible to see through it, but heavy metal music exploded through the walls. The smell of decay and rotting flesh was overwhelming in this part of the house, and I sank to my knees in front of the door, trying not to gag.

I jumped to my feet as Redfern pounded down the hall toward me, the usual look of displeasure on his face.

"Stop," I said, trying not to throw up from the smell. "You can't go in there."

With the pollen pail dangling from one wrist, I spread my limbs out, starfish style, across the door.

CHAPTER
FORTY-SIX

REDFERN REACHED OVER AND pried me off the door.

"Hey, hey! Watch the pollen." The pail slid from my wrist and rolled several metres down the hall. I dove after it. The lid was loose, but fortunately the duct tape held. I pulled the neck of my tee-shirt over my mouth and nose to stifle the stench, but it didn't help. Only the fact that I hadn't eaten since the egg salad sandwich at Timmy's kept me from hurling on Redfern's boots again. A girl could acquire quite a reputation for puking on the Chief of Police. If word got out, I'd never get a date.

Redfern slammed on the door with his fist, yelling the usual, "Open up! It's the police."

This was it. Once Redfern saw the marijuana plants, he was unlikely to allow Dougal to finish his pollination of Thor before he hauled my agoraphobic cousin away to be charged. By the time Dougal got back home, if he wasn't traumatized beyond salvation, Thor would be past his prime. And I would never get my money.

"It's not locked," I said with resignation. Good grief, testosterone has a lot to answer for.

Redfern threw me a "you just wait until later" look, not unlike the ones my parents used to give me when I misbehaved in public.

He pulled on the door and we both stepped back. Between the stench and the vibration of the music, I felt disoriented and dizzy. I pressed against Redfern for support, but he nudged me away and I reeled off to the side. I was resigned to what would follow as soon as Redfern spotted the cannabis plants.

But Redfern was staring at Thor, his eyes travelling up the length of the Titan's spadix. Soaring to within inches of the glass ceiling, Thor was magnificent.

The tall greenish spadix pretty much looked like a giant you-know-what. No wonder Victorian mamas kept their daughters away; mustn't make the young ladies titter, you know. But I bet the mamas couldn't take their own eyes off the tumescent splendour of the spadix.

The spathe was fully open now, the top curled back to display the glistening deep-burgundy interior. The plant was so unlike anything else in nature that if someone told me an alien spore had hurtled through deep space to land in Dougal's solarium and grow into this strange, beautiful creature, they'd get no argument from me.

But the smell! Holy shit what a stink. That it was coming from Thor was not in question. Orchids couldn't produce a strong scent if they tried. And we all know what marijuana smells like. Well, maybe I shouldn't make such a sweeping statement, but, believe me, pot can't drop you to your knees or make your head spin.

My streaming eyes locked on the open solarium windows — no doubt the escaping fumes had precipitated the emergency call to the police — and I dove for the nearest one.

On the way, I noticed a couple of things. First, Dougal, Chesley, and a third person were suited up in gowns and shower caps, like Glory, but these three took things to the next level. Their surgical masks were pulled up and they wore goggles. All had on latex gloves, and Dougal was brandishing a scalpel, or an X-acto knife — it was hard to tell in the brief glimpse I had on my way to the window.

There were no marijuana plants lined up against the windows. None. They were all gone. I sent an orchid flying when I draped my body halfway through the window, but I didn't pass any mature cannabis plants.

The air outside the solarium was only marginally sweeter than inside, and I was missing whatever was going on in the room behind me. I pulled my body back in and, with my hand over my nose, glanced into the far corners of the room. No tall green plants sagged under their burden of ripe buds. I knew better than to believe Dougal would stuff them all into green garbage bags and leave them out for trash pickup. They were close by.

Dougal resembled an insane scientist, not a big stretch. He held his hands up like a surgeon, the X-acto knife in one hand, the orange shower cap sliding down his forehead to rest on the top of his goggles. Chesley's shower cap was fuchsia, which did not co-ordinate with the eyes threatening to pop off his face into the cups of his goggles. Neither of them was smoking, but both seemed less concerned than they should have, facing an armed police officer, so they were likely stoned.

The third gowned figure was female by shape, but anonymous behind the getup. Here was Dougal's girl-friend, no doubt, and I would unmask her identity before I left if I had to rip away her mask to do it.

Dougal did not seem to notice Redfern, who was mute for once, his hand hovering near his gun. No, Dougal only had eyes for me.

"Bliss, have you got the pollen? Give it here."

He took the pail from my unresisting fingers. I forgot I was holding it.

He picked up a black marker and wrote something on the pail, then placed it carefully on the floor beside the concrete planter.

Only then did he seem to realize we had company. The music ceased abruptly.

"Oh. Hello. Is there something wrong?" Behind the goggles, his eyes were clear and centred. So, not stoned.

Redfern's eyes were streaming, but they darted every-where in the room, searching for the source of the stench.

It took a couple of tries, but he managed to choke out a few words. "Mr. Seabrook, we have had a report of a putrid smell emanating from your premises. The smell of decaying flesh is how it was described."

"It's my Titan Arum, Thor." Even through the mask, I could hear the pride in Dougal's voice.

"Uh huh. Care to explain what's going on?" Redfern finally gave in and wiped his face.

"Sure. When a Titan Arum blossoms, usually at night, the spadix, that's this tall structure here, heats up. The heat releases the smell, which is made up of sulphur compounds, and allows it to be carried farther afield. In the plant's natural habitat, the odour attracts flies and this increases the chances of pollination. In some cultures, the Titan Arum is referred to as the 'corpse flower,' since the odour mimics the smell of rotting flesh. I'm surprised Bliss didn't tell you."

"Tell him?" I screamed. "You didn't tell me! Yesterday, when I mentioned the smell, you ignored me. So don't go telling people I knew, you moron."

Dougal tugged his mask down, then quickly pulled it up again before mumbling, "Well, now you know."

The fumes were making me dizzy, or maybe it was rage at Dougal's arrogance. I staggered closer to the Titan's container and stopped cold.

"What have you done to Thor?" I asked. A neat square, about six inches by six, had been sliced into the base of the spathe. The interior was mostly pink with a row of cream on top.

"I'm preparing to dust on the pollen you just brought from Sif, and I'm collecting Thor's pollen for Sif. I'll have to make a few more holes. Ches and I are also going to dust some of Thor's own pollen on a few places and then wait to see which pollen works best. Glory's going to do the same at her end. We'll keep—"

"Yes, all very interesting," Redfern interrupted, coughing between words, "but how long will this smell last? You're gassing this whole end of town."

"Oh, did one of my neighbours complain? I think

I'll call around and ask everyone on the block to come over and see Thor. They can watch me pollinate."

"It's after midnight," I pointed out.

"But this is a once in a lifetime opportunity. I should have called in the Press, but at least I have it all on camera. Ches is taking photographs, and I have the video camera going."

"I suggest you don't alert the neighbourhood, but Mr. Sutton next door might appreciate a call." Redfern sounded rather nasal, like he was trying to talk through his nose and breathe through his mouth. Good luck to him; it wasn't working for me. Even my stomach was burning and the tears were trying to wash my eyeballs out.

Redfern appeared to have had enough of alien plants and mad botanists. He turned to leave, but just as I thought we were home free, Simon stuck his head out of his cage. It was a miracle the bird hadn't croaked from the stench. No such luck. He seemed fine, chipper even, as he fluttered to the floor.

Then, clear enough that I recognized my own voice, the bird shouted, "Pass the grass, please."

"It's that fucking parrot," Redfern observed with a stunning grasp of the obvious. He looked at me. I shrugged.

"Pass the grass!" Simon screamed again. Surely my voice never sounded that shrill.

Just when I believed the worst day of my life couldn't get any worse, I spotted an inch-long frond of *Cannabis sativa* leaf lying on the floor between Simon and Redfern.

CHAPTER
FORTY-SEVEN

"THE BIRD IS JUST learning to talk," I said, edging closer to the leaf. "He uses someone's voice and makes up absurd stories. Ignore him."

I planted my foot casually over the fragment of greenery. If the solarium didn't smell like an overripe corpse, Redfern would have spotted it first, and, thanks to Simon, I would probably be blamed.

To my relief, Redfern left without further comment, but not before giving me one of those "I'm watching you" looks on the way out. Strange how we communicated so well without words. I waited until the front door slammed, then reached down and picked up the leaf.

I walked over to Dougal and handed it to him "You should have told Redfern the address of the other Titan. If one of Glory's neighbours calls the police over the smell, Redfern will be pissed. He's running out of patience." And his reaction when he saw Glory's fine crop of cannabis would be nothing I wanted to witness, but I didn't tell Dougal that.

He shrugged and bent to pick up an aluminum pail from the floor. "I didn't think of it, and I don't have time to call her now. I have to harvest Thor's pollen, so you can take it over to her. You can warn her then. Now, stand out of the way, will you?"

I backed up a pace. "What happened to your … you know? Where is it?"

Chesley handed him a makeup brush. Dougal twirled it over the cream-coloured male parts, and I watched copious small specks fall into the pail he held underneath.

"My crop? I started to think about the odour Thor would produce and decided it would be prudent to move it. Turns out I was right. You led the cops right to the door."

"First of all, Dougal, I've been warning you for days to get rid of your pot. And I didn't bring Redfern. He arrived the same time I did. You should have warned me about the smell, which, by the way, is not getting any better."

"And it won't improve for another twenty-four hours. Go sit outside on the front steps and wait if you find the odour so offensive."

"So, where's your pot? I don't want to accidentally find it in the pantry or kitchen cabinet one fine day."

"It's nowhere you will stumble across it."

I gave up. Who cared, anyway? Then I looked over at Chesley and happened to catch his eyes blinking with guilty precision behind his goggles, like Morse code.

"It's in the back of your Volkswagen, isn't it, Chesley?"

"No!" Chesley moved closer to Dougal as though for protection. Dougal elbowed him aside and continued flicking his brush over Thor's male blossoms.

"How did you get the pots in that little car? Redfern walked right past the Beetle."

Chesley took umbrage at that question. He said, huffily, "The containers are all stacked neatly beside the garden shed. The plants are in bags."

"So, are you planning to hang the plants from the shower rod in your motel room to dry? Is your mother into toking, too?" I couldn't decide which one of them was the bigger idiot, my cousin who grew the stuff openly in his home, or Chesley who was planning to drive around with it in his car.

At the mention of Ivy, Chesley gave a full-body shudder and edged closer to the mystery woman. I turned my attention away from Chesley.

"Hi. Can we introduce ourselves? I'm Bliss Cornwall, Dougal's cousin. And you are?"

Dougal looked up from his brush and bucket. "Get lost, Bliss."

I'd had enough of him for one day. "Fuck off," I replied, and turned back to the woman. I waited expectantly.

She pulled her goggles up and the mask down. "It's me, Bliss. Holly."

Holly Duffett? From the Second Hand Rose Shop? She was Dougal's girlfriend? I was rendered speechless for a minute.

Her husband was a successful real estate developer who was throwing up high-end condos and McMansions all along the shores of Lake Huron, from Tobermory to Goderich.

No wonder it was such a big secret. Then I reminded myself it was Not My Business.

"Okay, well, good luck." I started to walk to the door to sit on the front stoop as suggested.

"Wait, Bliss." Holly put out a gloved hand and stopped me. "Dougal, honey, I think it's okay if we tell Bliss."

"She'll blab all over town, but it's up to you, Hol."

"She won't. She's family."

Dougal and I glowered at each other at that statement.

"Maybe we could go outside, Bliss?"

"Let's."

A door led from the solarium to the backyard. Light from the windows allowed us to locate a pair of deck chairs on the patio, and we pulled them closer. Thor's odour reached us there, too, but at least it was bearable.

I said, "Look, Holly. You don't have to tell me anything, really. What you and Dougal have going is your own business, and I'm making a real effort not to get involved with other peoples' lives. It's just that, with the agoraphobia this past year, he's needed me. In a way, I feel like the mother of a small child, not knowing if it's the right time to let go."

"I do understand, Bliss. Dougal would not have been able to get through this period in his life without your help. He still can't leave the house for more than a few minutes at a time, but he resents the fact he needs help at all, and takes it out on you. I know you two have a sibling relationship. You fight a lot, but care for each other deeply."

"Well, sure." Dougal and I had been raised almost as brother and sister, but he wouldn't take a bullet for me. And vice versa.

"Anyway, I want to tell you about our relationship."

"Please don't." I had heard enough from Simon's squawking and didn't want further details.

Holly laughed. "I mean, how we met and where it's going, and all that."

"So, how did you meet?" A house-bound agoraphobic would be the last man on my to-do list. On the other hand, you couldn't misplace him.

"Elise Boudreau called the shop about six months ago and said her employer had been going through the house and had gathered a lot of clothes and furniture together from his late parents. I stopped in to have a look and decide what the shop could resell. There was an immediate and very strong attraction between us."

Enough of that. When I got to know her a little better, I would suggest she put the parrot in another room during her intimate moments with my cousin.

I said, "Got it. Understood. But, what about your … um, husband?"

"Our marriage has been over for a long time. I know Harvey has a mistress, and I'm not sure why he hasn't left me yet, but …"

"Holly! Do something, now. Find an honest lawyer, not in Lockport, and make sure you get a fair settlement. Otherwise, you'll end up like me!"

"Bliss, I know. I've spent the past year trying to arrange my affairs. I've got quite a bit stashed away in a private account in my name, but I know Harvey has a lot more. I don't want to wipe him out, just ensure I can go back to school if I want and can invest enough to live on when I'm old. I've been scanning financial records and bank statements, anything I can find around the house. But I have no access to the business records."

"Never mind the honest lawyer. You need a shark."

"I have an appointment with a divorce lawyer in Toronto next week. I want to hit Harvey with a subpoena before he has time to hide our joint assets. Watching you struggle these past couple of years has taught me the value of awareness and stealth."

"Really? I taught you that?"

"Well, I didn't want to get blindsided, like you were. Harvey is probably arranging his business so it looks like he has no money on paper. I'll just get the house and a portion of our investments, but that's fine. That's all I want."

"I suggest you go for his throat."

"Anyway, I'm very fond of Dougal, and we'll see where fate takes us. As soon as he's able to travel, and my divorce is started, we plan to take a cruise. Just to see how we get along, away from familiar surroundings."

An agoraphobic, even a former one, on a cruise, with open skies and endless water? I'd sign on as a deckhand to see that.

"Sounds fun," I said to Holly. "Before I forget, I'm sorry I borrowed your skirt the other day. I was in dire need of some clothes and found it in Dougal's closet. I'll return it as soon as I can get back into my trailer."

"I couldn't believe it when you came in the store wearing that skirt. I was afraid my face would give me away."

"I'm just not that bright, Holly, as you'll soon learn."

"You're the bravest woman I know," Holly replied. "You could have given up years ago, but you've kept on fighting for your rights, and you inspire me to do the same."

Our situations were nothing alike, but, heck, I wasn't often admired, so I let it ride.

Dougal shouted through the open window, "Bliss! I've gathered the pollen. Get it over to Glory right away. Don't stop for anything."

I took the metal pail, and the stench emanating from the window surrounded me like a cloud of decaying ectoplasm. I called to Chesley, "If you don't call your mother and let her see Thor blossoming, she'll never forgive you. Just my opinion."

Before heading to Glory's, I walked around the house to the front door, still unlocked. In the kitchen, I foraged through the refrigerator. It was bare except for an empty milk carton and a plastic-wrapped slice of pizza. I sniffed it and decided I couldn't tell if it was edible due to Thor's body odour enveloping the kitchen. Hoping the green spots were olives, I slung the bucket of pollen over my arm and hit the sidewalk.

I felt like Little Red Riding Hood trotting off to the wolf's lair. For some reason, with that analogy in mind, I remembered I hadn't told Redfern about seeing Snake outside the cemetery.

Snake was still at large. And I had to wonder why Redfern turned up at Dougal's house in response to a nuisance call when he should be out hunting Snake. Maybe he was simply overtired and showed bad judgment. Or maybe ... Doubts concerning Redfern's motives hit me again. Maybe he was deliberately giving Snake time to escape. I felt more sad than angry at the thought.

I stopped and looked around at the quiet streets and misty darkness. Maybe it had been a mistake to leave my bike on the street in plain view of …

What if Snake was still in Lockport?

That was enough to take the skip out of my step. I started running, and didn't stop until I reached Glory's door. I looked back at my Savage parked at the curb as I rang the doorbell.

Pan answered this time, dressed in black pants and white smock.

He yanked the lime green shower cap from his head when he saw my glance.

"It's totally you," I said.

"Finally. The Royal Pain has been ripping strips off me ever since you picked up Sif's pollen. Give it here."

I passed over the pail. My job was done, and a thousand dollars was almost in my bank account. If the swamp deal and the Barrister house sale both fell through, at least I could pay my rent for the next couple of months. The thought of returning to Hemp Hollow made my stomach flip.

"Her Surliness said to remind you about Monday. You promised her three days a week, starting Monday."

I was tempted to shove the shower cap past his smirking lips and down his throat, but, instead, I said, "Pan, do me a favour? Do you see my bike parked on the other side of the fence? Would you watch from the door until I drive away?"

He grudgingly agreed and, before he changed his mind, I ran to the curb, started the Savage, and sped off.

I just wanted to shut myself into a motel room with my friend, the hooker, and hold off tomorrow.

CHAPTER
FORTY-EIGHT

A GIANT SPIDER CHASED me through the cemetery
and Redfern tried to shoot it. He had a yellow shower cap
on his head and was eating a brownie with his free hand.
The spider made a loud ringing sound as it snapped its
giant mandibles at the back of my fleeing head.

The spider morphed into my BlackBerry that I had
placed on the night stand before falling into the twin bed
beside Rae's. Without looking at the call display, I pushed
the talk button as my one open eye landed on the clock
radio. Seven a.m.?

"Yah, what?"

"Bliss? It's me. Can we meet?" a man's voice whispered.

"Do you realize what time it is? And, who are you?"

"It's me, Mike," he said. "I have a deal for you."

I bolted straight up in bed. "Tell me what you're
offering."

"Not on the phone. Can you meet me at Timmy's in
ten minutes?"

"Be serious. Make it an hour, and why are you whispering?"

"Because I don't want … Okay, an hour."

I ran to the bathroom, pulling down the hem of Rae's spare tee-shirt to cover my bare butt. Rae had thrown my underwear and tee-shirt into the shower with me when I arrived at the motel only five hours earlier. She made me shampoo my hair three times and I had been surprised at the debris that had washed out — sticks, leaves, a tiny pinecone, and a couple of things with legs.

I felt the underwear and tee-shirt. Damp. And my socks were sodden.

"Was that your ex-husband?" Rae asked from the doorway. Her pink pyjamas had purple penguins barbecuing tiny fish on them and her hair was dishevelled, but I was betting she would look gorgeous in half the time it would take me to get a comb through my one-ten-volt hairdo.

"Yes, he's going to make an offer. I'll have to run back to the trailer and get some clothes. I can wear my jeans and my jacket for the ride. God help me if I have another accident and wind up in the hospital with no underwear or bra. My mother would never forgive me."

"You know you can't go to Hemp Hollow today, Bliss. Give me those things and I'll throw them in the dryer. There's one in the office. In the meantime, take another shower and wash your hair again. And this time use conditioner. Oh, and I brought a new tooth-brush for you, too."

"You'll make somebody a wonderful wife, Rae."

She gave me a rueful smile and rushed out with my clothes. Twenty minutes later, I was wrapped in a couple of towels and Rae was French braiding my wet hair.

"This will stay in all day, even under your helmet," she said, and gave my hair another powerful twist.

"Oww, Rae, let up a bit, will you? At this rate, I won't need a face lift for another forty years."

She insisted on applying some makeup, just a little blush, mascara, and lip gloss. After I put my clothes on, she handed me my cell and jacket and shoved me out the door.

Chesley had his head inside the Beetle, sniffing the seats. His rear end was encased in black jeans, and was that pollen clinging to the back pockets?

"Just getting in, Chesley?"

He pulled his head out and whirled around, then glanced at the door next to Rae's.

"Yes. I came for Mum as you suggested so she could see Thor blossoming. We just got back and Mum has already gone to bed. I need to catch a few hours of sleep myself. Then ..."

His eyes slid to the trunk of the silver Beetle.

I followed his glance. "Are you telling me you shoved all Dougal's plants into that tiny space? No way."

"Shh." He moved closer. "I told you we pulled them out of the containers. We shook the dirt from the roots and then compressed the plants as much as possible. There are only two garbage bags in there."

"Well, what are you going to do with them?" He was as bad as my energy-sucking black hole of a cousin.

"I was hoping you would help me.... Wait, Bliss! I want to dump the plants somewhere outside of town where they can decompose organically. I thought you might know of a safe ditch or woodlot where I can scatter the plants."

"There are plenty of such places around here. Just find a back road and there you go. How did Dougal talk you into this anyhow?"

"He's my friend. He can't go outside yet, so I said I'd help him out. After Mum came over, we discussed the possibility of Dougal becoming a shareholder in our new venture here in Lockport. So, he's a partner now, as well as a friend. We talked to Glory on the phone, and she says she's interested, too."

"So, you and Ivy are serious about relocating to Lockport? Are you buying the Barrister house, that's what I need to know? And, what about my wetland? I'm just heading to a meeting now about selling it, so if you and your mother want it, you need to speak up now. Going, going, almost gone."

"Oh God, Bliss, yes! We decided on the Barrister property the first time we looked at it. The house may have to be demolished, despite what Mum thinks, but the land is just what we want. We're offering one-forty, so if you want to fill out the purchase agreement and bring it over later, we're prepared to finalize it today."

One-forty. I tried to do the commission calculation in my head, but my body overran with adrenaline and my brain shut down.

"What about the swamp?" I ran my fingers over the inside pocket where the tax receipt reposed, right next to the photo of the Weasel.

"I want to see it, of course. Mum can't negotiate uneven ground with her cane, so she has to rely on my opinion."

"I understand that, Chesley. And I want you and your mother to have the swamp. You don't know how much I want that, but what do I do if my other client makes a firm offer?"

"Can you stall your client, Bliss? Just for today? I want to see the *Cypripedium parviflorum* in blossom and take a look at the rest of the property first. And …" He paused and lowered his voice again. "I really have to get rid of the bags in the back." He patted the Beetle's trunk meaningfully.

Who was I to disparage blackmail? I had used it on Glory, and was on my way to do the same to the Weasel.

"Fine, Chesley. I'll see what I can do to stall my client. I'll be back around noon with the purchase papers for the Barrister place. Once you sign them, you and I will take a ride to the swamp to see the lady's slippers, with a little side trip for some organic composting."

CHAPTER
FORTY-NINE

I WAS TEN MINUTES late and, as I ordered a bottle of orange juice, a fruit explosion muffin, cheese croissant, and a large double double, I spotted the Weasel at a corner table. He was sipping coffee and pretending not to see me.

No one paid any attention to us as I sat opposite him and spread my food out on the table and started to eat. It was his move.

He watched me drain the juice bottle and scarf down the croissant. By the time I took the lid off my coffee and began picking away at the muffin, he still hadn't spoken. He had his lawyer face on, expressionless yet somehow arrogant. Only his rage-filled eyes gave any indication of emotion.

I smiled and plucked another finger-full of muffin. And waited. But my heart was hammering, and I knew this was the most meaningful discussion we would ever have.

Finally, he took a piece of paper out of his shirt pocket and threw it at me.

"This is what I'm prepared to give you."

I looked at the figure written on the scrap in Mike's neat hand. It wasn't a half million — just half of that. I folded the piece of paper once, then again and again, until it was too small to fold any more.

I looked into my former husband's hot eyes and said, "This is less than the house is worth. It doesn't even take into account our investments and savings."

"It's all I'm prepared to offer you. It's all I *can* offer you."

"Really? Somehow, I doubt that, but let me think a minute." I was silent for a few minutes, trying to weigh my odds of squeezing more out of the Weasel. They weren't high, I decided.

I took the picture out of my jacket pocket and looked at it.

Mike said furiously, "Put that away. Don't just wave it around like it was our wedding picture." His hand inched toward the picture, but I returned it to my pocket.

"To get back to the matter at hand," I said. "If I accept your offer, it doesn't include the swamp."

His face darkened with blood, and I was afraid he would throw himself across the table at my throat. Instead, he clenched his hands on the tabletop.

"Of course the fifty acres are included. What do you think I'm giving you this money for?" His voice was filled with restrained fury.

Now I felt anger flood my veins and explode in my brain. I was finding it difficult to think clearly, and had to make a concerted effort to stay calm.

"I was hoping you thought of handing over this money as doing the right thing, not buying something from me."

"I need the wetland, Bliss. You know I've promised to donate it to the province, and it might hurt my chances of nomination if I have to renege on that promise."

"That is not my problem, Mike. You can do one of two things: print a retraction in the paper saying the first article was a mistake, that you never meant to donate anything. Or pick up another swamp somewhere else in Bruce County and donate it. I'm sure if there are spotted turtles in my swamp, there will be spotted turtles in other swamps in the county. But you are not buying me off, as well as my swamp, for two-fifty."

"What will it take to get the sw ... the wetland?"

"It will take five hundred thousand."

"I won't pay it! You're crazy."

"Probably. But you asked me, and I told you."

"I'll give you three hundred."

I considered, but finally said, "Not enough." I doubted the Belcourts would offer fifty thousand for the swamp, but I did not want the Weasel to have it. I would donate it to the province myself before I'd hand it over to him.

"You ran me off the road Thursday night, didn't you?" I asked. It was quite clear he would do anything to get his hands on that land. Did he try to kill me, or just hope to incapacitate me for a while so the tax deadline would pass and he could scoop up the swamp?

"You're crazy," he said again, and leaned away from me. He did look shocked, but, then, guilt was not part of his emotional repertoire. "You'd better not say that in public, Bliss. I'll have you charged …"

"Sure. Okay. Let's move on, shall we? I think it's your turn." I caressed my pocket.

His eyes followed my fingers and he said tightly, "What do I get for two-fifty?"

"As I said earlier, you get to feel like an honest man, and maybe there will be a little bonus in it for you."

"How do I know you haven't made a copy and plan to post it on the Net?"

"As if I'd even know how to do that," I said truthfully.

He was silent for a long moment, then said, "Okay, give it here and I'll write you a cheque."

My heart gave a great leap, but I said, "I have a better idea. We'll leave here and meet at the bank. Once the money is in my account and I have a copy of the receipt, I promise to relinquish the item. How's that?"

"Why should I trust you?"

"Can you think of any other way to do it that doesn't involve a third party to witness the handover of the object in question?"

Of course he couldn't. We were the first customers when the bank opened for business, and it surprised me how quickly such a large transaction could take place. The teller couldn't keep the curiosity from her eyes as she transferred the money from the Weasel's account and deposited it into mine.

The photo handover took place in the alley between the bank and the Mason Jar Cafe. No words were exchanged. After I watched the Weasel walk away in the direction of the municipal building, moving like he had a nine-iron up his rear, I went back into the bank and withdrew two hundred dollars.

My next stop was Elaine Simms's realty office. Elaine was just on her way out, but she asked her sister Rachel to help me fill out the purchase forms on the Barrister property for the Belcourts to sign. Elaine was sure the Barrister heirs would accept the offer without a sign back. When I told her the Belcourts might make an offer on my fifty acres, she promised to help me with that, too, for a small fee, if the need arose.

With the purchase agreement in hand, I stopped at the Chin Chin Restaurant and bought a huge takeout order of Chinese food. It would be early for lunch when I got back to the motel, but I wanted Chesley and Ivy to sign the papers without delay. It was time to show me the colour of their money, or get their city asses out of my town.

And if they did come through, I needed to be fuelled up and ready to go with Chesley for our walk on the wild side. I didn't know which I found more daunting, a pack of spotted turtles, or two bags of wacky 'baccy.

CHAPTER
FIFTY

THE CEMENT PAD IN front of the motel units was a scene of chilling domesticity. Ivy, Chesley — and Rae — sat on webbed lawn chairs around a patio table. And the scariest part? Ivy was laughing at something Rae was saying, her red gash of a mouth open wide in hilarity. She thumped her cane on the cement with each guffaw. Even from the highway, I could see Chesley gazing at Rae with rapt attention and, as I drew closer, the expression on his face as she talked to his mother sent me a big uh-oh.

Chesley caught sight of me and jumped up, waving enthusiastically. I wanted to accelerate back to the highway and keep going, but the plastic bag of hot food was burning my thighs.

By the time I parked the Savage and extracted the purchase papers from the saddlebag, Chesley had gallantly produced another lawn chair for me.

"Chinese food for everyone," I called.

"Ms. Cornwall," Ivy said jovially, "your young friend here has been amusing us with stories of her clients' exploits."

The carton of chicken fried rice flew out of my hands into Chesley's lap. Luckily, I hadn't opened it yet.

"You know, Bliss," Rae said quickly, "my clients at the pool. I'm trying to convince Ivy to come out for some classes when she moves here. The exercises we do are beneficial for people with arthritis, and, with time, Ivy should be able to walk without her cane."

Chesley's lips opened and closed, but no sound came out. His eyes remained on Rae's face, worshipping her wholesomeness. Rae had done nothing more than brush her hair into a ponytail, throw on denim cut-offs and a black tee-shirt, and apply some discreet makeup over the last of the facial bruising. But that was plenty. She had charmed Chesley with her looks, and Ivy with her personality. It made me wish I had something to work with other than animal cunning and my candid wit. Yeah, I'm kidding, but I do have big brown eyes and killer cheekbones.

We were all silent for a few minutes as we sorted out the containers and heaped food onto our paper plates.

"Bliss, how did your, um, meeting go this morning?" Rae asked.

"It went great. Better than I thought it would," I replied. I gave her a thumbs-up, and the smile she sent me caused her face to glow. I thought Chesley would start drooling soon. He hadn't taken his eyes from her, not even to look at his fork as he lifted it from his plate.

"Chesley, wipe your chin," ordered Ivy. "You have orange sauce dripping onto your shirt."

"Bliss, guess what?" said Rae, seemingly unaware of what Chesley was doing to her in his mind. She was used to it, but I was betting it was new ground for him.

"Couldn't possibly," I replied, helping myself to more sesame chicken.

"Ivy — oh, and Chesley, too, of course ..." She bestowed such a dazzling smile on that unfortunate man that he vibrated in his chair. "... have offered me a job when their new greenhouse is ready."

I looked up from my food. "As what?"

Ivy's booming voice took over. "This dear child told us about her ambition to open her own day spa someday. But her dream can become reality only if she saves her money for a few more years, so Chesley and I want her to be the first person our customers see, or hear on the phone. We think she would be perfect."

Ivy's neatly groomed grey hair tickled my nose as she reached across the table and yanked the Mein Feng from my limp fingers. She emptied the container and looked around for more. I handed her the shrimp with broccoli.

"Shit," I said, looking down at my plate, "this chow mein is full of celery. I hate celery."

I sensed Ivy's attention shift from the shrimp and settle on me.

"And you, Ms. Cornwall. We shall have a job for you, too. If you would be interested, that is."

"That's very nice of you, Mrs. Belcourt," I replied politely as I pushed the celery to one side of my plate. "But I don't know anything about horticulture or botany. I don't even know the difference between the two."

"We feel you would be a superlative interface between our suppliers and the company. Someone with a … a strong personality is required to prevent the many mistakes in inventory to which our industry is prone. I feel certain you can keep everything organized for us. And we can teach you everything you need to know about the business."

The chances of me working in a humid greenhouse, especially one owned by the Belcourts, ranged from fat to slim. But, I couldn't bear to disappoint her, not until she signed the agreement to purchase.

"I had a frank discussion with your cousin, Dougal, and his ex-wife, Miss Glory Yates. This was last night, of course. Both Dougal and Glory are prepared to invest in our new Lockport business, and both Titan Arums will hold pride of place in the new greenhouse. We will be doing some groundbreaking work in attempting to hasten maturity of the new corms."

"You do know, Mrs. Belcourt, that Dougal and Glory are … well, there's still a bit of tension between them."

"I suspected that, but I'm sure they can act civilly toward one another on the few occasions they are forced to interact … board meetings for example."

As long as they don't hold board meetings in a glass-walled enclosure like a greenhouse.

"That's just great, Mrs. Belcourt, but don't you need to buy some property to fulfill this wonderful dream?"

"Of course I do, Ms. Cornwall. Is that the purchase agreement under your chair with a cellphone on top?"

Ivy read every word of the agreement, and only when the sun completed its balancing act on top of the world and began its slow descent to the west did she finally put her signature on the paper. I sighed with relief as Chesley signed in turn and handed the papers back to me.

"Now, are you in the mood for a nice piece of wet-land?" I asked Ivy. "I have a special, today only, on fifty acres of prime property along Bird River. It comes complete with spotted turtles and yellow lady's slippers, and there are many other botanical specimens to delight the most discriminating horticulturist."

"*Cypripedium parviflorum*, Mum," said Chesley, meaningfully.

Ivy's mouth turned up in a wintery smile. "Lovely. Ms. Cornwall, a firm offer will be contingent on Chesley's report. Chesley, take your camera when you accompany this young lady to the property. If it is indeed a spotted turtle sanctuary, we will honour that, but I want to see for myself."

Hell, if it made her happy, I'd strap one of the smaller turtles to the back of my Savage and transport it to the motel for her to personally inspect.

"Yes, Mum," Chesley replied.

Ivy had taken no prisoners, food-wise, and I began to scoop the empty containers into the plastic bag. If Chesley had forgotten his trunkful of contraband, I hadn't. Already, I was sure I could detect the sweet odour of cannabis oozing from the Beetle.

"But," Ivy put out a knobby, bejewelled hand to stop my cleanup efforts, "Ms. Cornwall, if Chesley returns with a positive report, we are prepared to offer forty-two thousand for your property."

"Gee, Mrs. Belcourt, I just turned down an offer for fifty this morning. But fifty-five will bring it home."

"Fifty-one," she countered.

"Fifty-four."

"Fifty-two, and that's my final offer." Ivy held my eyes, and I gave her a nod.

"Done," I said. In your face, Weasel. I wanted to do the happy dance, but resisted. It wasn't a done deal yet.

But I had won two victories already today — the Barrister house sale and, much more lucrative, my settlement with the Weasel. Not to mention the thousand dollars from Dougal for helping to pollinate Thor and Sif. And the day wasn't over.

Rae interrupted this pleasant reverie. "Bliss, you and Chesley go ahead. I'll clean up here, then I'll make some tea for Ivy. Do you like Earl Grey, Ivy?"

Chesley and I left them to debate the merits of Earl Grey versus the more delicate flavour of Lady Earl Grey. What the hell was Lady Earl Grey, anyhow?

"Bliss," Chesley whispered to me as we stopped by the side of the Beetle. "Do you know where we can drop the stuff?"

"Yes," I said. "Yes, I do." The idea had popped into my head that very minute. I decided not to tell him I could smell the stuff clearly over the skunk stink still rising from the leather seats. I pegged Chesley as the nervous sort and didn't want him driving up my fender.

"Well, can we do it first, before we look over the property?"

"A good idea, Chesley. The place I have in mind is just north of here, not far at all, so we won't have to pass the police station. After that, we'll circle back and I'll show you the home of the spotted turtle and the *Cypri*-whatsit."

"Is the dump site safe?"

Dump site? Somebody had been watching too much *CSI*.

"Yes, Chesley. It's safe, it's ironic, and just a little bit naughty."

"Naughty?"

"Let's ride. Follow me, but not too closely."

CHAPTER
FIFTY-ONE

THE SUN THRUST FINGERS of light through the canopy of pines and dusted the forest floor with golden flecks. A few birds called to one another above our heads, but otherwise the woodland behind Hemp Hollow was silent. It was a dead kind of quiet, and I thought of the mauled body of the unfortunate Jerry. Except the coywolf hadn't killed Jerry. He had been hacked to death by a human hand.

I shivered and lowered my voice to a whisper. "Right here, Chesley. Rip the bags and dump them, but fold up the bags and put them in your pocket. You don't want to leave any fingerprints."

"I wouldn't leave plastic bags lying around in the woods."

Through the trees, I glimpsed the small clearing behind the Quigley trailer and a pile of freshly cut firewood. I glanced at the roof of the lean-to at the back of the trailer, but no smoke drifted from the metal chimney.

Something wasn't right. Dumping Dougal's marijuana behind the home of the local pot dealer and Baker of earthly delights had seemed like a good idea when I was sitting on a lawn chair separating celery from the other vegetables on my plate. Now, it just seemed childish.

"Bliss, I'm done. Can we go now and see the wetland?"

I looked down at the pile of cannabis leaves at our feet. "Let's kick it around a bit so it can dry up faster. Wait!"

"What's wrong? That's all there is."

I moved the weed with the toe of my shoe.

"These are just leaves and stalks," I said to Chesley. "Where are the buds?"

Chesley managed to look insulted. "You can't throw out the flowering tops. There's more resin in the tops than the leaves, hence more THC, the active ingredient."

"It was my impression that Dougal was out of the pot-growing business."

"That's true. He isn't going to grow another crop, but that doesn't mean we're going to waste this batch."

"So, Dougal thinks he's doing a good thing by keeping the buds and asking you to dispose of the less valuable leaves?"

"Yes. Can we go now, Bliss? This place gives me the creeps." He hitched up his pants and looked around.

Chesley was the only man I knew who wore both a belt and suspenders. I guessed he was pantsed a lot in high school.

"First, I want to drop into my trailer and pick up a few things. Just a quick in and out and we'll be gone." I needed a change of clothes and Redfern surely couldn't freak out about that. I suspected Ewan Quigley was the second man in the cemetery last night with Snake and both of them had already been arrested, or had fled to a city where biker gangs were active.

"Come with me, Chesley." We moved through the trees and crossed over the path bisecting the woods until we came to the clearing behind my trailer.

"You live here, Bliss?" I could hear the wonder in Chesley's tone and bet Mum had always kept a better-appointed roof over his head than a rundown trailer on the wrong side of town.

"Not for long," I replied. "My ship just sailed into harbour. But I need some clothes. That's Rae's on the left, by the way."

As we walked between Rae's trailer and mine, we heard a bang, then several more.

"Rae's door is open, Bliss," Chesley said. "And look at the windows, they're broken. And so are yours."

"Check inside Rae's trailer, Chesley. I'll go into mine."

My door was closed, but the small window set into it had only a few jagged shards left. Glass from the rest of the windows lay on the ground, surrounding the front of the trailer. Someone had broken the glass in the door to gain entrance, then smashed the other windows from the inside.

I stepped inside the trailer.

Stuffing spilled from the bench to the floor like a waterfall of white cotton. The tabletop lay crookedly against one wall. Even the door of the fridge hung by one hinge. I had to step over the smashed microwave in the hallway to reach my bedroom, where I found the same degree of ruin. The mattress and bedclothes were in tatters and the plastic tote boxes where I kept my clothes had been upended onto the floor. The clothes had been ripped to shreds.

Only the bathroom had not been vandalized, and I was relieved my boxes of mementoes in the shower stall were intact.

I turned and ran for the door, where I found Chesley standing at the bottom of the steps. His Adam's apple bobbed as he tried to swallow.

"Rae's trailer has been totalled, Bliss. Even the metal support pole has been pulled down."

"I think we better get out of here, Chesley."

"Shouldn't we call the police?"

"We'll do it from the motel. Let's go."

I was halfway between the trailers, heading for the path, when I realized Chesley had stopped and was staring across the muddy compound. I went back and pulled on his sleeve.

He shook me off and said, "Look there, Bliss. The windows on that trailer are broken, too. And the door is open."

"That trailer belongs to the local drug dealer. Come on, Chesley, pick up those feet and let's make tracks."

"We have to check, Bliss. Someone could be in there, hurt." He started across the compound, and was at the Quigley's door by the time I caught up to him.

"Stop," I whispered. "Do you hear anything?"

We waited, but the only sound was a faucet dripping. I edged through the door first.

"Oh, God, what is that smell?" Chesley placed a hand over his mouth and nose.

"That's blood, Chesley, lots of it. Let's get out."

"Okay. No, wait! What's that?"

That was a body, splayed out on the floor, covered with debris and broken glass. The face had no discernible features. It was slashed in a dozen places, like Jerry's in the woods. The head tilted to one side, and I recognized the stubby grey ponytail at the back of the neck. A wide gash split the throat. The body lay in a puddle of blood, and more had spurted over the walls and cupboards. Crimson spray decorated the ceiling.

Ewan Quigley's drug dealing days were behind him.

Chesley ran out the door and pulled out his phone. I heard him tell the 911 operator a body had been found in a trailer. He looked questioningly at me, and I replied, "Hemp Hollow." I stumbled outside after him, finally able to tear my eyes away from Ewan's corpse.

Chopped to death by a hatchet. I felt hysterical laughter begin its ascent from deep in my throat, and to prevent its escape, I said quickly, "Right, run. Run between the other two trailers and through the path. Our vehicles are in the field. Go!"

Too late. Too late to run.

CHAPTER
FIFTY-TWO

SARAH QUIGLEY STEPPED IN front of us, blocking our escape. I heard Chesley choke on his breath as he backed up a step. My feet were rooted to the earth and my eyes could not translate an acceptable image to my brain.

Her naked body was striped with blood. Red rivulets ran down her face from her matted hair and dripped onto the ground.

I pushed against Chesley to make him move, but then stopped when I saw the axe in her right hand. I couldn't look away from the blade as she slowly raised her arm.

One glance at her expression and I knew Sarah had stepped through the door into insanity. In her hate-filled eyes, I saw the promise of my death.

"Get ready to run when I give the word, Chesley. Don't look back no matter what you hear. Keep running until you get to the highway."

Sarah took a step closer, and I said, "Now!"

Chesley's muscular legs carried him across the compound in seconds. Sarah turned to watch him run, but, as I hoped, she chose to concentrate on me. I used her momentary distraction to step sideways so my back was no longer against the trailer.

She advanced another step and I whispered, "Sarah, put the axe down and we'll talk. You don't want to do this." I could see Ewan's blood cracking on her skin as it dried. Her nude body was sinewy and tense, as dangerous as a cornered cobra.

"Yes. I do," she corrected, in a child-like voice. "I killed Jerry and I killed Ewan, too. Now I'll kill you. Then I'll look for that whore and kill her. Then it will be done."

Stall, Cornwall, stall. Chesley would have called 911 again. Redfern would come. He would be here any minute.

"Why did you kill Jerry and Ewan, Sarah?"

She hefted the axe, testing the weight of the handle. Reaching out, she felt the edge of the blood-stained blade with a thumb. I flinched, imagining the pain as the blade slammed into my body, over and over.

"Jerry was one of our runners. He wanted a bigger cut. Ewan and I knew we'd have to do something about him, so, when he came back after Ewan and Snake laid a beating on him for what he did to that whore, well, I decided to deal with it myself. You can't rely on men, you know. Sometimes you have to do things yourself."

"Where did you kill him?"

She cackled suddenly, then choked on some phlegm in her throat. "Did it right in the shed where we dry the product. It was an awful mess, but a few gallons of bleach took care of most of it. Ewan dragged Jerry out in the woods and left him. Damn fool! He should have put him in the truck right away and dumped the body far away. But he left it in our own backyard. He said he meant to move it later that night, but then you and that blonde whore found it. Bitches!"

"That explains Jerry, Sarah. But what about Ewan? Why did you kill your husband?" I knew I had to keep talking. But my brain was shutting down.

If I ran, I had no doubt she would swing that axe and drop me like a stone. The muscles running up her arms looked as strong as rope.

She could barely force words from lips twisted with rage.

"Ewan was going to leave me. He was packing, saying with Jerry's body and the cops poking around the product, he was leaving with Snake. Snake belongs to some biker gang and Ewan was going to join, too." She hawked and spat at my feet, but I didn't move. "He said he'd send for me later, but I knew I'd be in jail if he left me here."

"Then what happened, Sarah?"

"Why, then I killed him," she stated matter-of-factly, and every hair on the back of my neck snapped upright.

"I can see you would be angry with Ewan, Sarah. But why Rae? What did she do to you?"

"That piece of trash." Sarah moved the axe handle back and forth between her hands, but so far hadn't raised it. "She screwed my husband, then he expected me to take her in when she was hurt. He hasn't touched me in years, but he was quick to visit that tramp in her purple trailer. Can you imagine how that feels?"

"Yes, I sort of can, Sarah. But what about me?" My eyes were searching the woods behind the trailers, hoping to see movement, the flash of a cop's gun, anything.

"You." She cackled again, but didn't spit. Her breath was coming fast and loud. "I just plain don't like you. You have a smart mouth, and I knew you felt better than me every time you saw me outside. And you never came over and talked to me, not once."

"I didn't think you wanted me to, Sarah." My brain was no longer functioning and I couldn't keep talking much longer.

She raised the axe slightly higher, not yet high enough to take a swing.

With my last shred of composure, I said, "I live in a trailer in Hemp Hollow, same as you, Sarah. I'm not better than you."

"Maybe I won't have a chance to kill the whore before they catch me, but I will kill you."

"You'll go to prison, Sarah."

"I won't. I'll spend the rest of my days in a comfortable room in a nice hospital, where I don't have to cut wood to stay warm in winter. There will be food I don't have to cook, nobody to pick up after, or orders to fill." Her words were mixed with sobs, and the tears streamed through the dried blood on her contorted face.

I looked around frantically. I would have to make a break for it, but knew I wouldn't get far.

"You're the Baker," I said, hoping to keep her talking.

"People came from everywhere for my baking," she said with pride. "We made lots of money from my baking and Ewan's business. But I never saw any of it. It's been years since I've been out of Hemp Hollow. He wouldn't even take me into town. I'm glad I killed him. Now it's your turn."

The axe was on the upswing. I darted through the mud and between the two mutilated trailers.

The ragged efforts of her breathing and the footfalls of her bare feet were only metres behind. As I reached the clearing behind my trailer, there was a movement on my left.

I barely noticed the blond hair and the gun held between two hands. Sarah's steps didn't falter.

Just as Redfern screamed the words, "Halt. Police," she swung at him.

He dropped to the ground with a cry of pain. A shot rang out, but Sarah kept coming.

CHAPTER
FIFTY-THREE

SARAH SWUNG THE AXE again. The skin on the back of my right forearm split open, but I didn't stop. Not until I had a tree trunk between us. She swung again, and the axe blade burrowed into the trunk. As she struggled to dislodge it, I took a quick look at Redfern.

He was lying on the ground, a red stain spilling from his upper thigh onto his pants. He crawled toward his gun, which was lying a few feet away. If I kept Sarah occupied, Redfern could reach the gun.

With one hard wrench, she freed the axe. A pinecone bounced off her head and both of us looked up. Chesley was perched in a nearby pine, about eight feet from the ground. He was pulling at a cluster of immature pinecones, pitching them one after another at Sarah.

"Come down and throw some rocks at her," I screamed. The threat of rock throwing was enough to turn Sarah's attention to Chesley. She swung the axe with one hand, trying to reach his legs. He clambered a few feet higher and, before she could return her attention to me, I scooped a fist-sized rock from the ground and slammed it against the back of her head.

I didn't hit her hard enough. She whirled around, eyes black with madness, but before she could lift the axe handle again, I ducked in and smashed the rock into her temple. She crumpled to the ground.

I lifted the rock to hit her again, but Redfern called out, "Stop. She's out. Take my handcuffs and cuff her hands behind her back." His voice was weak.

Handcuffs were new to me, and Sarah was stirring before I got both her wrists behind her and snapped the cuffs closed. Chesley slid down the tree and stood a few feet away.

"Sit on her," I ordered Chesley.

"What? But, she's naked."

"Sit on her, or I'll kick your ass."

He sat, and I reached for his waist and unbuckled his belt. He didn't protest as I pulled it free. He still had his damn red suspenders to hold up his pants.

Running over to Redfern, I looped the belt around his upper thigh at the groin and pulled it tight. Keeping the pressure on with one hand, I took out my cell and called 911 again, ordering an ambulance and telling the dispatcher to alert the hospital about a possible severed artery.

Redfern had been applying pressure to his wound with his hands, but now he let go. He fell back on the ground and his eyes rolled slightly toward the back of his head.

"Hey, Redfern, you aren't going to faint, are you? Not

a tough cop like you." I struggled out of my jacket and spread it over his chest, using one hand while pulling the belt even tighter with the other. "Stay with me, Chief. Come on, don't go to sleep now. If you stay awake, I'll let you hit on me."

I was just saying any words that came to mind, trying to keep him from going into deeper shock. I continued to pull on the belt and the blood slowed to a trickle. I hoped that was because the tourniquet was working, not because he was running out of blood. But I wasn't sure. My St. John's Ambulance training in high school was a long time ago.

"Cornwall, you're really something," he said, his words nearly inaudible.

Sarah regained consciousness and tried to buck Chesley off her back. With no clothes to hang on to, he gamely latched onto her blood-soaked hair.

I threw another small rock over to Chesley. "Smash her with that." He reached for it, and Sarah suddenly went still again. Guess she wasn't up for another blow to the head. Maybe some part of Sarah's brain was still functioning.

Four of Redfern's officers, including Thea, thundered through the woods to surround us. It took only a few words for me to explain what had happened. Two of them relieved Chesley and held Sarah on the ground. The other two took over for me, holding the pressure with the belt. I was covered in Redfern's blood, and wobbled when I stood up. I stumbled over to Sarah and kicked her in the head. Just once, but it was a good one. Neither cop holding her down objected.

I leaned against Chesley and watched the ambulance arrive. The driver skillfully manoeuvred through the narrow opening in the trees, losing only one mirror to the lower branches of the pines.

The attendants ran an IV line into Redfern's arm. They threw my jacket aside and covered him with several thick blankets. I picked up my jacket and cell.

One of the attendants looked at me and said, "You're coming with us, Miss."

I stepped back. "This blood isn't mine. It's his."

"Not all of it. You have a nasty gash on your arm. That will need some stitches, so jump in with us and we'll get you fixed up."

They shoved me in after loading the stretcher with Redfern's unmoving body. I was pushed onto a bench while the two attendants worked on Redfern. I saw them release pressure on the belt, but when the blood spurted, they tightened it again.

Before the door closed on Chesley's white face, I called to him, "Don't tell your mother about this. Can we look at the swamp tomorrow?"

I wrapped my jacket around my injured arm, which throbbed in rhythm with my heart. When my cell rang, it took me a minute to answer it.

"It's me, Mike. Okay, Bliss, you win. I'll buy the fifty acres from you for sixty-five thousand dollars. And not a penny more."

Well, shit. I was feeling a bit spacey, not at my best, and I really didn't know what to tell him.

"I kind of promised the property to another party, Mike. I can't go back on my word now, but if they decide not to go through with it, I'll give you a call. That's the best I can do."

"Bliss, I'm tired of your games. Take it or leave it."

I was tired of hearing that phrase.

"I guess I'll have to leave it."

"I'll get you for this, Bliss."

"Go fuck yourself, Mike."

I leaned back and surrendered to exhaustion.

CHAPTER
FIFTY-FOUR

WHEN I RETURNED TO the hospital the next afternoon, Redfern was sleeping. They had finished topping him up with whole blood, but a clear fluid now dripped into the back of his hand. I sat in a chair by his bed and put my size fives on the steel railing. My arm had been stitched and wrapped, and a sling provided support for the healing tissue. Sun was pouring into the room, and I was as content as a cat on a windowsill.

The Belcourts bought my swamp that morning. Chesley had gone out at the crack of dawn to look over the property on his own, and had brought back enthusiastic reports and pictures of, not only the *Cypri-*thing, but other wondrous plants that, since he used the Latin names, I couldn't pretend to care about. He had taken several photos of the spotted turtles on their log. I had managed not to shudder as I looked at the strange, alien eyes peering into the lens.

Chesley could do no wrong as far as Ivy was concerned. Not once I relayed the story of his courage as he subdued a maniacal murderer until the police arrived. I left out the part about climbing a tree and tossing pinecones at Sarah. Now Chesley was basking in the glow of his mother's pride, and even Rae watched him with a soft look in her eye.

I put a stop to that mutual admiration rapport by sending Rae to clean Glory's house. Even Glory couldn't expect me to work with my arm in a sling and I knew Rae was a clean freak.

I looked at my watch. I would have to look in on Rae and make sure Glory hadn't already stuck her severed head on a pike at the front gates to warn off other aspiring cleaners. Glory was just going to have to get used to someone else vacuuming her Persian rugs and dusting the crown moulding.

I had been tossing around an idea and had decided to use some of my settlement money to start a cleaning business. Holly Duffett could help me out with the names of some women who shopped at the Second Hand Rose and who might be interested in working for me. Until I learned how to run a business, I would send Rae to Glory's three mornings a week. I remembered I had two new cleaning jobs lined up for Fridays, and Fern Brickle still needed me on Wednesday afternoons. I would have to get someone else on the payroll, fast.

My BlackBerry chirped. I looked up at Redfern, but he slumbered on, so I answered Dougal's call.

"Hey, Bliss. Where have you been? I hear you saved Chief Redfern's life. Good for you. Anyway, if you want to see Thor one last time, you better come over. He's starting to collapse."

"Is he still stinking up the place?"

"No, that's all gone. Mrs. Boudreau is back, though. The drug bust really upset her, but she's better now. She's making a sirloin roast for dinner, with mashed potatoes and salad, if you want to join me and Holly."

I heard Simon in the background, extolling the plea-sures of sex in the mud, or maybe it was sex in the tub. I couldn't quite make it out.

"Doesn't that bird talk about anything other than cannabis and fornication?"

"You're using pretty big words these days, Bliss. Don't let your new notoriety go to your head. You're still just a little freak with an oversized mouth."

"And, even though you may be a published author and part owner of a greenhouse, to me you will always be just my agoraphobic moron of a cousin."

"Fuck you." But I could tell his heart wasn't in it.

"No, fuck you. And tell Holly I'll be there for dinner, and have my thousand-dollar cheque ready."

I snapped the phone shut and placed it on the small table beside the bed.

"You're such a people person, Cornwall." Redfern sounded sleepy, but his voice was strong.

"That was Dougal. I'm fine with real people."

"How long have you been sitting here in my room?"

"Just long enough to realize you don't snore." I didn't want him to think I was keeping vigil at his bedside.

"That might turn out to be relevant some day."

"Get over your arrogant self, Redfern."

"It will be hard to remain my arrogant self around you, Cornwall."

"So long as we're clear on that."

"You saved my life."

"So, you owe me one," I replied.

A gravelly voice said from the doorway, "Why don't you two quit dancing and get at it?"

I almost didn't recognize the man leaning against the door jamb. He was clean-shaven, with a craggy, angular face, wearing jeans and a sand-coloured tee-shirt. But the smoke-damaged voice and the long, dark hair pulled back into a ponytail were the giveaways.

"Well," I said, "if it isn't Snake, the undercover cop from Toronto."

Both men looked at me, then at each other.

"When did you figure that out?" asked Redfern.

"Almost from the first time I met Snake, I knew he wasn't a regular biker," I said. That was one of the biggest whoppers I had ever told.

They both looked concerned, and Snake said, "Guess I'm not as good at undercover as I thought. What gave me away?"

I tried to backtrack. "Just instinct. Can you tell me what your real name is?" I hadn't noticed before how wide Snake's shoulders were, and his dark eyes crinkled at the corners when he frowned. I guessed he might be Italian, or maybe Greek.

"No, he can't," Redfern answered for him. "I'm sure you understand."

"Sure," I said. "Then, can you tell me why you were chasing me through the cemetery?"

"I didn't know it was you," Snake said. "A rival faction was trying to move in on the Quigley operation, and I thought we might have been followed to the cemetery. We were moving some inventory from the mausoleum that night."

"You came at me out of the fog later, though. You scared the shit out of me."

"You scared the shit out of me, too. And, my boys are still smarting from that sucker kick you gave me."

"Sorry about that. It was my knee, actually."

I thought for a moment. "I suppose it was Julian Barnfeather who thought of the mausoleum as a drop site."

"You don't need to know any more, Cornwall," said Redfern. "The details will come out at trial, and, in the meantime, the less you know the better."

"Whose trial? Surely everyone involved is dead — Julian, Jerry, Ewan. And Sarah is certifiably bonkers."

"We have hopes for a few arrests in the near future," acknowledged Snake. "But the war isn't over, and now I'm heading back to the city. I'd appreciate it, Miss Bliss, if you would keep to yourself the fact that there was an undercover officer involved in this exercise."

"My lips are permanently sealed," I promised.

Snake reached into his pocket. "Before I forget, I have something for you."

He handed me the snake's head buckle with the ruby eyes.

"Oh. Thanks, Snake. I love it." I held the object so the eyes caught the light. "This will look great with my red Savage."

Snake smiled, showing even, white teeth. "Glad I can help accessorize you."

"Probably not a good idea, bud," said Redfern. "She already thinks she's a bad-ass desperado on wheels."

"I have one question before you go," I said to Snake.

"Ask me anything, but I probably can't answer."

"Why such a big deal, undercover and everything, for pot? I mean, you guys were going at it like there was heroin involved."

"But it is a big deal, Miss Bliss. Somewhere at the end of all these small pot operations is a master criminal, likely the leader of one of the major outlaw biker gangs, who is shipping heroin and other bad shit all over this country. We begin at the bottom and follow the money, and would still be following Ewan Quigley if his wife hadn't murdered Jerry Corwin. Ewan and I knew she had done it, of course. And Neil and I knew we would have to shut down Ewan's operation, but we wanted to see where the marijuana from the mausoleum would take us. The other gentleman in the cemetery was a biker, and I hoped he would lead me further into the organization." Snake stopped and looked at Redfern, as if questioning whether he had said too much.

So the other man in the cemetery hadn't been Ewan Quigley. "Did you get the guy? Is he in jail now?"

"Somehow, in the confusion, he got away. With the cache, I'm afraid." Snake sighed dramatically.

"I see."

Snake and Redfern conferred silently again, and I got the idea there was more to this story than they would ever tell me. Fair enough. But ...

"But why didn't you arrest Sarah if you knew she killed Jerry. I mean, really, Rae and I were living right on her doorstep. And she tried to kill me!" I looked at Redfern as I said this, but Snake answered.

"Neil was asked to stand down for twenty-four hours. He did his best to make sure you and Rae stayed away from Hemp Hollow without actually telling you why. None of us believed Sarah would go after her own husband."

I had a few thoughts about that, but kept them to myself. Whoever was piloting this fight against drugs, some desk jockey high up in the hierarchy of the OPP or RCMP, could not have factored in a mentally ill woman driven to desperate action by neglect.

"Well, gotta go. I'll let you two get on with your courting." Snake's eyes met mine, and he winked.

He and Redfern did those strange male ritual things like bumping knuckles and whacking each other's shoulders. Then he left as suddenly as he arrived and we listened to his hoarse chuckle echo down the hall until it, too, disappeared.

"You're not leaving, too?" Redfern asked me. "I'll be all alone in my bed of pain."

"I'm pretty sure you're not in any pain, Redfern. You seem pretty cheerful for someone who almost had his leg sliced off. Good drugs?"

He winced. "You bet. And, it was just a nicked artery."

My BlackBerry sounded again, and I held a finger up to Redfern. He shook his head and lay back on his pillows.

"Hi, Dad. Is anything wrong?" My parents rarely called me, preferring their own weird brand of texting.

By the time I disconnected, I had more to smile about.

"I've got a place to live now," I told Redfern. "The MacPhersons are moving back to Hamilton. After the drug bust you spearheaded on the old and infirm, they've decided to blow this pot-intolerant town. Apparently their own tenants in Hamilton are moving out, so they're leaving Lockport by the end of the week. And I'm moving in. No more trailer for Bliss Cornwall."

"If that dollar amount I heard is your rent, your dad almost has to pay you to stay in his house."

"I might even make some money. I'm going to ask Rae if she wants to rent a room from me."

"Rae? You mean Rae from …"

"Yes, that Rae. Do you have a problem with that?"

"Not me, but you might. Once in the life, it's hard to get out and stay out. And I can't turn a blind eye forever."

"Everybody deserves a second chance. I have plans for Rae that will keep her hands busy in a wholly legitimate manner. And I'll be around to kick start her if she falters."

"We'll see," he said dubiously. "There's something else you need to know before you leave. You better sit down."

"What's that? Did somebody tell you I kicked Sarah Quigley in the head while she was handcuffed on the ground?"

He didn't look surprised. "Not that. After you were run off the road, I asked Dwayne to check all light-coloured SUVs in the area. He got several hits, one quite interesting."

"Who?"

"Dwayne found a silver metallic GMC Yukon registered to your ex-husband."

"The Weasel tried to kill me! I accused him, but he denied it."

"Take it easy, Cornwall. I dropped in on the mayor and his wife yesterday before all the excitement in Hemp Hollow. Naturally, they didn't admit anything. And, since the vehicle didn't actually hit you, there are no scratches or paint transfer to go on. By her demeanour, I think Mrs. Bains was driving the Yukon that night, and her husband didn't know about her intent. I don't believe she actually wanted to kill you. When Alyce's tricks didn't work, Andrea probably hoped to put you out of commission long enough to miss the tax deadline. Anyway, that's my opinion. I can't charge her, but you might want to stay out of her way."

The Weasel said he would get even with me? I had been ready to ask Dougal to delete the copies of the photo he had saved on his computer drives, but I changed my mind. I wanted to be done with the Weasels, but somehow I knew we would clash again. Next time, I'd be prepared.

Redfern watched me drop my BlackBerry and the snakes' head belt buckle into my tote bag.

"Cornwall? Do you still think I'm bent?"

"No."

"I'm glad to hear it."

I stood up and adjusted the sling while I waited for the throbbing in my arm to ease. "Gotta go. I've never actually been invited to Dougal's for dinner before, and I'd hate to miss it. Although I'll probably have to clear the table and take out the trash afterward."

"Before you leave, could you hand me that glass of water?"

I walked over to his bedside, but before I could reach for the water Redfern captured my hand. His grip was strong and inviting, and I let my hand rest in his for a moment.

He pulled me closer. "Do you know what you need, Cornwall?"

"I need a new BlackBerry. If you say I need a man, you'll be yelling for an extra shot of pain meds in a minute."

"There's the Cornwall I lust after. The correct answer is fun. You need to have fun again."

"Fun is my middle name. Everyone says so."

"When I have two good legs under me, we could take a ride in the country on our bikes, stop for a romantic dinner."

"Do you think your Goldwing can keep up with my Savage?"

He laughed, then winced and carefully straightened his leg. "I'm confused. Is that a yes?"

"Fine, let's do it."

What the heck.

"How about a kiss to seal the deal?"

I patted his good leg. "We'll talk about it tomorrow."

ACKNOWLEDGEMENTS

TO MY BETA READERS: Kathy Alessio, Cheryl Bellefeuille, Marlene Donaldson, Alyssa Ferris, Donna Houghton, Lara Ferris Inneo, Barb Lowe, Marilyn Pharoah, and Desneiges Roy. Thank you for critiques, suggestions, and, most of all, your friendship.

To Donna Warner, my sister/editor, thank you for your unflagging support and the countless hours you spent helping me with *Corpse Flower*. It's been a long road, but we had a lot of fun along the way. Now, on to the next project!

To Allison Hirst, my fabulous editor at Dundurn, thank you for patiently and good-naturedly guiding the book to publication.

To the Crime Writers of Canada judges who picked *Corpse Flower* as the winner of the 2010 Unhanged Arthur contest. It was truly an honour to be chosen, and I thank you all.

MORE GREAT FICTION FROM DUNDURN

A Green Place for Dying
A Meg Harris Mystery
R.J. Harlick
978-1926607245 | $17.99

Meg returns to her home to find that a friend's daughter has been missing from the Migiskan Reserve for more than two months. Meg vows to help find her and in the process discovers she isn't the only Native woman who has gone missing. Fearing the worst, Meg finds herself confronting an underside of life she would rather not know existed.

Twilight Is Not Good for Maidens
A Holly Martin Mystery
Lou Allin
978-1459706019 | $17.99

Holly Martin's RCMP detachment on Vancouver Island is rocked by an attack on a woman camping alone. At another beach a girl is garrotted. The case breaks open when a third woman is raped and gives a description of the assailant. Public outrage and harsh criticism of local law enforcement augment tensions in the frightened community, but as a mere corporal, Holly is kept on the periphery. She must assemble her own clues.

Spoiled Rotten
A Liz Walker Mystery
Mary Jackman
978-1459701410 | $11.99

When the body of Toronto restaurateur Liz Walker's meat supplier, Mr. Tony of Kensington Market, is found dismembered, her star chef, Daniel Chapin, becomes the lead suspect, then goes missing. More problems arise when two people are poisoned at the place where Daniel has been moonlighting.

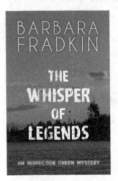

The Whisper of Legends
An Inspector Green Mystery
Barbara Fradkin
978-1459705678 | $17.99

When his teenage daughter goes missing on a wilderness canoe trip to the Nahanni River, Inspector Michael Green is forced into unfamiliar territory. Unable to mobilize the local RCMP, he enlists the help of his long-time friend, Staff Sergeant Brian Sullivan, to accompany him to the Northwest Territories. The park has 30,000 square kilometres of wilderness and 600 grizzlies. Even worse, Green soon discovers his daughter lied to him. The trip was organized not by a reputable tour company but by her new boyfriend. After the body of one of the group turns up at the bottom of a cliff, they begin to realize just what is at stake.

Almost Criminal
E.R. Brown
978-1459705838 | $17.99

Charming, wealthy Randle Kennedy has a secret: he's British Columbia's most prolific producer of boutique marijuana. Come legalization, he'll be the first on the market with marijuana's answer to single-malt Scotch. Until that day, he runs a tight operation with terrorist-cell security.

Tate MacLane is brilliant, miserable, and broke. Since graduating from high school at age 14, he's failed at university, failed to support his family, failed at everything except making a superb *caffe latte*.

Randle wants a fresh face to front his transactions. Tate desperately needs a mentor and yearns for respect. And money ... But he soon finds out that it's harder to get out of the business than to get in.

Exit Papers from Paradise
Liam Card
978-1459706118 | $19.99

Frustrated 35-year-old plumber Isaac Sullivan believes he has both the intellect and skill to be a surgeon. Forced to take over his father's plumbing business straight out of high school, Isaac's dreams of attending the University of Michigan fell by the wayside. However, the unfortunate setback didn't stop him entirely. For the past decade, he has absorbed every medical textbook and journal available to him. For practical experience, Isaac performs surgeries on the wildlife around his house. Yet the years continue to pass and Isaac remains stuck in Paradise, Michigan, as a plumber. That is, until this year, when an event pushes him to apply as an undergraduate for the first time.

Exit Papers from Paradise is about the gap between the person we are and the person we desperately want to be.

Available at your favourite bookseller.

VISIT US AT
Dundurn.com
@dundurnpress
Facebook.com/dundurnpress
Pinterest.com/dundurnpress